A TOXIC AMBITION

ERIK A. OTTO

ACKNOWLEDGEMENTS

So many helped this novel come to life. The first incarnation saw light through the assistance of my wife Sarah, my editor Michael Garrett, my cover designer James Cobb, and so many encouraging readers. This revised edition would not have seen publication without the support of my agent Laurie Blum Guest, my cover designer Karolis Zukas, and my editors Paul Witcover, Beth Dorward, and Doreen Martens.

My deepest gratitude.

PROLOGUE

Charles Hardin made a right turn on Divisadero, looking for the end of the rise that would deliver a view of Alcatraz and the crimson San Francisco sunset. His speed was such that driving required his uncompromised attention, and yet he was distracted. His momentum led him to inadvertently glide through a stop sign at the top of the hill. Fortunately, the cross street was devoid of traffic.

He regained his composure and slowed down. After several more intersections he turned onto a dimly lit avenue and pulled over to the side.

A neon sign on a convenience store beckoned fifty feet away. The avenue was quiet, with no pedestrians in sight. Energy conservation made the old houses lining the street look shadowy and amorphous. People could be watching him but there wasn't enough light to expose them.

Lurching over the steering column and closing his eyes, Charles relived the events of only minutes ago. A young caretaker had pulled him over. Charles had provided his ID, then bolted, driving away as the agent looked on. The caretaker was obviously stunned and hadn't chased him, at least not right away.

Charles massaged his prickly gray beard and calculated the repercussions.

The caretaker would let him go. Whatever traffic violation he'd committed was only a minor infraction, not worthy of pursuit. Charles would hide out in San Francisco for a few hours and then find a way to leave the Bay Area for good.

But it wasn't adding up. The stop didn't make sense. He wasn't speeding at the time, and he hadn't broken any other law. He jerkily looked at the backpack on the seat behind him. Could they know? He'd been meticulous in covering his tracks.

Maybe he'd been stopped on a whim by a caretaker bully flexing his muscles. Perhaps this agent hadn't been willing to chase Charles after a taunting episode that didn't quite go his way. Perhaps he'd been called away on a less capricious errand that offered more reward.

Charles raised his head and consciously chose this as the most likely scenario. The alternative was too dire, too hopeless.

He glanced in the rearview mirror. Comforted by the absence of pedestrian or vehicular pursuers, he stepped out of the car, grabbed his pack from the backseat, and jogged toward the convenience store. He would need supplies if he was going to leave the city.

The store was empty, with the exception of a middle-aged man behind the counter. He had an older-issue standard utility mask hanging loosely on his neck, which reminded Charles to pull up his own mask from his chest. He had taken it off at the caretaker's request. The tainted air was the least of his concerns at this point, and he reasoned that he might be more inconspicuous with it on.

Until a day ago, it had been almost twenty years since he'd worn a mask. It felt tight against his cheekbones, and the strap was uncomfortable around his ears.

The Inworld had made him soft.

He scavenged for a few food items in the store and stepped up to the counter.

"Was it me?" the man behind the counter said.

Charles was confused. In his paranoid state, he took a cautious step back from the counter.

"I mean, I haven't showered today, but is it really that bad?" The man gave him a gap-toothed grin. "Usually people take the mask *off* when they come into my store!"

Charles smiled back nervously under his mask. "Sorry, I...my head was somewhere else."

The man nodded as if he understood.

Charles left the store with lighter steps, more at ease after the benign interaction. Maybe he'd been too worried. If the young caretaker had guessed who he was, the Inworld would have dispatched security forces to go after him, but there had been no sign of pursuit after almost twenty minutes.

The door had scarcely closed behind him when he heard a faint noise borne on the air. It was hard to make out, barely a whisper in the now unbroken darkness, yet at the same time unmistakable. A series of low, muffled purring sounds. Joined to the sounds, a familiar array of lights flashed in the distance.

A weight of fear corrupted his good spirit.

He broke into a run, away from the convenience store, away from the car, away from the pulsating lights.

It was, in fact, more of a waddle than a run. His elderly limbs only moved so fast, and the pack swayed back and forth on his back, shifting his weight uncomfortably. The paper bag full of supplies began ripping, so he dropped it. The spilled contents rattled and rolled along the pavement.

He turned left on the corner of Webster Street. He would need more air, so he pulled off his mask again. The street was a steep downhill decline, steep enough that he had trouble running quickly. His speed challenged his control of his aching joints.

As he approached the next intersection, a whizzing sound came from ahead of him. The street ahead was dark. Any enercycle beams would be visible, but there were no lights to be seen.

The whizzing sound revealed itself to be from a gang of young teens coming down the cross street to his right, their bikes lit up only by faint blue glow ties. They were much closer than he'd anticipated. He tried to halt his stride, but his legs wouldn't obey. He stumbled on the steep grade and fell, tumbling into the intersection.

One of the bikes skidded out to his left. Another, following closely behind, skidded to the right, sideswiping another bike, and causing a crash next to Charles. A series of expletives was followed by a symphony of rubber squealing against pavement.

Charles stood up quickly, despite the objections of his limbs. "Listen to me. You have to help. Take my backpack and—"

"We'll be taking more than that, old man," said a tall, sinuous teen as he pushed himself up from the ground.

It was apparent Charles hadn't found the helpful sort. He nervously reached into his backpack while the teens circled him like a pack of dogs. After withdrawing a handful of items, he threw the pack at the tall teen and sprang to his right, splitting the closing circle.

One of the closer youths reacted quickly to the maneuver, jumping to intercept Charles just a few feet outside the circle. The weight of the teen's torso collapsed Charles's legs and dropped his knees to the ground. His face followed, smashing into the pavement painfully.

"This one's pretty jumpy," Charles heard from behind him. It was the tall teen again. "What else do you have for us, old man?"

This was the kind of thing the gangs thrived on. A stumbling old man was an easy victim, someone to taunt and toy with before mugging him or administering a savage beat-down. They probably expected him to beg for mercy.

But they had no idea how much adrenaline he had coursing through him, nor did they realize he had worse things to fear than a few bruises, so while his erstwhile tackler was getting up, looking proud of himself, Charles sprang to his feet, delivered a solid punch to the boy's nose, and took off again.

He was relieved the element of surprise had bought him a respectable lead. He ran downhill and away from the intersection as fast as his aching legs could carry him.

Before rounding a corner, he looked back. A few of the teens were sprinting after him, but he was looking for any sign of his original pursuers. Sure enough, the teen who he'd punched was looking up the hill, his arm raised to shield his eyes from the shimmering lights of enercycles.

Charles turned the corner, hoping the mess of bikes and teens would delay the caretakers.

He sprinted through another intersection, and yet another.

The streets were vacant except for him and his pursuers. The only sounds were the purr of the enercycles, a cacophony of footfalls, and his own heavy breathing drumming through the night.

Charles was quickly becoming exhausted. After several blocks, his lead had dwindled. He was headed down Greenwich Street, approaching the Divisadero thoroughfare. A small group of pedestrians was crossing the well-lit intersection ahead of him. For a moment he thought he might be able to lose himself among them. The prospect filled him with fresh energy.

Until several enercycles turned from Divisadero onto Greenwich, heading straight for him.

The grim reality took hold. This was it. There was no getting away. He came to a stop, turned, and walked forward, toward the oncoming teen assailants. They slowed down, not knowing what to make of Charles's about-face. He had already surprised them once, so they adopted a cautious stance.

When two of the gang members were less than a stone's throw away, Charles extended a hand to them, palm up. Cradled in it was a cylindrical sliver of metal, lined with parallel nodes—his last remaining data finger. Meanwhile, he was searching deep within his jacket pocket with his other hand. He spoke firmly. "It's critically important that you hide this from the caretakers. Find someone who can help you deci—"

Charles's words were cut off by a punch from a teen who'd snuck up on him from the side. He fell down but didn't avert his gaze from the youth he'd been addressing. The data finger tumbled across the pavement, but it was still close enough for him to retrieve it.

He pulled out what he had sought from his jacket. It was a pocketknife. He folded out the blade.

The teen who'd hit him stepped back, trying to mask his nerves with a smirk. "Gonna take a bigger knife than that, old man."

Charles didn't answer. He raised himself to his knees and looked down at the knife in his hand. It was small, but it would do the job.

When he looked up again, the teens were flinching at the lights from the enercycles. It was now or never.

He slit his throat and toppled over face-first in front of them.

There was a pulsing heat against his cheek, and his remaining energy fled quickly. He saw the teens in front of him from an awkward angle. His blood flowed toward them like wine from a shattered bottle.

All that work—for nothing.

The teen who'd punched him turned and fled. Another quickly followed, but the last hesitated. He was looking at something. The data finger Charles had dropped—it lay at the boy's feet. Charles tried to speak, but words wouldn't form.

As Charles's breathing became more laborious, the teen weighed the situation. This teen must have figured out Charles was no ordinary old man. He showed no fear of the teens, so his suicidal act wasn't out of cowardice. Charles put up a fight, and had killed himself for some important reason. The data finger had to be worth something, perhaps something significant.

The boy stooped, snatched up the data finger, and ran, disappearing from the enercycle beams and vanishing into the night.

Charles let his heavy eyelids close. He'd done what he could.

The whirring sounds of the enercycles drew closer. There were blotchy imprints on his retina—the only vestiges of the brilliant light beams that surrounded him.

Soon even the blotchy imprints faded, and there was nowhere else to go for his flagging consciousness. Weakness consumed him, and he relinquished his hold on the world.

PART I

OUTWORLD

CHAPTER 1

Tristan shuffled awkwardly forward, trying to find a place for his small feet among the morass of bigger brownish shoes. He was hemmed in between his parents at his back and an unidentified stranger at his front. He gazed down, swaying to and fro with the undulating horde of people.

Was it like this in the Inworld, he wondered, with all those people packed together all the time?

He gained some clearance and looked up to get his bearings. The shadowy purple sky had faded beyond dusk. Faint cascades of LED illumination met him from above whenever he reached a new intersection. It was at these crossings where he could make out the contours of the human heads bobbing around him, faces anonymous behind their safety masks.

When the crowd slowed, his parents took him by the hand, pulling him forward uncomfortably, sometimes painfully, squeezing him through the morass. The throng of people thickened even further, but his parents only pressed more relentlessly. His father's voice took on a note of urgency. "Tristan stay with us. Excuse me. Can we get by? Hold on tight, Tristan. Our son is in the square. Please. Thank you."

Tristan wanted to throw off his mask and cry out at the distressing ordeal. He wanted to ask if they could just go home. But he knew now wasn't the time. Today wasn't about him. Even in the whimsical mind of a nine-year-old, this fact had strong foundation.

They reached an incline in front of Union Square, where Tristan's perspective was illuminated by the flood lamps above him. His parents lifted him onto a concrete railing. Once steadied, he could bare full witness to his surroundings.

People had filled every corner of the square, and all were looking to the center with muffled sobriety. Tristan stood at a diagonal to the main stage, where he spotted Tom standing in the line-up, subdued and stoic. Set slightly closer to the crowd, over the line of outlaws, was a broad arch from which hung metallic rings. Farther behind and above, glowing eerily white, was an immense hollowvision cube that had been erected so all might view the spectacle.

It was Tristan's first time in Union Square. He had expected to see the shopping places his parents had told him about. Union Square, they had explained, was the last area used by the Inworlders before they left the Outworld completely. He'd even heard that at one time the famous Inworld founder Mother Myra owned a number of the buildings. Recently indoctrinated Inworlders would relive some vestige of their former lives by shopping in the historical old town.

But all that was decades ago, and the tunnel from the Parkdome to the square had been filled in. The shops had all but vanished. Large somber buildings dominated the periphery, but their function wasn't immediately apparent.

Many minutes were spent waiting. The crowd undulated and became noisier with time. An old man across the square began to yell in anger—a stream of curse words and threats. The caretaker guards immediately plowed through from multiple directions to pull him out. Doing so proved remarkably easy, since the Outworlder crowd knew to pull away from the incoming caretakers. No one would want to share the old man's fate.

After the miscreant was gone, the harsh education led to a fearful hush.

A caretaker officer appeared on the stage. He was wearing a dark shirt—not the typical blue and gold—and his safety mask was the standard issue gray, purposefully devoid of markings, and lacking any Ket team allegiance. He stomped around as if his feet were made of stone, assessing the line-up of outlaws in a weaving figure-eight path around them. Once satisfied with his inspection, he pushed the first young teen closer to the metallic rings.

A litany of words crystallized on the hollowvision, and the loudspeaker crackled with a voice reciting them aloud. Tristan flinched at the unnatural volume.

"Treason against the Inworld. Resisting arrest. This individual conspired to destroy our way of life, to destroy our safe haven. This individual's actions threatened to undermine Mother Myra's promise of salvation. Let it be known that anyone who commits these crimes against the Inworld will be subject to the same punishment, and their families subject to shame and persecution."

Tristan recognized the first Bluetoe gang member, though not by name. He was a tall, lanky kid he'd seen once with his brother. The carefree demeanor Tristan remembered in him was gone. His face was contorted, as if confused by emotions he'd never experienced before.

"Ricardo Silva, you are hereby sentenced to death," the speaker bellowed, partially distorted by static. The source of the voice was unclear. It could be someone speaking miles away in the Parkdome for all Tristan knew.

The masked caretaker pulled the wiry rope down and looped the metal ring at the end of it around the boy's neck. It snapped shut and he tightened a rusty wingnut in the back. Without any pause or ceremony, he proceeded to shove Ricardo over the edge of the stage.

Tristan turned away.

He'd heard of public hangings in other dome cities, but this was the first to take place in San Francisco. No one seemed to know how to react. There were a few gasps of surprised horror and some weeping, but mostly silent apprehension.

A knot tightened in his chest. Tristan finally felt the full weight of what was coming. His parents had told him, but he hadn't made the connection, not really known what it meant. Seeing Ricardo Silva hanging from his ring made it real.

Tristan felt his eyes swelling, defying his expressionless face. His father held him with firm hands around his waist on each side, as if the anguish might force him off his perch. His mother put her hand over his eyes. She said, "You don't need to see this, Tristan." But he could still see through a crack in her fingers, and with her body close to his, he could feel her resigned sobbing, further catalyzing his pain.

The loudspeaker reiterated the same list of crimes for Bavy Kimpton. Like Ricardo, he was sentenced to death. Three more Bluetoe gang member teens followed in swift succession.

The lesson learned from the earlier miscreant was forgotten by the fickle crowd. Soon people were cheering with each hanging, as if eager to be rid of the troublesome teens. Others taunted the youths as they were led forward. Amid the cheers and taunts Tristan also heard cries of anguish. Many silent spectators had faces streaked with tears, like his own.

The victims were pushed forward less ceremoniously after each loudspeaker recital. The first caretaker on the stage was joined by another. They looked impatient, as if they were tiring of the ordeal. The sixth victim was an older man named Hugh Percival, about the age of Tristan's parents.

When this older man was pushed over the ledge, a boy around Tristan's age climbed over the fence separating the watching crowd and ran toward the lineup. Caretaker guards intercepted the child and used batons to subdue him. The sticks hit him with sickening thuds as he let out a high-pitched wail. The guards held onto him as the seventh victim, a woman about the same age named Rena Percival, was also pushed over the ledge. The child continued to cry out in a disturbing combination of sorrow and baton-induced pain.

If it weren't for his parents' stern warnings that he should keep quiet, or for their firm grip on his waist, Tristan might have suffered the same fate as this boy who was being carried away by the caretakers.

Tom was eleventh in line.

Tristan still didn't understand why the caretaker agents had arrested Tom. He knew Tom had been in the Bluetoe gang, and they often were up to no good, but the gangs never messed with the caretakers. The penalty was too great. As a result, the caretakers usually left the gangs alone. They cared little if Outworlders fought among themselves.

Everything changed when the four caretaker agents came to their apartment and arrested Tom. Tristan and his parents were told his older brother had conspired with a man named Hardin to commit treason against the Inworld.

Why would Tom do such a thing?

Surely it was a mistake. It didn't make any sense.

And now, anyone who dared whisper a conjecture about this man Hardin was at risk of being included in the roundup. Perhaps that was why the two older people had been sentenced as well.

He looked at his parents to somehow glean further understanding, but only their eyes showed above their masks, and those eyes revealed despondency and little else.

It didn't matter now.

Tom was next.

Tom would turn on the rope, his neck hooked tightly by the metal ring, until his face came into a direct line of sight. Tristan knew his brother's eyes would be unnaturally pronounced, his skin a deathly blue, but he would always wake before fully establishing the image.

This was Tristan's dream. It was the worst kind of dream; a recurring nightmare grounded in reality. It was a dull knife constantly beneath him, ready to cut deep if he gave in to it, so he fought to suppress it, however he could.

He sat up in his bed, and his eye caught the picture on his desk. It was the only one he had of the two of them together, from when they were younger, two years before that day in Union Square. Yet the two boys in the picture seemed foreign. Perhaps it was because they had been so young, or perhaps because his smile had not yet been weathered by the events to come. These two could not be part of his family. Surely they were somebody else's kids.

He liked it better this way. He didn't want to make the bridge to that day. He reached over and turned the picture facedown, knowing that, as always, he would turn it back up sometime later in the day, when the dream reverberated less in his mind.

He jumped out of bed, pulled off his T-shirt, and searched for his outdoor garb.

His room was a mess. He had to sift through the two piles of clothes on the floor to find his Ket uniform and Ket team mask. He stuffed both items into his game pack. Then he found his heavy pants, hoodie, and nylon jacket in another pile and put them on.

His desk was also in disarray, with loose papers everywhere. To the chagrin of his parents, these were mostly Ket play diagrams and not homework. Only the masks on his wall were in any semblance of order, the four of them lined up neatly. Two were his Ket team masks from prior years, painted in team colors, and two others his mother had given him from the Seneca plant, each with unique flaws: a Tyband disposal mask with broken filter guard—making it look like an extra set of teeth—and a premium mask with a scratch that looked like a claw across the cheek. They were freak discards from the specialty mask assembly line.

There was something about the defective masks he liked, maybe because they might be collector's items someday, or maybe it was something else. Maybe he liked the fact that an accident could create something so unique.

He pulled the first mask off the wall—his standard utility mask—and fastened it loosely over his face. It was the usual gray except for the two sets of fluorescent green and blue lines painted on each cheek. The mask covered his nose and mouth, with straps that wrapped tightly around the back of his head. These Seneca brand masks had angular peaks that extended down from beneath the eyes. At the base of these peaks bulbous masses swelled out in the lower cheeks to accommodate the filtration apparatus, making the wearer look like some kind of baboon with inflamed jowls.

He tilted his closet door so he could stare at the mirror on the back. At only seventeen years of age, he didn't have any of the deep yellow coloring around the eyes that marked his parents' faces, but he knew it wouldn't be much longer before what looked like a tan became more permanent. He patted his head, correcting a few outliers in his short, raven-colored hair. He briefly stared into his russet eyes and breathed deeply between clenched teeth, his ritual for getting mentally prepared for game day.

He grabbed his Ket pack and opened the door to his room, stepping out carefully. It was quiet, which meant his father was probably still sleeping in the other room, so he treaded lightly through the apartment. He left out the rear door, heading toward his bike, which was locked up in the basement.

It was unusually bright outside. The sun was even visible—a distorted oblong orb of yellow fighting to be seen through strokes of beige mist. As he coasted down the street on his bike, Tristan leaned back at an angle most conducive to receiving sun on those parts of face not covered by his mask. He would maneuver through the streets hastily, deftly navigating around the paranoid, dreary masses, and he would take it all in.

Passing Masonic, he saw a pack of dogs roving for food. Pedestrians ignored them, sauntering down the street, going about their business as usual, with only red, watering eyes visible above their masks. Most were no older than his parents, although a few elderly folks were out, drooping and coughing.

Tristan's father often cursed elderly folks for venturing outside. He said they were being irresponsible. Tristan wasn't so sure. Surely they'd earned the right to do as they pleased. Either way they were unquestionably brave, or at least proud, especially those who looked desperately ill.

There were walkoffs, too. Tristan almost ran over one of them. He wasn't much older than his dad, laid out on the sidewalk with his legs sticking into the bike lane, people stepping over him, holding a wilted flower and a clutch of printed photos—probably of his family, alive or dead. His face was maskless and exposed, breathing ragged breaths.

Tristan ground his teeth as he went past. For the walkoffs, at least, he agreed with his father.

At the next intersection, Tristan snatched a quick glance to his left to see the sprawling Parkdome reaching toward the horizon. He would often visualize the hundreds of thousands of Inworld inhabitants behind those thick walls, tightly packed in claustrophobic rooms, sleeping in ten-level bunkbeds and resolutely elbowing through crowds to reach their work posts. In his vision all the Inworlders would be smiling, and with good reason. Their close confines were a small price to pay for being protected, for breathing clean air, and for never having to don a mask.

From his vantage point on the hill he could make out the busy panhandle entranceway for caretaker agents, who were coming and going in their blue and gold uniforms. There was also a bank of huge, glowing yellow windows at least ten stories up, but otherwise the Parkdome was mostly featureless, nondescript, and immutable, a glossy dark void against the hazy sky.

This was the goal—the promised land he had worked for years to attain. The myriad sickly faces of San Francisco reminded him that remaining in the Outworld was not a viable alternative.

He heard cheering as he approached Quanta Arena—the incantations of the other hopefuls. He began to fortify himself mentally for the match.

Tristan often wondered whether the games had really come about by accident, as he'd been taught in school, or whether they'd been contrived by the Inworld. The official story was that the revered Inworld climatologist Ernst Kettick had been developing a new form of energy-efficient air propulsion. During an experiment, he'd been wearing a prototype Ket suit and had nearly decapitated himself when it unexpectedly launched into a ceiling fan. This new energy field, later termed Ketrix, didn't end up being much use until Ernst tested it in a game format. And so, Ket was born.

Ket was played in an arena, which was specially designed to contain a Ketrix mobility field, and had a number of obstacles, or "blocks", placed throughout. Two teams would line up on opposite sides. Each player had a finite supply of Ket energy that could be used to fire a pulse weapon, for shielding, or to bound up through the air with anti-gravity assistance provided by the mobility field. A player's Ket field could also be combined with other players to create stronger shielding, and pulse fire could be concentrated by two or more players to overcome stronger shielding. When a player's shielding was overcome, they were eliminated. Ket packs, stowed in a pouch in the small of their backs, would lose power, Ket uniform light nodes would go dark, and players were to remain inanimate for the remainder of the match.

The object of the game was simple: to eliminate the other team, but the strategies were often complex. Teams that knew how to leverage their members' specific skill sets and exploited their numerical advantages tended to win.

Which was what happened today. Tristan's team Cold Fusion had been well prepared, and it paid off. Their opponent was Yellow Fury—a mediocre team that was often unpredictable. Fury had two hotshot snipers who had been too brazen, setting up in weak cover locations accessible from several angles. The snipers had knocked out two of his squad, but were overwhelmed by Cold Fusion's disciplined tactical advance. After the snipers were out of the picture, the rest of the Fury's players quickly followed.

Tristan had three kills, and according to the latest statistics, he was ranked nineteenth out of the two hundred and forty players in the North San Francisco league. More importantly, his team won games. The weekly chatter was about the individual rankings, and many thought that was all that mattered, but he knew the Inworlders were watching. He knew everything he did, both in and out of the game, mattered. So he kept his nose clean and wasn't flashy, and he made sure he won.

"You coming with us, Tristan?" Luisa asked.

Tristan had been sitting in the locker room after the match, replaying the game in his mind. Luisa had just finished packing up beside him. She'd only been in the games for two years and had shown real promise. She was ranked forty-second, and beyond that she was a great tactician, but her ranking mattered little. As one of the best female players, she was almost a lock for caretaker.

"Who's *us*?" Tristan said, wiping the sweat from his brow with a towel. He looked behind her to see whom she was referring to.

"Mugs, Keith, and I are going down to the wharf."

Tristan gazed at his watch thoughtfully. When he glanced back up, she gave him a sour face, intimating his lack of interest without saying a word.

He smiled. "Okay, okay, let's go."

After he showered and changed, they left the arena and hopped on their bikes. They rode up to the top of Pacific Heights and down past the Van Ness robot lanes.

There was more traffic than usual. Bots trundled slowly but methodically up the street from the wharf along the tracks. Some carried cargo, others were service units being redistributed to areas of the city in need. Fresh from the Inworld bot-works, the newest machines shone brightly through the haze, while most others were corroded and coated with blooms of grime.

Tristan was in the lead and Luisa was right on his tail, followed by Mugs and Keith. Mugs's real name was Raleigh, but he'd acquired the nickname because he liked to carry various tea mugs around with him everywhere he went. Keith was his sidekick, but it was hard to tell why, since Mugs and Keith were always bickering. Keith was tall for a Ket gamer, with a big shock of hair that would often flop about in games.

Tristan, Mugs, and Keith had all painted the Cold Fusion team colors on their utility masks, as most loyal Ket gamers did. These were fluorescent green and dark blue streaks over their cheeks. But for some reason Luisa hadn't. She kept her mask virgin-gray.

Was Luisa not fully invested in Cold Fusion? The prospect of losing her to another team made him nervous. She'd only been with them for two games, but she'd played very well—with four kills to her name and a number of well-executed advances. He was planning on making a formal request for her to commit.

They crossed over to Polk Street and rode down the hill to find a perch of crumbly concrete blocks near the cliff in old Fort Mason. There was a good view of the docks on one side and the bay on the other. A heavy, humid breeze came in off the ocean.

They sat peacefully for a while, until their silent contemplation was interrupted by Keith's brand of grating cynicism. "Fucking bots, can't they make them look more human? I mean, it wouldn't be hard." He was looking down toward the docks where the bots worked diligently lifting, hauling, and welding.

"They probably say the same about us," retorted Luisa. "I mean, why can't we look more like bots?"

Keith grimaced, and then chuckled.

It was evident Keith and Mugs were here on some obsequious mission to get into his and Luisa's good graces. There was no limit to what newbies would do to secure a place on good teams. Luisa, on the other hand, just wanted to hang out.

Or did she? She didn't seem like the type of girl to waste time hanging out at the wharf.

He'd first met Luisa when she'd approached him to talk about a match he'd won two months ago. In the competitive frenzy of games, it was unusual for top-ranked players to ask for pointers, or even hang out for that matter, but she seemed harmless enough, and he'd chatted with her politely. They'd compared notes, and he'd even gone out to eat with her and some of the other players.

He wondered if she might be interested in him on a more personal level. She was an attractive girl in a subtle way, with amber skin and brownish hair that she wore plainly. But she didn't give any clear signs of interest, and besides, truly dedicated gamers didn't have time for those kinds of distractions. He certainly didn't.

"Did anyone hear whether the Marindome is up and running?" Mugs asked after another brief silence. He jerked his mask to the north, across the bay, where the Marindome dominated the view. It was a source of some controversy. The Outworld officials were seeking higher admittance rates due to the increased capacity provided by the Marindome, but Inworld officials had protested on the grounds that it was already being crammed full—every room, closet, and utensil accounted for by Parkdome Inworlders.

"Oh yeah, I'm sure they've reserved a spot for you already," Keith responded sarcastically. Mugs didn't bother trying to one-up him.

From their current vantage, Tristan could see the opaque connector tube hanging off the base of the Golden Gate Bridge, which was the main Inworld transport artery from the Sidiodome to the Marindome. The Marindome had been half-finished for several months, but no one knew if it was being populated on the inside. Or at least, no Outworlder knew.

Tristan watched the tiny specks of cars and cycles moving on the bridge in the distance. He could only imagine how Inworlders traversed the same bridge via the connector tube. Undoubtedly they used vehicles too advanced for him to fathom.

There was more inane banter, mostly between Mugs and Keith, arguing over who was the better marksman, but Tristan was distracted thinking about what he needed to do for his training exercises. His cardio was lacking, and his motion shooting was rusty.

Why was he here? Tristan felt his *get on with it* internal alarm bell ring, and he stood up to go. As if joined by a string, Keith and Mugs rose at the same time.

Luisa remained seated, sighing as she stared out across the bay.

He'd noticed this sigh of hers before. Her chest would tremble ever so slightly, and at times the exhalation would trigger a low hum in her voice. It wasn't esophyxia, or even clearing her throat. It was as if she was singing a barely audible tune to herself.

"I've got to go," Tristan said as he turned away. "Always a pleasure." He didn't wait for them to acknowledge him. He'd wasted enough time.

He mounted his bike and began riding, hoping nobody followed.

No one did.

CHAPTER 2

Luisa left the cliff at Fort Mason shortly after Tristan. After he was gone, there was no benefit to staying. She bid her goodbyes to Mugs and Keith somewhat more tactfully than Tristan and hopped on her bike.

Tristan's dedication to winning in the games was overwhelmingly clear, but otherwise he was a closed book. She would need to talk to the others about whether they should approach him.

She wound southwest along the rippling roads until she reached the top of old Pacific Heights. As she made her way down the hill, the dark arc of the Parkdome rose in the distance.

Outworlders were taught the dark color of the domes was by design, to generate solar energy, but the domes did more than absorb sunlight. They took food from the Outworld, they took building materials, and they took jobs. The Parkdome was seeping it all away through its dark shell. She imagined the Inworlders sitting immediately behind the opaque exterior, clustered together tightly in pristine rooms, discussing ways to further exploit the Outworld to their benefit.

And Mother Myra was the queen of these ants, sending her minions to bring the next scrap of food back to their mound, all to her glory and adulation.

Luisa switched to the low-grade filter setting on her mask and ascended the last big hill before her apartment, huffing and puffing with the exertion. After gliding down the shallow decline that followed, she eventually reached her blocky beige and red apartment complex.

As apartments went, a flat in the housing developments in the New Mission was considered relatively upscale, even if it was a small, modest place.

She pulled into the complex and parked her bike in her designated spot. She locked it up, fumbled with her keys, then jogged up the steps to be met with two more locks on her front door. The multiple locks were annoying, but having them made her feel safe. There weren't many criminals in the New Mission, but occasionally bikes would be stolen. On the door, at least, it was more to keep out the walkoffs and drifters.

Once people gave up caring about living, they didn't seem to mind intruding.

She finally entered the door and locked it behind her. It was quiet, and she was alone, but it was home.

Well, not completely alone. Rex met her at the door with a friendly bark. She paused to give him a hug and rub the scruff on his sides. Rex was a crossbreed between a terrier and something else Luisa could never quite figure out. She had found him as a puppy out on the streets and took a liking to him. Rex's name came not from the inventory of classical dog monikers but rather from his big head, short forepaws, and ability to stand on his hind legs and walk through the apartment, resulting in an uncanny resemblance to the long-extinct Tyrannosaurus Rex.

After grabbing a protein bar from the fridge, Luisa sat on her old sofa in the living room. The apartment was sparsely furnished, with one couch and two other chairs in the living room, a bed in one room, and several dressers making up the bulk of it.

She had considered buying more, but every penny counted. In fact, these were the only possessions she had left after she'd sold off what she could of her parents' belongings. Combined with her parents' savings, the extra money had given her enough to live on for several more years, but only if she lived frugally.

Luisa looked up at her comlink handheld device docked in her home hub. The light was blinking. It was surely Fenton.

She sighed and let her voice hum ever so slightly. It was a bad habit, but the extra sound gave it more gravity. It made her feel lighter, and her worries less worrisome.

Minutes later she had packed her bag, stepped out the door, and locked her apartment once again.

Luisa was finding herself less content with her humble flat.

Granted, Fenton's whole apartment was only three rooms, but the main room must have been two thousand square feet, encompassing a kitchen, living room, office, and dining room, and there was a large bedroom and en suite bathroom that was extravagant to the point of being cheeky.

At eighteen, Fenton was only a year older than her, and physically well built, with sandy hair and smooth skin devoid of moles or freckles. He was amicable and seemed to find a way to get along with almost anyone. Quite a few people had said they were alike.

There were at least a few differences. Once you got to know him, his welcoming nature gave way to a sterner disposition, something she would often give him a hard time about. And Fenton's upbringing had been more privileged than her own, and, well, he still had parents.

Fenton's father was a businessman named Dale Kittredge. He ran a large logistics company that served the domes. They coordinated the various suppliers and maintenance engineers for the San Francisco robot transport system. A few of Fenton's distant relatives were in the Inworld, and they had been generous in extending support to those less-fortunate family members who remained in the Outworld, providing funds that allowed them to maintain a respectable—or, in Fenton's case, more than respectable—lifestyle.

Until the Inworld started clawing it back, with taxes on Inworld-to-

Outworld transfer payments. Fenton's mom refused to pay and was caught. She'd been in jail for several months, and still hadn't been properly sentenced.

Fenton joined Luisa in the living-room area. He brought a generous glass of synth-orange juice to Luisa and sat across from her. He was wearing a loose pullover and faux-tattered cords on the faux-suede recliner.

"Orange juice?" Luisa asked. Usually Fenton was all too keen to provide them with some kind of cocktail or spritzer.

"You may not know this, but we've got this thing called school early tomorrow." Fenton smiled and waved his hand dismissively. "So, what happened with Tristan?" he asked.

"I don't know. He's hard to read, but he would be a good addition."

He eyed her skeptically. "We have to be careful, Luisa."

"Remember what happened to his brother. He knows tattling on us could result in him being persecuted just by association."

"The more we expand the group, the more we're at risk of getting caught. We don't know how level-headed this guy is, and—"

"He's level-headed. You've seen him in the games."

Fenton frowned. "That's different. I know a lot of people who are dynamos in the games but certifiable in the outside world."

"He's fine. I don't know what he would think about our little secret, but he's not going to do anything stupid." Luisa bit her lip and looked down at her glass. She took another drink while averting her eyes from Fenton.

Fenton didn't answer. He stood up, ostensibly to get himself something else from the fridge, but perhaps more to let them both cool off. Luisa sat back and looked around. Fenton spent quite a while surveying the fridge contents.

The doorbell chimed.

With Fenton preoccupied, Luisa decided to answer the door herself. She navigated the maze of high-end furniture and opened the door to see Michaelis fidgeting in front of her.

"Well the rabbit finally came out of his hole," she said, smiling and pushing his shoulder amicably. "Been a while. How are you?"

"More like a spider leaving its web, but yes, sorry," Michaelis said. "I've been busy at the computer lab. I'm good." He glanced up sheepishly, only to quickly resume staring at the floor.

Standing no more than five and a half feet tall, Michaelis was stout verging on rotund, with a pasty complexion and poor posture, partly due to incessant coughing from Tanner's esophyxia. He wore archaic spectacles that looked like they'd been assembled by an amateur metalsmith on the first day of welding school. The spectacles, as well as his sea-green eyes, were usually gazing down, reluctant to engage. Nature's karma balanced these shortcomings with an incredible facility for logical reasoning and an unending stream of constructive ideas.

She had met Michaelis at school when she'd asked for his help on her math problems. She could tell he was smart, and it was apparent immediately he would be an asset to their cause. After noticing his grievance with the Inworld, which he only exhibited in subtle ways, she had carefully probed further and eventually recruited him into her and Fenton's two-person conspiracy.

Fenton finally returned to the couch area with a protein-yogurt and another glass of synth-juice for Michaelis. "So, Luisa spoke with Tristan today," Fenton said, bringing Michaelis up to speed, "but she couldn't get a good gauge of where his head is. We were just talking about whether we should approach him formally."

Michaelis processed the words impassively. "Tristan is a natural leader," he said. "He also scored ninety-three percent on the CSA exam."

"Sorry, what exam?" Fenton asked.

"It's a standardized computer systems aptitude test. It's quite hard to get that high, especially since I doubt he studied much."

"You think he could help you in the computer lab?" Luisa asked.

Michaelis snickered nervously. "No, no, he's not that good. I just mean he's smart. And as a Ket team captain, he could help us recruit more people, should we decide to. If Luisa doesn't think he poses any risk of exposure, I think we should engage him."

Fenton's discomfort was still evident but hearing this from

Michaelis seemed to make him retreat from any argument to the contrary. He sat back in his padded chair and pondered.

Luisa decided to push the issue. "Great, I'll bring him to the Marquis. Not sure when though. Not after our next game. We've got exams the next day. Maybe after class on Tuesday, or...after our game next Wednesday. I'll message you if he's going to show."

Michaelis and Fenton both nodded slowly.

They continued their conversation, but after the decision to recruit Tristan, the rest was trivial. As usual, it descended into a gripe session about the latest food distribution failures, or the increasing walkoffs, or their families' agonizing tolerance of the situation, or the fact that the caretakers would do nothing about any of it. Luisa was as guilty as the others. She needed the outlet just as much, if not more, but it was a form of procrastination that left her unsatisfied.

Of course, this procrastination was also fueled by fear, because any action would have profound consequences. In fact, if they recruited Tristan it would make things real. Tristan's intensity, his focus, wouldn't allow them to be idle.

Luisa wasn't that worried. So what if they were caught or killed? It would be like becoming a walkoff, but a walkoff the caretakers would actually need to clean up for a change.

CHAPTER 3

On some game days Tristan liked to be the last team member into the arena. He didn't need much time to warm up, and this way he could sit in solitude and visualize the game space, rehearsing commands and movements. As captain, it was important the many play options be fresh in his mind.

He glanced at his comlink display. Five minutes.

He finished wrestling on his tight-fitting, full-body Ket uniform and pushed the recharged Ket pack into the pouch strapped to the small of his back. Fluorescent green light nodes blinked on around his waist and collar. He pushed in his comlink-connected ear bud and strapped his cheek-mic around his ear. A tap on the mic sounded a crackle. Then he picked up his pulse rifle and fed the attached coiled wire into the Ket pack. Finally, he strapped on his utility mask and ran out of the locker room.

As the corridor opened into the arena, he could see a steady injection of spectators filling the stands from the various entryways.

The game was being held in Gander Arena. Gander's Ketrix mobility field was working, but it was one of the oldest and in need of maintenance. Today, in particular, it showed; a number of holes in the ceiling were admitting small gushers of rain. To make matters worse, there was no airlock and the air conditions were poor. As a result, Ket players would have to wear their outdoor masks, which could make breathing laborious during heavy exertion due to half-clogged filters.

It was a mostly homogenous crowd. Differences were only discerned through the colors of their masks; quite a few were standard utility gray, but a fair number boasted cheek line colors from the league-leading Ket teams. There were hundreds in fluorescent green and blue—Cold Fusion faithfuls. An equivalent number were striped red and black—Red Squall fans. Only a handful of caretaker guards were in attendance. Their heavy masks had filtration systems that looked like thick blue beards, raised from the mask surface with chiseled, angular lines. The rest of the caretaker masks were painted in a pristine gold.

Even on such an inclement day, with puddles pooling in the stands and on the arena floor, the diehards were coming out to watch their favorite Ket teams. It wasn't just a sport; it was *the game*, the main way Outworlders could gain a berth in the Inworld. Parents came to cheer their children on, hoping for a better life for their offspring. Others would come to bet on their favorite teams, or track players so they could enjoy the vicarious thrill of seeing their favorite player admitted to the Inworld.

When Tristan arrived at the bench, he shifted his attention from the stands to the roster to see who was on Cold Fusion today.

He still had the five team members he'd actively recruited, and the remaining six had been assigned randomly after the last game, which was a league rule for the first eight games. He noticed Luisa had accepted his commitment request and been formally moved to the team. This was certainly a positive development. His top six were some of the best in the league, although the other random sub-sixers were mediocre to poor. He did a quick scan of the randoms' playing histories and profiles to see how he could use them.

Their opponent today was the Red Squall, so named by their captain, Damian Thatcher, for use of a "blizzard" strategy. The team would scatter and attack the enemy from all angles to incite confusion and create mismatch opportunities. Every player's maneuvers were slightly different, so it was hard to know precisely what to expect on game day.

Tristan put down the roster and the latest league statistics. It was time to huddle with Cold Fusion and prepare for the match.

The teams assembled on opposite sides of the arena. They were a good hundred yards away from each other, and dozens of cover blocks of varying sizes lay between them. These were predominantly neck height; some were like sharp cones poking out of the ground toward the ceiling, others looked like inverted triangular prisms that had fallen from the ceiling and punctured the ground at odd angles, and others were more basic rectangular shapes. Flashes of Ket-powered uniforms could be discerned in the distance—in this case red nodes blinking around their collars and waists. These would show up as distant glows between the obstacles, and sometimes red and black striped masks peeping out from above them. It looked like the twelve Squall team members were spreading out along the length of the wall at the upper end. As expected, they were getting ready for some kind of blitz.

Despite the sparsely populated stands, the din of the crowd increased steadily as the teams prepared to start. Tristan looked back along the line of his team. Cold Fusion appeared ready, except for a few who were looking around the nearer cover blocks, still plotting their advance.

The buzzer sounded, and each team moved into action.

Tristan had decided to use four squads of three to drive out into the middle of the blizzard formation. He'd seen other teams use one or two squads, but these were unable to fend off the Squall due to lack of protection from enough angles. With four squads he could form a box and provide strong shielding from at least four directions.

The Squall dispersed along the arena sidewalls and in the array of blocks in front of Cold Fusion, and in the process began firing their pulse rifles. Tristan's squads ran ahead, cover to cover, and cohered into their square formation in the middle of the arena. The two foremost Cold Fusion squads concentrated their firepower on Damian Thatcher, who had hung back in the upper arena with two others, collectively forming a stronger Ket shield. Tristan hoped to overpower that group with sufficient firepower to dismantle the Red Squall command center.

The spectators always appreciated the blizzard strategy. They cheered as the frenetic ring formed around Cold Fusion's cadre, and crackling streaks of Ket pulse fire passed between the two teams. Most were stray shots. Several minutes of heated firing passed without either team suffering a casualty.

Several Cold Fusion players were hit, the pulses forming dissipating red circlets of light on their uniforms, but Cold Fusion's three-person formations were taking advantage of the increase in shield strength of collocated players. As a result, the Squall pulses were being absorbed with little effect.

The first casualty occurred on the Squall team as the squad at Tristan's back concentrated its firepower on one of the opponents who was isolated in a poor cover position. The combined shots, hitting in tandem, created a shockwave of blue static that moved in an expanding circle through the player's uniform. The hapless Squall player's suit powered down and the red power-lights around the player's neck and waist went dark.

Shortly afterward, confident in their numbers advantage, the Cold Fusion trio that had taken out the Squall player split off from Cold Fusion's square formation to chase two other Red Squall players on the upper left flank.

This wasn't part of the plan.

"Dammit Norm, what are you doing?" Tristan cursed into his comlink mic. "Jim, Norm, Dayton, get back here!" Norm was supposed to be leading the trio, but he was impulsive and reckless. Tristan had put up with him only because he was an excellent marksman. And Jim and Dayton were newbies he'd been assigned whose prior performance was lackluster at best.

"Norm, return to formation at once!" Tristan yelled.

It was too late. One of the Squall players waiting in the group of three with Damian Thatcher bounded up using a low-arc anti-gravity jump. The player's suit glowed red with Ket field consumption as he rose, his path followed by a faint crystalline contrail of orange sparks.

He'd found the opening made by the squad that had split off from the Cold Fusion cadre and—rising to a height of thirty feet—fired directly into the unprotected backs of two of Tristan's teammates on the opposite side of the Fusion formation.

Two casualties just like that.

The remaining member of the defunct Cold Fusion trio—a quick witted player named Nina—had the presence of mind to also bound up and turn around, firing at the bounding Red Squall assailant. She missed and moved away from the other three squads toward the arena sidewall. Nina probably wouldn't last long alone, but better to be a moving target.

The Cold Fusion formation had been compromised. Tristan needed to modify their strategy. "My trio follow," he commanded via broad-beam, and he bounded up in a low-arc anti-gravity jump toward the upper arena, feeling the static energy course through him while the air blew past. He looked back and saw his other trio members were indeed following. A Ket energy pulse flashed by his ear but nothing hit.

When he turned back to face forward, he was surprised to see his bounding trajectory was about to take him through a miniature water-fall coursing from an opening in the roof of the arena. There was nothing he could do to avoid it, so he put his hands up in an attempt to protect himself.

It didn't work. He splashed through it and was soaked. He didn't mind being wet, but he was worried it might disrupt his field energy. A flash of steam had come off his hot Ket pack on his back but fortunately his watch monitor still showed three-quarter charge. He could hear the crowd gasp at what must have been a small cloud of smoke left behind him, but he didn't look back.

His arc ended and he landed safely, hitting the ground running toward nearby cover. His trio assembled at the upper arena wall to the left of Damian Thatcher and another Squall player. Tristan called on Luisa to bring her own squad to assemble on the opposite side of Thatcher.

As Luisa and Tristan's respective trios maneuvered to crossfire Damian's duo, the other nine Red Squall players were working together to hunt down the four other Cold Fusion players. "I need help," Jim said via broadbeam.

"There's too many," Norm called out as well.

Tristan didn't respond. They were on their own now, in more ways than one. Tristan would have to expel them from the team after the game.

The crossfire on Thatcher was working. After several seconds of concentrated pulses, the shields of Thatcher and the other Red Squall player were overpowered and they went dark.

Tristan surveyed the field. The Squall players had taken down Norton's fledgling trio and were converging quickly on Nina—the last isolated Fusion player. There were now seven active players left for Cold Fusion and nine for Red Squall.

Nina lasted only a few more seconds, succumbing to firepower from the remaining nine Squall players, who were scrambling and firing at her from all directions.

Make that six for Cold Fusion.

But they were a talented group, and with significant Ket energy remaining.

Tristan broadbeamed his remaining players. "Six-player wall, upper arena. Concentrate firepower on the incoming Red Squall players from left to right." This would allow Tristan to keep the Cold Fusion shield strength at six and use the upper arena wall to protect their rear.

The Red Squall players kept to their blizzard strategy. They remained separated and spread out among the array of cover blocks. They moved one at a time, from cover block to cover block, closing in on the upper arena wall where Cold Fusion was entrenched.

"On the left, the cone block," Tristan broadbeamed. Cold Fusion directed all their fire at a Squall player who was advancing from his cover. They took him down.

"Conserve," he said, and firing stopped.

There were flashes of red for a few seconds, but no definitive targets.

"On the right. Two blocks up." It was Mugs on the comlink, from

Luisa's squad. They all concentrated their fire on the movement and managed to take down another Squall player.

It continued this way for some time. The incoming shots from Red Squall were deflected or absorbed. Conversely, as the disorganized Squall players advanced, they were being systematically eliminated by coordinated bursts of concentrated firepower from the Fusion line. Within a few short minutes, there were only three Red Squall left, and the six-member Cold Fusion shield was still holding firm.

Tristan split his team back into two squads of three to track down the remaining Squall players, who were now retreating to cover positions in the lower arena.

After a few shootouts, the battle was over, with five Cold Fusion players still standing.

Tristan's breathing became less labored as he took stock of the outcome. It was a sound victory, in the end, despite the fact that Norm's misstep almost cost them the match.

His focus dissipated, and he allowed a grin to surface. It was only then he registered the crowd cheering. They had enjoyed the match.

He sketched a bow to the stands. *Happy to oblige.*

CHAPTER 4

A decaying plastic bag blew up from the schoolyard and stuck to Luisa's leg. She wiped it away and it was taken by the wind, swirling up into the air until it snagged on a brick outcropping of the school building.

The schoolyard was mostly empty, except for the trash strewn about. A walkoff had been found there a week ago, and no one had been brave enough to clean up the grounds ever since. The school kept talking about barricading the schoolyard, but no one ever got around to that either.

The main doors opened and a student exited wearing a bulky coat, bracing herself against the wind, and protecting her books close to her body in tightly wrapped arms. Luisa waited by the bike rack and took out her handheld comlink. She pretended to read the screen while occasionally looking up at the stream of teenagers leaving the school. There were masks striped in red and black, salmon and white, maroon and yellow, and plain old gray masks, but no fluorescent green and blue masks.

She tired of waiting and entered the door. Tristan wasn't in the main lobby. She found him in his classroom. He was the only student left, leaning over pages on his desk, his fluorescent green and blue-striped mask hanging from his neck.

She took the seat next to him and raised her hand.

He flashed her a quick smile. "Class is over, Luisa."

"Apparently not, or you wouldn't be sitting here. And maybe my question isn't for the teacher."

"Oh really? Let's hear it."

"The question is—dinner, with me, do you want to have it?"

"That's not a very academic question."

"Hmm," she nodded. "Do you want me to write it in a haiku? Or maybe in the form of an algebraic equation? Or maybe—" she looked down at his notes. "—a Ket play." She nudged his shoulder. "Academic? You're not even studying!"

"This is more important. And yes, I am. I'm studying how to win."

Luisa could tell he was amused, but he was only half-grinning. "Come on," she said. "I'm being *extremely* charming. Why so glum? Mother Myra is watching."

He rolled his eyes and returned a weighty exhalation. "Yeah, sorry Luisa. I would ordinarily love to join you for dinner, but I have too much to do. Schoolwork, Ket pre-game planning, and now I have to go to the Seneca Mask Plant tonight. The warehouse lift droid broke down so if they don't move the pallets before tomorrow the assembly lines will be down. It's my mom's responsibility, but she's sick, and my dad's on his night shift, so he can't help, either."

"So now it's your responsibility." She said it with a positive inflection, nodding. It was important work.

He didn't seem to think so. "Yeah, it sucks." He was doodling on the corner of his arena map. There were cubes, spirals, and a profile of a woman—probably his mom, based on the Seneca plant coveralls. He was a good artist. Oddly, off in the corner there was a detailed mask on a face that was otherwise devoid of eyes or ears.

"Why don't I give you a hand?" Luisa said. "You'll be done in half the time."

He looked at her skeptically.

"What?" she asked, eyebrows raised. "I've always wanted to check out the mask plant. Masks are cool." She tapped her finger on his mask drawing doodle. "Don't you think?"

"No this is..." He pointed to the drawing, shook his head, and trailed off. "Sorry to be a buzz killer, but it's just a factory; boxes, pallets, molds, and assembly lines."

"Why don't you let me be the judge of that?"

His jaw muscles flexed as his mouth tightened. It was an expression she'd seen on him often.

"You're not going to have any teeth left if you keep gritting like that."

He was quiet for a moment, and she bit her lip, worried he would interpret her comment as snarky. He was a team captain, and probably used to being spoken to with more deference. It was a delicate balance, trying to be pushy but not too pushy.

Thankfully, his stubborn resolve melted away. He even allowed himself a laugh. "You're probably right," he said. "And fine, I guess I could use the help, but don't try any of your bounding maneuvers on the factory floor."

Her face gained heat. Earlier in the season she had once tried to jump away from an ambush, but instead she bounded into the arena wall. Bounding wasn't her forte. "Yes, touché. Trust me, that hurt. I don't plan on doing that ever again, never mind in a mask factory."

"Well, okay then."

"Okay then."

The Seneca Mask Plant was in the Dogpatch area of San Francisco, which didn't have dogs or much of anything else except a few factories and store houses. The main Seneca building was a big warehouse that stood out in a row of warehouses because it actually had fresh paint, unbroken windows, and a contemporary sign.

On the inside, the main length of the warehouse featured several assembly lines where masks of different varieties would be molded, cooled, have filter caches installed, and be fixed with straps and boxed.

At several points along the way on each line were inspection stations and supply depots.

Luisa and Tristan were actively pushing pallets on wheeled forks between the supply intake area—a seven-story maze of pallets near the bay doors at the back of the building—and the supply depot points on the assembly lines.

Luisa's scan gun pinged at her as she passed the QR code of the supply depot. The gun display said *Seneca P893872 High Grade Filters*. She quickly checked the inventory matrix on the clipboard dangling off her belt. When she confirmed it was the right item, she pump-raised the fork, pulled it out of the pallet, and pushed it aggressively back toward the intake area.

A sweat drop rolled into her eye and she blinked it away.

Tristan was coming out of the intake area with another pallet. His face was also flushed, and an arc of perspiration showed around his collar. "You're two behind," he said smugly. "Maybe I should go slower so you can catch up."

"Oh I'm just getting started," she said.

As Tristan was rounding a turn he clipped another pallet, pushing it back half a foot. "Who gave you a driver's license?" she said.

He smirked and pushed ahead, clearing the corner.

After the next pallet, Tristan's comlink alarm went off. "Okay, hands off the fork," he said. They both backed away from their pallets and went to have a drink at a cluster of plastic tables and chairs that served as a lunch area for workers.

Luisa said, "You know my cousin Chooly said they used to offer car insurance? It's too bad. You probably would have found it useful."

He snickered and took a sip of water. "I'm still two pallets ahead. You better get your rest."

Luisa stood up and stretched her arms over her head. She was in good shape, but they didn't do much pushing or lifting in the games. She was going to be sore tomorrow.

There was a block of offices that split off from the lunch area, along a corridor. Curious, she snagged her glass and meandered along the hall.

Three doors down was a corkboard pinned with news bulletins, quality procedures, and a few product diagrams. The diagrams were of various mask types, with lined arrows labeling the different components. She'd just spent the last hour hauling many of these components to the assembly line. It was interesting to see how they were incorporated into the masks.

"You weren't kidding, were you?" Tristan had followed her down the corridor. He was standing beside her.

"About what?" she asked.

"That you think masks are cool."

"You're the only one who doesn't."

"I like masks. I have a collection in my room. I just...sorry. They bring back annoying memories of when I was a kid."

She remembered his doodle. Could it be his brother? Best not to mention it here, though. It would be weird. "Yeah, I've got my fair share of those," she said instead.

She stared at the different mask classes—*Standard Utility*, *Ket Arena*, *Premium*, and *Heavy Duty*—and turned the top page of the blocky, broad-based *Heavy Duty* class. The page underneath revealed a layered schematic of the filter mechanisms.

"Have you ever worn a Heavy Duty?" Tristan asked.

"No, but I have a Premium I use sometimes."

He nodded. "Your mask probably has two filtration settings, but Heavy Duty ones have an additional high-grade setting for activities like working on the docks or for remediation. My dad uses one, but he has to be careful because the filters are so constrictive that he can hyperventilate when he's active."

"See, you *do* like masks." She smiled. "How come these masks don't have Tyband protection settings?"

"None of the Seneca brands have that setting. My mom says there's no proof you can filter out Tyband radiation with a mask, or any of the post-Tyband decay either. The masks are principally for preventing esophyxia and other respiratory illnesses."

She had spent quite a bit on her Premium mask. It was a Reliant brand with a Tyband protection setting. But she didn't argue. She'd never had any confidence the setting did anything useful.

Her eyes scanned past the other diagrams. There was an employee list with colored dots next to the name. Tristan's mom—Emilia Mardukas—was near the top.

"Your mom is the plant manager?" she asked. "What are all those marks next to her name? You didn't tell me she was so important."

"Yeah, she's the plant manager, but those are demerits for production delays. "She's always getting penalties, and for each one they dock her pay. It's like that every month. She might as well be working in the city remediation corps with my dad. She'd make the same amount of money."

Luisa frowned. "At least she gets to work indoors and making good quality masks is important for all of us. I mean, I can't think of many better jobs. It's better than protein farmer, or dock worker, or robot maintenance."

Tristan frowned thoughtfully and turned to focus on her. His eyes were burning. "Maybe, but whether she's a plant manager or dock worker, it's still an Outworlder job. We won't have to worry about that, because we'll be Inworlders."

It wasn't a quip, or even a wry comment. He was deadly serious. "Right," she said, biting her lip. She had been on the cusp of asking him if he wanted to meet with Michaelis and Fenton, but now it didn't seem right. It would be better on another day, one where he hadn't stated his intentions with such conviction.

Besides, she was enjoying herself.

"Yes, we'll be Inworlders," she said, "but for now, I think it's safe to say I'm a better pallet driver than you."

"You think so?"

"Oh, I think so."

Luisa jogged back toward the assembly line. Tristan was close behind her.

CHAPTER 5

Tristan was sitting in the locker room, reviewing the stat sheet. He had replaced the three players who had defied his orders in the game against the Red Squall. The three newbies were much more compliant, but they had other issues—they didn't shoot well. They kept blasting cover blocks, the ceiling, the floor, and their own teammates—anything but the opposition.

He would have to make more changes to the roster.

They had still won, with two players to spare, mostly thanks to Luisa who had performed a well-executed solo sneak attack on the enemy snipers.

He walked up to Luisa and gave her a collegial elbow to her shoulder. "Thanks, Luisa. Wow, am I glad you decided to commit."

"Hey, my pleasure," Luisa grinned. "And for what it's worth, I still think I'm a better pallet driver than you."

"Okay, okay, I give up." Tristan said, his hands up in mock defense. He began stuffing his gear into his duffel bag, filling all corners to ensure he could zip it up. Everyone else had left except Luisa. She was packed and ready, sitting on a metallic table nearby, swinging her feet. "Hey, Tristan," she said, catching him looking at her. "I'm pretty hungry. Do you want to get some chow?"

It was yet another inquiry from Luisa. He gave her a quizzical look. "Dinner again? Are Keith and Mugs coming?"

"No, just us, and maybe some friends who aren't into pandering." She winked.

It seemed safe enough, and he liked Luisa.

Of course, he would have gone either way. He would do anything to keep her on Cold Fusion.

"Sure thing," he said. "I'm famished."

Luisa wanted to bike all the way to a place called Marquis in North Beach, far from Quanta Arena. That was fine with Tristan. He was in no mood for arguing, and still experiencing the elation that came with victory. He only took his small day backpack and left his duffel bag full of Ket gear locked up in Quanta Arena.

After riding for more than half an hour, they pulled up to the Marquis and locked up their bikes to a rusty chain-link fence. At the entrance, a young woman greeted them. "Right this way," she said, coughing into her left elbow as she gestured into the restaurant with her right hand. She led them to the outdoor seating area—which of course wasn't really outdoors. In this part of the restaurant, customers were enclosed in a transparent plexmold half-dome so one could get the impression of being outside, while not actually being exposed to the elements.

Today, at least, it wasn't a comforting environment. The relatively tame weather from their ride over had given way to a sky full of dark, billowing clouds. The wind was picking up and howling around the plexmold. It made it feel colder inside, even if it probably wasn't.

Two teens were already sitting at their table. The taller of the two stood to greet him. His manner was formal and rushed. "Hi, you must be Tristan. I'm Fenton. I've seen you in the games."

Fenton had a probing look.

"Hi, Fenton," Tristan said. "Nice to meet you."

Fenton, Fenton. Yes, he'd seen Fenton before. He was a mediocre player in the games a couple of years ago. Tristan looked at Luisa. Had she misled him about the pandering? It seemed she knew what he was thinking, because she shook her head dismissively.

"Michaelis," the other, shorter teen said while remaining in his chair. He was a meek-looking fellow in big glasses. He pronounced his name with a guttural intonation, looking down at the table in front of him.

"Nice to meet you, Michaelis," Tristan responded in kind. Tristan turned to Luisa, an eyebrow raised. He hoped she might elaborate on her friends' skimpy introductions, but her eyes were just as evasive as Michaelis's.

Tristan shrugged and joined them. Maybe they were just shy. He kicked off the conversation enthusiastically. "So, how do you know Luisa?"

Fenton and Michaelis looked at each other but didn't offer any response. It was Luisa who answered for them. "Fenton and I are childhood friends," she said. "We grew up together in south SF. And Michaelis goes to school with me. He's from New York."

Fenton nodded slowly in confirmation, and Michaelis was still listless. Their demeanor seemed pretty serious for people who were supposedly friends.

Tristan sometimes felt out of his element in social gatherings. His relationships often faltered in the wake of his focus on the games. But the dry discourse between these supposed friends made him feel a little less lonely.

"How was the match?" Fenton asked.

"It was great," Tristan said, and he gave them a rundown of the game. They listened carefully and asked a few polite questions, the waitress took their order, and they asked a few more.

Large bowls of proto-chili—a synthetic bean mash smothered in brown oil—and side plates of fried synth-rice arrived, at which time everyone focused on eating. With an empty tank from his exertions, Tristan ate like he hadn't eaten in days. His safety mask was dangling from his neck and he had to pull it back at times to avoid getting it in his food.

When he looked up from his meal, he found Luisa gazing at him. He smiled back inquisitively, and she looked away. He started to lean back into his food until he saw that Michaelis had moved closer on his left and was looking in his direction. Fenton had also focused his eyes on him.

"Okay, what's up, guys? It's not my birthday."

They exchanged quizzical looks. Fenton spoke first. "We know about what happened to your brother."

Tristan hesitated in mid-chew, then shot up from his chair. He glanced around the restaurant for caretaker agents. A few people looked up from their meals, but just as soon paid him no mind. These people had thick yellowing around the eyes, and some were hunched over. They didn't look like caretakers, even if they weren't in uniform.

Luisa placed her hand on his forearm. "Relax, Tristan, this isn't a caretaker inquisition. My cousin knows the owner. This place is safe." If it had been anyone else, he would have shaken her arm off and walked away, but instead he stood firm.

Michaelis fidgeted with his glasses, correcting their placement on the bridge of his nose. "No, we're not caretakers," he said. "Quite the contrary. We also know you have good reason to have your reservations about them."

The comment put Tristan even more on edge. How much did they know about him? He couldn't hide a confused frown. "Okay, so what is this? Who *are* you with?"

Michaelis spoke up again, but quieter this time. "We aren't *with* anybody. We're...concerned citizens. We want to put an end to the injustice. The system—it's not working." He seemed to be trying to dispel the mystery of Fenton and Luisa's statements, yet he also seemed uncomfortable with his own words.

Tristan looked at him in disbelief. "Okay..." He began slowly inching back from the table.

"Just listen, will you?" Fenton said, gesturing to Tristan's empty chair. "Please?"

After some hesitation, Tristan sat back down and crossed his arms aloofly. "Fine, I'll listen," he said. He could feel his heart pounding.

Michaelis continued. "Basically, we want to bring down the dome system."

The boldness of the statement shocked Tristan. He'd heard of people wanting to lobby for a better life for the Outworlders—some basic medicines, a few more cleanup bots—but this was something different. It was ridiculous, or insane. The Inworld dome system dominated all forms of commerce. They enforced the laws through the caretakers. They could monitor everything—or nearly everything. He looked around the restaurant again nervously.

When he looked back at the table, Luisa and Fenton were cringing at the lack of subtlety of Michaelis's words.

"Okay...is this some kind of joke?" Tristan asked sincerely.

Michaelis spoke again, matter-of-factly. "Not a joke. We need to show people the system isn't working. Once we do that, people will start working toward making the Outworld a better place, rather than using the Outworld to make the Inworld a better place."

Tristan was becoming more agitated. "Really...so where's your army?" He put his hand to his brow and looked around, as if legions of militia might be waiting in the wings of the restaurant.

Michaelis returned to his former study of the tabletop. Luisa was unreadable. Fenton answered for them. "We're recruiting."

Tristan extended the line of questioning. "Okay, and once you get this army or whatever, how do you plan to take on the dome system?"

"We've got some ideas," Michaelis said.

It was an obvious question, and it was equally obvious they had no answer for it. Tristan frowned again.

Luisa was squirming. She interjected, "We need somebody with your skills, Tristan. Players in the games look up to you. We're not necessarily planning on doing anything extreme. We just want to make people see the unfairness of it all. We know we have a lot of work to do, and we're not going to do anything rash until we have a good plan in place, something with a good chance of success. Can't you just think about it?"

There was a sincerity to her words, and it was the first time Tristan had seen Luisa show genuine emotion. It blindsided him, temporarily derailing his train of thought. He pushed his chair back from the table and put his head in his hands, trying to process the situation.

The others let him be.

Tristan had only come to this meeting because Luisa had asked him to. Maybe this was the only reason she'd been talking to him all this time? Maybe it had all been an act—a means to an end? He felt used. These thoughts intermingled with consideration of their proposition. Challenging the Inworld system? He could be killed. Even if, by some miracle, it worked, what then? The goal he'd been working toward for years was to become a caretaker—to find refuge from the Outworld, but if the system changed, there might not be a refuge.

It was all so crazy.

He looked up. Fenton, Michaelis, and Luisa were whispering quietly. Luisa smiled at something Fenton said. He couldn't make out the words, but it seemed to him there was something smug in her smile.

That did it. The expression on Luisa's face fanned the embers of his distaste for the situation.

"Let me get this straight," Tristan said. "You've got no plan, no people. I'm sorry, I really have no love for the caretakers, but let's be realistic. It's the only way to get out of this place." He extended his hand and arced it at the plexmold around them. The wind howled ominously as if he'd called upon it with his hand. "I have a chance to make it," he continued, "and you're asking me to give that up? I'm sorry, I just can't be a part of this...whatever it is you're doing."

Tristan ran through this discourse quickly, and when he finished, he stood up from the table again. He was feeling anxious, as though he was falling into some kind of quicksand that would swallow him up if he didn't get away from these people, and this conversation. He tried to regain some composure and began backing away.

The others looked startled. Fenton reached out and grabbed his arm. "You can't leave."

It was said deadpan, and Tristan couldn't make out if it was a threat or a plea. There was fervor in Fenton's eyes.

To Tristan's surprise, the diminutive Michaelis put his hand on Fenton's outstretched arm. "He can do as he chooses," Michaelis stated.

After a pause, Fenton released Tristan's arm.

They glared at him while he stared back resolutely. The disconnect between him and them was palpable.

He turned and headed for the door without saying another word. The meeting was clearly over, and goodbyes weren't necessary.

Once outside, the weather had indeed changed. He was hit by a heavy, sulfurous wind. As he walked hastily up the hill toward his bike, he turned to see Luisa and her friends through the plexmold half-dome of the Marquis. Luisa was looking down at the table as the other two were engaged in animated conversation.

The image soon wavered as his eyes began chafing. He rubbed his irritated sockets and pulled out extra goggles from his backpack, wrapping them above his safety mask.

He unlocked his bike and rode hard, his mind spinning. The gusts of wind were so strong now that they whistled through the filters in his mask.

He almost crashed his bike on the way home—twice. It probably wasn't safe to ride. The wind was too strong. But he had to get away from that place, from that meeting, from Luisa, as quickly as possible.

CHAPTER 6

Luisa stepped out of the shower and toweled herself off in the cold morning air. Rex greeted her with a gruff bark and the clang of his dish at her feet.

"Yeah, yeah, I'll get to it."

She wrapped the towel around her midsection and pranced on the metallic floors into the kitchen with Rex's dish in hand. As she opened the fridge, the cheap electronic calendar she'd magnetized to the front caught her eye. She tilted the door back to the closed position to give it a quick scan.

Their next game was against Amber Lightning. This she already knew well, but its importance required her to repeatedly imprint the date into her gray matter to ensure there wasn't any chance she would forget.

The weeks following the dinner with Tristan had been difficult and uncomfortable. She'd stayed with Cold Fusion, even though she could have easily moved to another squad to make it more bearable for Tristan. She held out hope he would change his mind, but other than commands to her in practices or games, Tristan hadn't said as much as a word to her since that day.

It was such a disaster. Tristan had easily pointed out what they already knew but didn't discuss: the lack of any real support for their cause, and perhaps more importantly, the lack of a good plan. Michaelis and Fenton's tactless explanation, and surprising Tristan with their knowledge of his brother, hadn't helped matters. It must have all seemed so amateurish to Tristan.

She had to admit, they *were* amateurs.

The last meeting with Michaelis and Fenton had been uninspiring. She'd expected to have to put up with Fenton wearing an *I told you so* demeanor, but instead he'd been quiet. They discussed other recruiting targets and strategies, but their hearts weren't in it. Before approaching Tristan, they had spent several meetings focused on him alone. Now they were back to square one.

Rex's drool had formed a sizable puddle on the kitchen floor.

Luisa collected some kibble from the fridge and gave him a large serving, which Rex accepted greedily when the bowl was delivered to the floor.

"I've got to go, so you guard the fort." She scratched around Rex's collar.

She quickly dressed in her typical boyish fashion—tight pants and a T-shirt, with a brown vest overtop—and jogged out the door to collect her bike. She was running late for her meeting with her cousin.

Chooly was a good twenty years older than her and—at least by her estimation—had led a full and interesting life. He'd spent his early days in street gangs and then parlayed that into making a modest fortune selling black-market items to Outworlders. He'd dabbled in everything from reprogrammed helper robots to non-synth foods to therapeutics that had been banned by the caretakers. And that was just what she knew about. He was a cunning businessman who knew how to play the system.

She pictured Chooly as a role model for her own conspiratorial activities. Moreover, he had a wealth of information and was her only real source of intelligence. He'd known from his extensive contacts in the gangs about Tristan's brother being hanged for crimes against the Inworld, for example.

But her visit wasn't only business. Chooly was her only remaining family. He'd been with her in the waiting room when the doctor had given her and her mother the quick summary. With a shrug, the doctor had said matter-of-factly that because her father had worked by the docks, where the exposure to Tyband-contaminated materials was more prevalent than in other areas, he was more susceptible to cancer.

As for her mother, roughly a year later the same doctor had said just as matter-of-factly, again with Chooly by her side, that there was no rhyme or reason, except the usual risk of lung cancer. Chooly and his wife had taken Luisa in and watched over her. They stood by her in the inevitable aftermath when she cocooned herself in her room after her mother's death.

Eventually she came out of it, but with growing resentment. The Inworld could have saved her parents, but the greedy parasites refused to devote any resources to cleaning up the Outworld. They refused to allow Outworlders access to the advanced cancer treatment facilities, and instead, heaped luxury upon luxury on themselves in their pristine refuge.

And now it was Chooly's turn.

It was a rare form of bone marrow cancer. Chooly was on a number of anticancer therapies—many of which were black market. But the success rate of these therapies was so low that Outworlders had come to view the cures as death sentences in their own right. It had been several weeks since Luisa had seen him, and there was no telling how far he'd progressed in that time.

He was just one more fish in the ocean of Outworlder victims. The last number she'd heard from Michaelis was that in the Bay Area there was a forty percent incidence of terminal cancer by age fifty. You wouldn't hear much about most of them. They would die quietly at home, or one day they would just decide to not show up for work. They would relieve their families of the burden they had become, and walkoff to die.

Like her dad. They never did find his body.

And some people were genetically more susceptible than others. Of the family she'd known, the incidence had been more than eighty percent. She had long since written herself off as a cancer victim in waiting.

She was a ghost, cycling through a dying city.

Luisa rode west toward Junipero. It was the only affluent part of San Francisco outside of the dome system. It had been built up in large part over the last fifty years as Outworlders serving the Inworld had set up shop south of the Parkdome. This area was the main access point for commerce serving the Parkdome, Sidiodome, and the soon-to-be completed Marindome.

People claimed there was less pollution in this part of town, but everyone seemed to get sick just as much, and no scientist had ever supported the theory. It was probably a rumor circulated by the residents to prop up real estate values.

Luisa rode along the main bike thoroughfare on Holloway Avenue, past a bustling Junipero Boulevard and then over Nineteenth Avenue, which was dominated by the drone of boxy transport robots making a beeline to and from the Parkdome along zippers of sharp, bristling metal. As she labored each revolution of her bicycle wheels up the steep incline of the overpass, she looked north into the distance to see the mechanical ants entering the large dark Parkdome anthill on the horizon.

After several more blocks, she rolled to a stop outside Chooly's house. It was three stories tall, with wide peaked dormers and slate siding. The lawn was well kept, with a sprinkler currently arcing over a portion closer to the garden. It was full of yellow and red flowers in full bloom.

They were fake, of course, but well modeled after the kinds of expensive flowers she'd seen at the hydroponic farms south of the city.

She unstrapped her safety mask and rubbed the unsightly chafing marks left on her chin and cheeks before approaching the door. She parked the bike under the Fantonesta Residence sign on the front porch and rang the bell. She didn't worry about locking her bike. Crime was light here in Junipero, and besides, no one with half a brain was going to steal anything from Chooly's front yard, if they knew who he was.

Chooly's wife Melissa opened the door. She was a slightly overweight, middle-aged woman with a brilliant smile.

"Hello, Luisa, how are you?"

Luisa entered Melissa's outstretched arms for a warm embrace. "I'm great. How's Chooly?"

"He's just fine. You can find him out back." Melissa led Luisa through the house. In the living room were Chooly's favorite Ket team masks lined up along the wall, including one he'd painted in Cold Fusion colors. There were a few of Melissa's paintings—minimalist watercolors depicting tall buildings. The works were laden with heavy shadows that seemed to contrast with her friendly disposition. A written commendation from the mayor for Melissa's work was also there.

"Is Chooly doing okay?" Luisa asked

"He sure is," Melissa answered. "In fact, he's making dinner."

Luisa was surprised. Chooly had been in and out of bed for most of a year and unable to work, so she wasn't expecting him to be mobile. Maybe the black-market cancer treatments were working?

"I hope you didn't eat beforehand," Melissa chided.

"Of course not."

One of the great things about visiting her cousin was they always had good food. Luisa's never cooked anything half-decent, so it was always a treat.

They paused at the back door. Melissa said, "Before I let you go to the back, you have to give me the gossip. You know you're a beautiful young woman. You must tell me a story before I let you by." She turned to Luisa while her arms spanned the corridor, barring passage.

Melissa was always disarming. In fact, she and Chooly were the only people she knew who weren't tightly wound. She could feel the tension in her dissipate with every step into their home. "I wish I had more to tell you, but the good men are few and far between."

Melissa shook her head. "Tell me something I don't know."

As far back as she could remember, Luisa had never felt motivated to meet a mate. Sure, she'd had the occasional fling for fun or curiosity, but they were just distractions that never lasted. Inevitably someone in their circle would get sick, and they would pull away.

It's hard to have a love life when you're always in mourning.

In an attempt to avoid further inquiry, she turned it around on Melissa. "I've been waiting for you and Chooly to hook me up with some nice Junipero boys. What's the deal?"

Melissa smiled. "My mistake. We will get right on it." She saluted militarily. "But you should know there are no nice Junipero boys, just rich ones."

Luisa chuckled. "Right, sorry. The rich ones will have to do."

Looking only partially satisfied with Luisa's response, Melissa turned about and continued to the back of the house. "Well, I guess we'll just have to get Chooly to grill you, along with the hamburgers. He's much better at it than me."

"Oh, I know," Luisa responded cheerfully.

Chooly certainly was. Although almost every interaction she had with Chooly was good-natured and fun, she'd seen him when he was serious. When he was serious, she knew it, and she didn't joke around.

Melissa opened the patio door and hesitated. "I need to get the garnishes. I'll be back in a minute. You go ahead."

Luisa's mouth started watering when she smelled the grill. It seemed like forever since she'd had hamburgers that weren't synth-meat.

The Fantonestas were fortunate enough to have an enclosed back-yard. Similar to the Marquis, a half-dome arose from the back of the yard to the second floor of the house, keeping the heavily filtered air contained while also letting daylight in. The material used in the back-yard enclosure's construction was slightly different from that of the restaurant, however. It was less tinted, with discolorations only at the seams of the panels. She recognized it as one of the newer versions of plexmold that had come off the market. This might provide some comfort that it wasn't Tyband-contaminated, but no one knew for sure.

She also knew the material was scarce, and therefore controlled by the Inworld. It probably wasn't legal to use it for backyard enclosures, but the caretakers tended to overlook simple backyard half-domes, especially if you couldn't see them from the street. It was Chooly playing the system again.

Chooly was standing at the grill with a baseball cap on backward and his chef's apron that said *Kiss the Cook*. It was cheesy by Luisa's standards, but Chooly wore it well. The smoke rose up and was sucked out through a vent on the second floor of the house to a hidden exhaust on the side.

"Luisa! How's my girl doing?" Chooly raced over and gave her a big hug while lifting her a few inches off the ground, oblivious to the hamburger grease he was imprinting on her shirt with his apron.

Luisa was internally relieved. Chooly seemed to be doing better than ever. He did look pale, but his spirits were high. Any remaining tension melted away as Chooly dropped her to the ground.

"I'm very good, Chooly," she said. "Apparently I don't have to ask how you're doing."

After looking her up and down for a moment, Chooly responded, "Well, you better be hungry. I've got six burgers cooking, and at least two of them have your name on them."

"I'm always hungry. You know that."

Luisa, Chooly, and Melissa settled into the patio furniture and enjoyed a carefree conversation about next to nothing: food, the weather, and local Ket stars. Chooly did his impersonation of the new mayor. Luisa ate her fair share of hamburgers, to the Fantonestas's satisfaction.

Gradually the light began to fade as the sun merged with the western horizon. A smattering of clouds painted the sky a dull orange, and a chill began to permeate the backyard enclosure.

There was a lull in the conversation as the three admired the twilight spectacle from their safe haven without the burden of safety masks to diminish the experience.

Melissa broke the silence while rising from her seat. "Well, I better get this cleaned up, and don't think for a second you're going to offer to help, Luisa."

"Oh, I wouldn't dare." Luisa nodded in agreement.

As Melissa picked up whatever she could carry and left the yard,

Chooly leaned back in his chair, changing his posture to a thoughtful aloofness from his previously more carefree demeanor. Luisa had seen this change in Chooly before and knew it meant it was time to talk business.

"So?" Chooly began with his bushy eyebrows raised.

After a brief pause, Luisa realized Chooly wasn't going to offer any more context on his question, so she tried to answer as best she could. "We made the jump and tried to recruit Tristan."

Chooly's expression was unchanged, waiting for more. "It didn't go well," she continued. "Fenton and Michaelis laid it on thick, and he thought we were all crazy. Heck, even I thought we sounded crazy after I heard what we were saying. He didn't want any part of it. So as far as recruiting him..." She threw up her hands, not knowing what else to say.

"Well, it is crazy," Chooly offered coolly.

Luisa responded. "Yeah, I know. I think that—"

Chooly interrupted at a higher volume. "But that doesn't mean it isn't the right thing to do. Sure, people get by, but we have no control. Our puppet mayor has no say in what happens to our city, and that's just the beginning." He cleared his throat and continued. "I see the logistical reports. Those elbow-knockers are taking more and giving less than a few years ago, and they couldn't give a shit about you and me. I mean we have to clean up the filth and dead bodies piling up in the city. Sure, Junipero is fine, but last year in SOMA alone they found fifteen hundred people dead. Is it SOMA or is it a graveyard? And the caretakers just leave them there, watch from a distance, and make us do the dirty work. They don't even send their bots in, because they don't want them contaminated by our diseased hides. And just the other week I heard—well...never mind."

His face was getting flushed, but he caught himself before saying more. Chooly would often hint at some things he knew, but stop short of telling her, fearing she would eventually be incriminated just for knowing.

He held out his finger to hold her tongue as he took a drink. "Yes," he continued. "There needs to be change, although it won't be easy. In my life I made a modest contribution, but you're trying to do something bigger—a statement, a real focused attempt at something sustainable. Am I right? Is that what you want?"

"Yes," Luisa acknowledged. The simple word felt inadequate relative to the well of emotion backing the statement.

Chooly paused, as if to let her answer saturate the air. Eventually he responded, "So as far as Tristan goes, I wouldn't count him out. You said it yourself, they laid it on too thick. Maybe you should try again with a different tone?"

"Okay, sure, if you think so." But Luisa wasn't so sure. Chooly might just be trying to keep her spirits up.

"Hey, it's up to you, Luisa, I'm just offering my opinion. You're the crazy one who's trying to change the world, not me." Chooly smiled.

Luisa found it difficult to return his smile. Chooly was trying to make light of the situation, but his words were heavily weighted in truth. The joke was on her, really.

Chooly had been moving forward in his chair as he spoke. He sat back again. "Not that I think you shouldn't also explore other options in parallel."

"Do you have any idea who else we could recruit?"

"Yes, but give me time to think about it. They might be riskier and will need more investigation. I already knew a lot about Tristan. Others may be less clean in terms of understanding motivations, and I don't want you to get caught."

Luisa nodded. Chooly looked thoughtful as he took another sip of his drink. The sky was evolving to a mix of dark salmon and gray shades. Luisa shifted in her chair and held the seat with her arms straight against her torso to keep herself warm.

"What about Fenton and Michaelis?" Chooly asked. "How are they holding up in all this?" Chooly looked away as he said this. Although Chooly was generally supportive of their involvement, he'd always questioned her about their intentions. He said things like, "Well, they have the motivation, that's good," but in almost the same breath, "Just because they have the motivation doesn't mean they are right for the job."

Luisa answered, "They've taken it in stride, I think. I did talk with Michaelis the other day, and he said he's working on plans we can start to talk through."

"Yes. It's about time some concrete ideas were put on the table. I had a hard time understanding why you were recruiting when you don't know exactly what you're recruiting for."

Luisa could only nod. "Yes, well, Michaelis says he doesn't want to share his ideas until he fleshes them out. Knowing him, they should be creative and thorough."

"Hmm, good. I don't think it would be appropriate for me to help you there. You need to decide what you want to do, and own it. You're better off finding your own path. Either way, it's a tough nut to crack." He paused, and smirked. "Unless of course you can raise an army."

"Yeah, I know." Luisa cringed as she remembered what Tristan had said to them at the Marquis.

With a note of encouragement, Chooly added, "Hey, even if it's something small, it's better than ninety-nine percent of people in the Outworld. Somebody's got to stick it to those sneaky sardines." He gestured toward the Parkdome.

"Right," she said, nodding slowly.

"It's getting cold out here. Maybe we should pack it in?" Chooly offered.

"Okay. Thanks so much for your help, Chooly."

"My pleasure, Luisa. Just remember to be careful. You're only dreaming at this point, but the deeper you go, well...you know."

"I know, Chooly."

"And, oh yeah, you were late today."

There was always something that Chooly chided her on when she talked with him, some lesson or moral he made her take away with her. Today it was her punctuality.

"I'm sorry, Chooly, I know I said five p.m. It won't happen again."

"No worries." Chooly smiled as he lifted his significant frame up from his chair and gathered the remaining items on the table. She knew this wasn't a dismissal of the issue. Rather, it was Chooly's attempt to dispel any negativity that might hang between them.

They went inside and found Melissa reading in the living room. They continued their pre-dinner conversation for a few more minutes, while Luisa gradually made her way to the door. Melissa offered her a jacket for the ride home.

As Luisa rode back, the darkness claimed victory over the light. Junipero was well lit by the homes of the wealthy, but as she rode closer to the New Mission, the road lights were few and far between. It didn't matter. She knew the route well, and few people were out.

She made her way up Delores Hill, the biggest physical obstacle before the smooth ride downhill to her apartment. Her breathing reverberated in her safety mask, drowning out the sounds of dogs barking and wind whistling, and she reflected on her visit with Chooly and Melissa. The industrial plastic of the mask hid a grin prompted by her memory of Chooly's impersonation of the mayor.

CHAPTER 7

Tristan was alone in the arena after a bout of heavy training.

The confrontation at the Marquis reverberated in his mind. It infuriated him that Luisa and her friends had the audacity to proposition him—someone who was arguably a frontrunner for the Inworld. It also galled him that they had used his brother's death to try to manipulate him into their half-baked plot.

He considered kicking Luisa off the team, but he realized that was just his pride talking. She was good. He needed her. They didn't have be friends to be teammates.

He'd reacted to the experience the same way he did to anything that angered him. He used it as motivation. The anger would be his anchor, holding his focus steady, and allowing him to come back stronger. He was more determined than ever to win in the games and gain admission to the Inworld.

Yet despite everything, he realized he envied Luisa's ability to confide and share with Fenton and Michaelis. It brought home a simple fact: he couldn't make it to the Inworld without his own confidants, his own team—he needed more recruits for Cold Fusion.

He had made several attempts to approach gamers he thought would make good recruits; not just snipers or runners but smart tacticians. He was mostly met with bemused looks, polite dismissals, and sometimes a complete stonewall.

Admittedly, it was something he wasn't good at. The best recruits were usually pursued with compliments and outsized gestures, but Tristan couldn't find the right words, or the right gestures. Some were even given money, or drugs, or whatever else they wanted, but Tristan couldn't do that either. It just wasn't him, and it was difficult for him to understand why a spot on a good team wasn't enough.

Recognizing his attempts at recruiting had been in vain, he turned his thoughts to Cold Fusion's progress...or lack thereof. They had lost their last game, a game they should have won. He concentrated on doing a postmortem and revised his assessment of their prospects for the playoffs.

Cold Fusion had twelve wins and eight losses. It was a respectable tally, but they could have done much better. There were two teams ahead of them, which was two too many. The top two teams usually received the most publicity, and hence were recruited from the most for the Inworld. He still had time to catch up, however. There were another ten matches in the season before the playoffs began in November.

He glanced again at the standings stenciled electronically on the arena wall.

NSF League Standings: Top four teams as of October 7, 2140

Team; Record; Captain

Amber Lightning; 18–2; Sonny Joseph
Harry Karrie; 15–5; Karrie Hessle
Cold Fusion; 12–8; Tristan Mardukas
Red Squall; 11–9; Damian Thatcher

Amber Lightning was a force to be reckoned with. Sonny Joseph, the team captain, had recruited three of the top marksmen, including Vivek Patel, who had the best shot-to-kill ratio in the league. These hotshots had their caretaker ticket with Amber Lightning, so there was no way Tristan could get them to defect to Cold Fusion.

Deep in thought, Tristan had been oblivious to several other die-hards in the gym. They were practicing motion shooting and bounding around him. The voice of one of these players surprised him. "You're Tristan, right?"

Tristan gazed up to see a familiar-looking gangly young teen. "Yes. And you are?"

"Ardrey," he said, extending his hand. It was an unusual gesture among Ket players. Handshakes were more for stuffy businessmen.

Tristan recognized him now. Ardrey had transferred a year ago from the South San Francisco league and was quickly getting a reputation as a strong player. Many of the captains had been watching him, and some had been actively recruiting him. In fact, he was on Tristan's list.

Tristan shook his hand and automatically went into recruiting mode. "I saw you against the Golden Eagles last Tuesday," Tristan said. "You have impressive skills. That shot you made to eliminate Schneider was something else."

Ardrey appeared oblivious to Tristan's flattery. "What's wrong?"

Tristan was confused. He said, "I'm sorry, nothing's wrong."

"Was it your last game?"

Tristan tried to conceal the annoyance he felt at Ardrey's direct questioning. Was this newbie kid taunting him? He decided to go with honesty and humility, or at least partial honesty. The things you had to do to get the best recruits.

"Yeah, the last game. I'm working through the kinks."

Ardrey said, "I thought you could have used Nina more. She's fast. Use her to draw your opponents out."

Tristan was taken aback by the suggestion. It might actually be a good idea, but he was a captain, and Ardrey was a newbie. "It's worth considering," Tristan said carefully, and gritted his teeth. He wanted to change the subject. "Why are you here so late?"

"The new kids don't get any respect. They have to earn it." A barely discernible smirk crossed Ardrey's face as he looked back at the training floor. Behind him, two players were vaulting through the air, firing at a mannequin standing behind a cover block. "Hey, I know you're busy," Ardrey continued, "but do you think we could talk Ket strategy some day? I'm eager to learn."

This could be a veiled request to be part of Cold Fusion. Tristan was more than happy to use it as an opening. "Do you want to take a turn on our team? That way you can learn firsthand, even if you are a disrespected newbie." Tristan tried to offer a sardonic smile.

Ardrey didn't respond as he'd expected. He replied without affect. "No thanks, but if you want to ever talk shop, let me know."

Tristan was unsure how to react. Maybe Ardrey was still playing the field and not ready to commit. Tristan tried to find another opening.

But before he had a chance to figure out what to say next, Ardrey took the pause to extend his hand and bid goodbye. "Nice to meet you, Tristan. See you around."

Tristan took his hand and quickly ventured, "Yes, nice to meet you, Ardrey. Maybe we can chat again sometime?"

Ardrey shrugged and returned to his training exercises.

CHAPTER 8

When Sonny strolled into the arena he could feel envious eyes burning around him. It was easy, really. All he had to do was keep his snipers happy, they would keep winning, and he was a lock for the Inworld.

He had entered several levels up, giving him a good view of the warm-up activities and the arriving spectators. There were already a few people in the stands, mostly other Ket players. Many were wearing shoddy T-shirts and scraggly jeans or cords. Sonny, on the other hand, had on the black and blue Ket warm-up outfit he'd inherited from his cousin Olsen, who'd played in the Seattle Ket leagues a few years ago. The outfit looked similar to the typical dress of caretakers, although the colors were different.

Dress who you want to be, not who you are.

He turned and headed down the stairs to meet up with the rest of Amber Lightning in the locker room. They were silently preparing. He watched them donning their gear and pondered what was going through their heads when he gave them their orders. It didn't matter. Whatever it was, it worked.

Sonny had done his homework on Cold Fusion. They were a tough team and well balanced. His father, ever-present before and after games, had told him to take out the three top players, and they would fall apart. Maybe so, but it didn't matter. They would likely win anyway without any defined strategy. His hotshots would bring it home.

He was tired of hearing the nonstop yammering from his father. "Olsen practices on weekends," he would say. Or, "Olsen won more games with less talented players." It was annoying.

Sonny led Amber Lightning out of the change room, up the dusty staircase, and toward the main floor of the Quanta Arena. His team walked slowly, with heads up, the way Sonny had told them to. The growing crowd cheered as his hotshots broke into the opening. They hooted at the three best marksmen in the North San Francisco league. People in the stands carried placards with *Vivek One-Shot Patel* on them.

His father was waiting in his usual place in the lower stands. Sonny nodded in acknowledgment, but his father was gesturing emphatically for him to come over. Sonny met him on the sidelines.

He flinched as his father gripped his bicep firmly. "Remember to cut off the head. Do you hear me?"

Sonny only gave him a sideways nod in acknowledgement. He didn't need to look at his father's eyes; it felt like they were forever etched into him, watching every move.

Sonny would placate him and tell him he agreed. Sure, he was right, but it was obvious. Sonny knew that soon he would win the playoffs and become a caretaker, and then he'd be telling people what to do, and he wouldn't have his father's thumb on his back with every step he took.

After a brief silence, his father released his hold on Sonny's arm, and Sonny walked away to rejoin the team.

The buzzer sounded.

Amber Lightning was set up in their standard formation, in which the hotshots were paired with newbie sub-sixers. They fanned out into strategic sniper locations and began firing at will. Cold Fusion was adopting a full-line measured advance to maximize shield strength. They knew if they were static, they were sitting ducks against the Lightning hotshots.

Amber Lightning focused firepower on the left side of the

oncoming wall of Fusion with some success. By the time the Cold Fusion advance was close to the first hotshot group, two of the Fusion team had been eliminated by concentrated fire from his snipers. Sonny's first hotshot duo then did a lengthy joint bounding jump to get to a cover block farther away from the advancing Cold Fusion line. Cold Fusion kept advancing on the next hotshot duo in the same fashion, but now they had the first hotshot duo firing into their back. After a brief melee, three more Fusion were down, and only two of the Amber Lightning had been taken out—and these were just the newbies he'd been using as human shields.

Amber Lightning had seized the advantage.

Cold Fusion split into two teams, one of three and one of four. They raced in different directions at two Lightning squads of three isolated from the main fray. Sonny ordered one of his Lightning squads to stay put and shoot it out with the three oncoming Fusion players, focusing on Luisa Vincent. It was easier to get her when she was on the move. Two well-placed, coordinated shots took her down and she went dark. The other two Fusion players with her stopped charging and searched for cover.

On the other side of the arena, the Lightning were focusing on Tristan Mardukas, but he was well entrenched in his cover position.

It was time for Sonny to adjust his strategy. "Squad on arena left—pull back," Sonny said via broadbeam. "Let's finish the remaining two Fusion on arena right."

They lost a Lightning player in their retreat, but they made it back to cover and easily surrounded the two remaining Fusion players who had been in Luisa's squad. After some sporadic exchanges, and a few strategic cover block advances, those two Fusion were down as well.

There were only four Cold Fusion left against nine Lightning, and all three of the Lightning hotshot snipers were still active.

The rest was easy. Sonny just split them into three trios and moved toward the remaining Cold Fusion in arena left.

Sonny hadn't even needed to involve himself in the battle with the exception of a few shots here and there. He had just been staying back and issuing orders.

"Tristan Mardukas first," Sonny said, and he began firing more actively. He didn't need to say more, because they all knew what to do: look for the best line of sight at obtuse angles to Tristan's position. Tristan wouldn't be able to find cover from squads approaching from three different directions.

They found him behind a broad rectangular block and sure enough, the prevalence and precision of firepower was too much. Tristan went dark, thanks to well-placed shots from Vivek and Sonny hitting him at the same time.

It was only a matter of time. The remaining three Fusion players were cowering in defensive positions and were gradually eliminated by the overwhelming Lightning majority.

The match was over, and Amber Lightning had won convincingly.

CHAPTER 9

Tristan grew introspective in the days following the loss to Amber Lightning. The Lightning snipers were just too good. When they were having a good day, they seemed invincible.

Cold Fusion was on the bubble, and the playoffs were rapidly approaching. They would have to win both of their last two matches just to make the playoffs in fourth place. The importance of winning was becoming all too real.

There was a tendency for stars to falter at the end of the season. They would lose popularity if they didn't show up well in the last few games, and their standing would suffer significantly in the following year because they were seen as has-beens, brilliant flames who squandered their fuel too early. After next year, Tristan would turn nineteen and would no longer be eligible for the Inworld, so he didn't want to mess up his chances. He didn't want to be another fallen star.

It was a crucial time.

"Tristan?"

The voice was coming from a long way off. He shrugged it off, lost in reverie.

"Tristan?" his mother inquired again at a higher decibel. "Is everything okay?"

"It's fine, Mom." He briefly met her eyes and gave her a fake smile. "Just daydreaming again." They were sitting around the kitchen table, eating dinner. She had her black Seneca Corp coveralls on, and her hair was already up in tight braids. She would be heading to the factory for the night shift soon.

His father was also looking his way, an eyebrow raised over the jaundiced skin surrounding his eyes. He said nothing and went back to reading his tablet device.

Tristan didn't have a close relationship with his parents. He spent little time with them except for catching the occasional meal between Ket training and school. Even then, normally he would eat with such animal ferocity that there was little time for words. His meal etiquette was no different this evening.

"I'm worried about you," his mother continued. "All you do is practice and mope around." She was sitting across from him, cradling a cup of hot tea. "Your grades could be better. You're lucky, you know. You shouldn't take the opportunities you have for granted."

It reminded him what Luisa said about his mom at the Seneca plant. It was true. Tristan's parents both had jobs and, for now at least, weren't sick. A few kids in his class had to drop out of his school to get jobs or take care of their parents.

"I know, Mom," he said, "but I need to focus on Ket. Don't you want me to make it to the Inworld?" Tristan didn't hide his annoyance.

"Yes Tristan, but I just think you're getting too wrapped up in this. There's only so much you can do to win."

"Uh-huh," Tristan said, and he didn't offer more. He returned his attention to his food. It was bland rations—a clumpy mash of synth-rice and generic protein pellets without any red, brown, or green oil.

"I think what your mother is trying to say," his father added, "is that you shouldn't lose focus on other aspects of your life. We admire your dedication, but there's more to life than...what do you kids call it nowadays...being glossy?" He suppressed a cough when he finished.

"Shiny, Dad. They call the Inworlders shiny sardines—like they're stuck in a tin can." Tristan gave him one of the more unflattering descriptions, even though he thought it was wrong, because he didn't want to argue; he wanted to end the conversation. Without looking up, he added, "And I know, Dad."

That was that. The rest of the meal, all two minutes of it, was completed wordlessly.

Tristan knew they meant well, but they didn't recognize the importance of the coming days. Their lives were so different. His father, working in the city refurbishment corps all day, had never played in the games and didn't understand them. His life was hard. He would come home late, clad in his bulky protective gear, and often act comatose for the rest of the evening, nursing his back and worsening arthritis. And his mother was so wrapped up in her Seneca job, doing plant management or whatever, that she was rarely around.

What did they have to look forward to? The inevitable terminal health ailment would come soon. Both his parents were starting to show signs of Tanner's esophyxia. They would cough often, and sometimes he could hear them gagging in the bathroom. They would try to muffle it, but it was unmistakable. There was no masking the curdling sound. It was the first signs of interstitial lung disease. The countdown had started.

They couldn't defy the odds for long, and the future of his family would be a painful, destructive process. He'd seen it with other families countless times. Tristan didn't need to be here for that, just so he could repeat the process all over again.

With this resolve dominating his thoughts, after dinner he went to his room and revisited the Ket schedule for the upcoming weeks. To win, he would have to nail his strategy for the next two games and ratchet up the team's practices.

It might not be enough. Even if they did win the next two games, they would probably have to face Amber Lightning again. If that happened—when it happened—he would need a better plan of attack.

He decided to break the silence with Luisa to see if she had any ideas. At this point, he would take any help he could get. Tristan sent comlink messages to the team. They were to meet him at six a.m. for practice the next day. He asked Luisa to meet him at five-thirty. Then he spent time analyzing their next opponent and began running through scenarios.

Shortly after midnight he cleaned his teeth, applied anti-contaminant ointment around his eyes, and dizzily slinked into bed. The wheels continued to turn relentlessly in his mind as a shallow slumber overtook him.

CHAPTER 10

Luisa arrived at the arena at five-forty a.m. She'd been annoyed at the request to come so early but knew it was crunch time for the team.

She approached Tristan as he was putting the last of his gear on. He was alone. "Where's everyone else?" she inquired.

"You're late," Tristan remarked.

She remembered Chooly's reprimand from a few days ago, but Luisa wasn't about to be put in her place. "Looks to me more like I'm early," she said, waving her hand around at the empty arena. "Seriously, what's up?"

"I wanted to talk strategy before the rest of the team arrives." Luisa looked at her comlink again. He had indeed mentioned it but she'd forgotten. "Oh, okay." He seemed testy, so Luisa adopted a mechanical air, trying not to come off as antagonistic.

He said, "I would appreciate advice on how we can win. Any thoughts are welcome."

"Okay...can I see what you've put together?"

Tristan pulled out a binder from his backpack and handed it to her. It was full of scenarios and strategies, matchups, and random notes covering mostly each of the next two games. A few schematics showed plays, with probability distribution numbers on the side.

"What's this?" she pointed to the schematics. She'd never seen anything like it.

"I developed an app that uses historical Ket data. It helps me analyze probabilities of certain plays working."

Her eyebrows rose. It reminded her of what Michaelis had said about his computer systems aptitude test. She certainly didn't know anyone who'd gone to these lengths.

She leafed through the rest of it. "This is impressive," she said. "I need to take a thorough look at it, but I don't know if I can add anything. I saw what you did last year with Green Viper. Nobody thought you could have a winning record with that ragtag group. You're a good captain, Tristan, so I'm sure it's in good order."

Tristan looked impatient. "Please give me any feedback by tomorrow, and don't tell the rest of the team I'm asking you to do this."

"Of course," Luisa replied. She could sense the frustration in Tristan. Did he expect her to walk in at five-forty in the morning and dust off a bulletproof plan?

Tristan paced in silence along the sidelines as Luisa began putting the rest of her tight-fitting Ket uniform on over her spandex undergarments. This was the first time she'd really spoken with Tristan since the Marquis, and she wondered if she would ever get another chance. Chooly did say she might want to try again.

Luisa glanced around the empty arena, then ventured, "You know, Tristan, if this doesn't work out, I'd like to talk about what we discussed at dinner again. Our idea is more of a dream than anything else, but we're still interested in pursuing that dream. Fenton and Michaelis were just expressing their passion for the cause. If you give us a chance, maybe we can—"

"Listen to me carefully," Tristan interrupted, pointing a finger at her accusingly. "Never bring that up to me again, do you hear me? I'm not interested and never will be. I'm going to the Inworld."

Her face felt hot. "Okay, you got it."

The door to the arena opened and a tall wiry teen in full gear entered. It was Ardrey, the newbie Tristan had mentioned he'd spoken with before.

Ardrey still hadn't picked a squad. Each week he was taking a turn on the bottom six of various teams. It was strange a player of Ardrey's demonstrated ability still hadn't committed at this late stage of the season, especially considering he'd been heavily recruited by a number of teams.

Tristan stopped pacing immediately. He quickly shed his concerned frown and his eyes opened wide, brimming with a sense of opportunity. Luisa knew what he was thinking. His focus on the games hadn't wavered an inch at Luisa's previous comments.

Ardrey approached them. "Hey guys. You mind if I practice on the far side of the arena?"

"Ardrey," Tristan began, "I'm not sure if you remember me. We had a conversation a while back. I'm Tristan."

"Sure I remember. Everyone knows the team captains." He glanced over at Luisa. "And you're Luisa, right?"

Luisa acknowledged Ardrey with a nod. "Nice to meet you, Ardrey."

Tristan was eying the binder sitting on the chair next to Luisa. "Hey, do you remember you said you wanted to talk about strategy?"

Ardrey replied, "Yeah, sure."

"Well, I'd love to take you up on it. I'll even show you some of our plays for the next couple of games." Tristan opened the binder and scrolled through the pages so Ardrey could see it. He had put a significant amount of effort into devising plans for the next two games. Luisa doubted the other captains had anything as extensive.

Ardrey pouted in contemplation. He seemed to warm up to the idea. "That would be great. Thanks for offering."

Tristan nodded. "Good. We're about to practice, but why don't you give me your comlink ID, and we'll grab a bite to eat this week. You would be a good sanity check given your knowledge of the other teams."

"Okay, sure."

They exchanged contact information, and Ardrey bid farewell

curtly but politely and went to the far side of the arena to begin his training exercises.

Tristan's mood was uplifted by this exchange, but for Luisa's part, the development didn't excite her. She cared more about her second inquiry to Tristan—which had been flatly rejected.

The rest of the team arrived soon after.

While most other gamers slept, Tristan drove Luisa and the rest of Cold Fusion hard.

CHAPTER 11

There was a synth-garbanzo gyros place near where Tristan lived with reasonably good lighting and a few scattered tables that rarely had any takers. It was the kind of place that tried to be a restaurant but never made it past takeout. Although somewhat expensive, it was better than the typical synth-rice place, and they didn't skimp on the red oil. He didn't want to come off as cheap.

Tristan was at the table farthest from the food-ordering counter, reviewing his binder one more time and waiting for Ardrey to arrive. He looked down at his watch again. Eight p.m. on the nose.

He looked up, and Ardrey was standing in front of him.

Tristan began amicably. "Where did you come from? Have you been working on some stealth training?"

Ardrey managed a weak grin. After a brief pause, he offered, "I move fast when I'm hungry."

"Well, let's get some grub."

They headed up to the counter, ordered a couple of gyros, and made their way back to the table.

"Are you from South San Francisco originally?" Tristan asked.

"No, I was born in North San Francisco and spent my childhood here."

"Really? Where in NSF?"

Ardrey paused. "Russian Hill."

"Oh yeah? Where in Russian Hill?"

"The northern part." Ardrey looked mildly annoyed and didn't seem to be offering questions in return. So much for small talk.

Tristan began by discussing the most recent strategies he'd used against Amber Lightning and other opponents. He held back the binder at first but eventually brought it out onto the table. He wanted to share it as a gesture of good faith, but he also didn't want Ardrey to have too much time with it.

Ardrey listened intently. He interjected with the occasional question or expression of interest. They discussed various strategies—ones Tristan used, and ones the other teams used. Ardrey was engaged and caught on quickly, although Tristan couldn't read much else from him. It seemed like the meeting was all business for him, or maybe that was just his normal disposition?

Since the small talk wasn't working, Tristan decided he'd have to go with a blunt proposition rather than trying to befriend him. "Ardrey, I would like it if you would join our squad. We're the fourth-ranked team, and I'd be prepared to make you third in command of Cold Fusion. That would mean you could be second in command next year if all went well, maybe even first if Luisa made it into the Inworld. The chances of you captaining your own squad next year would be very high."

Ardrey contemplated this new turn in the conversation.

Tristan didn't want to corner him, even though he knew the offer was attractive. "Why don't you take some time to think about it?" he said. "I'm sure we can handle these two last games." Tristan actually wasn't that sure, but he wanted to sell Cold Fusion as a winner. "But I need to know before the playoffs."

"Okay," Ardrey said. "I'll think about it. Thanks for the offer."

"Of course, and I'd love to have you even sooner. It would be better for getting the right team chemistry in place before the playoffs."

"I understand." Ardrey nodded.

Having made his case, and seeing that Ardrey wasn't prepared to respond immediately, it appeared the brief meeting was nearing an end. Tristan made some more failed attempts at conversation, and they bid each other goodbye.

After Ardrey left, Tristan decided to stay for a few more minutes to noodle the meeting. He didn't know if Ardrey was shy, quiet, or just holding his cards close, but there was nothing else he could do. He doubted anyone else would give Ardrey third in command—not this late in the season. And he had demonstrated good faith by sharing his strategies. Hopefully that would put him in good standing.

Time would tell.

Tristan pushed Ardrey to the back of his mind and concentrated on the upcoming matches. He trained his team incessantly and spent even more hours in the gym doing individual exercises. He would sometimes awake in the middle of the night and some dark corner of his mind would place him in the arena, floating against the ceiling among the dark trusses, like he was on a high-arc anti-gravity bound that never ended.

The occasional gripe could be heard in the Cold Fusion locker-room talk, but it was short-lived, and Tristan chalked it up to exhaustion more than anything else. They were working hard, but the other teams were as well. No one would dare confront Tristan. It would be seen only as whining. They knew he just wanted to win. So did they.

The next game was a blowout. Their opponent, the Steel Panthers, were outmatched and outmaneuvered by a finely tuned machine. Tristan had adopted an unorthodox strategy of having his two fastest squads advance and then quickly draw back to feign a disorganized retreat. The two best Panther players had pursued them into a trap, exposing them in an arena corner where Tristan's two best marksmen were lying in wait.

In the end, Cold Fusion had eight players left standing, a sound thumping.

The victory changed nothing for Tristan. He called a practice for first thing the next morning and had them do more block-to-block sprints and bounding exercises.

The next team up was Razzle Dazzle. It was the last game of the regular season. Razzle was a more formidable adversary than the Panthers. In midseason, Razzle had climbed up the rankings with some impressive wins over Harrie Karrie and Cold Fusion. In other words, they were a key contributor to Cold Fusion's descent in the rankings. Regardless, all that mattered was if Cold Fusion lost, Razzle Dazzle would make the playoffs and Cold Fusion wouldn't.

CHAPTER 12

"Hi, Luisa, how are you?" Melissa's usually graceful expression was more weathered by worry, but her smile still maintained its charm.

Luisa entered Melissa's outstretched arms for an embrace. Melissa's arms squeezed all the way around, pushing her backpack against her spine. "I'm very good, and you?"

"We're okay. Please come in." Melissa signaled for Luisa to follow her. "Chooly has been expecting you but let me get you something to eat before you see him."

Luisa strolled into the kitchen as Melissa collected a piece of apple crumble cake on a plate and passed it to her. The crumble had green oil on it, so it would be sweeter than the bitter-tasting synth-crumbles you could get at the store. She also handed her a glass of water as she ushered her out of the room. Normally, Luisa would at least have a cursory chat with Melissa before meeting with Chooly, but maybe he wanted to see her immediately.

As she made her way to Chooly's room, she remembered Chooly's last words on her previous visit. She looked down at her watch and almost spilled the water in the process.

Shit.

"You're late," Chooly said. He was sitting up in his bed in a dark corner of the room. There was a stream of sunlight coming in from the window, dancing on the floor in front of him to the cadence of the patterned sheer curtains rippling from an external breeze. Chooly must have felt comfortable opening the window slightly given the low pollution index today.

"I'm really sorry, Chooly, the traffic was bad and—"

"Bullshit. You're always late. You need to fix that."

Luisa shifted her feet. Chooly was usually more good-humored with her, especially when he first saw her. He seemed to be in a terrible mood. She scolded herself again.

"Never mind," he said. "Sit down. Let's talk." In the shadowy corner, Chooly's outstretched hand motioned to a chair on the right side of the room. She sat in the chair, upright and at attention. The sunlight on the floor prodded at her feet as if toying with her. She ate a bite of her crumble cake and set it beside her chair next to her water. For some reason she'd lost her appetite.

"So, what happened with Tristan?" Chooly began. "He said no again, didn't he?"

"He said no. It didn't go well."

"I'm not surprised. Don't give up though."

Luisa didn't share his optimism. She wanted to change the subject. "So how have you been doing? Is there anything I can do to help you and Melissa?"

"I've been better. No need to help, but thanks."

"Do you and Melissa have plans for the holidays? If not I thought—"

Chooly cut her off. "Please. I have some important things I want to tell you." She could vaguely see his hand motion in the dark corner, dismissing what she was saying. "What you're trying to do is nothing like what I did in my life. The Inworld couldn't care less about the black market except to make a few examples. You're contemplating a direct attack on their way of life, and you probably won't succeed. You may even die, or at least be imprisoned for a long time." This was all said with increasing volume, giving the last sentence a certain finality and bluntness.

It was all true, of course. Hearing it aloud didn't change it. Was he trying to dissuade her? Was he telling her he didn't want to help?

He made a loud guttural sound to clear his throat. "Do you still want to do this?"

"Do what? You mean fight against the Inworld? Yes, absolutely. Actually, there is—"

"Let me get you something." Chooly cut her off again.

Chooly's form moved out from the gloom. He planted his feet wearily on the floor and stood up. Luisa raised herself slightly from her seat, intending to give him a hand, but he motioned for her to stay. As he stood up in front of her, the light finally caught his form escaping the shadows.

His face was heavily lined and stretched. He didn't stand fully erect, but rather partially hunched over, and she could see the contour of his spine. He'd always been a formidable man: six foot six inches in height with a stocky build. His stature had always commanded attention, and Chooly knew how to use it to his advantage in his business dealings.

It pained her to see him so diminished.

He slowly made his way over to his closet and grabbed at some clothes. He haphazardly pulled items off the hangers and let them drop to the floor behind him. Then he leaned over, entered the closet head-first, and lifted a piece of floorboard from the ground and placing it behind him. Eventually he backed out, carrying a metallic green dossier, which he handed to her.

Chooly slowly moved himself up onto the bed. "Write this down or memorize it. The combination is 5A6Z5N. If you get the combination wrong ten times, the contents will be destroyed. So don't get it wrong, and don't lose it."

Luisa hastily brought out the pen and pad she'd brought in her backpack. She wrote down the code.

Chooly said, "This contains much of what I learned in my years in the business. You may find it useful, but if anyone finds it, you could be killed, as well as Melissa."

Luisa listened carefully. This was serious. She wasn't sure she wanted this kind of responsibility.

"Please look through it. We can talk in a couple of weeks about how to make use of it. Until then, don't talk about it with anyone. It's too risky. Also, Melissa doesn't know about this. I don't want her to worry about this kind of thing, so just between us, okay?"

"Okay, I'll be careful. I understand the risks."

Chooly was silent, so Luisa continued. "Do you have any other ideas as to recruits we could try to find? We're kind of lost, and it would be good to have more leads to explore. Or is that in the dossier?"

Chooly retreated further onto his bed, into the corner of the room. She could hear him clear his throat again. "Not right now," he said. "Please go. I need my rest today."

"Oh, sorry." She stood up, but then hesitated. "You wouldn't...you're not going to walkoff, are you?"

"No, that's not me."

"My dad...I think it's cowardly."

"You're wrong."

"What?"

"The cancer he had, it would have been long, slow, and very expensive. He didn't want to force your mom to quit her job to take care of him. One of the reasons you have the savings you have—that you have the freedom to go to school and to fight against the Inworld —is because he walked off. His death gave you life, and freedom. Nobody wants to die, Luisa, but it's much worse to take from the living."

Chooly was the last person she would have expected to defend walkoffs, but here he was. And her dad...maybe he was right. Maybe he did do it for her.

"I'm lucky," Chooly continued. "I have the money to fight."

She wanted to argue, but she couldn't form the words. Instead, tears formed in her eyes. They were for Chooly, but also, maybe, for her dad as well.

"Sorry to cut the visit short," Chooly said, pulling up the covers. "Next time we can plan out the holidays."

"Okay," she said, holding back tears. "Thanks very much, Chooly. I hope you feel better soon."

Chooly raised his hand in a goodbye gesture between the shadows, clearing his throat again.

Not knowing what else to say, she put the dossier carefully in her backpack. She grabbed her plate and glass and turned to leave.

Just before she made it to the door, Chooly said, "We're rooting for you, Luisa."

As she left the room, a gust of wind caused the curtains to shift, and dancing light traveled up onto the bed. She looked back to see the faint glimmer of a grin cross Chooly's face. A moment later the curtains returned to their original position, and Chooly disappeared into the shadows.

CHAPTER 13

The game against Razzle Dazzle went well. Tristan used four teams of three and executed faster in getting to the best cover points. Luisa showed good leadership in taking her trio to cover almost directly behind six of the Razzle, catching them in a deadly crossfire with the rest of the Fusion, eliminating them quickly as the Razzle couldn't find the right directionality for their shielding. After that, it was a simple numbers game.

So they had won again, this time with five Cold Fusion left standing. Furthermore, they had made the playoffs with a strong finish to the season. Tristan had a good feeling about their momentum.

He hadn't heard from Ardrey yet, but there were still several days before the teams were frozen. Maybe he was waiting to see if Cold Fusion made it to the playoffs before committing? Now that he thought of it, that's what Tristan would do.

The real challenge was going to be Amber Lightning. The way the rankings worked it meant Cold Fusion would have to play them first. If they won against the Lightning, Cold Fusion had a serious chance of winning the league and, in turn, him making the Inworld. If they lost, it was anybody's guess. He would be on the bubble.

Practice with Cold Fusion began early the next day.

CHAPTER 14

S onny walked out of his house and felt a waft of hot air hit him. The amorphous blob of orange representing the sun was slowly lowering on the horizon, and a light breeze was the only respite from the oppressive humidity.

He began his gradual stroll to the nearby carport, walking down the driveway they never used. It was such a waste. When he was little, he'd asked his father why they didn't turn it into a garden or something more appealing than the harsh pavement. Father had ignored him and never answered. It was easier to maintain this way, Sonny guessed. The neighbors' fake plants discolored easily and constantly needed replacing.

He reached the gate and followed the familiar ritual of entering the code, going through the gate, closing it, and entering the code again to lock it.

As he reached the main street, he noticed small bands of heterogeneously appareled children running to and fro.

Right, it's Halloween.

This was one of the few neighborhoods where kids still went door to door to trick or treat. The poorer neighborhoods no longer participated in the pagan holiday.

It was such an odd tradition, one Sonny had never understood nor cared for. All the kids running around made him anxious. He liked the reassuring order of every other day, where children rarely went anywhere unaccompanied, and he didn't have to endure the shrieking sounds that went with the excitement of some carb nugget smothered in green oil. Thankfully, they never made it up to the estate. Since there had never been any candy, they'd stopped trying. There were better pickings for them down here on the main street.

A child ran up to him from across the road and stuck out his hand. He was dressed in all black and had white paint over his safety mask, making him look like some sort of robotic ghoul. His skin around the mask was red and blotchy from the heat, but it didn't seem to bother him.

"Trick or treat," the child said.

"Trick," Sonny answered as he brushed past. The child stood dumbfounded for a moment, then ran back to the group of friends on the other side.

Sonny reached the carport and again punched in his code at the gate. The guard gave him a cheery greeting. "Hello, Mr. Joseph. Happy Halloween, sir."

"Hello," Sonny replied, and he moved quickly through. He'd forgotten the guard's name and didn't want to be roped into an uncomfortable conversation.

Once in the sanctuary that was his car, he made his way east from Junipero toward the arena, and other thoughts began presiding, notably the playoffs that were beginning tomorrow.

While all the other captains were surely fretting every detail, he wasn't that worried. In fact, he'd never been more confident in his team. Sure, they would train and go through the motions, but they just had too much talent to lose.

Perhaps more importantly, his chances of getting into the Inworld were looking better every day. Sonny was already thinking about how he could keep his hotshots on his side when they all made it. Vivek had real star power and the others would also be useful as allies.

He pulled into the arena parking lot and made his way inside.

Sonny decided to sit out and watch the practice from afar. Besides running over the revised strategy against Cold Fusion one more time, it would mostly be shooting and bounding exercises. He also wanted to watch his new recruit in action from the stands.

He had been hesitant to sign Ardrey at first, but it turned out that not only was he a great player, he also had useful information about the other teams. To boot, all he wanted was a random spot on the roster, even if it was as a sub-sixer.

Heck, his motivations made sense. Obviously he'd want to be part of the best-ranked team, under Sonny's leadership. And with much of Sonny's team gone to the Inworld next year, he might be able to take a leadership role. So he'd decided to give Ardrey the fifth spot on the roster. Why not?

He let the Lightning do a brief scrimmage at the end of practice. Ardrey was quick and efficient. He snuck behind one of the hotshots and shot him in the back, helping his squad to victory. Yes, Sonny was quite satisfied with his decision.

He ended the practice half an hour early and announced a team dinner.

All he had to do was keep everybody happy, and he would be on his way.

CHAPTER 15

Tristan sat hunched over on the sidelines as he watched Cold Fusion warm up. When he'd learned Ardrey had chosen Amber Lightning, he was initially shocked and angry. After brooding for a while, he could see how it could be a good choice if he were in Ardrey's shoes. Amber Lightning was, after all, higher ranked, and they would lose quite a few good people to the Inworld next year. He couldn't fault Ardrey for picking them. What he didn't know was whether Ardrey had shared any of the information Tristan had showed him. He wasn't sure if he was angrier at Ardrey for the deception or at his own idiocy in giving an uncommitted player a look at Cold Fusion's strategies.

He tried to shrug it off, and he modified Cold Fusion's game plan from the one he'd shown Ardrey. Now Cold Fusion would use two groups to move up, gradually leveraging defensive positions; one group of six led by Luisa, one led by himself.

His team was ready. They were clearly on edge, but that could be a good thing. In practice they were firing on all cylinders, and their intensity was unmatched.

The buzzer sounded.

The game started out poorly for Cold Fusion. Within minutes of the opening, Luisa had been eliminated. The Lightning had ambushed her with highly concentrated fire before her squad could reach a good defensive position. Now the Lightning were concentrating their firepower on Tristan.

Luckily, Tristan had found a position with a lot of cover. Three cubical blocks were arrayed neatly in front of him to absorb incoming Ket pulses. On the other hand, he was alone and cut off from the rest of his team while fire from what seemed like all twelve Lightning players was directed toward him.

Keith pinged his comlink. "Tristan we're coming to give you back-up," he said. Tristan pushed back slightly from his cover block to broaden his line of sight. He saw them coming. Keith and Mugs had left their positions and were moving toward Tristan. Their intent was to give him additional shield strength, but the attempt left them exposed.

Before he could object, Lightning's fire switched from Tristan to his two would-be rescuers. Only Keith made it to his cover position.

Tristan wasn't even firing back. If he showed an inch of himself, he'd be done for in an instant.

And besides, firing back wasn't part of the plan.

So, he stayed under cover, as if glued to the block in front of him, and ordered his team to do the same over his comlink. He told them to shoot only if they had a good line of sight, but otherwise stay hidden.

Lightning's barrage was unrelenting. The team alternated between firing on his cover or on two other Fusion players. A few accurate sniper shots resulted in another Cold Fusion member falling. There were no casualties yet on the Lightning squad.

Tristan could feel tension coiling in his chest. This could be it for this season. He swore to himself, and at the same time resolved not to react.

Timing mattered. Patience mattered.

"What should we do, Tristan?" Keith was yelling in his ear in obvious exasperation.

"Nothing yet," Tristan replied. Keith could only glare at him in disbelief.

The unyielding Ket pulses continued to bear down on them. Cold Fusion stayed under cover. As the match continued, however, Tristan's hope grew. Lightning wasn't moving up yet. They were staying back, and firing at will, and the Lightning could only keep up their barrage for so long.

Finally, the firing relented somewhat. It came in waves. Eventually, it became even more sporadic. There were significant pauses between volleys. It was time.

"Tikashi, Nina, bound over the Lightning in the upper left," Tristan was barking into his comlink, startling Keith in the process. "Form an attack line."

Many game players had idiosyncrasies. Some were excellent shooters. Some were fast on their feet. Some followed orders well. Tristan was well rounded, but if he was known for anything, it was that he was a good bounder.

He jumped up and pressed the bounding button on his wrist. The Ket energy of his suit glowed as it collaborated with the Ketrix mobility field to lift him through the air. In one long arc he bounded halfway across the arena, sailing over two of the enemy Lightning players to join with Tikashi and Nina in the upper left arena.

He'd caught the Lightning by surprise, and they didn't begin firing at him until he'd reached the end of the arc. He made it to his target position safely, found cover, and began firing at the two Lightning players he'd sailed over. Tikashi and Nina took advantage of the crossfire position he'd created and started firing at the two Lightning as well. Meanwhile, the occasional Fusion, following his orders, would bound across and shoot down from above as they met up with Tristan on the other side.

The two Lightning were caught in a three-way crossfire and were quickly eliminated.

Tristan bounded to the upper right corner of the arena, and the same scenario played out again. They cornered three Lightning and took them apart from above, front, and behind. Fire from the Lightning players was still sporadic. It was exactly as Tristan had surmised: they had expended most of their Ket reserves on the initial attacks, leaving them with diminished shield, firing, and bounding energy.

Three more Lightning were down.

Tristan could feel the tide shifting and his hopes lifting. It was nine against seven in favor of Cold Fusion, and the seven on the Lightning squad had little Ket juice left. If Cold Fusion beat the Lightning, the playoffs were wide open for the taking.

Sweat dripped off his nose. He wiped his face with his forearm and checked his Ket gauge. He still had plenty left.

"Form attack squads," Tristan ordered. "Progressive advance." It was a typical strategy for taking advantage of superior odds to seek out a smaller force in defensive positions.

Cold Fusion quickly eliminated two more Lightning that were separated from the rest of the group, although one of the Fusion was lost in the offensive. It was eight to five in favor of Fusion, but the remaining five Lightning were in good defensive positions. There was nowhere to bound in behind them. They had good cover, and, well, they were good players. Vivek Patel, Sonny Joseph, and Ardrey all remained active.

Tristan sent a team of three to advance on the two Lightning on the upper left flank while the remaining five Fusion gave suppressing fire. Unfortunately, there was still fire coming from the five Lightning. A few of them still had a good amount of Ket juice left. The team he sent moved in stealthily on the left flank, arriving at an oversized inverted pyramid that made for a good cover location, then rushed the Lightning positions. In a quick skirmish with little cover on either side, the Fusion attack trio all fell, and only one of the Lightning players was neutralized.

During the skirmish, an isolated shot from the Lightning group took out the man on his left. No doubt it was Vivek Patel again.

It was tied, four against four.

But Tristan could see another opportunity. There was an opening on the left side of the arena where he could bound to and be well covered. He could take advantage of the confusion among the Lightning following the recent skirmish in that area.

He reacted instantly, bounding and simultaneously firing at the last

Lightning player on the left flank who remained after the recent skirmish. With intense concentration and a little luck, Tristan took out the surprised player with a pulse to his head. Then, landing near his target destination, he somersaulted into the cover position he sought. From there he should have a good angle to take out the other Lightning player.

Now that he was closer, he could see the Lightning player he had bounded close to was Sonny Joseph. Another Fusion player bounded in, near to Tristan's position, to back him up.

Sonny had nowhere to go. After a brief exchange, Sonny went dark, succumbing to the firepower coming from Tristan and the other nearby Fusion player.

It was four to two in favor of Cold Fusion. Tristan could see victory a few moves away in his mind. All he had to do was bound over to the right flank, and the remaining two could be attacked from three angles. The only issue was one of the remaining two was Vivek Patel, but he could see he'd been shooting sparingly lately. Did he have no juice left, or was he baiting them?

"Nina," he tightbeamed. "Head for the right flank."

Tristan started his bound, which, if all went well, would put Vivek in a compromised crossfire position.

As Tristan looked down and fired, Vivek didn't even fire back. *He must be out of juice entirely.* This was going to be easy.

But as he soon found out, Vivek had stopped firing for a different reason. There was another player in the air, a Lightning player.

The impact came from behind Tristan at the top of his arc over Vivek. Two arms wrapped around him in a bear hug, confining him. The force of it changed his trajectory. He had been redirected to a different location between Vivek and his remaining Cold Fusion teammates.

It was rare that Ket gamers would jump and collide in mid-air. Tristan had actually done it once, but it was tricky, and also dangerous. First, there was a significant chance you would miss your target, leaving yourself exposed. Second, if your bounding trajectory successfully intersected with your opponent's, not only did you not know where you were going to land, but there was a good chance you would injure yourself by landing awkwardly. Worse, your energy pack could become detached or deactivate in mid-air, leading to a catastrophic injury due to the lack of Ket energy buffering your downward arc. The latter had happened only a handful of times, as far as he knew, but nobody wanted to be that statistic—paralyzed or dead.

Luckily, Tristan's energy pack had stayed on. His assailant was taller than him, and in their current embrace would hit the ground first. Tristan struggled against him, trying to get to his pulse rifle. It had fallen out of his hand on impact and was dangling from the tether on his belt. But the grip on him was too tight. Fortunately, his assailant couldn't make a move for his rifle either. To do so he would have to let go of Tristan.

For a brief instant, all Ket pulses ceased as players on both teams watched the spectacle. The crowd was also atypically mute as all eyes focused on the extraordinary event.

To Tristan's surprise, as soon as they touched down on the ground his assailant fired on his anti-gravity operator and bounded up, pulling them both into the air again. He must have a great deal of Ket left. He must have been conserving it.

Tristan stuck his elbow back as they leapt skyward. It gave him enough space to turn around in his assailant's grasp. They struggled against each other in mid-air. His assailant had a hand under his chin and was pushing his head up so he couldn't see. Tristan struggled free and saw Ardrey staring him in the face.

Ardrey's eyes bristled with fury and determination.

Tristan took the opportunity created by their separation to punch Ardrey in the nose. Tristan had little leverage, so it was a weak blow. Nevertheless, there was a loud smack as Ardrey flew away from him, blood streaming from his nostrils.

Their separation was fleeting. Ardrey had used his left hand to grab on to Tristan's pulse rifle tether. Using the recoil from the punch and his leverage on the tether, Ardrey managed to swing Tristan back into a bear hug position from behind, this time getting Tristan's right arm locked behind him. They struggled again, but Tristan was even more immobilized than before. His only hope was to get his pulse rifle out when he landed.

There was a cluster of blocks ahead of them: pyramids, misshaped trapezoids, and cones. Great cover, but not favorable terrain for the landing of two struggling, intertwined bodies.

They careened off two cover blocks in sequence and landed in a messy heap.

There was a loud scream. Tristan didn't realize it was coming from his own mouth until he saw his flaccid arm waving under his shoulder, having several additional degrees of freedom. His weapon lay a foot away, still on its tether, but he just stared at it, his synapses in disarray. His shooting hand was useless, dangling at his side.

Ardrey got to his feet beside him. His nose was steadily streaming blood, but otherwise he appeared no worse for wear. He coolly pointed his weapon at Tristan.

Before he fired, he stared at Tristan with an odd expression. The look reminded Tristan of something, but he couldn't say what. It was as though he'd just eaten a whole lemon and was reacting to the sour taste. Maybe it was Tristan's mutilated arm or just his pathetic position, sitting upright but helpless, like a rag doll.

He said, "Sorry, Tristan," and he fired on Tristan's exposed and defenseless body, eliminating him. Tristan's suit powered down and went dark.

Tristan sat there watching the rest of the match in a state of disbelief, with his grotesque arm flailing under him out of the corner of his eye.

He watched as Ardrey rejoined the fray and caught two of the remaining Cold Fusion in a crossfire pattern between him and Vivek Patel. With their cover compromised, the Fusion tried to run for safer haven, but they were both easily picked off by Vivek in two rapid shots.

Vivek had six kills this match, and the fans were ecstatic. The huge banner with his name on it rippled in the stands.

After what seemed like hours, Ardrey and Vivek gradually, methodically encroached upon Nina—the one remaining Fusion player cowering on the right flank. Nina was hopelessly outmatched by the more talented Lightning opponents and was easily eliminated.

Tristan watched helplessly as Cold Fusion lost the game. Shock and pain gave way to the realization he was watching his chances of getting into the Inworld this year disappear. His arm, swelling and colored, expounded the situation for him.

His hopes for next year could be dashed as well.

PART II

MALIGNANCY

CHAPTER 16

"Maybe you need the new mask that exfoliates while it protects?" Fenton teased as Luisa's fingers traced the lines the mask had left on her temple and jaw.

Luisa glared back at him while mimicking the deep debutant voice of Abuella, the popular vids star. "I prefer weekly plastic surgery. Better long-term results and saves you so much time with makeup."

"Right." Fenton nodded, smiling.

Luisa was sitting with Fenton, his friend Rick, and Luisa's friend Sophini in a club that could best be described as dingy. They were in one of the two occupied booths. Across from them there were a dozen empty tables surrounded by scratched polymer seats. A couple of the tables were replete with untended buckets full of dirty glasses. Bass-heavy music thrummed on the dance floor where half a dozen people thrashed around in vigorous gyrations.

The booth was accessorized by a spread of mixed drinks, beer, and wine at various states of consumption. When the odd flash of light would, on occasion, manage to survive the journey from the dance floor strobes, the colorful glasses on the table would refract the rays into rainbow patterns.

Sophini threw a bottle cap into a glass on the far side of the table. "Yes," she said.

"I don't think one out of five is enough to declare victory," Rick said. Rick was tall and slim, with sleepy eyes. He was a quiet sort, from out in the hydroponic sectors. It was mind-numbing, isolating work, according to Rick, but safer than city living.

"The rest were obviously just practice," Sophini said, smiling in return.

Sophini was a friend from school. She was petite, with wavy black hair, wearing a loose-fitting mauve blouse and tight black skirt, whereas Luisa was wearing a black blouse and red nylon pants like the ones she'd seen on some Junipero girls. It wasn't anything special, but it was dressier than Luisa was used to.

Sophini loved the little things; extremely sweet minty drinks, steaming hot showers, and fashionable clothing. She tended to bring out Luisa's more feminine side. Every month they would get together, and Luisa would be reminded that she wasn't, in fact, a boy, and that maybe the universe didn't revolve around the Ket games.

The bartender approached their table. She was older, her face paved into lines that formed a constant grimace. She served Fenton another beer and collected a few of the empty glasses. "Aren't you all a little young to be drinking?" she remarked sourly, barely looking up at them.

"Probably," Sophini said, and giggled.

The bartender just nodded and left.

Chooly had told Luisa that a few decades ago teenagers couldn't drink alcohol, but the caretakers had abolished a lot of laws, especially ones they found annoying to enforce. The drinking age limit was an easy one.

The bartender went into the back again. They probably wouldn't see her for another half an hour. There weren't many patrons around so they couldn't blame her.

Luisa took another sip of her gin-spritzer and nudged Sophini. "Probably?" she mocked. Sophini giggled again.

Luisa was enjoying herself, or at least was trying to.

The games had really brought her down. Even though she didn't really care about making it to the Inworld, she felt terrible for her other Cold Fusion teammates, especially Tristan. They had given it their all and had their dreams shattered. She'd also avoided the group meetings with Michaelis and Fenton, and she'd even skipped a few days of school.

It was all just too much.

She wondered what she would have done if she'd been selected to be a caretaker. Maybe she could try to change the Inworld from the inside out? Deep down she was worried she would enjoy it, and the experience would drive her to complacency. Chooly had once noted this about her—that she could be swayed easily. She wasn't sure if it was a warning or a just a comment in passing, but either way, she knew it should be heeded.

Speaking of Chooly, she was reminded that the dossier he'd given her still lay in the bottom of her closet, untouched. She knew the act of opening it would pull her down avenues of contemplation she wasn't ready for. She would often awaken and see her closet door left open, and the dossier beckoned to her. No, she would think, she was on vacation.

As the night wore on, she let go of these nervous thoughts and worries. She was able to forget about the Ket games and the dossier. She let herself float along a river of conversation that led to a sea of laughing and dancing.

She floated happily as the tide took her out.

Luisa woke to a heavy head and the smell of sweat flavored with metabolized alcohol. Given the state she had been in the night before, she felt more lucid than she might have expected. Beside her, lying partially clothed with his back to her, was Fenton. He was breathing softly, still in slumber. Luisa turned and stared at his oblique profile, not yet ready to stand and exacerbate the pounding of her head, nor force her heart to labor any more than it already did.

Luisa had an on-again, off-again relationship with Fenton. They had, at one point, been a couple. For whatever reason, they broke apart, but remained friends. Since then, they might share a kiss or fool around on occasion, but it was always fleeting.

She forced herself onto her feet and walked out to the kitchen, looking to rehydrate. She grabbed two glasses of water and went back to the room. After a few minutes of Luisa staring at Fenton's back, he eventually stirred and turned around.

She handed him the glass.

"Oh, thanks," he said. "How long have you been up?"

"Just a few minutes."

He surveyed her appreciatively and moved toward her on the bed. Luisa smiled back at him. She sat upright and aloof, not wanting to engage any further.

He got the hint and settled for a kiss on her shoulder before taking a drink. "What's up with you today?" he asked.

Luisa shrugged.

Fenton finished his glass and pulled his pants off the floor onto his legs in a slow but deliberate movement. "When's our next meeting with Michaelis?" he asked. "Last we spoke with him, he said he wanted to show us something, right?"

Luisa nodded. She looked over to the closet door, slightly ajar, holding the dossier. She hadn't told Fenton and Michaelis about it.

There was no reason she could think of for not meeting, and she knew Michaelis wouldn't appreciate any more delays.

It looked like her vacation was over.

"I have something I want to talk about as well, but I need some time first. Let's try to meet later in the week."

Luisa waited for Fenton to get dressed. They had a quick breakfast, and Fenton left, being sure not to part with a kiss, as if to ensure clarity in their relationship status.

Luisa showered, brushed, creamed her eyes, and went back to bed. After several more hours of rest, she opened the closet door and took out the dossier.

She sat with it on her bed, feeling the outline of it with her palms.

The cover was nothing special, just a rectangular prism of hard green plastic. There were quite a few scratch marks on it. The lock system was an electronic interface and keypad.

She sometimes wondered why she was doing any of this. Why open the dossier and expose herself to even more malaise?

She hadn't always felt this way. When she was growing up her parents had told her the Inworlders weren't much different, citing the example of her grandfather Ernesto who had been granted a berth in the Parkdome. Ernesto had supported Luisa's late relatives by sending money.

But as she grew older, she learned more of the untold parts of the story. Ernesto and his Outworld relatives grew apart, and within a generation they rarely spoke. Nowadays the Inworlders rarely, if ever, left the domes, and only the caretakers braved the toxic environment of the Outworld as their agents. Ernesto and his offspring were no different.

Other gaps in the story would remain a void, forever lost with the death of her parents, but she knew there was no new information that would change her mind. Ernesto and any children he might have were dead to her. They had neglected her family, and she could no longer name them her kin.

Meanwhile the Outworld continued on its warpath against her family, unrelenting.

She could not be Ernesto. She could not be a part of the complacent killing machine. It was a foundation wrought of emotional granite, forcing her to inevitable action.

She sighed, hummed softly, entered the code Chooly had given her, and opened the dossier.

CHAPTER 17

Sonny didn't know whether his caretaker enercycle was brand new or just extremely well maintained. Even in the haze of San Francisco, the chrome shone brightly. And despite the muggy air, he enjoyed driving it through the streets. He would often pull up next to bicyclists and other vehicles so they could compare their sooty and rusted-out machines with his own.

At the moment he was stopped at an intersection near the docks, surveying the traffic going by, watching for infractions and waiting for a dispatch call. Sitting beside Sonny, and ignoring him for the time being, was his superior officer and mentor. Rafael Maiyor was about twenty years his senior, a scrawny man with a stubby nose and sunken face. After a few days under his tutelage, Sonny hadn't learned much about him. He suspected there wasn't much to learn.

Sonny had been in the Inworld for more than a month. Most other new recruits were still in training, but Sonny and a select few others had been chosen to go on probationary patrols already, doing the rounds of San Francisco. Sonny took this as a good sign. Maybe he'd already made an impression, and maybe this would mean he would have a better chance of advancing past the caretaker sectors of the Parkdome, and into the *real* Inworld.

Father said to never be satisfied. There's always something better.

At first he'd been mesmerized by the Inworld. There was a lush paradise in the center of the caretaker sector called the "Theater Chamber" where one could exercise or just wander through greenery without being encumbered by a safety mask. There were always bots around doing some sort of cleaning or other menial function to make life easier. He'd seen for the first time one of the gigantic crystalline hollowvision cubes, where vids always appeared to be three-dimensional. It was easy to forget about the depressing Outworld when he was inside.

And it was way more spacious than he expected. They weren't packed in like sardines at all. Maiyor told him the Inworlders needed to make the caretaker section more hospitable, as an incentive for winning in the games, but the "Old Inworld"—in the western part of the Parkdome—was still claustrophobic and tightly confined.

He soon realized that although his new caretaker world was more spacious, it was still small in scale relative to the Old Inworld section. Old Inworld this and Old Inworld that—there were so many stories of luxuries he had yet to see: virtual reality areas, sophisticated transport systems, museums, elaborate baths, and multilevel gardens. He heard speculation about it, often through whispered conversation. For all he knew, these could be just rumors, but it did make him want to know more.

Maiyor was taking a call on his headset, but speaking low enough that Sonny was unable to hear. Earlier, Maiyor had shut off Sonny's caretaker comlink, saying gruffly that he "hadn't proven he was smart enough to use it yet."

Maiyor finished his discussion, fired up his enercycle, and said, "Follow me." A low purr began to emanate from the undercarriage. Maiyor pulled out, cut right, and headed north. Sonny started up his own enercycle and turned to follow.

They traveled in sequence, winding down the hill to the most desiccated part of Market Street, sometimes putting sirens on to halt traffic around them so they could get by without delay. They swung left through a few side streets and took circuitous cutbacks up another series of hills. Maiyor paused and waited for him at a pullout that looked over Noe Valley.

"See that, there," Maiyor was pointing to a small brown house with a perforated roof. "That's where I used to live."

"Good location," Sonny said, hoping it was tactful enough. "Does your family still live there?"

"I don't know. That's not why I'm showing you. I went back, twice, but that was years ago. We're supposed to police them, not socialize with them. And it makes conversations difficult, because nothing about the Inworld can be communicated to the Outworld—you know, to maintain the peace. In fact, *any* association with Outworlders is frowned upon."

"Got it," Sonny replied.

"Don't worry, new caretakers usually get it out of their system in the first year or so."

Maiyor didn't wait for Sonny to acknowledge him. He pulled out again and Sonny followed. They eventually ended up on the southeast side of the domes near Twin Peaks. Here they pulled up to the corner of an intersection. Maiyor pointed to the opposite corner, where a crumpled pile of lumber, brick, and mortar lay on a collapsed hillside. A small corner of a house could be seen at the top of a hill some forty or fifty feet up.

"The rains last night took down the house." Maiyor gestured at the remains of the house up the hill with his palm up, then lowered his hand, as if he was gently bringing the house to lie neatly on the ground. However, the house clearly had not landed neatly. It was a crumpled ruin.

These hillsides had become heavily eroded over the years. The monsoon rains happened with greater frequency in the winters, and the last day of a several-day deluge had ended the previous evening. In many parts of the city, the landscape had fallen into disrepair, and the rains tended to accelerate these kinds of events.

So why were they here? He knew Maiyor was baiting him with his silence, which was fine. He could play the part of the ignorant caretaker recruit if it suited his interests. "Might I ask what the call was for, Sergeant?" he asked.

Maiyor took a breath under his mask and said, "You see, private, there was a report that someone was leafing through the wreckage this morning. Possible theft. We're here to ensure only qualified medical professionals and search-and-rescue workers venture onto the premises." He was staring Sonny down as he spoke. Sonny nodded in acknowledgement.

So they sat at the intersection, watching and waiting. Sonny wondered, was there someone in the house when it fell? Was that why Maiyor mentioned medical professionals?

Half an hour later, the paramedics arrived. There were only two of them. They worked through the rubble to find any signs of life. Some family members came by. They began crying and screaming, and tried to search through the rubble. At Maiyor's request, Sonny held them back, saying the medical professionals needed to handle it. It seemed strange to Sonny, but it may have been a test of Maiyor's authority. He did what he was told.

Eventually the paramedics pulled two people out of the ruin. One was dead, the other barely alive. There was wailing and screaming from onlookers as the bodies were taken away. Soon afterward, the site was quiet again.

Maiyor had been watching the vid screen on his enercycle monitor, ignoring the scene. He looked up at Sonny and said, "Good work today, Sonny. I can tell you're going to be a useful addition to the security detail."

Maiyor looked up at the sky, which was rapidly clouding over. "I have a specific job for you," he said. "It's an important assignment, so you should feel privileged."

"Sir?"

"It seems, given your success last year and connections in the Outworld, the higher-ups think you might be of greater service. We would like to clamp down on some more...nefarious Outworlder activity. It will involve some detective work."

"Yes sir," Sonny replied without hesitating. "I'm honored, sir, and I won't let you down."

Without offering more, Maiyor started up his enercycle again. "Uh-huh," he mumbled over the purring sound. "I'll brief you back at the dome. I'm getting out of shitsville. Make sure no one goes through the wreckage for the next thirty minutes or so. Then report back to me at four p.m."

Maiyor peeled away.

No one went through the wreckage, nor did anyone ask questions. People who wandered through kept their heads down and gave his blue and gold uniform a wide berth.

On his way back to the dome, he resisted the urge to visit his father. His old house was nearby, and he had the time, but he decided against it. He was moving up in the Inworld and couldn't let his ties to the Outworld hold him back. Besides, it might be some kind of test by Maiyor. They could keep tabs on him at all times, with the chip that the Inworld doctors had implanted in his shoulder.

So he went straight back to the dome, allowing himself ample time to psychologically prepare himself for the meeting with Maiyor, as well as any further patronizing he might have to endure.

CHAPTER 18

Tristan heard the sound of his own muffled sobbing, the scream of the child being beaten by the caretakers, and saw the grotesque view of his brother twisting in his metal noose. He again woke up just before his brother's face could be seen. It was strange that he'd had this dream so many times, but he could barely remember what his own brother looked like. Other aspects of his dream could be so vivid, so real.

The dream had come to him more often in the past few weeks. During the intensity of the Ket playoffs he'd been given a respite as his subconscious mind was dominated by other concerns, but it was back, and with greater intensity.

Tristan wiped the drool from his lip and felt at a crook in his neck. He was sitting on a bullet train. He corrected his posture and turned to the window to watch the hills roll by. This was how he'd spent most of the trip, even though he was mostly oblivious to the landscape. It did nothing to diminish his malaise.

A girl about his age with long blond spiral curls had been sitting across from him. She was dressed in dark, tight-fitting attire with many buttons and ruffles—maybe she was going to a formal event, or maybe it was a school outfit. She started a conversation or two, or rather tried to. He answered her politely but curtly, and offered nothing to reciprocate.

Eventually she moved away, taking an open seat farther down the train. She probably perceived his lack of responsiveness as some form of rejection.

At the next stop she was replaced by an older woman in a beige frock who smiled at him. He smiled back politely. She didn't initiate any conversation. Occasionally she would look down at his arm in the sling, obviously curious, but not enough to ask about it. Tristan was glad for that.

As the train cut its way north through Nevada, the barren hills gave way to light brush, then desert. The windows were buffeted by the occasional sandstorm, sullying the windows, and limiting his visibility. It would be this way for many miles. The great interior dustbowl was just beginning.

After glancing down at his watch, he calculated he would arrive at his uncle's farm in Montana in about eight hours. It was to be his new home for a while. According to the gospel of his parents, it would be "good for him to be away." He needed to "get perspective on his life again."

It was also because he'd made it unbearable for them. As he went through the two painful operations on his arm, putting their family into even greater debt, he would respond to their conscientious inquiries about his progress with one or two-word answers. He did try, at first, to make light of his situation, but he soon felt sickened by any attempt at levity. When people asked, he would grit his teeth and give an accurate, albeit short, account of events. His stark tone would ensure his statements were conclusive and not subject to debate.

His arm was bad. According to the overwhelmed Outworld doctor, it was a compound fracture in two places with a fair amount of tissue damage. Tristan may not have the ability to play in the games next year, or at least not with a good shooting arm. He had assumed as much. Tristan absorbed it all and did what he was told. He listened to sympathies and thanked sympathizers unemotionally. He went through the surgeries stoically and didn't complain.

The train was braking. Looking ahead, he could see a track junction in the distance. A windowless, sleek-looking robot transport was running across their path. The train gradually slowed to a crawl and then stalled as the boxy, segmented transport blocked their progress.

It reminded him of a similar occurrence on his last trip on a train, many years ago. Tristan had traveled outside of San Francisco only once before. He'd gone to a Ket training school in Seattle and had enjoyed it immensely. Those many years ago he'd also kept his nose to the window, but because he was excited, rather than to keep to himself. His parents had reluctantly financed the travel, knowing he would never forgive them if they didn't.

Seeing the world-renowned dome system of Seattle had further fueled his aspirations. The infrastructure was so much more efficient. Hundreds of transport lanes and tubes fed the dome system from all directions. In San Francisco, by comparison, there were only two robot lanes and no sky tubes linking any of the large domes.

He vividly remembered his excitement as he told his parents and his friends about the city and the ride up and down the coast. But now, as he looked out at the Nevada dust bowl, he felt the scenery sapping his will, parching his spirit with every dry gust of wind. This was nothing to talk about, and he didn't see how staying at a farm would serve his aspirations. He would be lucky if he ever played again, never mind making it to the Inworld. Being distracted at a farm for several weeks wouldn't help his meager chances.

The train finally jerked to a full stop. He watched the segmented structure continue to pass by. As far as he could see on the dusty horizon, there appeared to be no end to the train. They were stuck.

"Fuck," he said, gritting his teeth.

The elderly lady looked at him wide-eyed, uncomfortable with his language.

"Sorry," he offered.

The lady didn't respond, but acknowledged the apology with a nod. She looked back at her book while shrugging off the indiscretion.

He returned his gaze toward the window and shook his head. The minor delay was no excuse to cuss aloud.

He didn't really care though. What did it matter? The elderly woman was no one, and he was on a train to nowhere.

CHAPTER 19

Michaelis had much to discuss with Luisa and Fenton.

He pulled out several folders of notes and printouts from his pack and stacked them on Fenton's black marbled table. Mentally he rehearsed key points from the contents; options with arguments for and against, risks, unknowns, open questions, sources, and a list of action items. It was all there, written neatly in report format, for him just as much as for Luisa and Fenton.

The work reminded Michaelis of his time in school, before he was expelled. He had actually enjoyed the assignments, with all the analysis, synthesis, and reporting. And yet, then, as now, he never felt eager to present his work. He would wait for others to speak first. First does not mean best, and there was no need to be boastful.

Luisa also had a collection of documents in front of her, from the dossier. She had given Michaelis a copy of the contents two days earlier, and he'd read it over eagerly. Fenton had pulled out a pad of paper and pen and was sitting forward in his chair, watching Michaelis arrange himself at the table.

"So who wants to start?" Fenton ventured.

Luisa's gaze turned to Michaelis. He coughed into his elbow and gestured with a brief sweep of an open hand at the table, giving the floor to her.

She tilted her head back and forth—a window into some kind of internal debate. Finally she said, "So I'm not sure where to start except to talk about the dossier. Like I told you, my cousin was heavily involved in, um, the black market and contraband."

Michaelis and Fenton both nodded, alleviating any necessity for her to elaborate.

"I'm not sure what to make of the stuff in it," she continued fingering the papers in front of her. "I'm still trying to figure out what it all means."

Fenton asked, "Did the dossier offer any suggestions on what we could do to call out the Inworld?"

"It's not like that. It's a bunch of random information from Chooly's life like contact names with footnotes, bills of materials for black-market products, news articles, and contracts. There are scribbles everywhere I haven't read through in detail."

She hesitated.

"Go on," Fenton urged.

"Well, there are a few things that might be interesting. For example, many of his contacts weren't on good terms with the Inworld, so we could use them as resources, if not recruit them into our group directly."

"Many are also criminals, I'm sure," Fenton cautioned. "No honor among thieves." Fenton had always been nervous about Luisa discussing matters with Chooly, perhaps fearful Chooly's past would come back to haunt him, and they'd be found guilty by association.

Luisa responded, "Fair enough, but some may have a genuine motivation against the Inworld. They may not be doing it out of greed. One of the contact names is even a former caretaker, according to a note in the dossier."

Michaelis had seen the annotation in his review. There were rumors of people who were former caretakers living in the Outworld, but he'd never met one.

"But can we contact this person?" Michaelis asked. "What was his name…" Michaelis opened his copy of the dossier to the reference. "Peter Hastings? There's only a time and place to meet: Friday, April 3 at nine p.m. in a SOMA bar called Flip."

"That's in four months," Fenton said.

Luisa jumped in. "Yes, but I think where Michaelis is going is there is no indication the meeting isn't from several years ago, when Chooly was actually going to meet with him. There are other places in the dossier where Chooly did this, putting dates and times for meetings but not the year, so we don't know exactly when they may have happened."

Fenton stated the obvious. "That's not much to go on."

"Even if that doesn't work out, we have other options." Luisa pointed to a stack of papers in the dossier. "Look, it's a lot better than what we had before. These people won't report us to the Inworld if we reach out to them, and it's a lot less risky than asking people at random."

"Agreed." Michaelis nodded. There was indeed a rich list of contacts. It included many wealthy individuals who traded in contraband, people in the transportation trade, electronics industry, even mercenaries, all of whom probably had something to lose if they reported them, which thereby minimized the risk.

Fenton reluctantly agreed, nodding.

Luisa continued. "We may be able to access weapons through these people. There are references to 'home defense' and 'security' for some of the suppliers and contracts."

"Whoa," Fenton said. "Wait a second. Weapons? Let's not get ahead of ourselves. My mom is in jail for trumped-up tax evasion charges. Imagine what they would do if they caught us with illegal weapons."

Luisa looked unsure of herself. She glanced over at Michaelis.

"Yes," Michaelis said. "Maybe we should look at the bigger picture here. I have some ideas on the dossier as well, but first maybe we should talk about what our objectives are."

Luisa confirmed with a nod. She looked relieved to pass the baton to Michaelis.

Michaelis had expected Fenton and Luisa would look to him, with his ability to access more information and his technical background, to make sense of the dossier. Freed from her leadership of the discussion, Luisa stood up and wandered across the loft to the kitchen where she opened a box and poured some chips into a bowl.

Luisa wandered back to the table with a half-filled bowl, rubbing her right hand on her trousers to free it of the crumbly castoff of the synth-rice chips. The oval chips were lined with beige arcs—she had dribbled some savory brown oil on them for flavor.

Fenton grabbed a handful and began chewing.

Michaelis began. "So, I spent a lot of time reviewing the dossier and thinking about courses of action. I'm assuming we essentially have two general approaches here, which are not necessarily mutually exclusive. We've talked about a few tactics under these two umbrellas, but never put them systematically into a plan, so that's what I suggest we discuss first."

He paused to let them absorb this while at the same time clearing his throat aggressively and fingering the rough welding on the rim of his glasses. "The first general approach," he continued, "is to sway public opinion against the Inworld to such an extent it would lead to a dissolution of the dome system, or at least lead to significant changes. This would reveal secrets about the Inworld such as the uninformative public reports or outright misinformation. Essentially we could set out on a counter-propaganda campaign."

They both nodded.

"The second general approach, as I see it, is to covertly take or destroy, by force, some element of the Inworld dome system. This would essentially be a coup or an act of terrorism. There are shades of gray in between, but that's what we're talking about, right? If we want to make a real change to the system, those are the only paths?"

Luisa mulled it over for a moment. "I guess so," she said.

"I agree with the general approaches," Fenton said. "Thank you, Michaelis. I think swaying public opinion should be our main objective. We won't have enough resources to take any meaningful military action against the Inworld. Imagine the technology, security, and firepower the Inworld has at their disposal. We should focus on where we can have the most impact. Also, even if we do cause some physical damage, what then? Will things really change, or will they just quell the rebellion, and clamp down on the Outworld more?"

Luisa was squirming. "I see your point Fenton, but I have to say I disagree. Without a big symbolic resistance, nothing will change. As soon as they're aware of any anti-Inworld propaganda they'll put an end to it and silently wipe us out without so much as a whisper, and in that case there'll be even less of a sign there was any opposition. We need to do something to show people change can be made—that we can stand up to the Inworld. If it means using force, I think we should be prepared to do so."

They were both looking uneasy and almost apologetic, but not enough to give ground. It was a conversation that, as a group, they had been circling around.

Michaelis decided to shift topics before it became too heated. "Why don't I give you an example of a way we could use the dossier? There is a report by an Outworld tech team that worked on the Inworld IT systems." He showed them the stapled report. "I can't be sure, but based on this report, I do think San Francisco's systems are not as effective at proactive security measures as other dome cities like Seattle. This is probably because San Francisco is one of the oldest and most entrenched dome cities, and they haven't bothered to upgrade systems simply because there haven't been any attempts to test security."

Luisa raised her eyebrows, either in contemplation or bewilderment, Michaelis couldn't be sure.

Fenton said, "So you're saying...maybe we could get away with broad electronic communications to the masses without risk of getting caught?"

Not to be outdone, Luisa said, "Or maybe it wouldn't be hard to crack the dome security codes and gain entrance?"

They were both staring at Michaelis, as if he had all the answers. He let out a short laugh, almost a giggle. "I'm not sure either option is that simple, but yes, exactly. Those are areas to investigate. Maybe we can try to find weaknesses for both purposes."

They nodded as if it was a simple request—like fetching more synth-rice chips at the store. It was frustrating to try to get Luisa and

Fenton to understand, but they couldn't be held accountable for their knowledge gap on technology.

He liked Fenton and Luisa, but he missed his old New York friends at times like these. Ella, Tuan, and Harjit had easily been the smartest kids in school, and often they would finish each other's sentences. On the many inclement days in New York, they would stay inside his mother's cramped apartment and play games for hours. He didn't feel that same kinship with Fenton and Luisa, and he sometimes wondered if he should give up on these meetings.

For the time being, he tried to stay focused on the conversation at hand. He said, "Another thing I found is an inordinate amount of underwater work being done at Ocean Beach, near the Parkdome. It may mean they are planning to expand the Parkdome over the ocean."

"So what?" Fenton said.

"They promised the mayor they wouldn't do that, several times. The land is owned by the city, and the Ocean Beach waters are being preserved."

"If true, we could use that against them," Luisa said, "to show the people they are breaking the law."

"Exactly," Michaelis said.

"What else do you have?" Fenton asked, eyebrows raised.

Michaelis took out his list from his folder and placed it in front of them.

"What's that?" Luisa asked.

"I have a list of other proposed leads we could follow up on, action items and the like. Should I read them off?"

Luisa nodded, more slowly this time. Fenton followed suit. They could tell by the amount of writing it was about to get serious.

Michaelis began working his way through the list, and they listened intently, rarely objecting, although at times requesting clarification. Some of the action items involved researching dubious contradictions in the Inworlder propaganda. Others involved exploring Inworld security defenses. And of course, they had to review the dossier in full, and perhaps go through it another time to be thorough.

It took a long time. They ended up sitting there for many hours, with several pauses for trips to the chip bag, and also to order some falafel-protein cakes. If caloric intake was their goal, they certainly accomplished it that evening.

As the night was winding down, Michaelis reflected on their progress. They had discussed real, tangible options—more than in all their previous meetings combined. Things were moving.

As a result, he left Fenton's flat walking with purpose. His mind kept working as he pushed quickly through the thick evening air. After several blocks, he felt the familiar constriction in his neck coming on, and a brief coughing fit overtook him. He chided himself for rushing, readjusted his mask, and changed to the low-grade filtration setting to allow more airflow.

When he continued to plod onward, the cadence of his stream of consciousness remained, as did the sense of exhilaration—a feeling he hadn't felt in a long time.

It reminded him of how he felt playing Hex Strategem in New York —a game where players tried to amass riches and territories across six fictional cityscapes from the pre-dome world, and then, of course, try to destroy each other's empires. Ella, Tuan, and Harjit would be beside him, fingering their cards, plotting their maneuvers, and it was his turn. It was that feeling—the anticipation of a well-thought-out move—that he felt on his way home that evening.

Maybe these meetings with Fenton and Luisa weren't so bad after all.

<h1 style="text-align:center">CHAPTER 20</h1>

In the days after their meeting, Luisa tried to speak with representatives of Parkdome supply outfits about how they dealt with the Inworld. She also asked a few specialty contractors if they knew of underwater repair work being done near the part of the Parkdome that extended near Ocean Beach. The more polite responses were looks of suspicion or scorn. Usually they would outright tell her to get lost.

When she'd received her fill of rejection, she decided to instead scout the Parkdome defenses, taking notes of entry procedures, emergency exits, and security staffing shifts. She enjoyed this much more, since she could ride her bike while doing it, even though the weather was turning bitterly cold. Her hands were numb half the time, so taking notes was time-consuming.

She'd only done a quarter of her planned route when her comlink chimed.

It was Melissa. Luisa's heart sunk as she tapped her comlink handheld to accept the call. Melissa's voice croaked. "He's awake and wants to talk to you. Come quickly." She hung up.

Chooly had fallen into a coma a few days before. Since then Luisa had gone to see him in the hospital a few times. He hadn't been conscious during any of her visits.

Luisa immediately rode with purpose toward the hospital, navigating the dim streets with speed and efficiency. Maybe Chooly was on the mend again?

When she arrived, Melissa was sitting next to Chooly, holding his hand. His eyes were closed.

Luisa entered the room with some hesitation.

Melissa walked over to hug her. "I'm sorry I was short with you earlier," she said. "I wanted every minute with Chooly while he was up. I hope you understand." The yellow coloring around her eyes was mottled pink from crying.

"I understand completely," Luisa said. "How is he?"

"We spoke. He wanted to see you, but he was...so tired. He fell back asleep. I'm sure he'll be awake again soon."

"Okay."

Chooly's form on the hospital bed ate at her. He had wasted away to almost nothing. His skin was pasty and white, painted over with networks of prominent green veins. A tautened grimace replaced the sleepy grin he would have worn in better times.

Chooly had relapsed before, but always came out of it. His indomitable spirit had persevered as long as she could recall, but the sight of him defied her confidence.

They took a seat and Luisa held Melissa's hand.

"Did he say anything else when he was awake?" Luisa asked.

"Yes, we talked for some time." Melissa was smiling her usual benevolent smile, but her eyes began to well with tears. The droplets spilled down the fair contour of her nose. She began heaving, holding onto Luisa. "He wasn't the same," she said. "Something wasn't right."

"He'll be alright," Luisa said. "Waking up is the first step to recovery."

Melissa kept crying on Luisa's shoulder.

Melissa regained her composure, finally lifting her head off her shoulder. "Thank you, Luisa. You're so kind."

Luisa didn't ask what the doctor said; it was too near, too raw.

Melissa sat erect in her chair. "If you don't mind," she said, "I'd like to be alone with him. When he wakes I'll be sure to call you right away. Chooly wouldn't like us both worrying so much over him."

"Okay. Just let me know if I can help."

Melissa hugged her again. "You've already been a tremendous help. Know that Chooly really does love you. He said so." She looked away from Luisa, averting her eyes.

"Oh. Okay. Goodbye Melissa, and take care."

Luisa rode home, confused, and no less concerned.

Not more than an hour later she got a call from a nurse at the hospital.

"Ms. Luisa Vincent? Yes. Hello I have some terrible news. Your cousin has passed away. I'm terribly sorry. Mrs. Fantonesta wanted you to know. She said services will be next week and she will reach out to you. I'm terribly sorry."

"Oh. Okay, thank you." The comlink disconnected.

Chooly was dead.

Melissa seemed to know he was at the end. And with this realization, the full force of Chooly's death hit Luisa, along with an aching lack of closure. She sat on her couch, head in her hands, and sobbed.

A profound loneliness burrowed into her, like a thick wedge piercing her chest—a sensation she hadn't felt since her mom died.

The world had been further sullied. It was an even darker place. The light of a valiant knight had been extinguished.

Luisa remembered how her parents would console her when someone died. They would say the deceased person would be fine because Mother Myra had taken them. Myra would come in the night and take the toxins out of the dying person and escort them away to a mythical world to dream in an endless sleep.

There were many stories about Mother Myra. There was one about how she founded the most innovative greentech company in the world and became a trillionaire, or another about how she devoted her life to founding the Inworld so she could save humanity. Those stories might have had some kernels of truth, but this particular story about Mother

Myra coming to visit dead people was a fairy tale—a way to placate children and avoid telling them the truth.

After her parents died, she ceased believing in Mother Myra. The truth was whoever had died, often painfully, was not escorted to any magical place.

No, Chooly wasn't dreaming in an endless sleep somewhere. He no longer existed. The only thing he'd left behind was his cancer. It would lurk in the shadows until it was ready to take someone else, and again, and again, until everyone died and there was no one left.

She continued to weep.

She wished she could be with someone. She wanted to call her friends, but she didn't think Fenton or Michaelis would understand, and, judging by the nurse's message, Melissa wanted to be alone.

There was no one.

Seeking an escape, she glanced down at the dossier in front of her, seeing the note Chooly made about meeting the caretaker agent who'd left the Inworld. Why not go to this Flip Bar, where this mysterious man was supposed to meet Chooly years ago?

She knew it was a long shot, but she justified it as a noble task.

Her mind made up, she hurried to leave her suffocating apartment, eager for any refuge from her loneliness, and aching for a drink.

And drink she did. She sat at the bar in Flip, and after four shots, loosened up to the patrons. At one point she flirted with a bearded fellow in his early twenties who was at the bar next to her. He had a ready smile and calm voice. He played along. It was fun, but he was cautious.

"Hey, I'm not a walkoff," she said when he turned to talk with his friend.

He turned back, forced a smile, and said, "You have a nice night."

He left the bar soon after.

The rejection didn't make Luisa feel any better.

She occasionally spoke with the bartender, a man named Horatio.

He was probably in his mid-forties, with slicked back hair and unyellowing foundation pasted around his eyes.

"Who are your favorite Ket players?" she asked.

"Sorry, I don't watch Ket much. Vivek Patel, I guess. He's pretty good, isn't he?"

She clenched her jaw. "Yeah. He made it to the Inworld."

"Oh. Good for him."

"Where are you from?"

"The southeast."

"Really? No domes around there, right? Must be nice."

He frowned. "Not really. It's a hamster wheel. There's a synth-rice plant in my town and a few hydroponic farms, so we've got jobs at least, but it's owned by the Inworld, so no one has enough money to reinvest in the community. That's why I came out here, to look for better opportunities in a dome city."

"What have you found?"

He smiled broadly, and some of the dried foundation cracked around his eyes. "Good people," he said nebulously. He moved away to take care of other customers for a while.

People moving to dome cities was a common thread. A good portion of San Franciscans were transplants. The Inworld and mayor both encouraged it and often cited immigration numbers to promote the cities' favorability. It was the only way they could keep replenishing the population.

After ordering her eighth drink from Horatio, she asked, "Hey do you remember a guy named Peter? Sorry I can't remember his last name. The guy was a former caretaker—must have had quite a story."

He eyed her curiously, although that wasn't unusual. He'd been doing it all night. "Haven't heard of him."

"Oh, come on," she said. "He was here all the time."

"Sorry." He shrugged.

"How long have you tended bar here?"

"Six years."

"I'm not leaving until you tell me about Peter." She said it with a smile.

He half-grinned in return and shook his head. "We close at two a.m.," he said, and moved down the bar to collect a few used glasses. Was he trying to call her bluff? It was two hours away.

He took the order of another patron, then stayed at the far end of the bar, ignoring her.

People came and went. A few came up to the bar. She asked them their names, or if they played Ket. She spoke a little too loud and laughed a little too much. She was drunk.

Eventually, as the blended haze of exhaustion and liquor took hold, she stood up to leave. Horatio called her a taxi, which she clearly needed.

It wasn't until later the next day she realized her conversation with Horatio was dangerous and imprudent. What if he had Inworld contacts? Asking questions about caretakers could get her into all kinds of trouble. Of course, at the time it seemed like the most logical line of questioning in the world.

CHAPTER 21

The farm was in a secluded area of Montana near a town named Whitefish. It was nestled next to a small lake in a fertile green and golden valley that extended for several miles. It was a peaceful place. His parents were at least right about that.

His uncle Jobe was a widower, so it was just the two of them. For the first couple of weeks his uncle barely said a word, as if the many years of being a hermit had robbed him of the art of conversation.

What was worse than his silence, however, were Jobe's occasional bouts of curiosity, which consisted of stark inquisitions about his arm or how he was *feeling*. That was what Tristan wanted to avoid more than anything. They were probably questions planted by his parents, because it certainly didn't seem natural for Jobe to care about anything outside of his farm.

So he avoided his uncle much of the time, even though he was the only human contact he had.

In his disabled state, Tristan had a lot of time on his hands. His chores consisted of anything that could be done with one arm, which was very little. After a few days his uncle had relegated him to domestic chores inside the house and make-work projects that didn't serve much purpose like rearranging the woodpile. In the evenings he would go for long walks or runs along the road that led along the lake or up the hill into the forest. He kept up his fitness with zeal; anything to keep busy.

He dreaded the discomfort of his idle thoughts.

Today was something different, however. Today they were going into town. The only time he'd been to Whitefish was when his uncle came to pick him up at the train station. Tristan was even moderately excited. Anything to break the monotony.

With one of the few remaining train stops left in Montana, Whitefish had about ten thousand inhabitants. It was isolated and strangely had some newer construction, something Tristan hadn't seen in San Francisco in recent memory. Tristan asked his uncle about the buildings, expecting there was some new industry he hadn't seen near the town, but that wasn't it at all.

"It's complicated," Jobe said as he turned onto the quiet main street of the town. "You see, avoiding the use of Tyband materials was a good thing sixty or seventy years ago, but when a whole city avoided Tyband altogether, these 'clean towns' were later seen as a bastion of raw materials for Inworld construction. Many clean towns were removed by armies of robots, which left little trace of their existence in less than a year."

They pulled up at a stoplight. Jobe waved at a pedestrian who walked by. It wasn't clear whether they actually knew each other.

Jobe continued. "After the bots had their way, it was like a sandstorm had swept the landscape clean in a whirlwind of deconstruction. This happened to most small towns in Montana, but Whitefish struck the happy medium of harboring just enough Tyband-contaminated material to keep the robots away. For a while, people migrated to Whitefish as other towns nearby were disassembled or withered away and died like so many did. Whitefish actually grew in size, so they had to build the newer buildings."

"Oh. Thanks."

"But now the population is decreasing just like everywhere else. Only smaller construction projects seem to be the order. And those can be dangerous, so we have to be smart about it."

Jobe was being unusually forthcoming. Maybe the change in

scenery was making him feel more conversational. "What do you mean by dangerous?" Tristan asked.

"Like cutting corners, not building to code, using unqualified materials. The hardest part is that Outworld factories skimp on quality so they can build cheap and quick. It's like...take your mom's plant for example. I'm sure she's told you. In masks there's a lot of competition, and not much money to go around. It's like that with building materials too."

Tristan said, "Yeah. I sometimes wonder if the Inworld could do a better job manufacturing masks, with all their robots and automated systems. My poor mom is always getting demerits."

Jobe stopped at another stop sign and cast Tristan a dark look. "Did you ever wonder why she's getting those demerits?" Jobe's eyes returned to the road and they continued on.

"Well, I just assumed—"

"That they were incompetence? Laziness? No, that's not your mom. Sis gets on my nerves, trust me. She talks way too much, but she's neither of those things. She gets those demerits because she does extra testing for Tyband, testing that's not sponsored by the Inworld investors. As a result she finds—and rejects—more contaminated masks than other plants. That's why I would never buy anything other than a Seneca mask."

"Why would they give her demerits for that? Surely the Inworld wants good quality masks?"

"Oh they do, which is why they moved their own mask production to inside the domes, but they could care less about Outworlder masks. They have their output quotas to hit, and their quality standards are about a mile from what's reasonable." He sighed and shook his head. "So they dock her pay. The investors even tried to have her fired, until the whole staff threatened to quit, and they backed down."

They had passed by the newer buildings in Whitefish and reached the main urban area, consisting of a few larger stores and warehouses that were pretty ramshackle. Jobe finished. "Sis takes it on the chin, for you, and me, and all Outworlders."

"Sorry Uncle, I...didn't know." A flash of guilt stirred in his chest.

The story still seemed fishy though. There was no space for mask production plants in the Inworld. The Inworlders were packed in tight, with barely enough air to breathe, which was why the Outworld had to supply everything. Everyone knew that.

They were pulling up to a hardware store.

"Stay in the car," Jobe commanded.

Tristan did as he was told. People went in and out of the store, middle-aged men and women mostly. They looked serious and focused. Greetings were mumbled. The occasional hand wave was made as a quick distraction.

There was a small shack being renovated nearby where a few carpenters labored industriously. As Tristan watched, an old man was slowly making his way to the hardware store from the site. He was walking incredibly slowly, with his back bent.

It made Tristan think of his father. He also had a troubled gait, and he was fraught with body aches brought on by years of manual labor in the streets of San Francisco. Would his father look like this poor man in a few years? The man wasn't clad in the same heavy protective material his father had to wear, but that didn't give Tristan any comfort.

Jobe was coming back from the store carrying a number of lengthy wooden beams. He also was barely clutching a bucket filled with nails.

Abruptly, he tripped on a stone obscured by his conglomeration of wood and dropped everything onto the ground.

Tristan hopped out of the car and walked over to help. Without thinking, he grabbed a piece of wood with his casted arm and instantly felt shooting pain. "Dammit," he cursed. The piece of wood he grabbed clattered to the ground again.

His uncle looked up at him from his crouched position and shook his head reprovingly.

With his bad arm still smarting, Tristan picked up what he could with his good arm and brought it to the car. Jobe dutifully opened the door and deposited the goods. Tristan expected some rebuke or derogatory remark, but Jobe said nothing. The look he'd given him was enough.

Once back in the car, his arm ached with greater force. Tristan reminded himself that every movement could cause it to set improperly or delay healing.

As they drove out of the lot and continued their rounds in Whitefish, he ignored Jobe and the people of the town and instead turned inward. He focused his anger and told himself he would heal. He would get better and play in the games next year, against all odds. He dug deep, like he always did, to find his anchor, and his resolve.

He didn't find what he was looking for. The usual pyre of willpower that burned within him wasn't there. Only a dim flicker of defiance would acknowledge his call.

CHAPTER 22

Luisa felt numb as she went through the motions at Chooly's funeral. She had trouble remembering their time together. Her mind wouldn't let her. Maybe it was a means of self-preservation.

She tried to spend time with Melissa, but Melissa was preoccupied with the arrangements or with her other friends. Perhaps Luisa's relationship with Melissa had only been an extension of her relationship with Chooly. It seemed this branch was about to wither and die with him.

Fenton and Michaelis had asked to meet again, but she hadn't returned their call. They knew Chooly had died. They knew she needed time. They could wait.

When she was alone in her apartment, it felt like the walls were heavy, as if they were about to fall in on her. So she went out. Her recent forays had been the only reprieves from the unrelenting sadness. She longed to talk to strangers because they knew nothing of her pain.

In fact she'd been out four of the last five evenings, and she was still hung over from the previous night, but the worst of those nights was the night she stayed home, alone with her thoughts, unable to escape.

Rex let out a bark, wanting to be fed. She ignored him and left the apartment.

She'd been back to Flip twice since Chooly's death. Horatio was nice enough, or at least willing to put up with her. The last time she was there she'd had some good conversations with other patrons. It was the kind of distraction she needed.

For lack of any better option, she went to Flip again. Maybe she just needed time. Maybe the weight in her chest would be gone when she woke up the next day.

She sat at a table this time, instead of the bar area. She was drinking slowly, away from the main action, but watching the people in the bar intently.

She would mingle, or read the news on her handheld comlink, or stare off into space. All the while she was steadily sipping cocktails. Occasionally Horatio would look toward her. "Yes, that's right," she whispered to herself. "There she is, back again today at the same bar. Get used to it, mister barkeep."

A group of three men entered and removed their masks, their heads were swiveling like they were casing the joint. They were somewhat brutish, with big beards and rounded torsos. One had a mask with amber and florescent yellow stripes on it—Amber Lightning's colors— but he didn't look like one of the players. He was probably just a fan. He caught Luisa's eye and stepped toward her. "Can we join you?" he asked. "We'll buy you a drink."

She looked at the table. She already had a drink. Did they think she was a drunk? Maybe she was. "Get lost, losers," she said. After raising their eyebrows, they moved away. They stood around looking perplexed, then left the bar.

She laughed to herself. It was a cheap laugh that ended quickly.

The bar was quiet, with only a few people milling about, whispering in a muted fashion. Having squandered her only real opportunity for conversation, she focused on steadily sipping whatever suited her fancy. She'd had about five drinks; her untended table did the math all too easily.

When she looked up again, Horatio was standing in front of her, holding a tray he began filling with her empty glasses. "Are you okay?"

he asked. Although he ignored her most of the time, Horatio had at least correctly surmised something was indeed wrong.

She didn't want anyone's pity. "Everything's good here, Horatio, just having a drink. You want to sit down and chat?" She pulled out a chair. "Tell me about that town of yours, in the southeast."

"You were serious, weren't you?"

She shrugged. "What are you talking about? Come on." She patted the seat again.

He stared at her for an uncomfortable moment. "If you're going to kill yourself, I'd prefer it not be on my account—at my bar." His face became stern, his brow furrowing. "The man you're looking for goes by the name of Hastings—Peter Hastings. I'll warn you, he's a crazy drunk. Actually, you two should get along." He half chuckled, stopping himself partway as if realizing it may be in poor taste. "He frequents the bars in the Old Mission now. Try Zed. That's all I know."

Without waiting for a response, he marched back to the bar.

"Well, that was rude," she whispered. She wasn't sure if he was trying to get rid of her or help her.

Probably both.

She called back at him. "Thank you."

His eyes wouldn't meet hers, but he grimaced at her unnatural volume. He remained focused on the glasses he was washing.

She had something. It was a gift really—a much needed justification for returning to Flip so many times.

And it was also a good reason to leave. She had harassed Horatio long enough. Maybe she should help him by removing the cantankerous girl who was beginning to be bad for business.

She stood up, steadied herself, dropped too much change on the table, and walked out the door.

CHAPTER 23

Michaelis rubbed the ridge of his nose and pushed up his glasses. His fingers lingered on the bumpy metal rims, contouring the poorly welded seams.

He glanced up at the clock on the dingy wall of the computer lab. It was after eleven p.m., and there was no one else in the room except the caretaker monitor. He'd already received several furtive glances from the shifty-looking agent, who undoubtedly was hoping Michaelis would leave so he could get back to his Parkdome sanctuary. But he looked young, and therefore new to his role. He was probably less callous to the Outworld, and also not as willing to bend the rules, which meant he probably wasn't going to shut the lab until midnight.

Michaelis still had time.

Luisa and Fenton often questioned why he would go to the computer labs. If he was trying to be secretive, why would he do this right under the nose of the caretaker agents?

It was because he knew the Inworld had intelligent agents tracking searches. Michaelis had to change his identity, location, and search patterns randomly to throw off the scent of any netbot. And at home e-mail addresses or other login credentials were required, whereas lab logins only required a name, for which he entered the name of someone else, real or imaginary.

He entered another code string into the software prompt. It would compile malware that would reveal the underlying search algorithm encoded in the network browser, so he could see how the Inworld was manipulating search results. The screen spat back a page of code that he tried to digest while keeping one eye on the caretaker monitor.

This wasn't how Michaelis had imagined his skills being used. His interest in network intelligence was initially driven by the same ultimate aspiration of so many youth. He was a terrible athlete with Tanner's esophyxia so the Ket games were out of the question, but he knew he still had a shot at entering the Inworld because a select few had been chosen after demonstrating exceptional expertise in technical fields.

With his mom's encouragement, he'd joined a gifted systems-computing stream in school with this objective in mind. Unfortunately, the Inworld selection process was far from a pure meritocracy, and it often seemed capricious. For a while they had started selecting structural engineers, and several were plucked out of the best programs. As a result, there was an influx of ambitious, motivated students that swelled the ranks of structural engineers. Then, rather abruptly, no more were taken in. No one knew why. Now there was an army of well-trained engineers with nothing to do. It seemed like the selection process was predicated on some scientific fashion trend.

It had been a pipe dream, really.

And it all came crashing down in the first year of the program in San Francisco, when Michaelis went too far, too deep. His intent hadn't been malicious; all he wanted to do was learn. And he did learn, more than most Outworlders ever did. His knowledge empowered and drove him, until he made a mistake. They figured out he was testing the boundaries of network security, and he was expelled and forbidden to pursue his studies in any academic institution.

Ironically, a year after his expulsion he was doing the same thing, only his intent *was* malicious. If only they had been willing to share their knowledge, he would have been perfectly content.

Out of the corner of his eye he saw the caretaker monitor move. Michaelis didn't avert his eyes from the display but he closed his search algorithm software program and opened a newsreel window. The caretaker navigated through a few empty rows of terminals, gradually wandering around to the space behind him. "What's new?" he asked.

The article Michaelis had pulled up was entitled *Rezoning for robot lanes behind schedule* but he otherwise had no idea what it was about. He said, "I'm trying to find out if my apartment is going to be affected by the new robot lanes."

"Is it?"

"Not sure. Not yet, at least."

"It's late."

"Yeah, sorry. I'm almost finished."

There was a pause. "Good," the caretaker said, and he moved away.

When the caretaker returned to his station, Michaelis went back to work, but as the night wore on it was getting harder to make sense of the code. He could only process two or three logical operators at a time when usually he would make sense of them by the dozen.

Michaelis unglued his eyes from the computer screen, picked up his work folder, and sat back in the uncomfortable plastic chair. He took the sheet he'd hidden in the back and glanced at his list to check his progress.

Much of his time was spent puzzling over what they were up against in terms of both Parkdome security and network security, but he might as well have been banging his head against the wall. Anything pertaining to Parkdome security was highly classified. They would have to scope it out on their own, on foot.

For network security, there were signs San Francisco was more lax than other dome cities. Case in point, in the computer labs you didn't need personal information to get on the net. The San Francisco dome system was also too lazy to put firewalls in place for broad comlink communications. As a result, with some work, they might have a shot at reaching everyone on the nets with a broad communication—a real chance to sway public opinion.

He couldn't be sure, however. Any rogue communication he planted might not even make it out beyond the first server, especially if some sort of Inworld security alarm was triggered beforehand. For this reason, if he had his way, he would prefer to avoid the nets altogether and find some other medium for communication.

He began skimming through the dossier one more time. It included a number of press releases he'd paid little attention to, mostly because they appeared to be related to mundane business transactions. Reading these seemed only mildly more entertaining than the searches he'd been doing. He scanned through them again until he arrived at one that caught his eye.

Among the press releases was a newspaper article. It was a story about the street kids who'd been caught by the caretakers eight years ago, including Tristan's brother. This by itself wasn't interesting. The story of street hooligans being detained and hanged was well known. Everyone was aware of the infamous day in Union Square. What was interesting was that it claimed they were arrested for their part in some form of conspiracy with a man named Hardin, a caretaker who worked on Inworld security systems and who'd reportedly stolen highly sensitive material.

According to the article, the gang had taken "data fingers" from Hardin, presumably containing secret information about the Inworlder security systems. A list of the perpetrators was included in the article. It didn't say what happened to these data fingers, except to mention they "may expose a serious flaw in Inworlder security."

He could see why Chooly would have kept the article. These data fingers, if found, could be worth a lot to people like him.

How could the Inworlders have let this happen?

When Michaelis looked for the same article on the nets, it didn't exist in the archives. Furthermore, he couldn't find any articles by the same journalist any time after the article was written. It was as if the author had vanished.

This old article, if correct, finally provided an explanation for why the Inworlders had gone to such extreme measures that day in Union Square. It was possible the article was later removed to prevent people from looking for the data fingers, and they may have even censored the journalist.

Why would they go to those lengths? The only reason he could think of was they hadn't found all the missing data fingers.

He would have to tell Luisa and Fenton. Perhaps they knew some of these kids, or their friends, just as they knew Tristan. Michaelis also made a mental note to be extra careful searching on these topics on the nets. There could be targeted netbots skulking around, waiting to snare the overly curious.

Maybe, just maybe, if they could get their hands on one of these data fingers, or at least find out what flaw it exposed, they would have something. It provided a modicum of hope that his diligence over the past two weeks hadn't been completely in vain.

He looked across the room again.

The caretaker agent was staring at him, this time without flinching, no longer satisfied with the occasional look of disdain.

It was time to go.

CHAPTER 24

Luisa massaged her calf muscle as she sat in the arena stands. Another season was about to begin and there was a fresh breed of new stars in the making. No teams had been formalized yet, but people lined up outside the arena to get in on pickup games. Luisa had played earlier so she could relax and check out the field.

Her game had gone well. She liked the pickup games because the best individual tacticians tended to stand out. People who could quickly survey a situation and capitalize on it were at an advantage in the pre-season anarchy. Today she'd been fortunate to be placed with a few veterans from last year, and they used numbers advantages well throughout the match, eventually winning.

A couple of newbies on the other team were good, however—really good. As excellent shooters and sprinters, these newbies would certainly be picked up by good teams. She could tell they were, ultimately, more talented than she was, and with a little more experience, her opponents would have easily bested her team.

That was fine with her. She could accept that. What worried her was how she felt. What she gained in wisdom was lost in her lack of excitement. She could see the drive in these newbies and felt the same lacking in her. It could be her clandestine activities were taking away from her passion for the games, or maybe it was her nights out on the town.

Or maybe she was just plain getting older.

She scanned the stands. There were a few players she recognized. Many had played last year but hadn't made it to the Inworld. Other faces were missing, however—those who made it: Sonny Joseph and his gaggle of hotshots, Damian Thatcher, and a few more.

They had been so close. Tristan might have made it if he hadn't shattered his arm. Well, maybe not, she reconsidered. The loss was disastrous for him as the captain. But it didn't matter; his arm sealed the deal. No way.

There was no sign of Tristan. She'd been to the arena many times expecting to see him and wondering how he would handle the crushing defeat. She might never see him again. Many a gamer vanished once the dream was gone.

Ardrey was there. Some people thought he might be pulled into the Inworld as early as last year given his stellar performance, but he had two years of eligibility left, and they never pulled anyone out that early.

He played in the game after hers and won. She watched his efficient and calculating maneuvers on the arena floor. There were many rumors about Ardrey. Everyone said what happened to Tristan was an accident, but was it? Did he steal Tristan's plays and give them to Sonny Joseph? The games weren't about making friends. Many perceived them as life or death, so it wasn't out of the question.

Either way, Ardrey had become a force to be reckoned with, and if anything, the incident with Tristan increased his popularity. Six months ago he was seen as a promising fledgling recruit, but now he was a star, if not the top player in the league. He was made captain and could handpick his own recruits.

She shuddered at the thought. It just didn't seem right after what happened.

Luisa left the noisy arena to be met with the patter of heavy rainfall. The streets were flooded with miniature streams of muddy water following the contours of the asphalt. She threw on her overcoat and safety mask and reluctantly ran out to the bike stand. There she wrestled with her lock, hopped on her bike, and headed toward the Old Mission.

Luisa shook off the drops on her overcoat in the entranceway to the bar, mimicking Rex after a walk in the rain. She removed her mask and jacket and peered into the establishment.

Zed was a darkly lit lounge with an eerie red glow, sparsely populated with a diverse collection of individuals from all walks of life. It was never busy, but also never empty. She knew Peter Hastings, for his part, took it upon himself as a matter of pride that there was at least one patron. He was sitting with Fenton and Michaelis in the back corner of the bar. They looked at her expectantly.

Luisa had found Peter the second time she'd gone to Zed after the tipoff from Horatio. Partly through feminine guile and partly through a kinship born of a fondness for liquor, she had connected with Peter. She had bided her time before she broached any incriminating questions. Luckily, he was intoxicated so her moment came quickly. While he was hesitant to reveal his identity, it was clear he had a profound distaste for the Inworld, judging by the expletives he used when the subject came up. He also seemed to be lonely, and aimless. Eventually she had convinced him to meet with their little trio.

"You're late," Fenton noted, mildly annoyed. He stared blankly at her as she strolled over to the table.

Luisa ignored him. "Well, how about a round of drinks? This one is on me, Mr. Hastings." She extended her hand, which he gladly took. His eyes were bulging and his face pallid. He had a shabbily cut peppered beard, and wore his long greasy hair in a part lying partially over his forehead. She didn't know whether this appearance was to mask his identity or if being unkempt was his style.

"So did Peter tell you he used be ranked in the top ten in the South SF league?" Luisa asked.

Michaelis and Fenton nodded.

"He played with Waylen Samuel. Remember him?"

They nodded again.

How late had she been? An uncomfortable silence ensued as Luisa tried to come up with another conversation starter.

Before she could continue, Peter interjected, "Listen here kids. I don't really have much to live for anymore, but on the level..." He paused and cleared his throat. It was a profoundly unattractive sound, almost a yell if it weren't for the audible phlegm-curdling component. "I'd rather enjoy my remaining time here on earth than be caught by those Myra-lovers. The only reason I'm here is because Luisa told me you want to put a dent in that shiny black eight ball." He pointed through the wall in the direction of the Parkdome. "Tell me what you've got, and convince me I'm not here for some kind of bullshit setup." He glared at each of them individually. Satisfied they'd all been listening, he raised his glass to his lips.

Fenton and Michaelis raised their eyebrows. Although crass, his monologue was succinct enough.

Luisa chimed in. "Absolutely, Peter. We appreciate you agreeing to talk with us, and we recognize this is a precarious situation. Michaelis, do you want to fill him in?"

They had discussed beforehand that they might need to be forthcoming to convince him to help, and Michaelis would be the best person to explain the situation. Michaelis hesitated, as if running through some final analysis before deciding it was okay to proceed. When it appeared the machinery of his mind stopped churning, he began.

He described their motivations against the Inworld, the two philosophical approaches they were considering, samples of his findings from the computer lab, some of the findings from Chooly's dossier, and finally how they had come to find him. Meanwhile, the three others listened intently, taking the occasional sip of their cocktails.

During the description, Peter's expression only revealed only a furrowed brow. "Humph," was all he ventured in response.

Fenton said, "So what do you think, Mr. Hastings? Do you think you can help us?"

Peter was still digesting the information. "Hmm," was all he replied after another moment of consideration. After a longer pause, Fenton threw up his arms. Luisa kicked him under the table, urging patience.

Luisa went to the bar to collect another tray of drinks. When she returned Michaelis was squirming at the uncomfortable situation, or perhaps at the rate of alcohol consumption. Sometimes Michaelis would act like this—like he was a concerned parent taking care of misbehaving children. Fenton shrugged and grabbed another glass of cider to cradle. It went without saying that Peter did as well.

"Well, let's see now," Peter broke the silence. "It all sounds plausible. I don't think you have a batshit's chance in hell, of course." He smiled at Luisa, and she smiled back politely. "And you know you're all going to get caught and face lifelong imprisonment, if not the caretaker death squad." He looked somberly at Fenton who nodded carefully. "But what the hell, should make for something interesting to do to pass the time, right?" As he finished, he punched Michaelis in the shoulder. Michaelis mouthed *ow* to Fenton, who let out a chuckle.

Peter opened up after that. Fenton, Luisa, and Michaelis sat on the edge of their seats firing one question after another, and to be sure Peter's tongue would stay lubricated, Luisa kept the alcohol flowing.

He told them about his time in the Inworld. Apparently even when granted access to the Inworld as a caretaker, you didn't have freedom to go wherever you pleased. In fact, you needed to earn the ability to access the Old Inworld, in the western part of the Parkdome. Privileges like advanced healthcare and interdome network access weren't available to new caretakers either.

It wasn't the utopia people on the Outworld made it out to be. Maybe on a relative basis, as the caretakers on the lowest rank of the Inworld still had much more than anyone in the Outworld, but the Inworld class system was a surprise. In fact, Peter claimed he rarely saw an "Old" Inworlder, someone who was born and raised in the dome system. He'd spent most of his time with the other new caretakers— predominantly former Ket stars—in their segregated section, enjoying what they could of their new life and its benefits.

"Why did you leave?" Michaelis asked. It was a sensitive question, but Peter was probably expecting it.

"I'd been part of a kind of special forces Outworld security detail, which was one part police force and two parts fucking propaganda engine, with a dollop of corruption to boot. I was in an altercation with one of the higher ranked caretakers over what I thought was the unjust handling of an Outworlder. It wasn't a smart career move. I could have been put in jail, or perhaps relegated to some dirty job on the lower echelon of Inworld society, but before they could consign me to my new fate, I ran."

He savored his drink for a moment. "It was during one of my regular security details," Peter explained. "I stole an enercycle and took flight to the ruins of Oakland, then hid out in one of the desert shanty-towns. It was there I had my microchip removed by a hermit at a hydroponic farm—the guy was a former surgeon, or at least that's what he told me. It was a bloody operation, let me tell you, and it took weeks to fully recover from it. The guy had to cut out part of my shoulder blade, and I'm not sure if it was because it was a requirement of the operation or if it was because he was just an asshole."

Peter sipped his drink again and squinted into the memory. "They came for me with a full security force of twenty-odd caretakers, murdered some of the farm workers, and in some cases destroyed the only leads to my whereabouts. So, I dug up one of the recently deceased, inserted my old chip into the shoulder blade of the corpse, and burnt the body. I wasn't sure if they thought it was me or not, but I didn't see them again. After that I laid low for months, traveling around the East Bay, occasionally stealing food or other essentials. When the inhabitants of the shanty towns were becoming wary of me, I made my way back to San Francisco proper."

Although the story had been interesting, Luisa's optimism was beginning to wane. Peter had been in the Inworld for only three years, and in a sequestered part of it, so what information could he really provide? His monologue also exposed the challenges they faced. If a former caretaker knew little about the Inworld's inner workings, how could a few young Outworlders find a way to infiltrate it?

At this point Michaelis took over, dissecting the story in more detail, and trying to extract as much information as he could. Luisa wasn't hopeful.

She headed to the bar again.

"Same thing, Luisa?" The bartender approached her, wringing his hands.

"Yep, another round." This bartender was different from Horatio. He was younger—gruff but well built. She smiled, and he smiled back.

After receiving the drinks, she hesitated to go back to the table. She'd much rather stay here and hang out with this bartender, maybe flirt a little, talk about the games, the vids—something less serious.

She peered over at Michaelis who was firing questions at Peter. Peter looked exasperated. It wasn't until Fenton glanced in surprise at Michaelis, and showed increased attention to Peter by sitting up in his chair, that she decided to go back and join the conversation.

Peter was gazing at Michaelis with a look of curiosity, as if seeing him in a different light. He was choosing his words carefully. "Yes, I did hear about that through a caretaker who'd been transferred to Marindome construction duty from the Parkdome. You would have liked this guy. He could really shovel the shit." Peter made a shoveling motion with his hands, as if it needed some explanation.

"I'm sure he's high up in the caretaker ranks by now—a real ass-kisser. Anyway, I was always questioning things, and he once told me about a fellow named Hardin, who was some kind of computer genius. He was working on advancing the security systems, and he was under tight watch because he was from the Outworld originally. It was unusual for anyone not at least several generations shiny to be working on the most sensitive security systems, you see, but apparently he was that good."

Peter paused to take another healthy gulp of his full drink. "So anyway, he told me about how this guy had stolen some access codes to the San Francisco dome system. Apparently, he could control the whole security system with a computer program called the Security Countermand Application, or SCA for short. He downloaded it onto data fingers made of a biological matrix that wouldn't be detected in security checkpoints. The caretakers were in a state of panic. They weren't sure what he'd stolen because it was so secretive even to them. They only knew it related to some powerful computer program.

"Anyway they found the guy. Apparently he slit his own throat, the sicko, and tried to give away copies of the data fingers to some street gang kids. They rounded up all the kids but were never sure they found all the data fingers. Of course, they covered this up the best they could by killing all those involved, even the freaking kids. They must have been really worried."

When Peter's monologue ended he looked away from them in contemplation.

"How much of the system could these data fingers—this Security Countermand Application—control?" Michaelis asked.

"Most of it, I think. Sorry the details are hazy."

"Do you know where the missing data fingers could be?" Fenton asked.

"No idea. Sorry kid."

They tried a number of additional questions, tracking through his story, pulling it apart, but little else came of it, so they switched topics.

They managed to define the entry points to the domes and better understand security protocols, including how the caretaker enforcement organization functioned, but otherwise there was little additional information they could glean from Peter.

It was past midnight, and Peter was drunk. He was diverting the conversation to—by his own admission—more entertaining topics. As his lips became more lubricated, they also became more laced with sarcasm.

"Why don't you walk up to the Parkdome and state your intentions? I'm sure they'll surrender to three kids. Just go up there and threaten them with your pulse rifles." He laughed to himself and continued on this tack for some time, calling them the "Dream Team."

Michaelis grimaced and Fenton sat there with eyes barely open. He had too much to drink as well. Luisa laughed at their situation along with Peter, to the chagrin of Michaelis.

After succumbing to a few more minutes of abuse, Michaelis stood up to leave, pulling Fenton along with him and gesturing to Luisa to come as well. She shook her head no. She was having fun.

Luisa stayed with Peter, making light of their little group. It was self-deprecating, she reasoned. Although later, when she was sober, she realized it might have seemed pathetic. She even danced with Peter—albeit clumsily—later in the night. Zed had filled with about ten or twelve patrons. The eyes of the bar were on them.

At one point, she fell forward during a dance, and Peter caught her. "You okay? We can't have you going down. The dream team needs you!" he laughed.

Much later—it must have been after two a.m., when there were only a few stragglers left in the bar—she barely recalled their last conversation of the evening. Luisa was griping about the impossible odds. At this point, even Peter was embarrassed for her, trying to get her to leave. He grabbed her arm and escorted her toward the door.

They spilled onto the street.

"It's not fair," she said. "No one cares."

It was then that Peter said something, but it didn't quite register with her until the next day. He was angry about having to take care of this misfit drunkard, and tired of her complaining. "You don't think you're the only game in town, do you? You're so naïve. Come on, let's go."

That was the last she remembered of the evening.

CHAPTER 25

In the frosty night air Michaelis was scanning the descent toward the waves rolling in below. Fenton was teetering on the edge of the cliff in front of him, wearing the bulky underwater suit, his weight secured by the old towline. Michaelis could see a faint frown of concentration behind the transparent faceplate of his helmet, with sweat droplets visible on his forehead.

"Are you ready?" Michaelis asked. Fenton returned a scowl.

Michaelis looked down at his handset to check on the most recent comlink message from Luisa. It read *Clear*. The time stamp was less than a minute ago.

"Okay it's time," Michaelis said, and he nodded to Fenton.

Fenton began rappelling down the cliff while Michaelis moved to position himself against the nearby tree next to the winch.

Fenton had borrowed the winch and suit from an uncle whose family had a history of deep-sea diving. He claimed it was an antique from before the Tyband era, and he was most certainly being honest—the suit was so old and rusted that it barely worked. So while Michaelis craned his neck to get a line of sight on the cliff where Fenton descended, he made sure he was close enough to the winch to apply the brake if necessary.

After several light jumps down the crags of the cliff face, Fenton was within reach of the water. Directly to his right was a cornice, which would occasionally cause the waves smashing against it to shoot frothy water up the wall and shower seawater over him. He continued descending and the outcropping absorbed the impact of the next wave.

In another quick jump off the wall Fenton splashed into the water and was submerged.

Soon there was nothing more to see of Fenton, only the light of his headlamp stabbing a distorted dagger of illumination into the frothy murk. Michaelis pulled up the cable and rolled over to sit up closer to a nearby tree trunk and check the tracking console he'd configured. It showed a blip representing Fenton on the grid, moving westward, away from the cliff face.

Michaelis let out a wheezy sigh into his mask. Everything seemed to be working.

For the second time that evening Michaelis questioned why they were doing this. Yes, there was a pattern in the dossier: repeated mentions of work being done underwater near Ocean Beach, and that it was kept under wraps by the Inworlders. So it could be something worth exploring, but it seemed like the venture was forced into play simply because it was the only thing they could think of, and Luisa kept pushing for them to do *something*. There was little reassurance that there was nothing illegal about what they were doing. The Inworld would easily find some way to justify a penalty for snooping around.

The group had hit a wall. Obtaining one of the enigmatic security program data fingers was a long shot, and they had pulled up no leads since their discussion with Peter. According to Luisa, Peter had made her believe there was some other rebel group, but now he was denying it. It was hard to say for sure, since Peter and her were both half-drunk much of the time.

They had also been trying to recruit from Chooly's list of contacts without success. Some of the potential recruits were hardened criminals who couldn't be trusted. The two individuals they finally decided to approach gave them only looks of fear and incredulity. They wanted nothing to do with them.

The transponder beeped.

Michaelis hit the acknowledgement button on his arm. He checked his earpiece to see if it was functioning.

"How are the fishies down there, Fenny?" Luisa's voice came through, answering Fenton's call first.

Fenton responded, "I'm having enough trouble seeing my feet, never mind any fish."

"You mean you can't see the stars? It's such a beautiful night here at the Cliff House. I might go have some synth-chowder and a beer. You interested?"

Fenton replied, "Sure, just get Michaelis to pour the beer into the air tank next time."

There was a pause.

Luisa adopted a more serious tone. "How is everything working?"

"I'm fine. Air tank is good. No suit leaks. I'll be heading west along the bottom for about a thousand more feet, then I'll hang a left."

"Okay. Keep in touch."

It was nice to hear Luisa in a good mood again. The last few times he'd seen her she'd been either listless or tipsy. Michaelis hoped she hadn't chosen the Cliff House for access to alcohol, but rather what they had discussed—it was the best lookout point to track any caretaker activity nearby.

According to the positioning system, he still had another six hundred feet to go until he was supposed to turn. The blip continued forward through the grid.

Fenton opened the line again. "The bottom is sandy, with some trash or rock outcroppings I'm having to walk around. Nothing interesting. I still have fifty minutes in my air tank."

Fenton reached the turning point. "Turning left now," he said.

The Parkdome extended out about three hundred feet from the beach area into the water. Michaelis's hypothesis was that the Inworld might be working on extending it further, which they had vehemently denied in the media. Soon they would know, and hopefully they would also be able to document evidence of work being done.

Fenton's tracker slowed. He was about five hundred feet from the Parkdome.

"Lots more trash here. Hard to make out the bottom from the junk." Michaelis shivered at the thought that some of it could be Tyband-contaminated.

"I've hit a rock wall about five feet high. Can't get around so I'm going to hop over it."

"Sounds good," Luisa responded. "Be careful."

There was silence for a moment.

"Had some trouble getting over the wall. Was pretty jagged. Water clearer here. No visible obstacles ahead. Wait. There are stacks of wood —no, metal beams of some kind. And indentations. The ground is harder, as if they swept away the sand. It must be shallow. It's brighter here. Turning off my headlamp."

Michaelis did some quick calculations, looking at his position and the decline into the ocean. "You should still be quite deep in the water," he said.

"I am pretty sure it's brighter here than..." Fenton trailed off.

"Fenton?" Luisa asked.

"Sorry, I had to duck behind the beams," Fenton said. "There is some kind of underwater bot patrolling around. It nearly shined a search light right on me."

"Can you take any pictures?" Luisa asked.

"Not without being seen by the bot. Shit. There's another one coming this way."

"Get out of there," Michaelis urged, "right away."

"Got it. I'm...whoa, a light came on from below me, if that's possible."

Michaelis's heart began beating more rapidly. Fenton had surely triggered some kind of motion sensor, possibly a security alarm.

"Keep us updated Fenton," Luisa said, "and keep moving."

"Okay. I stirred up the murk so it's hard to know where I came from. How's my line?"

"Fine according to the transponder," Michaelis said. "Keep moving."

The comlink was quiet for a while. The tracker beeped. The waves continued to break against the cliff. Michaelis's heart pounded.

"What's going on, guys?" Fenton asked. "Any sign of trouble up there? I must be getting closer." His blip was moving quickly. He would be nearing the cliff wall soon.

"You're two hundred feet away," Michaelis said. "I'll get the winch ready."

"Hey, don't worry, Fenton," Luisa said. "No sign of elbow-knockers up here, but let's not wait around for any to show up."

"I'm near the rock face. Michaelis, drop the cable."

Michaelis began winching the cable down.

The channel from Luisa opened up again. "Spoke too soon. caretakers. Nine or ten of them. Not normal. Searching for something. Signing off." A disconnection could be heard.

Fenton responded, "Luisa? Are you there?" There was a pause. "Michaelis, can you drop the cable?"

"Give me a minute, Fenton. I think we should cut the channel soon, though."

"No shit, but drop the cable!"

"Okay, it's down."

"Where? Oh, I see it. Okay, pull me up." The cable jerked twice as a confirmation signal.

Michaelis turned on the winch and it started rewinding slowly. It was quite loud, and it would occasionally sputter.

"Can you go any faster?"

"I don't think that's a good idea," Michaelis said. But Fenton was right. The winch was taking too long.

The old winch engine sputtered again and began making a disconcerting grinding noise. Then it stopped altogether.

"Hold on," Michaelis said. He examined the old contraption. The cable wasn't stuck, so it was something in the gearbox. They didn't have time to try to fix it.

Thinking quickly, Michaelis looped one end of the cable around the tree, disconnected the lift component of the winch, and placed his feet against the base of the same tree for leverage. He held onto the taut end of the cable that led over the cliff.

"We're doing it manually. You've still got the cable?"

"Manually?" Fenton said, and after some hesitation. "Yeah, I guess so." The cable jerked twice again. Michaelis braced himself against the tree and pulled on the cable in sequential bursts of effort, elevating Fenton in jerks up the rocky embankment.

Michaelis's neck was feeling bloated, sinewy. It was coming, the first signs.

He continued to pull. Fenton was heavy with all his gear. Michaelis was sure Fenton was also pulling up with all his might, and possibly even climbing the cliff face, or he would never have been able to do this.

After a few painful minutes, Fenton's suited body angled over the cliff edge. Michaelis greeted him with a flushed face and a bout of coughing.

"Let's go—" Michaelis said between gasps, "—we don't have much time before they start searching here." He pulled off his mask and let it hang from his neck. He wasn't getting enough oxygen.

Fenton hurriedly took off the helmet. "What's going on?" Fenton asked. "Is Luisa okay?"

"All I know...is what you heard...I think you might have set off... some sort of...I haven't heard from her since—"

Michaelis doubled over, gasping feverishly. He waved off Fenton, who was trying to hold him up. All of Michaelis's energy was focused on pulling oxygen into his lungs.

Thankfully, Fenton was unfazed by Michaelis's troubles, and in a decisive state of mind. "Okay let's go. We can't wait for Luisa to respond. They could be nearby."

Michaelis coughed and nodded at the same time. Further conversation was out of the question.

Fenton had taken off the full suit and put on slacks and a loose sweatshirt. Michaelis was able to unloop the cable from the tree and throw it down into the ocean, together with the useless winch.

Fenton hefted his duffel bag with all the gear in it and began hiking up the hill in the dark, with Michaelis close behind. He had turned off the light so progress was difficult. Michaelis staggered after him.

They made it up to a pebble-strewn pathway sometimes used by hikers. Fenton decided to take a fork leading through a wooded area. Both ways would get them back to the car, but this way would provide them with more cover.

Eventually, as they progressed up an incline on the path, they could see down the hill that led to the Cliff House. It was a beacon of light perched above dark ocean swells. In front of the building were a number of enercycles. Several caretakers were milling about, but there was no sign of Luisa.

In front of them was another split in the path.

Fenton paused to assess the situation while Michaelis held his head in his hands. He was absorbed by his ailment, his trachea constricted, but he was still able to offer some insight on the situation. He put his arm out and pointed down the longer path. If they took the more direct route, they'd be out in the open longer before they made it to the car.

Fenton seemed to agree. They skulked down the path, around some turns, looking back occasionally.

Suddenly, lights appeared at their backs, shimmering behind them.

"Come on!" Fenton whispered loudly while grabbing Michaelis. He threw him into the underbrush. Fenton pulled at Michaelis's underarm to help him through the shrubs and up a light grade. They scrambled until they threw themselves over a cleft. Looking back down they saw two caretakers driving down the path on enercycles. The caretakers stopped below them.

Michaelis and Fenton kept low and moved on, scaling the rest of the grade under the foliage, eventually reaching another pathway that led them to the trailhead, where they broke from the forest. Fenton ran first and pulled Michaelis along behind him. The car was just down the street.

Michaelis just couldn't move fast enough, so Fenton let go and ran toward the car on his own while Michaelis limped after him, hunched over. Blue spots were showing in his peripheral vision.

Michaelis fell over after tripping on what was barely a pothole. He managed to stand up, but his momentum had been lost. He felt like a zombie, rising from the dead. He cursed his feeble body and dysfunctional airways, all the while challenging himself to stay standing. He coughed and coughed. All his energy went into filling his lungs.

Ahead of him, Fenton had made it to the car. He was throwing the gear on the backseat and looking back to see whether they were being followed. In quick succession he started the car and drove the distance to Michaelis, who had slowed to pathetic baby steps. The car stopped and Michaelis fell onto the side door. He managed to snag the door handle, open it, and roll into the backseat of the car, panting desperately.

Fenton pulled away.

Michaelis felt the motion of the car, but it felt more like a boat at sea, the sensations dull and prolonged. The peripheral spots in his vision were expanding. The grungy seat cushion in front of him became the only object that wasn't some shade of blue.

He rolled over on his side. It felt better this way. He could only concentrate on breathing. Each inhalation was a monumental feat.

Fenton was at the steering wheel, looking over his shoulder. He was agitated, yelling at him, but no words registered for Michaelis. The periphery of his vision began to collapse completely, closing inward until there was nothing. There was no car, no Fenton, only blue.

The blue turned to black, and Michaelis fell unconscious.

CHAPTER 26

Tristan's cast had been removed two days before, but he still wore a rough splint on his forearm. The doctor said it was healing well.

It was hard for him to agree that his emaciated yellow limb was looking "well". He could grip things, but nothing heavy, and it would be another month before he could do anything practical with it.

Tristan was going home in a few days, and he felt like he should make a better effort to get to know his uncle. Their only real conversation had been on their trip to Whitefish, and it had been more of a lecture. So on this particular evening, Tristan had used one of his mother's old recipes to prepare a large dinner, consisting of a real pot roast that wasn't synth-meat, potatoes, and even dessert. Maybe it would catalyze some sort of discussion.

Jobe definitely looked excited. He didn't cook much, mostly eating one food item at a time, like a bowl of beans or a boiled egg. The concept of eating a meal with a variety of courses was foreign to him.

"This looks great," Jobe said. He spent little time surveying the spread of food and began eating, efficiently apportioning morsels from the serving dishes to his plate and mouth simultaneously.

Tristan opened his mouth to speak but decided to wait for a pause in Jobe's food assembly line.

When Jobe had made good headway on the meal, he tried again. "So, Jobe, I wondered why you never remarried."

After a few more chewing bouts, Jobe said, "Not many eligible women in Whitefish," and he laughed. He sometimes cracked himself up, as if recalling a joke he'd made, or a situation that was humorous to him, but he never explained why it was funny.

"Oh," Tristan said.

Another bout of feeding followed.

"How come you don't visit us in San Francisco? There are lots of eligible women there."

Jobe looked up with his eyes but continued to lean into the meal. "I went to visit six years ago. You probably don't remember. It's too far for me. I need to take care of the farm, and I can't afford it."

Tristan tried another subject. "Do you think Mr. Findley's property is going to sell soon? It's a great piece of land." It was something Jobe had mentioned before.

"No, way too expensive. He's lost his head, that old curmudgeon."

This was followed by silence interspersed with chewing and the clink of eating utensils.

After a few more noble attempts on Tristan's part, little headway had been made. Jobe seemed resigned to enjoy the food and not participate in any kind of intelligent dialogue. Maybe he was just boring? Tristan watched as Jobe scraped clean the second helping of food and pulled the dessert closer to his plate to prepare it for consumption.

After eating the dessert in silence, Jobe paused and looked up at Tristan. "So, is that it?" he asked, making an odd open-mouthed sweep of his teeth with his tongue to collect any remaining food items.

"I'm sorry, what do you mean?" Tristan asked.

Jobe dismissed his comment with a wave of his hand. "How's the arm today?"

It was hardly real conversation—he asked the same question every morning.

"It's okay," Tristan responded. "I've been working at improving my grip strength."

Jobe just stared at him.

Tristan explained. "In the games it's important to have good grip strength."

Jobe nodded. "You know, I was in the games, too."

"Really? My parents never told me. Where did you play?"

"I was in Seattle." Jobe was watching Tristan's reaction carefully. "I hear you're a good bounder. That takes a lot of skill. It's rare to get someone who can bound while being able to fire accurately at the same time."

Tristan didn't interrupt. He didn't want to stem the tide of verbiage coming from Jobe's mouth.

"I was a sniper," Jobe continued. "I made it to the playoffs every time, but my team never made it to the finals. In my last year, people said I was a fifty-fifty shot for the Inworld, but I didn't make it, obviously."

Tristan had a sinking feeling. This had to be some sort of setup. Maybe his parents wanted him to learn from his washed-up uncle and come back happy because he was just as screwed—destined to live a life as a hermit farmer, or on the docks, or in Tyband disposal. He sat rigidly and listened, knowing there would be some misguided lesson coming soon. It was just one more humiliating speech he would have to endure.

Jobe continued. "Of course I was crushed when I didn't get in. For many years I was angry, reaching back, you know, trying to get back what I lost—that feeling of hope. But I later realized life isn't just about getting into the Inworld. I realized there's more to it than that."

Tristan took the bait with some resignation. "What do you think it's about?"

"Well, it's about living what life you've been given. About being good to your family and friends and making do with what you have."

Tristan kept his face deadpan, trying to hide his annoyance. Jobe was still elaborating. "I live every day and enjoy it," he said. "I try to stay healthy and keep my friends healthy so we can all push our lives as far as they will go. I realized this slowly, though. It wasn't until Marie died that it really hit me."

He seemed to be repeating himself, but his uncle thought every word had unique meaning. Finally, Jobe finished. "I realized that, because I had been so focused on it, so caught up in it, that my time in the games had taken away from what I had with Marie. It was then, too, I realized I was glad I never made it into the Inworld at all." He said it matter-of-factly, moving away from his dessert and back to the remains of dinner, trying to gnaw meat off a meatless bone.

A thrust of anger surged through Tristan. This superficial tripe was lame and patronizing. "Living your life" was the answer? What a crock. If you don't make it to the Inworld, you're going to die early. Yeah, sure, he was glad he never made it in.

What a bunch of horseshit.

Tristan gritted his teeth and looked down at his empty plate. He grabbed it and stood up.

Without glancing back to see Jobe's face, Tristan said, "Well, thanks Jobe. I didn't know you were also in the games. I'm going for a run." Tristan pushed his plate onto the counter and abruptly walked out of the room, trying to contain himself.

Tristan did run, despite the food sloshing around in his stomach. He ran through the field covered with islands of snow, then up the road toward the mountain path. The sun was surely going to set soon but Tristan didn't care. His thoughts raced while his feet paced. He had to get as far away from Jobe—from that conversation—as possible.

Tristan never had much respect for his uncle. And now, what? His parents thought he would be just like him? Give up on the Inworld and live in the middle of nowhere? Tristan wasn't going to sugarcoat his loss. Yes, the odds were stacked against him, but he was still going out to win next year. He wasn't going to be a loser.

He ran faster. His uncle's house repelled him up the mountain trail, but he knew something else was pulling him from higher up on the mountain. A nagging feeling of uncertainty had held him since the day before, when he had walked this path.

After twenty minutes he stopped and bent over, panting. He lifted his gaze from his knees, and looked off to the right.

Yesterday he'd seen a deer by the path. Stricken by sickness, the deer had fallen. Whether it was related to Tyband, other pollutants, or some other disease it was impossible to tell. The animal had been gasping for breath, looking up at him, its neck trying to jerk away from Tristan, but otherwise unable to move. The deer's eyes were vivid and wide, glistening with fear.

The deer had frozen Tristan in his stride, and he'd stood there for many minutes, not knowing what to do, but he'd done nothing. Eventually he'd kept walking down the path back to the farm.

He hadn't told his uncle about the animal.

Now, in the declining light, Tristan could see the deer was still there. It had expired, and maggots had formed several holes in the otherwise plush fur of the animal. They were diligently burrowing into the carcass.

He was pulled toward it. He sat on a soft bed of pine needles next to it.

Tristan reached over and touched the animal's fur in an area undisturbed by the scavenging worms. The day before he hadn't tried to find a way to save the animal—he hadn't even tried to comfort it. Instead, he'd stood there, helpless. For some reason, he felt guilty—as though he'd personally invited the maggots to compete for their place on the diminishing carcass.

His talk with his uncle must have precipitated this. Was there something his uncle had said that pushed him back to this clearing?

Tristan allowed himself to cry for the deer. And then, he cried for himself, and his broken arm. Like a child lost in the woods, his grief was directionless and immature. Many minutes passed this way, Tristan's gaze alternating between the deer and his emaciated arm. Sweat had dried on his shirt, and tears formed dark rivulets where the sweat had begun to dry.

He felt spent and pathetic. Memories flooded his mind, as if there had been a vast dam holding them back that had broken, and each memory that passed the threshold into his conscience eroded the dam further, bringing a torrent of others. They were images from his last league game, of Luisa, of his parents, and his brother. Eventually, as he wept, the flood slowed. Out of the turbulence, some images became clearer, surfacing to the top.

The visions of his brother, Tom, tormented him most. One was from just before they took him away. They were sitting in their modest living room, Tom talking to him about a run-in with a caretaker aerial drone with his gang buddies. Tristan had been bursting with questions but he'd said nothing, worried about sounding ignorant in front of his brother.

This quickly transitioned into Tristan watching Tom's hanging with his parents in Union square. He knew the image that was coming next. It was the one he'd learned to evade but was always there, lurking in hiding—the one that made him wake up from his dream before it ever resolved. With the dam broken, he couldn't stop it from projecting in his mind. He held his head in his hands awaiting the inevitable. It came, with full force. He saw his dying brother turning in the metal noose, his face fully resolved, a grotesque mask distorted by pain.

It was so detailed, so real, as if he was seeing it for the first time.

Tristan wept again. His brother's face had broken free from his subconscious and taken hold.

He struggled to regain his composure. In the past, when he had been faced with failure, or despair, he had pulled himself out of his hole in a forge of new will. He searched deep within himself to find an anchor for his anguish, an objective to reset and recover. His anchor had always been the games. His motivation had led to incessant practicing and strategizing. It had kept him focused and sane.

But now, that was gone. What was left of his old flame had been extinguished by the river of memories that overwhelmed him.

He again reached back and forced himself to visualize the games. He pictured himself on the arena floor, firing his pulse rifle in earnest, but in his reverie the games around him stopped, his imagination refusing to cooperate. Amid the frozen battle scene, a figure approached him. It was Tom again, his face still distorted by the hanging.

Tom took Tristan by the arm and, in a flash, he had returned to Union Square eight years ago. Tom's head was encircled by a noose, not yet tightened. He was still holding on to Tristan firmly, looking at him squarely as he floated like a surreal ghost above the stage. The executioner caretaker was coming to push his brother over the ledge. Soon the metal noose would tighten around his neck.

But the executioner didn't push Tom. Instead he turned to Tristan, as if waiting for instructions. The executioner wore a gray, lifeless utility mask, like he did on that day, to hide his identity. It had no team colors. It wasn't even standard caretaker issue. It was devoid of allegiance.

Tom said, "Take off the mask."

A series of masks peeled off the executioner's face, each one revealing another underneath. The standard utility mask came off to reveal a Heavy Duty mask, which came off to reveal a Ket arena mask painted with Cold Fusion colors. Finally, the Ket arena mask fragmented and fell away, revealing the gray executioner's mask again.

He knew what was behind the executioner's mask.

It would be his own face, staring back at him.

A ripple of anguish coursed through him. He broke out of the reverie, stood up, and paced about the clearing, looking for something —anything—to distract him from what was surely there. His mind thrashed in upheaval. Tears and expletives escaped him.

Tom's apparition stayed with him, as did the executioner's. They wouldn't let go. He had to choose between them. Only then would the tornado of emotion begin to dissipate. His brother's broken body, finally released from the depths of his mind, made the choice clear. There was nothing in the world that could let him be that person, that murderer of his brother.

He chose not to remove the executioner's mask. Instead he reached out to Tom and pulled him carefully from his metal noose, away from the stage. Tom's face returned to normal, and he smiled. Union Square disappeared, and the whirlwind inside Tristan slowly died away.

A switch had been flipped.

His old motivation had withered and died, and the seed of something different was deeply rooted and growing within him. Tristan had found his new anchor.

Now, when he looked back across the clearing at the deer carcass, he knew he couldn't be a part of the disease, sickening the deer, or a parasite devouring it. If he were faced with the dying deer again, the only option would be, against all odds, to try to save the deer, to help the deer thrive. That was the right path.

It became the only path.

The daylight was all but gone, and only the stars were left to provide faint contrast of the surroundings. When he walked away from the clearing he knew he shouldn't be able to see the deer, yet it appeared to him when he looked back, etched permanently in his mind's eye.

He walked on, back toward the farm.

Soon he began running again, and in the faint light, his focus shifted to making careful footfalls on the rocky path.

CHAPTER 27

Michaelis walked along the sterile, gray-tiled corridor, down the steps and toward the front door. He was careful to moderate his breathing, remembering the incident near the Cliff House from several days prior. He didn't want to experience that again anytime soon.

It had been a close call. Michaelis eventually came to and recovered after Fenton gave him oxygen that he had stowed in his road kit. Luisa had thrown her comlink handheld away, in case the caretakers were tracking her. She met up with them at Fenton's later.

They were relieved to have all made it out safely. The group had scrambled communications and used unlisted comlink IDs, but who knew what kind of probes, sensors, or other security devices the caretakers had at their disposal.

It had been too close.

Luisa tried to highlight the positives—they knew the Inworlders were lying, and they were surely working on extending the Parkdome into the ocean. But it was a trivial find relative to the risks they'd taken, and they didn't obtain any real proof they could use for practical purposes.

The near-tragedy had impacted their already-precarious morale.

Michaelis left the building and walked down the concrete steps, under the red awning emblazoned with the City Utility stencil, shining in a yellow, blocky font. It was one of the caretaker-managed buildings that served as a catchall for any municipal functions the caretakers didn't want to maintain inside the domes. Just as many Outworlders as caretakers toiled away in such buildings, simply because caretakers didn't like to do much of the actual work.

And, of course, although only frequented by a few, it also had a public computer lab.

There was a biting cold that morning, so he zipped his jacket right up to the base of his mask. Frost covered the few cars lining the street.

After walking down a steep hill, Michaelis stopped at the Central H mail depot—a slotted cylinder wider than a bathtub that was too full to take mail half the time, but fortunately not today. He dropped off his weekly letter for Harjit and continued on his way to his intended destination, a quaint coffee place north of the panhandle.

He ordered a mint tea and waited patiently by the counter for the attendant to prepare his order. He hoped the tea would help him warm up.

To add to his anxiety about Ocean Beach, the infernal caretakers had been all over the lab. A lab tech caretaker was wandering around constantly, checking everyone's screens. The caretaker decided to strike up a conversation with a young lady next to him, giving him a direct line of sight to Michaelis's screen for the better part of thirty minutes. When the caretaker finally did tire of his exceedingly boring conversation and sat back at his desk, Michaelis was hit with numerous warnings by the virtual lab monitor.

So, he'd decided to move to the coffee shop to do what he could without a computer terminal.

The tea was only slightly warm when he received it, but he didn't argue with the semiconscious shop attendant.

He grabbed a stool next to the window, where there was plenty of counter space. Here he could see people walk by. In this part of the city, just north of the Parkdome, many people worked in service jobs, whether they be accounting, managerial, or maintenance for the city utility. They wore conservative, monochromatic styles of clothing, similar to Michaelis. Coupled with the prevalence of generic, unpainted gray masks, it was hard to tell anyone apart. They all walked with purpose with shoulders raised in the sharp cold of the morning.

Pushing his tea aside, Michaelis opened his file folder and began perusing. In it was the latest report published by the Inworld Health Authority, which he'd been anxious to read.

As expected, it was mostly about Tyband.

There was always much conjecture about the Tyband scourge but so little was known with certainty. What no one debated was that China and Mongolia had made trillions of dollars by creating stronger and lighter polymeric structures, but the process they used permeated the materials with an undetectable form of radioactivity. The materials were disseminated all over the world to be used in virtually every form of plastic packaging and building material. The problem was identified only after twenty years of increasing cancer incidences. By then, it was everywhere.

There wasn't much agreed upon in terms of health solutions, at least according to Inworld sources, although they claimed much research was underway. They always claimed much research was underway.

Michaelis had low expectations, but he was still disappointed in the report. Much of it was a copy-and-paste from the prior year, with the same stale articulation of computer-generated verbiage.

...still little known about the original Tyband Bayandeigr Manufacturing Process; determining the root cause and reversing process pose a challenge. Existing data:
- Polymers and plastics root contaminants
- Construction material tends to over index
- Geographic root Ulaanbataar, Mongolia, (aka "The Ash Lands")
- Geographic contamination over index highest to lowest: East Asia, American Alliance, European continent, Australia. No discernment known within American Alliance.

He jumped further down the page to information about transfer between Tyband and Tyband-free materials, something they'd been working to understand since well before he was born.

...toxicity transfer rate unknown. Tyband contamination levels below limits of quantitation may still be carcinogenic...

They also showed polystyrix production at its lowest levels in a decade. Polystyrix was the composite material used to build the Inworld dome walls. It supposedly was Tyband-resistant, but it was made using many trace elements that were difficult to source, so it was extremely scarce. The limited polystyrix supply was the main reason the Inworld gave for being unable to accept new Outworlders. Michaelis often wondered if they could have used other materials that were less scarce, but they chose polystyrix simply because it was so novel that it couldn't be Tyband-contaminated. Or maybe they just didn't want to accept more Outworlders, and the scarcity of polystyrix was a convenient excuse.

The second half of the report was even less informative. He read through the nauseating platitudes on the research fronts being pursued by the Inworld and skimmed down to the end:

In conclusion, Inworlder scientists have been working diligently for many years and are making great progress; however, there are still unknowns about Tyband contamination. There is good news, however, because it is now believed that toxicity transfer has reached its peak and is set to decline in the next twenty years.

Michaelis had been hearing more about the "Tyband Decline" theory over the past few years. Yet in this report there was a complete lack of any evidence, scientific theory, or even a plausible hypothesis to back up these assertions. At least in the last health report they had listed some statistics and actuarial studies that, on the surface, appeared plausible. They again included the same rhetoric about the evidence being lost in the eleven-year war with the East Asia Cooperative that wiped out almost all of Mongolia's population.

He looked around the coffee shop, imagining the degree to which the various materials in the shop were contaminated. It was impossible to tell.

For all he knew, things could be getting worse. These reports were no more than propaganda under the guise of science, written to keep people appeased. Without any data to back up the theory, Michaelis reasoned the situation was more likely headed in the opposite direction.

Michaelis put down the report in frustration.

Outside a man ambled by without his mask on, oblivious to the elements, the only exposed face in a sea of gray masks. His chin was high, and his teeth clenched. He looked proud, as if he was bravely defying the odds. The others steered around him, giving him a wide berth.

He was surely a walkoff, already afflicted by some terminal illness, choosing to live his remaining days unencumbered. He might end up on the docks, or in a park, or in some favorite place where he proposed to his wife or won his last Ket match. Or maybe he would just keep walking until he couldn't walk anymore.

Even if he wasn't dying, he would be soon.

After another sip of tea, Michaelis begrudgingly continued to skim other sections of the health report. He noticed Tanner's esophyxia wasn't even mentioned. Last year the Inworld had put forward a ten-year plan to shut down the alimentary fermentation plants that spawned the disease-causing airborne mites, but those plans had vanished.

The rest of the document was about new appointments in research and hopeful anecdotes from political figures. This was the most scientific publication from the Inworld they were allowed to see, and it was pure fluff.

He should be thankful. Aside from his esophyxia, he was in good health. San Francisco was one of the better cities when it came to the ravages of pollution and climate. In his youth, when he walked through the streets of New York, the grandeur of the city had been lost to the polluted smog banks. The air was so bad that some people not only wore safety masks, but also bulky oxygen tanks. It was there he developed his esophyxia, and if his mother, rest her soul, had not moved them west when he was younger he might not have lasted this long.

Like Tuan, and probably Ella—wherever she was. Of his New York friends, Harjit was the only one he knew was still alive, probably because his family moved to the Iowa protein farms. Harjit complained about the monotony of it all the time—that he missed the city, their gaming, and their discussions.

But complaining was a privilege. Michaelis had reminded Harjit of that in his letter.

His tea had turned from barely warm to quite cold. He didn't have the heart to finish it. He left it on the table and stood up, fastening on his unpainted mask, and checking it twice before heading out onto the streets. After regulating his breathing, he stepped into the frosty morning and blended in with the clusters of gray-masked pedestrians.

CHAPTER 28

Luisa reached out and turned off her alarm clock.

It was the first official league game of the season. She needed to get up early.

She stared at the ceiling.

It was the first official league game of the season, she reminded herself again. She needed to get up.

Only when she reminded herself a third time did she muster the will to unfurl the covers and put her feet on the floor. Once standing, she quickly dressed and tossed her backpack over her shoulders, nearly tripping over Rex on her way out the door.

"Don't worry, Rex. I'll get you later."

Rex answered her with an ambiguous bark.

Luisa hopped on her bike and headed for the arena.

It was a foggy day, so she had to pedal cautiously through thick banks of opaque mist. When she arrived and entered the main foyer of the arena, hordes of gamers were milling about, all with a sense of purpose.

She was on a good team, composed mostly of remnants of Harry Karrie from last year. They lost Karrie to the Inworld, and a couple of the more senior players were ineligible, but they had picked up one good sniper and a couple of experienced bounders. The new captain, Tina Reed, wasn't any great talent, but she instilled loyalty. Luisa was optimistic about their chances.

They had changed their team name to Black Barracuda.

The game went poorly. They hesitated in executing even the simplest tactics, and it was enough for the other team to take the advantage. Eventually the Barracudas broke down entirely, and the other team hunted them down individually. Luisa had managed to survive until the end, and her statistics were good—two opponents eliminated—but anyone who watched the match wouldn't care.

Luisa had always enjoyed the spirit of camaraderie of Ket. She used to hang around after games for hours, refueling with the energy that hope provided, but she'd been less interested recently. The infectious vibe had less allure. Nevertheless, she forced herself to stay, given that it was the first day of the regular season.

Besides, she didn't have much else she wanted to do.

She climbed high into the stands of the sparsely populated arena and took a seat, scanning the spectators who were focused on the match. She had grabbed an NSF league guide earlier and pulled it out of her backpack, combing the rosters for familiar faces. She doubted there was anything she hadn't seen before.

Except there he was.

Near the bottom, on the team called Purple Scream, was listed Tristan Mardukas. He must have just joined. She hadn't seen him since he'd crushed his arm in their tragic playoff loss last season. She cringed at the memory.

Purple Scream wasn't a good team. They were pretty much bottom of the league. She looked down to the game times. He was on after the next game, so she decided to stick around and watch.

The game was a blowout. Purple Scream played against one of the top-ranked teams. For the most part they just sat back and used their snipers to pick off the slower-moving Scream players.

Tristan was rusty and was having trouble shooting, but his

bounding was excellent. He managed to confuse and distract the other team with a few well-placed jumps, eliminating one of the opposition before being taken out. Many would see this kind of play as reckless, but he was the only Scream player who had a kill. That had to be worth something by her arithmetic.

Luisa was glad she stayed, and she was happy to see Tristan play again. After an injury like the one he'd sustained, she had worried he would never recover. But here he was, back at it again. She had to give him credit.

Poor Rex. She still hadn't fed him.

She picked up her pack and headed along the circuitous corridors toward the arena exit, where she was met by the same flood of hazy fog she had encountered on the way in, but now combined with rain. It was better than the monsoons, at least.

"Luisa?"

Tristan was standing beside the exit, safety mask off, his face still heated and dripping with sweat.

Luisa didn't know how to greet him. She smiled and raised her hand in an awkward salute. He was deadpan, unmoved.

"Can you walk with me a second?" he asked.

"Sure," she said, pulling off her mask. "How are you? You played well." Luisa felt giddy, like she was meeting a long-lost friend.

"You were better," Tristan responded.

He had watched her game.

Tristan led her away from the cluster of gamers at the exit, toward a concrete overhang that sheltered them from the weather. He turned to face her as she caught up.

His unyielding eyes reminded her of when they played together on Cold Fusion. There was an intensity to him during the game that was palpable. His glance pierced through the haze. For a moment they stood there, locked in attention.

"Are you still involved?" he asked.

"Um, I'm not sure what you mean. Involved in what?"

Tristan's gaze softened. He looked down briefly. "I'm the same guy you met last year, Luisa. You were right about me. Tell me you're still working toward your goal."

Her head swiveled. There was nobody close enough to hear. She was shocked at his boldness, and at a loss for words.

"No Luisa, I'm not a caretaker spy," he said. "I want in."

PART III

———

METASTASIS

Luisa tapped her hand nervously on the arm of Fenton's couch. The deep-seated chairs were covered in a velvety ochre material. Four of them of different sizes ringed an oak coffee table. They were comfortable. Or at least, they should have been comfortable.

Luisa was worried how Tristan might interpret their dysfunctional group. They were doing fine two months ago. Why couldn't he have approached her then?

At the request of the group, she'd led Tristan over to Fenton's apartment rather than just given him the address. She'd even frisked him. He was quiet but cordial. He'd stated repeatedly he'd do anything to prove he was worthy of the group's trust.

If he knew how much trouble they were having recruiting new members, he might not be so humble.

Tristan was in the restroom, and Fenton was sitting across from her, also fidgeting. Michaelis and Peter hadn't arrived yet.

"How is your mom doing, Fenny?" Luisa asked.

"I only get to speak to her once a week, but she's doing well. It looks like they might accept a plea deal to reduce her sentence to eighteen months."

"Oh, that's really great," Luisa smiled, and he nodded. She hadn't known a deal was even on the table. It meant his mom could be out in three months.

"But don't worry," he said. "It doesn't change anything for me. I'm as committed as ever to sticking it to those elbow-knockers. You should see how much she's going to have to pay in penalties and back-taxes."

"Glad to hear it, Fenny," Luisa said, smiling.

Indeed, she was happy for Fenton but a small part of her resented this turn of events. The way she saw it, she'd lost three people to the Inworld. Fenton was getting the only person he lost back in only a year. How was that fair?

"So he was in Montana all this time?" Fenton whispered, nudging his chin toward the bathroom. He'd always been suspicious of Tristan, and Tristan's recent disappearance only made things worse. Michaelis, on the other hand, had been quickly sold on the idea of bringing him in, even though he'd been growing more critical of their options lately.

Luisa also kept her voice low. "Yes, his arm was healing—after the accident in the games. He has good reason to hate the caretakers. You know what happened to his brother."

Fenton nodded. "Sure, but we were all there, in the Marquis. It wasn't that long ago when he implied we were all crazy."

She didn't have time to respond. Tristan opened the restroom door and returned to the couches. He said, "Fenton, I again want to thank you for giving me a chance to make my case for inclusion."

Fenton said, "Sure. We...we're glad to have your help." It sounded insincere, but Luisa thanked him under her breath for at least saying the words.

After a moment of silence, Fenton pushed up from his chair. "Maybe I should get us some snacks. It's nothing like the food at the Marquis—just synth-rice chips."

Luisa chimed in quickly, "Of course. We wouldn't dare have a meeting without synth-rice." She chuckled nervously. Tristan smiled politely. He didn't seem put off by Fenton's insensitive comment.

Michaelis and Peter arrived while Fenton prepared the synth-rice chips. Peter had become a regular at their meetings, though he said little. He would shake his head or make a sound to signify his distaste for an idea, but rarely contribute in any other way.

Michaelis pulled a chair up from the table, Peter sat on his favorite reclining couch, and they huddled around the synth-rice chips bowl Fenton had prepared. He used red oil this time, so they would be spicy.

At first much of the discussion centered on superficial questions directed to Tristan; why he was interested in joining their group, who his parents were, platitudes for his brother. When those were exhausted, Michaelis started to explain their status. Fenton's facial expression showed some concern about opening up to Tristan, but he didn't openly object.

Tristan absorbed it all and said, "We need to get inside. That's the only way we can make a statement."

Michaelis raised his eyebrows. "Any attempts at trying to get through the layered security system unnoticed have been foiled. Not one attempt by an unauthorized Outworlder has been successful. Of course, that information may have been deleted from the nets, or never posted at all."

"What about using force? If we can't sneak in, maybe we need to find another way."

Fenton scoffed out loud, but Michaelis was unperturbed. "Believe it or not, the dome structures have been attacked by explosives or accelerants on a number of occasions in other cities, but these attacks have done little damage and created no viable access points. This is primarily due to a force field built into the polystyrix dome surface material—it helps bind it together."

"That's right, kid," Peter confirmed with a gruff snort. "You've got your facts straight." Luisa was a bit startled by Peter's comment. She thought Peter had been asleep.

Tristan said, "The Ket interleague finals will be in the Parkdome this year. Is that a way we could gain access?"

The group went silent.

Michaelis had never followed the Ket games, as he was interested in more academic pursuits. Neither did Fenton. This was probably news to them, but Luisa was the most surprised. She had noticed the finals game in the Parkdome on the schedule, but hadn't put two and two together. "Yes. He's right," Luisa chimed in.

"It's on the vids," Tristan continued. "They had plans to do it for a while, but only confirmed it a few days ago. The Inworlders want to see a live game, and they have a special Ket arena on the inside."

Luisa and Michaelis took some time to digest this possibility. Fenton was already ahead of them. "Well, they're not going to let Outworld spectators in, are they? I doubt it, and if that's the case, it means we need someone playing in the game if we're going to take advantage of it. Even then, I imagine the security would be intense."

Fenton was right, of course, but Luisa didn't want to say it. She was surprised Tristan even brought it up, given that the door was almost certainly closed for him.

Tristan was the picture of calm, however, acknowledging the truth of the matter. "You're absolutely right. Even if we could get in by being on one of the top teams, without more information about security it would be risky. I'm probably a lost cause, and anybody else on the best teams would be hard to sway since they are on the verge of making it to the Inworld. I do think Luisa could have a reasonable chance of making it to the final game, though."

Fenton was nodding through all this. "Yeah but low likelihood I would think."

"Low likelihood but we should at least acknowledge that it's a possibility," Tristan said, "even if it's a remote one. I mean, if we're talking probabilities of success, it's not too far removed from the other options you've outlined."

Fenton was frowning. "Okay, it's a possibility, but even if we were to gain entry, anything we do on the inside is pointless. It would be a suicide mission."

There was silence for a moment.

The pause led Fenton to believe he'd made some progress. He seemed smug, disengaged, having said his piece.

Tristan persisted. "Maybe, but we should keep our options open. Messaging the people about what the Inworld is hiding may be just as dangerous. The only difference between an attempt to sway opinion and an attack from within might be lifelong imprisonment instead of death, but the risks of being caught are probably similar."

Fenton was about to argue, but Michaelis chimed in first. "That's probably true."

Since Michaelis was the resident expert on communications and net security, Fenton had to let it rest. "Okay, I guess we'll keep it in mind." But Fenton waved his words away with his hand as if to suggest he wouldn't keep it in mind at all, except to squash it if it ever came up again.

The rest of the meeting was tedious. They went through nearly everything they had learned or discussed in detail with Tristan. He even looked through much of Chooly's dossier. They were there for three hours before Tristan realized he might be overstaying his welcome.

He thanked the group for all their attention and apologized for taking up too much of their time. He took on a number of homework assignments to fill in any gaps.

Luisa wanted to ensure his enthusiasm was recognized. "It's our pleasure, Tristan. We're happy you could come."

When it was clear Fenton and Michaelis weren't getting up to leave, Tristan hesitated at the door. Luisa spoke for them. "The rest of us need to talk. I'm sure you understand." She smiled.

"I understand." He nodded.

"Don't worry. It's just some housekeeping stuff we have to take care of. We definitely want your help, so don't go defecting to any other rebel groups just yet."

Tristan smiled briefly, paused to absorb what she said, then asked, "Are there other rebel groups?"

Luisa hissed. Fenton and Michaelis unconsciously glanced over at Peter, who was staring at the wall, either to ignore the looks of her friends or because he was off on one of his daydreams. Tristan surveyed the scene with one eyebrow raised, waiting for a response. The glances to Peter revealed whom he should address for an answer.

"There's another group? Who's in this other group?" Tristan walked back into the room to confront Peter.

Peter had succumbed to his urges after the second hour of the meeting, after finding an old bottle of schnapps in Fenton's liquor cabinet, so he couldn't be easily roused from his quasi-stupor on the recliner. His gaze had moved from the wall to staring downward at the floor, as if counting the fibers of the carpet.

"Excuse me, Peter? Do you know anything about this other group?"

Peter gradually lifted his heavy head to look up at Tristan. "Yes, hotshot, there's another group," he said.

Tristan pressed on. "Who are they? Are we working with them?" Tristan looked around at the rest of the group after addressing Peter, but again received no clues.

Peter finally responded. "I don't think it's a good idea for you to meet them. You guys need to get your act together."

Luisa thought Tristan was going to lose his cool, but he kept an even keel. He enunciated a controlled and measured response. "Okay, Peter. Why don't you tell us what we have to do to show this group we're ready? Tell us and we'll do it."

It looked as though Peter hadn't expected his question. "You're a persistent little bugger, aren't you? How about this, I'll find out and get back to you."

Tristan nodded. "When do you think we can find out?"

Peter looked annoyed. "I'll try to get back to you by next week."

Luisa, Michaelis, and Fenton looked at each other with eyebrows raised. This might be progress.

"Thank you, Peter." Tristan looked around at the group, then at his watch. "I'm sorry, I'll get out of here." He headed to the door. "Thanks again."

Luisa hurried to follow him out into the stairwell outside Fenton's apartment. "Thanks Tristan. I'll give you a call."

He paused and looked back at her curiously.

Luisa felt odd. There was a frost of formality around Tristan, and she wanted to melt it away. What happened to the more carefree banter from before his accident, those many months ago?

He tilted his head sideways, as if he was trying to solve a puzzle. She didn't know how to respond. Finally, he nodded, opened the stairwell door, and left without further hesitation.

Luisa slowly turned and went back into the apartment, feeling unsettled about the parting transaction.

Their follow-up discussion was short and revealed no dissension about Tristan. Fenton may have been concerned, but he didn't have a credible argument.

What wasn't voiced, but was apparent to all, was the increased tension in the room. Time would tell if it would be a constructive influence or a destructive one.

CHAPTER 30

Tristan sat on the bench in the change room and took a deep breath. He smelled sweat and damp towels, and the aromatic powder players used to avoid chafing.

He had been firing on all cylinders, rarely pausing to take a break from the mental machinery that had been put into operation at his uncle's place in Montana.

Sure, he'd "rested" by staring at the ceiling in his room or by trying to watch the vids, but his thoughts rarely strayed from the task. He would often jump from his bed or his chair with some pressing idea to explore, usually involving research on the nets or exposing a weakness in the dome system. He knew it wasn't healthy to stay in this state of mind for long, and lately he'd tried to sway his thoughts—to turn off the machine to do some maintenance, even if just for a short time.

"Good job today, Tristan." It was Giorgi, the team captain. "I knew you would be a good addition." Giorgi's statement was betrayed by a slight inflection of surprise that he failed to mask.

"Glad to be of service. Thank you for letting me join the Scream."

Giorgi nodded and walked off to glad-hand some of his other teammates. He was one of those captains who looked like he fit the role, and checked all the boxes, but he didn't really know how to win. He'd heard others joke about him in the corners of the locker room, calling him *Neander-strategist.*

Giorgi had needed a good bounder for a new play he wanted to try out, and there were few to pick from who weren't already taken, so he tried his luck with Tristan. To the surprise of many, including Tristan, Giorgi's play was successful—when adapted with some of Tristan's personal modifications—and Giorgi kept him on the team. Unfortunately, they only had one win and five losses, and were in the bottom quartile of the league—the dregs. Even with a thirty-game season, it was hard to recover from that kind of abysmal start.

Tristan *had* played well lately—better than his own expectations. Of course, he couldn't shoot well...at all. He was ranked deep in the bottom half of the league in marksmanship. Today this was painfully apparent to anyone who watched. He should have had an easy kill of one of the bounders he'd knocked off-trajectory in mid-air. His target was defenseless after his fall, not more than sixty feet away, and he had three clear shots at him. All three missed, and his intended victim was able to return fire on Tristan and eliminate him.

Tristan had worked to improve his shooting, but after countless hours spent trying he decided it was a lost cause. So instead he focused on his strengths—he'd become a bounding specialist. Today he'd knocked two of his opponents out of the air and caused significant confusion, derailing their opponent's strategy almost completely.

He felt a bit like one of the reject masks that hung on the wall of his room. They could work fine, and fulfill a function, but nobody wanted one. People were mystified by him, and in some cases, even afraid of him. He was the estranged kid with the shattered arm who was playing against any hope of making the Inworld. Why didn't he give up?

This enigmatic persona was magnified by his bounding specialization. The best players were usually quick on their feet, or more often, excellent snipers. There weren't individual player stats that could quantify a good bound, because often they resulted in elimination, even if the move helped your team. And the Inworld didn't select people for their bounding ability. Sure, a player needed to know how to do it, but no one was ever chosen for it.

And bounding was dangerous. More than ninety percent of injuries were related to some form of bounding. Yet here he was, probably the most infamous victim of a bounding accident, specializing in bounding.

When the locker room had fully emptied, he decided he would rather wash up at home. It was almost definitely still raining—a monsoon again—and there was no point in taking a shower if he was going to get soaked.

He headed up to the exit and glanced through the glass at the main arena causeway. The sheets of rain were coming down on the windows in blustering waves. Underneath the overhang of the arena was a cluster of individuals fully garbed in masks. Perhaps they were waiting for someone to pick them up, or perhaps they were waiting for a break in the rain.

His father had told him it never used to rain like this in San Francisco. Sure, it rained, he said, but only a "spitting" rain. Tristan wasn't sure what that meant, and it was hard to believe when he would often get soaked through to his skin in seconds during the winter months.

He wrapped himself as much as he could, donned his safety mask, opened the exit door, and waltzed past the onlookers into the torrent.

Visibility was so poor that navigating his cycle required his uncompromised attention. He gritted his teeth and gripped the handlebars firmly as he made his way up the street away from the arena. As he passed through an open intersection on the crest of the hill, out of force of habit he glanced to his right to catch a glimpse of the looming Parkdome. Instead, he was met with a blinding gale, nearly throwing him off his bike. No, he wouldn't be able to see the Parkdome today.

San Franciscans were lucky to have this weather. Many other cities had become arid wastelands, or swamps, or were pummeled by even nastier storms half of the year. Here they only had to deal with the rising ocean and monsoons. The climate might be an impediment to daily life, but in some other places, nature was lethal.

Somehow these musings didn't provide any consolation in his current circumstances. It would be quite a trial just to get home.

Before he continued on, he remembered he was supposed to meet with Luisa. He'd asked her if he could stop by to talk.

That's what happens when you let your mind stray.

At the crest of the next hill he looked to the south, down toward the New Mission. It felt as if he was facing directly into an oncoming squall. He sighed, braced himself, and rode down the slope into the torrent.

After trying the doorbell a few times, Tristan decided to just go inside. They had agreed to meet, and the door was unlocked, so he hoped it would be okay.

Tristan was met in Luisa's front entrance by a dog standing on its hind legs, barking feverishly. He froze, trying not to incite any violent response. He was dripping wet and starting a minor flood in the front hallway.

"Luisa?" Tristan yelled into the apartment.

Luisa came out of her room, looking disheveled. "Yes? I'm sorry, I fell asleep."

She was rubbing her face to get the blood flowing.

"This may be a bit late, but do you mind if I come in?" Tristan asked.

She smiled. "Sure, sure. Rex you get down. Down, boy. Go to your room." She scratched his back, and the dog turned tail and headed deeper into the apartment.

"You should really lock your door," Tristan said. "There are some bad Outworlders out there."

He was gesturing to himself, but she was looking down, and so didn't get the joke. "Yeah," she said, "lately I keep forgetting."

Tristan took off his jacket and the nylon rain guards he used to cover his pants, taking care to sequester the dripping to the front-door area. "I hope you don't have nice cushions on your chairs like Fenton. I don't think it's possible to strip down enough to be completely dry."

Luisa raised her eyebrows and gestured to her basic-looking kitchen table and plastic molded chairs. "What do you think?" she said. "I'm just glad they're not Tyband-contaminated."

"Great. I'll be back in a second." He stepped into the bathroom. Tristan decided to change his soaked shirt top. He had a dry sweatshirt that had been reasonably well protected in his backpack. It would keep him warm even if his wet pants sapped the heat from him.

When he returned, Luisa was sitting at the table, drinking a glass of water.

"So what did you want to talk about?" she asked.

Tristan didn't know where to start. There were a few details to discuss about the research they'd been doing and some ideas he wanted to bounce off her, but nothing pressing. Those weren't the reasons he'd wanted to see her.

He got right to the point. "I'm concerned about you," he said. "Whenever I see you, whether at the arena or in our meetings, you look either depressed, tired, or hungover."

Luisa let out a shrill laugh. "Oh, don't worry, I'm fine. I probably shouldn't be going out so much, but hey, you only live once, right?" She said it with a grin, but her wry smile was diminished by the gray bags under her eyes.

He didn't understand why Fenton and Michaelis weren't showing more concern for Luisa. Maybe they didn't want to confront their friend, or maybe they just couldn't see it? It was possible the change had been too gradual for them to notice.

He decided not to take the bait with her casual response—to not make this into a superficial conversation by glossing over the problem. "You're destroying yourself." He said it with all seriousness.

She laughed again and brushed it off with a shrug. "Okay, now you're acting weird." She stood up and walked to the fridge.

"I'm worried it's affecting the group. You're not contributing anymore. I know it's not because you can't or because you don't want to, but because you're preoccupied."

She hesitated at the fridge, poured another glass of filtered water, and brought it to the table, avoiding eye contact. She was silent, a small mock smile occupying her face, as if preparing for the next brush-off statement. But none came, and the smile eventually withered.

The trembling sigh escaped her, but it was quieter, without the subtle hum of her voice. "What do you want from me, Tristan?" There was no more superficial politeness left in her tone. "I brought you into this group, and now what, you're accusing me of...being useless?"

"I didn't say you were useless. I said something was distracting you. There's a difference."

"You know what? Fuck you, Tristan. Mister fucking stone-cold. Mister fucking enigma. You don't have the right to do this." She stood up and crossed her arms.

Tristan tried to explain. "You know there's a higher purpose here, and we can't afford to—"

"A higher purpose? Listen to yourself...you fucking machine. That's it! I couldn't put my finger on it, but that's it. Are you even human or are you some Inworld protocol droid we've never seen before?"

It was Tristan's turn to stand up. "What would your parents think? Do you think this is who they thought their daughter would turn out to be?" Without giving her time to respond, Tristan continued. "What about Chooly? Do you think he gave you the dossier so you could find the best gin joint in town?"

Luisa was fuming. A misty veil had covered her eyes. "I can't believe you would say that."

Tristan looked down. He'd gone too far. What she said about his lack of feeling had struck a nerve. He looked at her again and truly saw her. She was wounded, a mask of pain and anger.

She brought her hands to her face. "Chooly was like a father to me."

"I'm sorry, Luisa. You're right. I just want us to succeed so badly and...it bothers me to see you this way, I guess. Especially when I know it's not really you." Tristan was stammering, but he kept on, coming to further realizations as he blundered, and declaring them in turn. "I don't know what it's like to lose my parents, and I know you were close to Chooly. It must have been hard when he passed."

Luisa still looked pained, but the anger had subsided. She looked side to side, seeking some means of escape.

Tristan continued. "And I wasn't thinking, since you don't really have any family at all, I guess, anymore." It flowed out of his mouth, the logical cause and effect. He winced as the sentence came to an end, only realizing it was cruel after the words came out.

His filter had been compromised by his own emotional state. His words were a dagger, and he was twisting it.

Her face contorted, and she began to weep, holding her face in her hands to hide the tears.

"Dammit, I shouldn't have said that," Tristan chided himself, "I feel like an ass." He could only hope he sounded sincere.

Luisa looked up at him. "No, it's the truth, I think. Everything you said is the truth."

She held her head in her hands again.

Tristan slowly reached out to her, enveloping her in his arms. She flinched at the initial contact but didn't move away. He was holding her, but it wasn't condescending. It was one part apology, one part for his own consolation.

Eventually she pulled her hands down from her face and wrapped them around him, returning the embrace and resting her head on his shoulder.

They were interlocked for some time, his pants still dripping from the rain. The impact of droplets falling to the floor was the only sound in the quiet apartment.

Tristan eventually left her embrace. "I should probably go. I'm sorry for the things I said."

There was silence as he collected his things. He put on his jacket but didn't bother with his rain guards. He would put them on outside.

"I just wanted to help," he said from the doorway, "but I think I may have missed the mark. You know I'm one of the worst marksmen in the league."

Luisa offered a feeble smile. "No, no, you're right. I've been a real screw-up." After wiping her eyes, she smirked and continued. "But yeah, you're a crappy shot."

"Right." Tristan returned her smile and took the opportunity to leave on a relative high note.

"Bye Luisa."

He closed the apartment door carefully behind him.

CHAPTER 31

Sonny was sitting in an open area of the Quanta Arena stands at the moment, with no other spectators in his vicinity. He was a king looking over his kingdom, watching the peasants fire back and forth at each other in their little wars. A myriad of Ket energy pulses would cross his field of vision. The crowd would cheer and jeer and sigh. Games would start and end, and the players would come and go. He particularly enjoyed watching players from last year, and seeing how they had changed, some for the better, some for the worse. They were so intense, so hopeful, and always so intent on winning.

Ardrey had blossomed. He was routing team after team, a star of the league. Ardrey clearly owed Sonny for this—for allowing him to hitch a ride on Amber Lightning.

The other interesting but sad story was that of Tristan Mardukas. He had become a pathetic sideshow, living out his last season of eligibility bounding around like a circus performer. He should have given up after his arm injury. Someday, when Sonny was running things, he would implement a rule so broken players like Tristan weren't allowed to play. It took away from the purity of the games.

A buzzing vibration came from his earpiece. He looked at the ID on his handheld comlink device. It was his father.

Sonny ignored it. What was the point? His father couldn't help him anymore.

Instead he pulled out his tablet and opened the list Maiyor had given him. Maiyor had explained that there were criminal Outworlders who might try to do more than the usual theft or selling contraband. They might even consider taking aggressive actions toward the caretakers. These were mostly protesters and idealists with a warped sense of morality.

The list was eleven hundred names long, each with some "hypotheses" attached to them. Yes, eleven hundred. Maiyor had explained there was an Inworlder AI system that identified these suspects based on lifestyle, demographics, acquaintances, family, criminal records, phone records, and other personal data. When he asked more about how the list was generated, Maiyor got stern and told him it was none of his business. That may be, but he doubted Maiyor knew much about it either, and Maiyor was out of the picture, anyway.

Sonny now reported to a different supervisor by the name of Flippy Broderick. Broderick was a brute of a man who rarely left his office in the Parkdome. His only distraction was watching the Ket games religiously. During their meetings he would often make Sonny wait until he was finished watching a match. Sonny wouldn't even be allowed to speak until the game was over.

He'd heard that someone had once commented on Broderick's first name, making reference to the name of a dolphin from an old children's book. Broderick had reassigned the person to the slums of Oakland. No, he wasn't a lovable sea creature. He was a decision-maker, whereas Maiyor was more of an errand boy. Broderick reported directly to the Security Marshal of the Inworld, and he was given expansive authority. At Sonny's recommendation, he could mobilize caretaker forces on short notice to apprehend anyone Sonny wanted.

Broderick would at times mention specific infractions that were annoying him, but not Sonny's responsibility to investigate. Like the time he overheard Broderick talking to the Security Marshall about an incident where someone was snooping around Ocean Beach near the

Parkdome. There was a big stink over it because a lot of the Old Inworlders lived closer to the ocean, so some higher-ups were frazzled.

Sonny paid close attention to these conversations. If he wanted to move up in the ranks, he would need to find these perpetrators. These were real gems, the kind that could help him make a name for himself, even if they weren't his responsibility.

Given the number of names on Maiyor's list, Sonny quickly realized he wasn't going to be able to investigate them on his own. Also, as a caretaker, he would never be trusted by the Outworlders, so direct inquiries would be pointless. If he could get Outworlders under his wing, however, he could do some real intelligence work.

So he needed to do some recruiting.

He decided he would have fun with it. It reminded him of his days on Amber Lightning. This was hardly different. Maybe the type of recruits weren't the same, nor the ultimate objective, but it was a similar process.

He looked around at all the envious eyes in the stands. And where better to start than his old stomping grounds at the arena? It would be easy to take a few of these young hopefuls under his wing. Also, a few of the names on the list were actually Ket gamers, so it was a good place to start. Heck, the gamers might think he had some say in the selection process for the Inworld.

While the Ket gamers fired and bounded below him, Sonny made another, different list—a list of people he would approach to help him find Outworlder criminals.

CHAPTER 32

Michaelis peered out of the side window into the night as their car hummed along, heading south on the 280. A constellation of lights dotted the hills. He tried to discern a shape or a pattern to them, but the points were too disparate and random. At times the hum of the car turned into a rattle when the wind whipped at them. They were riding in a cheap Van-Rite vehicle that was like a cube on wheels. Aerodynamics took a backseat to environmental protection and cheap manufacturing.

Luisa sat in the front passenger seat, looking sanguine, staring ahead through the windshield. Michaelis thought she might complain about all the planning and secrecy, but she'd been quiet and complicit, not saying a word.

Peter was also behaving, without the usual mumbling under his breath. He sat in the driver's seat, navigating the car confidently forward. It was as if driving required him to be a different person altogether from his usual agitated, intoxicated, babbling self.

It had taken much cajoling to convince Peter to talk to his contacts. Eventually Peter told the group he'd arranged a date and time to meet them, but there were conditions. There was to be only two of them, and it would be under cover of darkness in a secret location.

Michaelis hoped these weren't militants, but rather intellectuals, because a young girl and a pudgy dropout with esophyxia wouldn't present an aura of strength. If they were military types, it might have been better to send Tristan and Fenton as the more physically imposing members of their group.

For better or for worse, here they were, going somewhere on the peninsula only Peter knew, to be met by people only Peter knew. The only thing Peter revealed was the group was called the OPM, or Outworlder Peoples Movement.

The car wound around expansive bends. The 280 had once been a much greater thoroughfare with several lanes in each direction, but now only one lane was maintained. The other lanes were filled with rotting tree trunks, trash heaps, and rusted-out cars that would occasionally wink reflected headlights back at them as they drove past.

Their current location, according to Peter, was Portola Valley. The valley was a community with a number of protein farms, including a main plant for Portola synth-lamb. Synth-lamb was considered a delicacy by some, but Michaelis wasn't sure why since it tasted like all the other synth-protein products. Maybe it was because there was a billboard depicting Mother Myra eating synth-lamb near Quanta Arena.

Peter leaned into the windshield of the car, as if analyzing a smudge on the glass. They turned on a side road and continued to wind down a series of innocuous-sounding streets such as Alpine Road, Westridge Crescent, and Plant Avenue. They entered a small residential area, which although lit, showed little trace of humanity. A carpenter bot was disassembling a pre-Tyband era house on a side street as they passed.

They pulled into the parking lot of a blocky, industrial-looking building and stepped out of the car. Beige and brown discolorations ran across the brick, as if a giant hand had randomly unleashed two bursts of spray-paint from above. A sign read Grace Hospice Services. Peter gestured for them to exit the car and brought out some hats and bandanas.

Luisa took a step toward Peter, closing her eyes. "I'll go first," she said.

Peter pulled the bandana over her head, and did the same for Michaelis.

"I don't think we're going to be missing much in the pitch-black," Michaelis remarked.

After Peter securely—almost violently—pulled a hat over the blindfold to ensure it was tight, he led them toward the hospice building.

Michaelis quickly lost any sense of direction. They were maneuvered through what appeared to be several doors and hallways, and up and down stairs. Finally they came to a halt.

"Ah, our guests have arrived." The man's baritone voice was deep and confident. "You can call me John. Please forgive the secrecy. I hope you understand."

They had decided beforehand that Michaelis would do most of the talking. "Yes, certainly," Michaelis said, not sure which direction to face. "I'm Michaelis, and this is Luisa."

"Is it safe to remove our blindfolds?" Luisa asked.

"No. Do not attempt to remove your blindfolds."

Michaelis cringed at Luisa's naïve question. Maybe they would never see "John," if that was his real name, and it was important to not appear like incompetent amateurs here, whether or not it was the truth. He was thankful that John's stern tone would probably dissuade her from saying anything for a while.

The series of inspections could have been worse. First they were patted down, then moved to a room where they went through what sounded like a full body scan to detect any foreign objects.

When their hosts were satisfied, the party was brought to a vehicle for a twenty-minute drive, and the doors opened for them.

Michaelis stepped out.

The air outside was cool, infected only by the sound of faint whispering.

A voice could be heard above the whispers. "John?" a man said.

"They're clean," John replied.

Their hats and blindfolds were unceremoniously removed. Michaelis rubbed his eyes, donned his spectacles, and took in his surroundings. It was a wooded area with three twelve-foot high lamps blaring in the direction of Michaelis, Peter, and Luisa. The silhouettes of five human figures could be discerned lined up just behind the large posts, out of the light.

After his eyes adjusted, Michaelis could make out outlines of the figures, but they were wearing safety masks, and their eyes were only shadowy sockets. It would be impossible to identify them.

The one named John, was standing close by, and could be discerned with much greater clarity. He was a squat, powerfully built man dressed in dark brown coveralls. His apparel and mask did not hide his gregarious smile. "Apologies for the secrecy, Michaelis and Luisa," John beamed, "and welcome."

John walked around to join the other figures lurking in the dark. "Peter has told us a little about your group," he said, "but we're eager to hear more. First let us tell you about the Outworlder Peoples' Movement."

The voice changed seamlessly over to another man's, as if the exchange was rehearsed. The outline of a lankier, taller figure on John's right began speaking. "You can call me Max. Before we begin, you must recognize whatever information we give you here is told in confidence and cannot be repeated. You may brief your two colleagues at some point, in a location you're sure is secure, but from then on you should never discuss this until we meet again. Is that understood?"

Michaelis nodded in concert with Peter and Luisa.

"Good. My associates and I represent the Outworlder Peoples' Movement, or OPM. We would like to see significant change in the government and social rights of individuals in San Francisco and the rest of our country—the kind of change that would require a substantial upheaval of the dome system. It would seem we have similar interests, would you agree?"

Michaelis said, "Yes, it would seem that we do." He noted the reference to "country." So this was more than a San Francisco-based outfit. He felt more and more like they were way out of their league.

Max continued. "We have substantial resources that we can bring to bear, but we need to be extremely careful about being discovered. For that reason, we need to pick our allies closely and also choose what we do with those allies even more carefully."

He waited for more nods from the group.

"Peter has said you're interested in working with us, as an independent group. That is no easy task. The OPM has been in existence more than twenty years and never collaborated with others. We have seen other groups try to formulate some form of resistance and fail. Sometimes we know what happens to them, and it's not pretty, and sometimes, well, they just vanish without a trace."

Max let this settle in before continuing. "We know you would be valuable additions, and we share the same cause, so we have agreed to see if you would want to join the OPM, but under our command. We would tell you what to do, and when. We would convey very little direction—no strategy or names. You would simply have to be ready, and if called upon, you would perform tasks asked of you. These tasks could also include personal hazards."

Luisa and Michaelis looked at each other. Peter was fidgeting.

"This is simply how it has to be," Max continued. "We respect your ambitions, but will not risk greater involvement due to security concerns. We have been building this movement for a long time and can't afford to jeopardize it. If your wish is to truly make a difference, history has shown small splinter groups like yours have not been successful. Joining us may be your only chance not only of making an impact, but of survival."

John was standing in front of them in the light, but Max still lurked in the shadows. Except for the lack of a cloak, Max could have been mistaken for the grim reaper, crooning about their near-certain death from the darkness.

"Any questions?" Max finished.

Michaelis tried to read Luisa's expression. She was biting her lip, and Michaelis could tell she had concerns. He nodded, encouraging her.

"So, um..." She hesitated, then changed course. "First of all, thank you for the opportunity to meet. I guess we'd like to know as much as we can about the OPM to help me—us—make the decision. Is there any way we could prove ourselves to you enough that we could be involved in the decision making?"

Max responded, "If you prove your worth, and your discretion, we may invite you into our directors' circle, but I wouldn't expect it for several years."

Michaelis asked, "And how do we know whether it's dangerous or not? Would you at least give us some sense of the danger, or *hazard*, as you put it, involved in a task you ask us to perform?"

"We are all working for the same goal, and we assure you we would not send you on any dangerous errands without at least giving you a sense of the level of risk."

Another man spoke out of the shadows. "And yet you would be expected to live up to your commitment, potentially risking your life. If you join, that would be your oath to us."

There was silence. Michaelis continued. "Can you give us some sense of the resources you have at hand? I'm sure you understand we would want to be part of something big—something impactful."

There was whispering among the group lurking in the shadows. Max answered after the inaudible debate. "I can say we have more than fifty individual members and access to military resources that can be applied."

It wasn't much help. "Firearms? Explosives?"

Another man answered, "Yes."

"What about attack robots or armed vehicles?"

There was whispering in the shadows again. "We have access to armed vehicles."

"What kind of explosives? How many people could you mobilize?"

There was more whispering. If the increased volume of the whispering was any measure, the OPM representatives were getting agitated. "I think you have enough information, or rather, all we are willing to give."

It was a lot to digest, and Michaelis couldn't think of any further questions. He said, "Thank you for meeting with us. I think we'll need to talk to our colleagues and get back to you."

Luisa nodded in turn.

"Understood," John responded. He looked back at the shadows and faced them again. "I will escort you back."

They were refurbished with blindfolds and hats and ushered into the car. There was more whispering in the distance, superseded by Max's parting words. "Be safe."

John drove them back to the hospice building, probably taking the same route, if the duration of the trip was the appropriate indicator of this. He would ask them the occasional question about the Ket games or their families. They responded truthfully.

Before leaving them in the parking lot, John said, "I'm to give you one more message. We have many sentinels. If you compromise the OPM in any way, we will take action, including eliminating you if we have to. I'm sure you understand."

"We understand," Michaelis said.

They did now.

CHAPTER 33

Tristan arrived at the cliffside perch in Lincoln Park before the others. Michaelis had insisted they meet in a discreet location where there was no chance they were going to be heard. Fenton said if his apartment was bugged, they would have been caught already, but he agreed. They needed to leave nothing to chance, even if just as a show of faith to the OPM group—in case they were being watched.

It was late in the afternoon. The sky was full of warm tones—hot streaks of orange and red. From the vista Tristan could see low-hanging clouds of mist envelop the Golden Gate Bridge, the suspension towers jutting out above the wispy layers.

The rest of the group gradually arrived and walked their bikes to drop them behind a bush, slightly removed from the path. Peter's face was beet red from the ride.

Michaelis said, "We need to make a decision."

After some head scratching, Tristan asked, "Well, you guys were there. What do you think? What kind of a feeling did you get?"

Michaelis answered, "I think they're legit, but I don't know how competent they are. And I don't know if they're just a secret club or if they are intent on action."

Luisa was standing back, not fully committed to the conversation.

Since her breakdown in front of Tristan, she'd been more disengaged in their meetings, but she also seemed more thoughtful and—to put it bluntly—less hungover.

Michaelis continued. "We need to think hard on this. They do appear to be organized, and no offense to the present company, but we're lacking in that department."

The group digested his words.

Luisa stepped forward. "Peter, you have more experience with the OPM. What do you think?"

Peter looked up from his latest waking dream. He frowned and squirmed, but didn't immediately respond.

Luisa had a good point. Peter must have formed an opinion over the years. Tristan continued in the same vein. "Maybe we could start closer to the beginning. How did you first come in contact with them?"

Peter nodded. "Sure, sure. Good point. I don't know what I'm allowed to tell you, though."

Luisa said, "Tell us whatever you're comfortable with."

Peter grimaced. "Well, I first met them, um, three years ago. At that time I was still running, looking for hiding places. I found out about them through one of the people I met in the Oakland slums. He was actually a friend of your cousin Chooly's, Luisa. They took me out to the woods, just like they did with you, and gave me the same spiel. So yeah, I did it."

"So...you're a part of their group already?" Fenton asked.

Peter waved his hand to imply he shouldn't be interrupted. "I went through a security authorization and training program, as they called it. I didn't realize until later they were mainly just pumping me for information. You know, about the Inworld, my experience as a caretaker, all that shit. I told them everything, just like I told you guys. I didn't care. I wanted people who matter to know.

"After they said I was in, I wasn't called upon for a long time, like months, and when they did call me, it was a kind of show-off routine where they took me through a hidden area and showed me some of the stuff they mentioned to you. You know, trucks, weapons, and explosives. They actually have an old pre-Tyband tank. They probably do this for everybody—to get them excited. Then I didn't hear from them for a while. When I did, it was just to check in and do the show-off routine again."

Peter held his chin thoughtfully. "I only knew maybe three of their people the whole time I was involved, and I was never asked to do anything. Maybe they didn't involve me because of my past, or because I drink too much, or maybe that's what they do with all the lower-level recruits? I don't know. I just don't fucking know."

Peter squinted, turned away from them, and looked at the waters of the bay. It was shimmering, reflecting the red sky. "About ten months ago, I asked to get out, because I couldn't stand not knowing what was going on. They said there would be serious consequences. I knew they might hunt me down, just like they said. I told them I would keep it a secret, and they still gave me all kinds of grief, but you know when you've been through what I've been through, threats don't worry me much."

He shrugged. "And here I am. They didn't hunt me down. Not sure if I missed out on anything because they never asked me to do anything. I guess they were okay with it because they agreed to let me introduce you to them." He showed his palms. He had nothing more to offer.

Michaelis asked the obvious question again. "So what do we want to do?"

"Do we have to decide right now?" Fenton asked. "I mean really, what's the rush?" He looked annoyed, which was increasingly common at their meetings. His annoyance was often directed at Tristan, so he was acutely aware of it.

"Well, yes, I think we should decide on a course of action," Michaelis said.

Tristan pushed further. "Why aren't you in a rush? We're all here, together. Things are getting worse, not better. And I hate to say it, but the longer we procrastinate, the more chance we get caught, and the more nothing changes. Let's decide and move forward."

Fenton looked at Luisa and Michaelis. It didn't look like any support would be coming from them. He put his hands up. "Fine, fine. Let's just make sure we think it through."

Tristan decided to volunteer his opinion, since no one else seemed to be doing so. "Frankly, I'm worried about joining them. Based on Peter's story, we may just be sitting around doing nothing. They've been in business for twenty years, right? What have they done? Maybe it's all been undercover but I sure haven't seen any impact. Also—"

Fenton cut him off. "Wait just a minute. Peter said they might not have used him because of his history as a caretaker. Also, who knows if things could be worse? Maybe they are making a real impact or just waiting for the right time. Maybe that's what we should be doing?"

Tristan bit his lip. All Fenton seemed to want to do was buy more time. Tristan could see how Peter's story would sound great to him. They could join the OPM, then sit around and do nothing. That's what Fenton wanted. He wanted to feel like he was doing something, apparently indefinitely, but never actually do it.

"I wasn't finished," Tristan said. "Who's to say having one big group is the best idea? In the Ket games, most strategies rely on gaining a numbers advantage, but not all. Sometimes the best strategy is to have several smaller squads be more nimble and flexible rather than combining forces. So if you lose one, you can still win. Why not have two as long as our interests are aligned?"

Luisa seemed to get the gist of his argument, but it may have been lost on the others.

Michaelis said, "We should also consider the possibility the whole thing is a trap."

"A trap?" Fenton asked, his face gaining color. "Why would they bother going through this charade if they were working with the Inworld?"

"If they don't do anything but impress people and make them feel like they're part of something, it's a way to neutralize anyone they recruit. They can watch potential perpetrators and control them. They give people a sense of purpose, but don't actually have any impact. Granted, I think the possibility is small, but it *is* a possibility based on what we've seen so far."

They pondered this for a moment. Fenton was looking around at them, frowning. He looked exasperated. "This is ridiculous," he said. "Are we only going to be satisfied if we do some kind of suicide mission? How can you be so risk-averse with the OPM but then be so whimsical about other things? Like the freaking underwater escapade —that was crazy, and now we're afraid a rational, well-resourced group of individuals may not be able to help us?"

Luisa tried to calm him, touching his arm. "We're just putting all thoughts and opinions on the table, Fenton. We don't know what we're going to do yet."

Fenton pulled his arm away. "What else are we going to do? Are we going to walk to the Parkdome entrance laced with explosives and blow ourselves up? Why don't we just jump off this cliff? It would have about the same effect." He walked over to the cliff and pretended to lead them theatrically over the ledge with his arms.

He turned and made his way back to them. "Seriously, though, what are we going to do without them? Do we have any real leads? Sure, we've had some ideas, but none have proven promising." He looked away, disgusted.

There was silence for a moment. Tristan knew Luisa and Michaelis had a tendency to placate Fenton, but he didn't want that to happen today. He didn't want to lose this argument; it was too important.

He chimed in before the others could. "We still haven't found all the people from the article in Chooly's dossier who may know about this data finger. Also, we may be able to enlist somebody who's in the final league game to do reconnaissance of the dome weaknesses. And Michaelis has developed malware that may be able to drop a broad message to most people in the city, revealing what we know. I'm pretty sure we wouldn't be permitted to push all these opportunities forward if we were with the OPM."

"Those are just random shots in the dark!" Fenton was almost yelling. "My god, Luisa and Michaelis, can you help me here? I think Tristan has gone mad. He's trying to kill us all. Okay, maybe Michaelis's program could work, but we'd be caught or dead shortly after. Not my idea of a productive work effort. Guys, come on!"

Michaelis and Luisa looked torn, not wanting to take sides. There was a long, tense pause in the conversation, with no one willing to speak. It had to be Luisa or Michaelis to break this. There was nothing either Fenton or Tristan could say to progress the debate.

To Tristan's surprise, however, it was neither Michaelis nor Luisa who broke the stalemate. It was Peter.

He began slowly. "I think you should—you know—all do what's best for you, individually. But I should say that, um, my opinion is it may not be right for you kids—this OPM thing. I'm not just saying that because I didn't get much out of it. I'm saying it because if you want to do something, you've got to do it yourselves. Everyone's points have all been good here, but I feel like I've gotten to know you—"

Fenton was about to speak but Peter held his hand up, signaling he wasn't finished.

"I've gotten to know you and I think you'll lose the fire you have if you join them. It's too easy. I'm getting old, and I can see what happens. I can see you have a chance. Yes, maybe a small chance, but a real chance, to make some kind of change happen. It's been a while since I've actually been a part of something I'm excited about. That means something. Don't give it away."

It was repetitive, but it was the first time Tristan had seen Peter genuinely sincere. He usually had only two settings: ornery or intoxicated.

Peter immediately tried to downplay it. "Sorry. Not well said. Just my opinion on things, I guess." He put his head down.

Fenton was livid. "You know what? Fuck this! This is a joke. I can't be part of this. It's totally insane."

He threw his hands up and marched over to his bike. Tristan thought someone would go after him, maybe Michaelis, more likely Luisa. Again, they didn't; Peter did.

He ran after him, trying to catch up to him on his bike. Peter had an awkward gait because his right arm hung lower than his left, an artifact of his shoulder blade operation. Since Fenton wasn't slowing down, Peter was out of earshot of Luisa and Michaelis by the time he reached him. It looked like they spoke a few words Tristan couldn't quite make out. Fenton left, and Peter returned to the group.

Luisa looked at Peter hopefully. "What did you say to him?"

"I wanted to give him the option to join the OPM, so I gave him the means to contact them."

"Oh. Good thinking," Luisa said. She looked downcast, disappointed. She was probably hoping Peter was asking Fenton to reconsider. "So I guess we're not going to join the OPM, is that right?" Luisa asked.

Michaelis nodded, and Tristan also confirmed. Luisa agreed more reluctantly.

It was decided. They all looked at each other sheepishly, yet with an air of determination.

"So, what do we do now?" Luisa asked. She was looking directly at Tristan.

He needed something new—something to justify their decision. But Fenton, for all his bluster, was right that they had little to go on. They needed more. They needed action.

"Well, for one, I think Luisa and I should try to get on the winning team in the league, so we can get into the Parkdome for the final game."

Luisa said, "Just like that? There are people who work their whole lives to get on the best team in the league so they can have a *chance* at the Inworld."

"You don't give yourself enough credit," Tristan said. "You've been playing well lately. You should at least try. As for myself, I know I'm an anomaly and my chances are few, but I might be needed for my skills, even if I have no chance of winning a berth in the Inworld. Remember, we just need to have any position on the winning team to gain access to the Inworld. We could even be sub-sixers."

She stared him down for a minute, testing his mettle, then said, "Okay. Let's do it."

Tristan was surprised she agreed so readily. She was more focused than a few weeks ago, in a resigned sort of way. "Okay. Okay great. We'll try to get in contact with the best teams right away."

Luisa pressed. "Anything else?"

Tristan said, "Can we devise a detailed plan for what we do when we get into the Parkdome, should we ever get there? I think it's time we at least mapped out, step by step, a way to make a big symbolic resistance. It would be something tangible we can build upon, rather than just high-level conversations."

Michaelis's eyebrows were raised. He was the obvious choice to give this a go since he surely had many of the pieces together already. "Okay," he said. "I have a rough draft already. I'll finish it and present it at the next meeting."

Luisa said, "I'm going to talk to Fenton again, to see if I can make him come around. Maybe he'll change his mind after he cools off." She didn't look hopeful.

After a few more open questions about their next moves, they decided to end the meeting and regroup at the same place in a week's time.

Tristan waited for Luisa and Michaelis to leave. They seemed shaken by the loss of their long-time friend from the group, and sobered by the knowledge they were taking on more risk.

Peter had decided to stay on the perch for a while, looking out over the bay in the fading light. He moved to sit near the cliff to better take in the view.

Of the four of them, Peter appeared to be the most satisfied with the day's discussions. Tristan was thankful for his contribution, and wanted to make that known. After the others had left, Tristan sat down next to him. "Thanks for your support today," he said.

Peter's eyes were squinting as if he was trying to make something out in the distance. He was slow to respond. "You're welcome," Peter finally said. "You know, Tristan, I think you've got a shot. The Inworld, for all its air of invincibility, has grown complacent."

"You think so?"

"Yeah, and there's something else you should know. I didn't say it at first, because I didn't trust you guys. I think I trust you more now. Even if it's a batshit's chance in hell, I think it's worth the risk."

This sounded important. Tristan looked back for Luisa and Michaelis, but they were long gone.

Peter said, "I was on the team that hunted down your brother and his friends. Well, not on the team, but part of the whole thing. Almost every caretaker had some part in it, it seemed. Fucking nightmare."

Peter shook his head, not taking his eyes off the horizon. "It was one of the main reasons I left the Inworld. I couldn't sleep after that. Anyway, I had nothing to do with capturing them, but I was involved in the interrogations. Lots of bad things went on in those interrogations."

He looked over at Tristan, meeting his gaze squarely in his eyes. "They found several data fingers, the ones you know about, and anyone who had one was hanged or killed in the interrogation. The problem was, they didn't know how many copies this Charles Hardin guy made and he seemed to be throwing them all over the place before he finally filleted himself like a lunatic. Like I said before, the data fingers were made of a biologically derived material that couldn't be identified by any scanner, so they were hard to find. The caretakers didn't want to take any chances. So if there was any possible link, if there was any way the kids could have even seen the data fingers, they were hanged. And after that day, after the hanging, lots of people were killed in other ways. Believe me."

He continued to hold Tristan's eyes with his own. "You're lucky you're alive. Your brother obviously didn't have one of the data fingers. Be thankful for that."

Peter looked back to the water in the bay. "Why am I telling you all this? You may remember that day in Union Square. There was a kid who was killed along with his parents. It was because they thought for sure they had one of the data fingers, but they could never find it, and they were really tough to crack in the interrogations. They were going to hang the other kid, too—the little brother. What was his name, Zachary Percival, or something? Jeez. I can't remember his name. Too many drinks. There was a big stink, some people saying he was too young. He made an impression on one of the higher-ups because he was a cute kid. So anyway, he was saved, at first."

Tristan cringed at the memory of the young child screaming as he watched his parents and brother hanging. And then, Tom...Tristan shook it off, focusing, holding onto the train of the story. He extrapolated to where he thought Peter was heading. "So you think this kid may have a data finger? Is that what you're saying? Is he still alive? Michaelis checked on him. He said he died in a robot lane accident."

"Yeah that's right. You guys have done your homework. Let me explain. So I was on the detail taking care of the kid, and we found out he had an uncle who owned a cabin up north in Treble—you know the hippy place? So we took him up there."

Tristan was confused. "I don't understand. You think he didn't die on the robot lanes? You think he's still alive, living up in Treble?"

"No, no, no, you're not getting it. I'm sure after the higher-ups forgot about him, one of the other security details went after him and killed him. You don't stay cute for long, you know. They may have even thrown him on the robot lanes, but more likely they just shot him and made up the report. The report did look fake, missing some typical caretaker protocol stuff, but nobody cared, and everyone just assumed the obvious—that they'd killed him."

Tristan was still confused as to where this was going, but decided to withhold further questions while he digested the information.

Peter sighed. "What I'm saying is you might find something up in the cabin up north, that's all. They interrogated the uncle a number of times. They killed him too, but I still think they were hiding it some-where. A few years later they weren't as careful. It became more of a bunch of goon squads, intent on terrorizing rather than finding the data fingers. As the caretakers lost interest I don't think they did a thor-ough job of cleaning up the loose ends. So, who knows? You might find something up there, that's all."

"Wow, Peter." Tristan's excitement was resonant in his voice. "We'll definitely check it out. Thanks for your help."

"Hey, don't thank me yet. You probably won't find anything, and it could be dangerous, but what isn't these days?"

"Still, thanks a lot."

"You got it. Hey, do you want to grab a beer or something?" It was a rare gesture of camaraderie from Peter.

Tristan considered it. It would be a good way to thank him, but he was eager to share this news with Michaelis and Luisa. "I have to go, but I'll definitely take a rain check."

"Okay. See you next time."

Tristan shook Peter's hand and stood up to leave, hoping he could catch up to Michaelis or Luisa on his bike. This was a great lead. He was also glad Peter was more trusting of them. He was turning out to be a valuable member of the team.

Later, in hindsight, Tristan regretted not having the beer with Peter that evening. Sure, Peter was rough around the edges and had a drinking problem, but he definitely cared about their cause, and it showed in spades that evening. A beer would have been a nice gesture to show his appreciation.

Of course, if it were any other day Tristan would probably not have beat himself up over something so trivial. That day was different, though, because it was the last day he saw Peter alive.

CHAPTER 34

Luisa's current Ket team—Black Barracuda—had potential, but it was a real outside shot that they would make it to the league title game. There were three other teams that were more serious contenders, so Luisa tried to negotiate her way onto one of those teams. She would also see if Tristan could join with her, but only if it worked for the captain.

The meetings were far from easy. They had to exercise extreme care to not reveal their true intentions. The captains of these teams were a near lock for caretaker, so any smell of trouble and they would hand them over to the authorities.

Thus far they had spoken with the team captains of the Wired Warriors and Red Rebels, the first- and third-position teams, respectively. They had gone in trying to sell strategies for victory that involved Tristan's bounding expertise and her more balanced skill set. The captains had listened politely and said they would consider it. After the meetings, Tristan said he was hopeful.

But Luisa could see it in their eyes. They weren't *really* listening. Luisa was a has-been for which this kind of end-of-season pleading was customarily turned down, and the captains had no idea what to make of Tristan.

Which left the second-place team, the Shock Hawks.

They had intentionally left Ardrey's team for the end, hoping against hope one of the other teams would take them. Tristan would have trouble confronting the person who conceivably betrayed them to end their season, not to mention shattering his shooting arm and squashing any hope for him of making it into the Inworld.

Tristan said he had nothing against Ardrey, but despite his downplaying there was a fire in his eyes when she mentioned Ardrey's name. His mind seemed to retreat into a sort of suppressed rage. She couldn't blame him. Whether Ardrey's intentions were malicious or not, it would be difficult for Tristan not to associate him with all the pain he'd endured.

She would have to handle the meeting carefully.

Luisa rode with Tristan through the foggy streets eastward down toward old Union Square, toward Ardrey's suggested meeting place. She watched Tristan run his hands through his oily dark hair when they stopped their bikes at the intersection. He did it with force and concentration, as if the act would exorcise any lingering demons. She imagined him gritting his teeth under his mask.

In this part of the city, the buildings were in various states of abandonment, with the few ghostly inhabitants they came across looking just as dilapidated. It was as if the shabby buildings would occasionally produce offspring in the form of similarly unkempt humans.

She hated biking through this area. It felt eerie and reeked of a kind of ancient death. Not the death of people, although some of the smells came close. Rather, the death of a bustling, energetic world, where people would mingle and shop like in the pictures she'd seen. The buildings stood in despair, weeping stucco, brick, paint, and glass over the loss of their former grandeur.

The bar Ardrey had proposed was one she knew; she'd been to it once in the last few months. It wasn't a surprise—she'd been to many. Ardrey was up at the front, a full beer in front of him, reading a book with the help of an ornate table lamp that looked oddly out of place in the minimalist decor. There were a few other people in the bar, minding their own business.

His look went sour when he saw her enter. It wasn't a good start, considering his usually unreadable countenance. He looked down at his watch.

Shit. Again.

She glanced over to Tristan to apologize, but he was off in his own world, concerns over tardiness taking a backseat to taming himself before the discussion.

They arrived at the front and took seats beside Ardrey. Luisa made sure she was between the two of them. "I'm sorry I'm late," Luisa said. "I know your time is important, especially this late in the season."

Ardrey nodded. He was looking around her, glancing curiously at Tristan. "It's okay. What's up?"

Luisa spoke with confidence, even though the premise was shaky. "As I mentioned, we wanted to make our case for getting on the Hawks. We think together we can be valuable additions going into the play-offs." She looked to Tristan for support, but his eyes had glazed over.

She was about to continue, but Ardrey spoke first. "First of all," he said, his words directed toward Tristan, "I wanted to say I feel bad about what happened last year. It was an accident, and I wouldn't wish that upon anyone." It may or may not have been sincere, but something melted in Tristan's eyes. Luisa was heartened that the chance this meeting would result in violence had decreased considerably.

Ardrey continued. "I know your stats, fine, I know your skills and specializations as well, but what I don't get is why now? I've had people trying to be a part of my team for months, and I've only taken one newbie since the early part of the season. Why weren't you asking then?"

Tristan had awakened from his coma. He responded for them both. "I was in recuperation for my arm in the early part of the season, and it wasn't until a few weeks ago that I demonstrated I could be in any way effective. Luisa has also put in some great numbers recently. So frankly we didn't think we'd have had a shot at joining early in the season. Also, we know how to work together, so we thought we'd propose this as a kind of package deal."

It sounded reasonable. Luisa was relieved.

Ardrey thought about it for a while. While stewing, his eyes were half closed. "What would I tell the team? You know Jared, and particularly Emma, two of my best—might not take kindly to giving the spotlight to others who could take their places in the Inworld if we win."

Tristan had a ready answer. "I think you know I'm not going to be selected for the Inworld. I'm perceived as damaged goods, and reckless to boot, according to almost anyone you talk to. I just want to win."

Ardrey shifted his gaze to Luisa. It only answered the question for Tristan.

Luisa's mind raced. Here it was again. The primary reason they would be denied by the captains was the propensity to upset the team dynamic with new recruits at the end of a season. Luisa could take away someone else's chance to make it to the Inworld. She needed to take this concern away.

"I don't want to go to the Inworld," she said. "I'll sign it in my player contract if I have to. That should keep your people satisfied, and if we could help you win, they should be quite happy."

This was quite a bomb to drop, and it may have been too much.

Strangely, Ardrey didn't show any shock or surprise. Or maybe it was just his lack of affect. After a moment of contemplation, however, he began to look at her more inquisitively. "And why not?" he asked.

Luisa looked down. "I simply don't believe in what the Inworld stands for. Nothing against it, really, I just don't think it's for me." It was easier to lie if she mixed in some half-truths, but her response wasn't really an answer, and she dreaded the inevitable follow-up.

Ardrey didn't push further, though. "I can't say I understand it, but I guess it's not unprecedented."

"Really? Who do you mean?" Tristan asked. Luisa looked at Tristan reprovingly, and he immediately bit his lip. He was surely trying to identify another recruit, but it was too suggestive, too revealing, and she was trying to get off the topic. Neither of them were choosing their words carefully enough.

Ardrey looked annoyed. He answered tersely. "No one I know specifically. I've heard of players in the past." He looked thoughtful. "Luisa, the more I think about it, the more I'm surprised. I mean, given your family history, what possible reason could you have for staying in the Outworld?"

A tense silence hung in the air. Luisa searched for the right words while Tristan was lost in his own regret, having invited the question. An invisible pendulum swung toward her, gathering momentum as Luisa searched for a reason, something rational besides the well of anger that seethed beneath the surface.

But before she could find a path away from exposure, Ardrey seemed to tire of waiting. "I suppose that's personal, and none of my business," he said. His quizzical gaze remained, however.

Luisa tried to take the opportunity to push through. "Thanks for your understanding, Ardrey. Tristan and I just want to win."

The tension dissipated, and they went on to discuss roles they could have on Ardrey's team. Luisa did most of the talking, and Ardrey listened politely. Tristan appeared distracted again.

Luisa tried to lighten the mood. She wanted to build some rapport with Ardrey. She talked about some of the players' idiosyncrasies, like how Rowan Mojibe was always inadvertently pulling his hand before high-fives.

She had presumed Tristan's comments about Ardrey being cold and calculating were born of some sort of inherent bias, but as she tried to engage him in normal conversation she had to admit they might be founded in truth. Ardrey listened to her, but didn't offer her much in return.

Eventually Ardrey looked at his watch again. "I'm sorry I have to go. I'll consider your proposal and get back to you."

He packed up his things and left them at the bar.

They may have hinted too much about their true intentions, although it didn't faze Ardrey. He seemed rational, and he took the proposal remarkably well. In the end, though, it was the same answer they'd received from the other team captains, almost word for word.

She compared her notes with Tristan, and he agreed with her sentiments on the meeting. He also thanked her for handling it the way she did, and apologized for being distracted. She understood.

To Luisa's surprise, Tristan offered to buy her a drink. He stressed the "a" in "a drink." So they each had a soda, nothing more. Tristan took some friendly abuse about being a space cadet. It was good to see him take it easy. When their drinks were done, they left, back onto the decrepit streets.

When Luisa arrived at home, she fed Rex and sat with him on her empty couch, reflecting on the day's events.

She was alone, and beginning to get that familiar urge to leave—to escape—but she didn't want to jeopardize her efforts to stay out of trouble.

The quiet openness of her apartment continued to eat at her. She tried to tease Rex into barking, if just to fill the void, but all she managed to get was a weak growl.

She turned on the vids as a distraction. Eventually it did the job, lulling her into a slumber on the couch.

CHAPTER 35

Treble was the remains of one of the newfangled Rebirth communities that sprang up thirty years ago. Trying to create an Inworld of their own, groups of Outworlders, mostly hippy types, had banded together to form self-sustaining cooperatives with additional protection from the environment. The communities were poorly organized and under-resourced by mostly uneducated, idealistic individuals, and doomed to failure from the start.

The Inworld never even tried to stop them. The micro-economies of the American continent revolved around servicing the domes, and nothing was going to change unless someone could marshal new resources that weren't dome-dependent. Since the Rebirth people had nothing of value to begin with, there was no reason for the Inworlders to be worried about competition.

The main Rebirth structure in Treble was a decaying system of underground tunnels that webbed around the Russian River region. These tunnels were mostly unoccupied, and all that remained in the town of Treble was a gaggle of cottages dotting the wooded area, inhabited predominantly by hermits and small-scale hydroponic farmers.

The most concentrated area of Treble was a small downtown—a couple city blocks that ran near the river. It was here that Michaelis had been loitering, having encountered only two inhabitants thus far. He could be here a long time at this rate, and the drive alone had taken a good two hours, when he could have been devoting that time to the computer lab and saving money not renting the expensive motorcycle. Still, Luisa and Tristan were right that the lead should be investigated, and they were probably right again that he was the appropriate one to do it. If he did find this elusive data finger, it would be well worth it.

So yes, the logic made sense, but Michaelis didn't have to be happy about it. He'd drawn the short straw because Luisa and Tristan were busy with the Ket games.

He didn't stay grumpy for long. The two people he'd met so far were remarkably friendly, and it lifted his spirits. He had worked his way up the street and was approaching the grocery store. There were two more people in the store, chatting away, an elderly lady and a rather homely-looking young man with a red rash on his cheeks.

The young man ventured, "Well, hello, sir, how are you?"

Michaelis smiled under his safety mask. "Very good," he said. "Thank you. Would you happen to know how I could find Zachary Percival? He's an old school friend, and I was going to drop in for a surprise visit, but I left his address in San Francisco." He patted his pant pockets and shrugged.

The young man thought for a moment. "You know what? I don't know of any Zachary Percival. He wasn't part of the Rebirth, was he? They've all gotten up and left, and good riddance."

It was the same answer he'd received from the other two people he'd asked. Michaelis shrugged. "No, I don't think so, but thanks anyway."

Michaelis picked up a fresh apple from one of the produce bins in the store and polished it on a disinfecting wipe he kept in his jacket pocket. It was bruised and had worm holes, but real fruit produce that wasn't shriveled up or blight-infested was hard to come by. "This is nice country up here," he said. "You're lucky to be living in Treble—and real apples to boot."

The older lady took a step forward, wagging her finger thoughtfully.

"You know, son, I don't know a Zachary, but there used to be the Percivals who had an old cabin up in the woods off Ozark Avenue."

Michaelis brightened. "Great, I think that's them. I'll be able to surprise him."

She hadn't finished wagging her finger. "You may be disappointed. We haven't seen the Percivals for years. There was a lot of talk of them being in trouble with the caretakers. But the cabin is up there, on the ridge at the end of Ozark, I think. Yes, that's right." She was tapping her head and nodding.

"Okay, thanks for the warning. I'll just hope for the best."

Michaelis bought the apple and thanked the two of them before returning to his motorcycle and proceeding to Ozark Avenue.

The property wasn't clearly marked. After skulking around the end of the street, he found a driveway that had an old Percival emblem as a burnt stencil in the wood paneling of an uprooted mailbox.

The cabin was a decent size, but rustic. Michaelis tried to get some sense of whether it might be inhabited. The façade looked old and dirty, but not completely unkempt. Foliage was encroaching significantly on the driveway, which suggested it hadn't been maintained for some time.

That was as much as Michaelis could discern from the outside. He backed away and parked the motorcycle, returning cautiously on foot.

He knocked on the door.

Nothing.

He knocked again.

Nothing again.

He yelled, "Hello, is anybody home?"

Silence.

In the game Hex Strategem there was a maneuver you could make when you had surrounded your opponent. It was tempting to go in for the kill but if you weren't careful about your assault they could escape to another game plane and re-establish another resource base. So you needed to skulk around until the player made a mistake and revealed all their hidden escape routes. The problem was, this could take ten or more turns. It was extremely boring, and his friends found it aggravating. Michaelis hated doing it, but he did it anyway, in order to be sure he won.

It was how he felt now. He hated the idea of breaking into the cabin, and nobody would be happy about it, but it was something he had to do, and it was certainly better than going back to San Francisco empty-handed.

So he walked around the cabin, looking for an easy entry point. The back area was similarly neglected, overtaken by the encroaching forest. The building was on a hill, and what looked like a bungalow from the driveway became a two-level cottage on the other side, with a sliding door on each floor.

He tried the bottom door. It was locked, so he climbed up the side of the hill and hopped over the deck railing. He felt the tightening in his neck. He paused, and put his hands down on his knees, taking labored breaths through his safety mask.

The view was nice from the deck, despite the overgrowth around the cottage. It looked over a lush, evergreen valley. It felt alien to him, a far cry from the collapsing Edwardians of San Francisco or the walled-in streets of New York.

Refocusing on his task, he examined the deck door and tried it. It was unlocked. "Yes," he said under his breath. It saved him the need to inelegantly smash a window with a rock or tree branch. But did it mean somebody was home? He doubted it. The house didn't appear to have been used in years.

The room beyond the sliding door opened up into a right angle of cozy-looking couches next to woody, knotted side tables. A mess of magazines and newsprint was piled on a coffee table in the center, spilling onto the deep shag carpet. A stale smell stung at his nostrils, and a layer of dust coated every surface.

Michaelis's beating heart reverberated in his ears. This kind of activity wasn't something he was accustomed to. Physical exploits were the domain of Tristan and Luisa.

He made cautious advances through the cabin. There were two bedrooms that looked like they hadn't been used in years. Many of the other common rooms appeared used, but unclean and messy. One of the rooms was locked. There was nothing to suggest who the owners were. It was almost like a rental cabin. The magazines and books on the coffee table covered business, sports, and pop culture; pretty typical and dated from four years ago.

He began searching through drawers and cabinets. One room appeared to be an adult's room. There were old clothes in the closet that were musty and moth-eaten, apparently unused for years. There were places where it looked like things had been removed from the room, like picture frames and jewelry. Subtle indentations in the dust were all that remained.

After exhaustively searching the rest of the cabin, he still needed to access the one locked room. He couldn't see a key anywhere, so he decided to try to kick it in. It took several tries, even though the interior door and lock were flimsy. Again, this wasn't his thing.

It looked like a child's room. Clothes and other items were strewn about the floor and bed. Dresser drawers had been left open, disemboweled. The room was dusty like the others, but it had been disturbed more recently. There were no picture frames or anything to reveal anything about the former inhabitants, aside from maybe the poster of *Notre Dame*, a popular vid about old Europe, which was quite old.

He wondered if this might be Zachary's old room.

He rummaged through the drawers and under the rug and bed. There was no sign of any data fingers.

He tapped and pried at the floorboards and side panels and looked behind the desk. Then he noticed something unusual: a small hole in the top right corner of the room. He pushed the desk over and climbed on top. Dust particles circulated, cascading around him in the faint light.

He peeled back a loose board, which revealed a black metallic apparatus. Pulling it further exposed a video camera. A green light on the bottom of the camera was visible.

Michaelis immediately ducked out of the camera's line of sight.

What was that doing here?

He reached up and violently ripped the camera out of its perch. He tried to tear open the loose paneling around the opening and look inside the hole. It took him several attempts. The expanded hole revealed that the camera had been connected to a trailing wire that led to a comlinked modem.

Someone could have been watching him. He thanked himself for leaving his safety mask on; it might at least prevent someone easily recognizing him. Still, if someone was watching, they could be on their way to the cabin now.

Dammit.

There was no point in cleaning up. He abruptly left the cabin through the back door, climbed down the wall, and scurried up the embankment to the motorcycle.

It wasn't until he was back on the highway, after frequent looks over his shoulder, that his pulse slowed enough to give it more serious consideration.

The camera didn't look like Inworld technology. He'd seen the ones caretakers used in places throughout the city. They were smaller, with rounded corners and obscured lenses behind tinted glass. This was more like something you could get at your local electronics store, jury-rigged for the room. But if it wasn't Inworld tech, whose was it?

It was impossible to say.

Tristan and Luisa would be disappointed the search hadn't turned up anything, and they would be concerned about the video camera. It reminded him of Ocean Beach. Once again they were perilously close to getting caught. And they could never go back, in case whoever set up the camera set up a more elaborate trap.

He had to admit he was fine with never returning. He would have much preferred another trip to the computer lab.

CHAPTER 36

It was a cold day for May. Tristan had to counterbalance chilling gusts as he cycled through the streets. Their exposed cliffside meeting place was only going to be worse.

Even with the weather as it was, he decided to take a longer ride than usual. His route took him eastward, around the Embarcadero. From the Embarcadero he made his way to the marina. The huge Van Ness pier spanned out below him into the bay as the tireless courier bots carried supplies to and from an autonomous freighter docked there.

When Tristan was a child, any Outworlder was allowed in the shipyard area. Today there were still a few caretaker personnel working on the periphery, doing mostly robot maintenance, but otherwise the area was almost completely run by the bots.

Some said this was a good thing. The shipyards were often the hardest-hit areas of Tyband contamination—not a good place for people of any stripe to be working—but he was sure the increasing automation wasn't adopted out of a desire to be more humane. It was simply to drive more efficiency, control, and profit for the Inworld.

Tristan took the Van Ness overpass at Lombard, watching the bots humming along in the robot lane below him.

The Sidiodome grew on the horizon, monopolizing the view. Outworlders knew little about the Sidiodome. It wasn't like they had much info about the Parkdome either, but at least they knew it was the main entrance into the system of domes, and where the bots and caretakers came and went. Except for some safety exits, there was no outside access to the Sidiodome. What was inside it? Did it serve administrative functions or was it full of plush Inworld residences? Was it as crammed full of Inworlders as the Parkdome? He had asked himself these questions hundreds of times.

Eventually he made it to Lincoln Park, which was once slated to have a dome as well, but he'd heard the ground composition was too unstable. Tristan was glad. It was one of the few green spaces left in San Francisco, and it actually had a view.

But even the view would be encumbered by domes, eventually. Cranes and scaffolding rose out of the Marindome construction across the bay.

Luisa arrived shortly afterward, the lines in the corners of her eyes evidence of a subtle grin under her mask. "So guess what?" she said.

Without any immediate inspiration, Tristan didn't bother guessing.

Luisa continued. "I heard from Ardrey. He wants us on his team."

Tristan didn't know how to react. It was a long shot for any captain to agree, especially Ardrey. So while he knew his reaction should be elation, his first inclination was to lean toward suspicion. "Really? Why do you think he agreed?"

Luisa was noticeably unhappy with his reaction. "Does it really matter? Aren't you just a bit excited?"

Excited? That was one way to describe it. It was all becoming real. If they made it to the finals, it meant they would be able to put their plan in action, but pinning their hopes on being on Ardrey's team? His stomach turned. "Yes, yes, I guess so. I just don't trust anyone, you know, especially Ardrey. Maybe he really does think we can help his team, but we have to be careful."

Luisa squinted at him, trying to read deeper than his words.

A wheezing sound could be heard. Michaelis pulled up next to them and dropped his bike on the ground. He leaned over, catching his breath. They could hear the filters of his mask whistling, working overtime.

"So guess what?" Luisa said. "Ardrey wants us on his team."

Michaelis looked at her from his stooped-over position with eyebrows raised. "Then there's something you should know," he said between gasps.

They waited patiently. It didn't appear he would be providing the enthusiastic response Luisa was looking for either.

"I've been following Sonny Joseph," Michaelis said, still struggling for air.

This had come about when Tristan had seen Trevor Nikino, a well-known Ket gamer, surreptitiously asking some other gamers about "renegades" in the locker room. Tristan wouldn't have thought much of it, except he saw Trevor debating with Sonny Joseph in the stands, and their interaction didn't appear to be amicable. So they had asked Michaelis to track Sonny and Trevor, when he had the opportunity. Michaelis was the only viable candidate for this, since he wasn't known in the Ket game world.

Michaelis took another deep breath. "I was following him today, and there was an interesting development." He put his hand up and looked down, indicating they should wait.

After a minute Michaelis' breathing began to regulate. "Someone came up to talk to Sonny in the stands, just like you said Trevor did. It didn't seem friendly, more like a business meeting. Again, just like you said. Sonny left the stands with this person, and I followed them. They made their way into the basement of the arena, toward the old offices. The fellow who met him left, and I managed to hide in an old office to avoid being seen, but a few moments later I heard Sonny talking to someone else. It was an animated discussion, but I couldn't quite make out what they were saying. So I glanced around the corner and saw he was speaking with Ardrey Wren."

"Oh, great." Tristan threw his hands up in the air.

"Now wait a minute," Luisa said. "They used to be teammates, and they won the playoffs together. Couldn't they just be talking about the good old days? Or hey, maybe they're friends." She emphasized *friends,* as if it was a word that Tristan and Michaelis were unfamiliar with.

Michaelis said, "Based on what we've seen, and what you heard from Trevor Nikino, Sonny is no regular caretaker. My guess is he's working as a sort of detective for the Inworld. He has people coming and going and doing his bidding. You can tell when he's talking to people in the stands. It's never casual. It looks like this friend of yours—"

"No," Tristan interjected, feeling a flush of anger. "Ardrey is not a friend."

Michaelis looked confused.

Tristan tried to calm himself. Michaelis couldn't possibly understand the depth of resentment Tristan had for Ardrey.

"Okay, okay," Michaelis said. "Your *potential future captain* could be working with Sonny."

Tristan tried to analyze this new development objectively. Ardrey wasn't the type to engage in chatter with an ex-teammate in the bowels of the arena unless it was for some purpose. This same person had just invited them to be on their team unexpectedly. It smelled like foul play from every angle, and at its core was Ardrey, the cold, calculating cause of so much of his angst.

Michaelis added, "One more thing, I think he saw me."

"Who saw you?" Tristan asked.

"Well, I'm not sure if Sonny Joseph did, but when I looked down the hall, I'm pretty sure Ardrey did. I tried to walk away nonchalantly, pretending I was lost, but I doubt they bought it. I'm not sure I can trail them anymore."

Michaelis eyed Tristan, waiting for his response. Luisa was frowning. He knew what they expected. They expected him to nix their plan to join Ardrey's team.

But he didn't give them an immediate response. He wrestled with his emotions, trying to rein them in, and walked away to peer over the cliff.

What else could they do? There was no direct proof Ardrey knew about their group. Ardrey could be getting into Sonny's good graces for other reasons. He could be sucking up to him so he would get a good position once he made it to the Inworld.

But there were so many strange coincidences.

Even if it was some kind of trap, they had a chance, and a chance was more than they'd ever have if they weren't on Ardrey's team. This thought grounded him and held his tongue. Their only plan of any substance hinged upon getting through dome security, and the only realistic way to do that was to get into the Inworld for the interleague game finals.

When he considered the alternative, he was confronted with the powerful images of his past; his brother turning on his noose, the deer dying by the path. It was his subconscious telling him he couldn't go back. If it was a trap, he would have to find a way to counter Ardrey, to figure out his plan and use it to their advantage.

He finally turned back to Michaelis and Luisa. "This is our only chance. Let's take it." He managed a meager smile.

Luisa's posture became more relaxed, as if she had been donning armor for an anticipated debate, but now she could let it fall away. She smiled. "Let's do it!"

For the rest of their meeting they talked about ways to monitor Ardrey so they could look for signs of foul play. It wasn't until some time later they realized Peter hadn't arrived. Despite his drinking problem, he'd never missed one of their meetings. It was another ominous development they didn't need. They decided to go by his place and check in on him after the meeting.

When they adjourned, Tristan remained satisfied with their decision. They hadn't taken the easy way out. They hadn't chosen the well-trodden path of fear and complacency.

But a lingering worry ate at him. Why wasn't it one of the other captains? His teeth clenched as they rode in tandem, away from Lincoln Park, and toward Peter's apartment.

CHAPTER 37

Luisa had been to Peter's apartment once before, months ago, so she knew where to go. The door was unlocked. Until they reached the living room, the apartment looked remarkably clean. This was the first sign something was amiss—Peter wasn't one for cleanliness.

They found him on the couch. A stench of vomit and alcohol permeated the air. There was a deposit of crusty bile as the source, dried up and integrated into the carpet beside the couch. There were two empty bottles of vodka on the coffee table and an empty vial of sleeping pills tipped over on a side table.

The scene might lead one to believe Peter had drunk himself to death or overdosed on sleeping pills, or both. Sure, Peter was a drunk, but he'd been curtailing his activities. Her suspicions were enhanced by discolorations on his cheek—probably bruises. But what was most out of place was the fact that Peter was particular about his spirits, and he hated vodka.

They cleared out of the apartment soon after, leaving him as he was, worried they were being monitored. They did a sweep to ensure they'd left no traces.

Sometime later, Michaelis and Tristan asked Luisa what she

thought, and she gave them her take. They all agreed murder was the rational conclusion.

Peter's death was difficult to stomach. He had been growing on her, and they all felt the loss more than they would have expected.

Over the next few days they tried to make a list of the many possible suspects. Peter had a colorful past. Maybe the OPM didn't like him revealing their group to the four of them? Although the manner of his death would be a little extreme for making a statement. Or did the caretakers finally find him and kill him? It was possible, but if it was the caretakers, how did they find him, and did he reveal anything?

Luisa was at the greatest risk because she'd been Peter's main contact. She would be in his comlink call list several times. Even though they were using aliases and unregistered call IDs, one never knew how the Inworld might be able to track them.

Peter's death also made her reflect on Fenton. She went to visit him and warned him of what happened. She tried to let him know she still valued him as a friend. They hung out, and watched some vids together, but he'd been cold and distant.

Fenton did give her the means to contact the OPM, and he tried to convince her to call them. Luisa found it odd that he pushed it on her even though he hadn't bothered to call them himself. It was a culmination of her realization that Fenton's heart was never fully in it, especially after his mom had made the deal to reduce her sentence. He'd been there for his friends, but that just wasn't enough. Giving this OPM contact information to her was his catharsis of the whole affair. After that, their connection could be easily severed.

All of this could have easily pulled her back down, but it didn't. Luisa was more focused. She felt youthful again. It was the Ket games. They were invigorating, and they distracted her from the symphony of death surrounding her.

The Shock Hawks—Ardrey's team—were firing on all cylinders. They had won the last of their regular season games, and their first playoff game was behind them. It had been a blowout where nine of her teammates had been left standing. The momentum drove her forward, and kept her from wallowing.

They had been watching Ardrey closely. His skill in the games was clear. He would easily switch between roles as a commander, sniper, or runner, and he even gave Tristan a run for his money as a bounder. He didn't offer much praise or inspiration, yet his teammates followed him religiously.

There were no indications of conspiracy, and no sign of allegiance with the caretakers—at least not yet.

The Shock Hawks were ranked first, but they still had to win the NSF playoffs to make it to the interleague game in the Parkdome. There were two games left against two tough teams.

She was hopeful. Michaelis had come up with a solid plan about what they could do if they made it inside the Parkdome. It was risky, and fraught with uncertainty, but it also gave her a sense of purpose, and kept her looking ahead.

She dared not look back, for behind her were the ghosts of her past; her mom, her dad, Chooly, Peter. She dared not look back, for she knew her own death might be close on her heels.

CHAPTER 38

The NSF League Finals was a momentous day. Quanta Arena was packed to the rafters with fans from across the city. It was exactly how Tristan had remembered it: a dynamic living organism of sound and energy. This was the sporting event of the year—the one game that defined the players' futures more than any other, and everyone knew it.

For years he'd fantasized about playing in this game, but so much had changed. If they won, they would play in the interleague game in the Inworld, and they were as prepared as they could be for what was to come. After Peter's death, and with Fenton leaving, the group gravitated toward the extreme. Something needed to be done, and soon, never mind the consequences.

The buzzer sounded, and the players moved into their positions.

To Tristan's surprise, the Wired Warriors came out by concentrating their firepower on him. His cover position was being bombarded. No doubt they were anticipating his typical suicide bounding rush.

Ardrey tightbeamed him. "Tristan, hold." Tristan wasn't planning on bounding anyway. The maneuver would be ineffective if he hardly managed to get off the ground.

It was never a good sign when your opponent anticipated your first move. Nevertheless, Ardrey had his share of contingency plans.

Tristan heard Ardrey on his comlink. "Number three, left flank."

The Shock Hawks were in a spread-out formation, maximizing the use of cover. Play number three involved the four Shock Hawks on the far left flank taking the offensive, two bounding and two running to strategic cover positions closer to the Warriors. The objective was to create a beachhead on the opponent's flank so they could fire at them from two angles rather than one.

The firestorm shifted away from Tristan's covered position, and he peered out to see his teammates on the left taking the offensive. The first Shock Hawk bounded far and deep toward the upper left. This was followed by another Shock Hawk ascending in a poorly executed low arc behind him, while two others scurried hastily forward on the ground underneath them.

The ploy had mixed results. The first bounder made it to his intended position, but not to a place with optimal cover. The second bounder, through some excellent shooting, was taken out in midair by Wired Warrior snipers. The two Shock Hawk ground troops made it some way out, but not that far. The result was they did have somewhat of a beachhead on the left flank, but it was a precarious one, and it was a costly maneuver with one player down and one alone in the distant upper left.

The Wired Warriors focused on Jared—the isolated Shock Hawk. It didn't look good for him, and he couldn't fire at any exposed Wired Warriors because of the barrage he was under. The other two Shock Hawks that were part of the advance weren't deep enough into the arena to support him.

"Tristan, go," Ardrey broadbeamed. "Line, advance."

Tristan bounded up, firing under him as he went, leaving his Shock Hawk teammates behind as they advanced forward under him more cautiously. A few Wired Warriors fired up at him, but most tried to pick off the advancing Shock Hawks on the ground. From Tristan's vantage he could see the intense melee brewing. Out of the corner of his eye, he saw Jared taken out even before he landed.

But they hadn't hit Tristan.

Tristan landed just off the upper-right flank. He found cover and began firing at the two Wired Warrior positions closest to him. At least he could keep these two occupied and distract them from the main Shock Hawk advance.

What seemed like an eternity passed in his new position, with sporadic fire between him and the two Wired Warriors. The Warriors occasionally looked the other way, sometimes firing toward the main fray, but they were apprehensive with Tristan at their back.

The crowd was deafening. There was no clear favorite in this game, so the undulating roars gave him little sense of which way the match was going. Tristan could only hope some of the roars were for his team.

After more trading of Ket pulses, one of the two Warriors he was closest to left his position. Tristan took the opportunity to run to another cover block, one that gave him a better attack angle. He took out the other Wired Warrior nearby after a few focused shots.

Now where to go? His question was answered by a Wired Warrior bounding up in a broad arc in front of him. He was looking away from Tristan.

Low-hanging fruit.

Last year he would have been much more cautious. He would have tried to sniper him, but he didn't have the same confidence in his long-range aim. So instead he bounded up on an intercept course, firing intensely all the way.

He took out the wayward Warrior on the first part of his upward arc.

As he was reaching the crest of the bound, he looked down and surveyed the situation. There were a lot of dark uniforms. Of those that were still active, he counted three other Shock Hawks, and five Wired Warriors.

"Tristan, lower right." It was Ardrey, wanting support. The Warrior Tristan had intercepted had been bounding in to corner him.

Tristan's Ket energy was running low, which was the problem with doing huge bounds and extended shootouts. When he landed in the upper left corner of the arena, he ran as fast as he could to help Ardrey.

"Tristan, can you bound over him?" Ardrey asked by tightbeam. He was referring to the Warrior pinning Ardrey down.

"No, running out of juice. Might not make it."

The comlink was quiet for a moment. Tristan found cover near the sporadic exchange of Ket pulses between Ardrey and the Wired Warrior.

"Okay. Charge at him, then find cover," Ardrey ordered.

Tristan wasn't sure what Ardrey was thinking, but he nevertheless followed the command. He charged in, firing at will, then sidestepped behind a cover block close by. The skinny, wave-shaped block didn't provide him with much protection. Initially surprised, the Warrior turned to fire back at Tristan while seeking better cover for herself. Then the Warrior turned to look back toward her original prey —Ardrey.

Of course, Ardrey wasn't in his original position. He'd found another angle. The Warrior was taken out with a solid blast to the chest before she even managed to find Ardrey in her field of vision.

No longer pinned down, Tristan and Ardrey turned and ran toward the rest of the fray.

"Status," Ardrey sent via broadbeam.

"Reno and Emma active here on the left flank. Three Warriors on top of us."

Luisa didn't report. She must be out.

"Hold defensive positions," Ardrey commanded. "Tristan and I are heading to upper center."

They arrived at the upper center and took cover a short distance from the main melee. The closest Warriors were looking back periodically, but they didn't appear to have seen Tristan and Ardrey approaching.

Ardrey had a concerned look on his face. "How's your juice?"

"I've got enough for basic shield and about ten shots, I think."

"Okay. I'm all out."

"You're...all out?" Tristan exclaimed. Ardrey would be essentially useless except for issuing commands.

Ardrey didn't answer the rhetorical question. Instead he said, "We're charging them. I'm going to come in by stealth from the right. You draw their attention from the front left. Got it?"

Tristan nodded, wondering what Ardrey could possibly be thinking.

Tristan made his way forward. When his position was revealed, he fired twice and ducked behind cover. The two Wired Warriors turned to fire back at him. He stayed in position for a few more seconds, then jumped up to continue the charge.

What he saw next amazed him. Ardrey ran in from the right side at full speed. One of the Warriors turned to fire, but was too late. Unbelievably, Ardrey tackled him and began grappling with him on the ground.

The other Warrior was standing nearby, shocked into inaction by the physical display. Should he fire at the grappling duo? Should he try to separate them? But in the games, any time spent dwelling in uncertainty could be disastrous. Tristan took advantage of the surprise of the Warrior player. After a few stray shots, his Ket pulses hit the mark and the dumbfounded Warrior went dark.

Tristan had been running forward as he fired, and he'd almost reached the skirmish.

Ardrey had pinned the Warrior to the ground with his body and was methodically unstrapping his Ket pack off his back. This had been done a few times in the games, but it had been years since it had happened in the NSF. There was a look of fury on Ardrey's face that Tristan would remember long after the match. The visceral emotion reminded Tristan of the moment just before Ardrey had taken him out in the last season. It almost made him feel a kind of bizarre kinship with Ardrey. He could have been like Ardrey, or maybe he had been—a year ago.

Ardrey finished ripping the Ket energy pack from the Warrior, making him power down and go dark. The desperate look on Ardrey's face vanished and his cold focus returned. Ardrey met Tristan's eyes, and Tristan nodded.

Tristan took stock of the situation. There was only one Wired Warrior left and four Hawks. The volume in the arena was deafening—almost painful to his ears. The crowd knew the deathblow had been dealt.

Ardrey stayed back and commanded the three remaining Hawks to surround the lone Warrior, who was swiftly eliminated.

The Shock Hawks had won the NSF league.

The tension burned off quickly in the wake of victory, and Tristan allowed himself to be taken away in the wave of jubilation that followed. There were trophies, awards, and speeches. Fans hooted and hollered when they finally left the arena.

The team went out for a dinner and drinks, and they all relived the match and the season. Even Ardrey was full of smiles in his reserved way. Tristan was given much praise for his role in the match.

Later in the evening, many left to be with their families—to share their excitement with people they cared about. Tristan stayed with a few of his teammates who remained, including Luisa. They reveled in the day as much as they could.

When the dinner ended, Tristan escorted Luisa home. She was as excited as he was, and it felt good to be with somebody who under-stood him—who knew what this meant, and could mean, for both of them.

They arrived at her blocky apartment in the New Mission and stood quietly, not wanting the day to end. Whether it was the connection he felt at the moment, the exuberance of the day, or just long overdue, he kissed her, and she returned the kiss eagerly.

They went inside to Rex's cheerful barking and found themselves on the couch, where their lips met again.

Tristan knew it would all return the next morning: the nervous anticipation, the concerns about Ardrey, and even the images of his brother. They always did, so he was happy to have buried it away that night. It felt good to shine brightly this one time and share himself with someone.

The exhilaration of the evening was also spurred by a growing awareness in both of them. The real fight was coming soon. Knowing their time left in this world might be limited, each moment took on a greater virtue.

It wasn't until Rex dropped his bowl in front of the couch that they returned to reality. It was the sound of duty, of responsibility. This was not a true victory. Now was not the time to celebrate—now, more than ever, was the time to focus.

Luisa stood up to fill Rex's bowl and Tristan bid his goodbyes shortly afterward.

PART IV

INWORLD

CHAPTER 39

Tristan had become less fearful of the dream, so he didn't try to suppress it. He didn't embrace it either. Instead, he patiently let it come. Other details would reveal themselves on occasion: the feeling of his mother's hands on his shoulders, trying to reassure him, or the wailing of the child who lost his parents, or the loudspeaker blaring out the sentencing of his brother in stark monotones.

It would always return to his brother's oblique body, turning slowly, his face a grotesque mask. The image was much clearer after his revelation in Montana, as if in his youth his subconscious had amputated the memory to save the rest of the mind, and now the lost gray matter was regenerating.

He dressed in his tight-fitting Ket uniform and headed to the kitchen. His parents were eating breakfast absentmindedly, his father distracted by his tablet. Tristan sat at the table.

"Morning," his father said.

"Morning," Tristan responded.

Ordinarily, little else would be said, but as the interleague game day grew closer, Tristan felt detached from his parents. It wasn't sitting well.

"How's work going, Dad?" Tristan asked.

His father barely looked up. "Not bad. Well, you know—my

back...and I have walkoff duty in Noe Valley tomorrow, but I can't complain."

"Why do you do it, Dad?"

"What do you mean?"

"Your job."

"To put food on the table. To put a roof over your head."

"Oh."

His father's eyes eventually strayed upward. He must have recognized that Tristan starting a conversation was unusual. He said, "Remember those pictures I showed you when you were young—the Painted Ladies houses, and those mansions in Pacific Heights?"

"Yeah."

"A hundred years ago all the houses in San Francisco were that beautiful; immaculately painted, with rounded windows, and steep arches—each one with so much individual character. We lost something when we let them fall into ruin. That's why I do this. Sure, we need the money. And yes, I have to deal with walkoff duty, or waste disposal, but every once in a while the remediation corps gets to refurbish an old Edwardian. We bring back beauty, and respect, to the city I love."

Tristan remembered the way his father looked at the old houses in the pictures, as if he were lost in them. He wanted to thank him for all he did—to tell him what he did mattered, but instead all he said was, "That's cool, Dad."

His mom said, "Are you ready for the interleague game, Tristan? It's so exciting!"

It was nice to see that his parents were proud of him—the sports celebrity. They wanted to relish this moment of fame, even though it might be fleeting.

They might have a different opinion if they knew he might not return. They didn't understand the gravity well Tristan was in, pulling him away. He was torn between letting them enjoy their proud day and confronting them with the truth.

"I wanted to let you both know I...appreciate what you've done for me," he said. It sounded silly, and it was out of character. His parents shared a confused look, not knowing how to react. There was no point in telling them anything else. It would only make them more susceptible to persecution if, or when, he was caught.

Eventually his mother's eyes softened. "Well, thank you, Tristan. We know, and we love you too."

He slowly stood up and made his way to the door, grabbing his safety mask and game gear on the way out. His parents hollered an amiable "bye" as he left.

It was an overcast day, but the dark somber clouds would part on occasion, revealing beigy patches of light behind them. Tristan felt an impulse to take his mask off, but decided against it. That was walkoff mentality.

He rode leisurely, watching the people in the street, and looking at the buildings on his route. He took the time to appreciate the old Edwardians again, trying to find the arches and rounded windows his dad had mentioned. He felt like he was seeing them for the first time.

People were moving purposefully, focused on their worldly pursuits. They didn't share his reflective state of mind. He crossed the robot lanes and watched the lines of blocky metalloids advancing along the tracks.

In time, he made it to the perch in Lincoln Park. He was the first to arrive, so he sat on the edge and stared over the bay.

Luisa arrived a few minutes later. Tristan greeted her with a smile.

"Where's the brains of this operation?" Luisa asked.

"Hey, what are you saying?" Tristan frowned in amusement and pointed at his chest. "Okay who am I kidding. I think our brain trust doesn't have much idle time these days. Let's hope he's just late."

"Right," Luisa acknowledged.

Michaelis did arrive shortly afterward. He had transformed since Tristan first met him. He must have lost twenty pounds, and while he would still finger his glasses and speak in quiet tones, he hardly ever looked down when he spoke.

"Luisa, I didn't see you look back once," Michaelis said.

"What? You were following me?" Luisa asked.

"You bet I was," Michaelis chided. "And you're wearing your mask with Shock Hawk colors on it. People recognized you along your little carefree ride. I made sure no one followed you into the park, but you need to be more careful. Both of you should wear generic masks that don't draw attention."

Michaelis was right. He was covering all the bases, thinking through every detail. They would be lost without him.

They reviewed the plan, and reviewed it again for good measure. Michaelis relayed his most recent discussion with the OPM who, to their surprise, was actually warming to their ideas, and offering a few of their own. When they finished, Tristan said, "So are we all ready? We're about to face the lion...in the lion's den."

"I prefer to think of them as sardines in a can," Luisa said.

"Okay," Tristan said, grinning. "That sounds better. Let's show these sardines what we're made of."

They all fidgeted in silence until Luisa broke the uncomfortable moment by hugging them both in turn. "Good luck," she said.

And with that, they parted ways. It was to be their last meeting before the interleague game. The pressure was mounting as the media was beginning to follow Tristan and Luisa, so they needed to minimize their interaction.

Tristan left knowing they were ready, and feeling confident he could trust Luisa and Michaelis. Ardrey was the biggest concern. He had dashed his hopes once before. Was he mobilizing his enigmatic energy to do so again? The plans for getting through security, convincing OPM to help, and execute other aspects of their plan were fraught with enough risk.

He reminded himself again that it was their best chance because it was their only chance.

Tristan took a circuitous route home, this time looking behind him on occasion to ensure he wasn't being followed. His path through the city gave him the opportunity to get a good vantage of their target. The Parkdome loomed, its dark shell eating into the cityscape, ever present, taunting him. He still couldn't picture what lurked underneath, even after the descriptions Peter had provided.

He pedaled on. If all went to plan, he would find out soon enough.

CHAPTER 40

Luisa lifted her pack off the couch and sighed her usual sigh—her heart fluttering and her vocal cords contributing a gentle hum—then closed the door to her apartment behind her.

Rex barked behind the door. He certainly didn't understand why he had received a shower of affection that morning, but he'd enjoyed every minute of it.

Melissa would take care of him if she didn't make it back.

She rode to the Parkdome. It was a cold, overcast day, and a thick breeze pushed and pulled at her.

She shifted her weight carefully on her bicycle. The explosive biogel packs felt uncomfortable concealed under her Ket uniform. Even though Michaelis said they were completely safe when not mixed, she felt obliged to avoid any harsh movements.

Her greater concern was the Inworlders had some form of detection mechanism for them. Michaelis said this was a "calculated risk." In other words, there was a real chance she could be in jail or under who knows what form of brutal interrogation in less than an hour.

She arrived at the main entry to the Parkdome in the old Panhandle and was slowed down by heavy pedestrian traffic. She maneuvered to lock her bike up at the rack near the Mother Myra statue—a ten-foot-tall depiction of Myra leaning into the elements, her right elbow wrapped around her forehead to protect her face, with a baby carefully shielded in the other arm. Of course Mother Myra never had any children of her own, and she was always wearing a mask before she founded the first Inworld enclaves, but that didn't stop the sculptor from exercising artistic license.

It would have been more accurate to show Mother Myra cowering in fear with a bag of cash nestled in her arm.

The Panhandle entrance was usually quiet except for the few caretakers coming and going, but today it was a zoo. There must have been fifty caretakers buzzing around on enercycles, talking to just as many reporters, cameramen, and casual observers. The caretakers had formed a human periphery around an assembly area where a few Shock Hawk players could be seen, their black and teal suits contrasting with the sea of blue and gold caretakers milling about.

Luisa was increasingly nervous as she approached the scene, cognizant of what was concealed under her clothing. She hung back until a roving reporter noticed her and tried to intercept her. He had a sweat-marred collar, a flushed face, and slick hair. "How are you feeling today Luisa?" he asked. "Any insights on today's game?"

"No comment," she said, not meeting his eyes. She brushed past him.

As she came closer to the entrance, she saw Tristan arriving. The wall of caretakers stopped him. They compared his face to a comlink image and let him into the periphery.

She joined him inside the ring and he flashed a determined smile at her. "Have you sharpened your talons, Shock Hawk?" he asked.

"I'm trying to avoid sharp objects." Her eyes darted down at her midsection, where the biogel packs were hidden.

"Right, sorry."

Outside the ring of caretakers and reporters, the occasional cheer could be heard. The Shock Hawk fan base had grown with the team's success, and Luisa was amazed by the diverse crowd of hundreds of spectators willing to support their team, *her team*, for today's match. Their opponents, Phaser Frenzy, were supposed to arrive soon after, and would be greeted with a similar flourish.

Ardrey arrived next, and a roar from the crowd ensued. He frowned stoically as he made his way through the onlookers, reporters, and care-takers, an uncomfortable hero who shied from the spotlight. It was unusual he would be on time because he was typically early to every-thing. Maybe he'd been told to arrive last, for dramatic flair? Much of this was scripted by the caretaker organizers.

Ardrey was ushered into the enclosure. Pictures and vids were taken as the Hawks gathered, talking informally.

The caretakers prodded them into a line and they moved single file toward the main entrance. They each brought their faces close to a retinal scanner next to a caretaker sentry, and all were allowed to pass through after a quick exam.

So far, so good.

They weren't in the Parkdome itself, but in the main gangway entrance the caretakers used. This, in itself, was farther into the dome system than any Outworlders ever ventured.

The gangway walls were made of a salmon-colored material, brightly lit by floodlights, a contrast from the black, glossy polystyrix material that contoured the outside. They maneuvered onto a moving sidewalk. To their left they could see the primary robot and vehicle entrance sloping down deep into the ground. The vehicle laneway was quiet, closed for the day's events.

Four caretaker agents led them on, their heavy boots echoing along the corridor. Four more pulled up the rear.

At the end of the walkway two caretakers stood at the entrance to what looked like another security checkpoint, while two others were perched on a balcony above it, holding standard-issue shockers—stun guns that caretakers sometimes used to immobilize Outworlders.

The caretakers who accompanied them wore bright gold and blue uniforms typical of those seen on the street, but these other four care-takers were wearing conservative-looking black and gray pants and tucked-in white shirts. It gave them a more businesslike air. Their skin was paler compared to the blue and gold clad caretakers, and they had virtually no yellowing around the eyes, probably because they rarely left the Inworld.

The ceiling at the edge of the security entrance shimmered with orange incandescence, creating a faint strobe-light effect on the guards and checkpoint workers.

Luisa looked on as the caretakers leading the column put their belongings in a black box with grid marks on the sides, then walked through a tall cylindrical enclosure topped with a display panel that periodically flashed green. It had to be some sort of full-body scanner. The Shock Hawks ahead of her all went through, first taking off their backpacks and giving them to the more business-like caretakers, who put these items in yet another form of scanner.

This was a crucial checkpoint. She looked back at Tristan, who shrugged. He was right; there was nothing they could do now.

The green light flashed for her and her anxiety diminished. Her bag followed on the conveyor shortly thereafter.

Michaelis had been right. The Inworlders have been safe in their protected Inworld for so long, they wouldn't contemplate anyone taking on a plan so audacious. Of course she couldn't be sure there weren't sensors to scan for the components of the biogel packs later.

Tristan emerged behind her, and they walked together into a brightly lit hallway that led into a large atrium. It was several stories high, with multiple exits. To each side stood a number of cylindrical elevator shafts, and in front of them was a see-through wall with large glass doors rising to the ceiling. Sunlight streamed in through the pane of glass above, which defied rational explanation since it was an overcast day outside.

Caretakers—the blue and gold kind—dotted the sidewalls of the room, watching the Outworlders as they stepped into the atrium. The caretakers were pointing at them, making remarks. Some were laughing, but most were serious. The Outworlders must have looked like rats out of their cage.

A blue and gold caretaker at the head of the column said, "You can take off your safety masks."

Luisa had forgotten she was wearing her mask. She began to unstrap it, along with the rest of the Shock Hawks. Before they could finish, the caretaker continued, "This way," and motioned for them to follow.

There were two black-clad caretakers waiting at the large-paned window. One of these took over the lead in front of the column and beckoned them forward to the large semicircular plexmold doors cut out of the huge pane.

The doors opened automatically, and the column marched through. Four more caretakers fell in step on both sides. Luisa realized they were entering the Theater Chamber, according to what Peter had told them. This was the synthetic outdoors area for the caretakers. Based on Peter's cursory description, she had imagined this chamber as a large, brightly lit, hollowed-out room, with the occasional hydroponic plant installation positioned throughout.

It was much more than that. The "sky" was brighter and clearer than any day she'd ever seen in San Francisco. It was hard to believe the dark shell was somewhere above her head. The roof, if there was indeed a roof, was an all-encompassing light blue expanse.

The scene was alien to her. There was no cloud, fog, smog, or mist. There were no purple, ochre, beige, red, or orange colors typical of the San Francisco sky. The group all stared at the ceiling, if it could be called that, searching for seams, curvature, or anything else that might reveal the truth behind this mirage. Luisa couldn't find any source of the illusion. It was as though she had been transported to some other world, or to some other time, under a bright blue sunny sky.

And the synthetic sun beat down on them. Luisa looked at the skin on her arm as if seeing it for the first time. Strangely, it didn't feel warm, the way it would on a day not even half as bright in the Outworld.

They were led down a pathway made of tight, perfectly cut cobblestones. Ornate towers rose high into the sky on each side, decorated in an elaborate Edwardian style typical of old San Francisco. But unlike the Outworld city, the buildings were perfectly maintained. Every panel, window frame, and doorknob was flawless, clean, and freshly painted. Between the towers were pathways that led to areas with trees and what appeared to be small lakes or ponds. Ahead of them, probably half a mile away, was an even larger building with a similar facade, dominating the view on the virtual horizon from right to left. That was where they were heading—the arena.

There was so much space. Peter had said the caretaker portion of the Inworld wasn't as confining as the Old Inworld in the western part of the Parkdome, but this still exceeded her expectations. It was like she was in a huge outdoor park with the occasional large tower placed throughout.

Luisa was beginning to feel a bit faint. The Inworld's perfection felt disorienting, like a caricature from an animated vid, with immaculate cleanliness and exhausting color. The somber downtown would actually be a welcome reprieve at the moment.

A multitude of Inworlder eyes were bearing down on them. The caretakers loitered in doorways, open windows, and adjoining pathways, watching them go by. In contrast to the Outworlders outside the panhandle entrance, these people hardly made a sound—no cheers, and no jeers. They just chatted idly among themselves as they monitored the parade of Outworlders marching by.

She looked back at Tristan. He was gazing straight ahead, his jaw clenched and teeth grinding, uninterested in the spectacle around him. Something about his grim determination in this cartoon world made her smile. He noticed her expression and lifted his hands uncomprehendingly.

"I'm surprised you have any teeth left," she said.

He scowled back at her.

They were closing in on their destination. The loiterers beside the path were becoming more numerous.

Eventually the column of gamers and their caretaker escort reached the face of the large building, walked up the steps, and entered. Four of the admin caretakers peeled off and remained behind at the door, facing outwards, into the Theater chamber.

The trek continued through a series of sliding doors and passageways, eventually leading to the arena. It was the same size as the Outworlder arenas, except the playing area was boxed in from the floor to the ceiling with heavily tinted translucent plexmold. The ceiling was lined with a matrix of exposed nodes necessary to create the Ketrix field, whereas in the Outworld the nodes would be behind protective paneling.

Luisa looked for a division in the stands. Peter had said the middle of the arena marked the split between two distinct sections of the Inworld, one side being the caretaker zone and the other being the Old Inworld that few caretakers would ever see. The caretakers would sit on one side of the stands and the Old Inworlders would sit on the other.

The division was barely visible—a dark line in the plexmold on each side. As they continued to walk around the caretaker side of the stands, she could discern some movement on the Old Inworlder side, but it was hard to make out behind the heavily tinted plexmold. All she could see were vague humanoid shapes or the mechanical movements of service bots.

At long last, they made it to their locker room and had the opportunity to sit down. Several blue and gold caretakers remained with them, hanging back and staring at them coldly. The Shock Hawks were quiet and meditative after the trek through the Inworld.

Luisa smiled and nudged Tristan, who sat beside her. He angled his eyes upward. She followed his glance and saw Ardrey sitting directly across the room, staring at them. She forced a smile for Ardrey while suppressing a shudder.

The game wasn't for another hour, so they made nervous chatter in front of the caretaker guards and Ardrey's watchful eye. The Shock Hawks went through the motions of their strategy. Ardrey made a speech about them representing the NSF and that they should have fun, and, of course, win the game and show the Inworlders what the NSF is made of.

Even though this interleague game wasn't as important as the league finals for Inworld selection, it was an opportunity for those not in their last year of eligibility to make a name for themselves before the next season. So yes, it was still an important game, and it began to show on the faces of her teammates.

For Tristan and Luisa, today was the only day, and the only game. They ignored the Shock Hawks around them and rehearsed their plan in their minds. Once the game began there would be little time for reflection.

CHAPTER 41

Michaelis paused his bike at a stoplight and glanced down at his watch. It had been a busy day, but he was on time. If all was going well, Luisa and Tristan would be sitting in the locker room preparing for the game. Earlier he'd watched them from among the gathering crowd at the panhandle gates. They had entered the Park-dome unimpeded, but there was no way to know if they'd made it through the internal security hurdles.

Prior to that, he'd met with John at an abandoned gas station just up from the docks where the caretakers hated patrolling. It was quite out of the way, and possibly Tyband-contaminated, but in the end he would do whatever he could to ensure they had OPM involved.

John confirmed the OPM would have their people near the bomb sites, armed and ready for action. Of course, they wouldn't move a muscle until they exploded. If no bombs went off, the OPM would do nothing and disavow any involvement with them. That was the deal.

Michaelis couldn't have asked for more.

It was a big turnaround from his meeting with John earlier in the week. They had hemmed and hawed about the risk—about how if it didn't work they would be set back years after more stringent security protocols were put in place—but he could see their minds turning in a way that suggested it just might work.

It was a calculated risk getting the OPM involved at all. Michaelis had previously made the point they could have even been a clandestine front for capturing potential conspirators. But Peter didn't think they were a bad bunch, even if they were in a perpetual state of procrastination.

Of course, Peter had been murdered.

In the end, there was no other choice. They needed the OPM for the plan to work, period.

He was nearing his apartment. After traversing the upper Pacific Heights area, the rest was easy: a few flat stretches intermingled with just as many easy downhill rides.

Michaelis set his bike against the house and entered. He lived on the first floor of a four-bedroom flat with two other young bachelors close to the Van Ness docks. It was a quiet place, and his roommates were friendly enough.

He couldn't stay long. He wanted to get to a computer lab and go over the messaging code one last time before joining John and the OPM at the rendezvous point.

His roommate Hector was sitting in the front room of the house. "Hey, why's the door open?" Michaelis asked in passing, while walking toward the hall, but his greeting didn't register the response he'd expected, so he backtracked. Hector was sitting straight up and staring at the vid screen, but nothing was on. Hector didn't normally have good posture. He was normally inattentive, melting into the couch, sloth-like. And his eyes were wide open, glaring.

Hector put a finger to his lips and pointed with his other hand down the hall.

"What is it?" Michaelis asked quietly. Hector had beads of sweat on his brow. This was no roommate prank. Something was wrong.

Without speaking, Hector silently mouthed *caretakers* or at least, that's what it looked like, and he again pointed down the hall. Hector then mouthed *leave,* and stabbed his finger desperately at the door.

Michaelis needed no more convincing. He turned and tried to squeeze past the open door silently.

He glanced back as he left. Down at the end of the hall, the doorway to his room opened, and a man clad in gold and blue stepped out.

"Hey you, stop!" the caretaker hollered.

Michaelis slammed the door behind him and ran down the entryway steps. He hopped on his bike and pedaled vigorously around the corner, only now noticing two caretaker enercycles parked neatly on the other side of the building.

His mind raced as he pedaled. He couldn't disable the enercycles. They were tamperproof, requiring fingerprint authorization to access the ignition hub. He could only think to get as far away from the caretakers as possible before they could properly chase him. To get away you need speed. To have speed, you need to go downhill.

He turned left on the next street and pedaled hard toward the intersection offering the closest downhill route. Even with the increasing distance he heard the high-pitched spark of a caretaker enercycle powering up.

He didn't have much time. They could easily go twice as fast as he could.

He turned left at the intersection and gathered momentum on the downhill slope. He could feel his heart pounding. Already his lungs were clenching and his throat tingling. "Not now...give me just...a few more minutes." Michaelis's inhalations and exhalations were increasingly strained. His mask filters were already whistling at him, even though he was on the lowest filtration setting.

If he kept heading in the current direction, he might end up cornered. The bay was straight ahead, and the robot lanes leading to the docks were on his right. If he turned left, eventually he'd be boxed in by the hills leading up to the Sidiodome. There were still many blocks between his current location and the bay, so hiding out or ducking into an alley seemed to be the best bet, but no good hiding places were presenting themselves.

He had reached the Lombard Street intersection. Traffic was light, but heavy enough to make him have to wait for an opening or turn. He pulled off his safety mask and let it hang off his neck. He was breathing in a forced, rhythmic fashion, knowing he'd need every oxygen molecule.

They had to be close on his heels.

He had an idea.

He turned right on Lombard and pedaled furiously. People on the street looked at him curiously, but for the most part paid him no mind. His red face and dire expression weren't that unusual. He was just one more desperate person in a sea of desperate people.

Franklin Street was clear of traffic, so he passed through the intersection without delay. He climbed the small hill to the fence at the end. This marked the barrier between the street and the Van Ness robot lanes.

The last push had put him over the edge. When he stopped at the fence, he doubled over and was wracked by a fit of coughing. His esophyxia was in full tilt, his throat dangerously nearing full constriction. It forced him to his knees. He stabilized himself on the ground with his hand, for fear he might fall on his face.

Looking back, he saw what he feared. The two caretaker enercycles had reached the Franklin–Lombard intersection and were turning in his direction. They had seen him.

One was the caretaker he'd seen coming out of his room. The second was also familiar, even under his mask; it was Sonny Joseph.

Had he been trailed? Maybe Tristan and Luisa had been found out?

But this was no time for conjecture.

Thankfully, traffic had picked up on Franklin, and the caretakers were held up. It would give him precious seconds.

Michaelis picked himself up off the ground, still wracked by the occasional disabling cough, and staggered to his right, running along the fence, leaving his bike where it lay. There was a slim corridor between the fence and the decaying houses. He had hoped to find a spot to hide in the various dead-end alleyways that ran up to the Van Ness robot lanes. Unfortunately, now that they'd seen him, hiding here was out of the question.

He cursed himself and his esophyxia. If he'd just taken a few more steps to hide the bike and jump into the corridor along the fence earlier, the caretakers might not have seen him.

Beyond the fence, and down the steep ramp on his left, the robots moved earnestly forward in their tracks along the lanes, unconcerned with his plight. Some were transportation drones that looked like boxy modified railcars, others were more humanoid in appearance, carrying customized equipment they could self-transport after reaching the end of the lanes.

There were intermittent holes in the fence. Troubled youths would often play a sort of Russian roulette by running across the robot lanes at night, gaining access via these holes. Sure there were cameras, but usually the kids wore masks. Caretakers never did anything about it because running across the lanes, in itself, did nothing to halt the perpetual progress of the robots, even if occasionally a tragic accident occurred. There was also an element of self-policing. When a youth would get caught up in the tracks and mangled it would be highly publicized. Lane-crossing incidents would reduce for a while afterward.

Michaelis had thought about the possibility of having to cross the lanes, even as he'd turned on Lombard. Now that hiding was out of the question, he had no choice.

With this realization, he boldly jumped through the next fence hole, sliding down the sloped wall to the tracks. He had to immediately roll out of the way to avoid a humanoid robot rushing at him at thirty miles an hour on the lane closest to the fence.

His jacket was caught up in the sharp metallic belt of the second lane. With some force he tore himself off and stood up, leaving a rip in the material of his jacket. Now he was facing down another robot, this one shaped more like a bulldozer. There was also a large boxy railcar robot that had just passed by him in the third lane. That could be his ticket.

With every ounce of effort, he ran away from the bulldozer bot bearing down on him and toward the slower moving railcar heading in the opposite direction. He had to stare at his feet to ensure he was running on solid components of the tracks and not on the sharp, moving elements. After barely looking up, he snagged a handhold on the railcar and held on. His feet dragged painfully under him as he tried to pull himself up. The skin on his ankle was gashed open by a jagged edge of one of the tracks. Eventually, with another thrust of effort, he pulled himself onto the top of the car.

He sprawled out on the roof of the boxy transport, wheezing emphatically. He checked his lower legs; they were bloodied, but the cuts appeared to be superficial. Glancing back, he saw one of the Care-takers standing at the fence hole he'd used, staring at him, looking unsure of what to do. It was the Caretaker who'd first seen him at his house.

"Who says I'm not...cut out for this," Michaelis rasped from atop the railcar, leaving the caretaker behind. "Luisa...Tristan...eat your heart out."

A fit of coughing overtook him, but his pulse was slowing, his need for air reducing. He was going to recover.

Sonny Joseph ran down the fence line from the other direction. He had tried to circle around so they could corner Michaelis. He spotted him when the other caretaker pointed in his direction.

As the lanes went up the hill, Michaelis's line of sight with the care-takers was becoming obscured. Shortly before he lost his view of them entirely, he thought he saw Sonny strike the other caretaker, but it was hard to be sure.

The metal mass plodded onward, taking him out of sight, and giving him precious time to think. There was a place to hide just a few blocks up, if he could get to the other side of the lanes.

Once he'd gained enough distance from the caretakers, and the way across the lanes appeared safe, he jumped off the railcar and made a break for it. He ran the rest of the way across the lanes and scaled the canyon wall, scrambling through another fence hole to safety.

CHAPTER 42

Sonny was fuming. He had to restrain himself from throwing Franz onto the robot lanes. Instead he settled for a relatively benign scoffing on the head. Franz deserved way worse, but right now he needed all the help he could get, however incompetent.

Sonny immediately called in a description of Michaelis and put out an Urgent Apprehension Request.

He wasn't confident they would catch him. Michaelis could get off the robot lanes anywhere along the line, and the search radius was probably too wide to find him easily. They could reduce the radius if they found the right security camera footage, but that would take hours.

Two caretaker teams acknowledged his request and went to look up and down the lanes on either side. Maybe they would turn up something.

He also requested help from two other caretaker agents to go back to the house. He hoped Michaelis's roommate hadn't fled.

He walked stiffly back along the fence to his enercycle, fired it up, and regrouped with Franz on the way back to the house.

Even though they had lost Michaelis, it did prove Sonny was onto something. Hopefully when he unraveled the whole thing, Sonny would stop being patronized by the other caretakers for his "methods."

Building his army of informants had been a long process. Rather than prosecute a bunch of misdemeanors, he tracked down the perpetrators and blackmailed them with harsh penalties for their illicit activities. One of these Outworlders was involved in black-market deals, so Sonny threatened him with the prospect of a jail sentence that included Tyband disposal if he didn't give him something better. The man was wide-eyed and afraid. He told Sonny about Peter Hastings, and he even proceeded to track him down and deliver him.

Hastings was a big find—one of the most significant failures of caretaker security in San Francisco history—but Sonny had a feeling Hastings would also be a great source for new leads. So he pushed him and pushed him. He used barbiturates and pain agents to get him to talk. Yes, he might have been a bit overeager, and he took him too far on one of his interrogations, but the guy was on his last legs anyway. Anyone stupid enough to leave the Inworld had it coming.

He had thought Flippy Broderick would have been fine with Hastings dying, even happy. Broderick wouldn't care about his methods, as long as he made progress and gave him some real criminals. But Sonny had been wrong. Broderick had wanted to make an example of Hastings by having him publicly executed, rather than dying in an interrogation. So after being on the receiving end of a barrage of expletives and insults, Sonny promised the leads he generated would result in an even better story for the Inworld public relations department.

At the time he wasn't sure he'd be able to deliver on his promise. Hastings was remarkably strong, perhaps because as a drunk he was less sensitive to the drugs Sonny was using. It wasn't until days after Hastings died that Sonny's brain teased something out of it.

There was one thing Hastings had said that stuck with him. After hours of pain treatments, he started getting testy, and, in a fit of stammering rage, he had lashed out, "Fuck you, caretaker. You better watch your back in the arena. I bet your little flunkies are going to be the death of you."

He was babbling about many things at the time, so Sonny

thought it was just more defiant incoherence, but later he would think more about what he said. Peter was no longer a Ket gamer; that much was clear. So how did he know about Sonny spending time in the arena? And his "flunkies?" Had Peter been watching him? It seemed strange.

Then he remembered the spectacled Outworlder from that day outside his basement office. He had no place being there, and his physique wasn't that of a game player. It would be nearly impossible to get lost that deep in the arena, so there was a good chance he'd been following Sonny or one of his recruits.

So he'd put his army of minions to work, collecting security footage in the arena, and asking around. Eventually Sonny had identified and profiled the little snoop—Michaelis Dejong. He even found he had a record of illegal computer hacking, and was on the list Maiyor had originally given him.

The two backup caretakers had arrived at Michaelis's place already. These were veterans, but Sonny already outranked them. They sneered at him and Franz as they entered the front room. Sonny wasn't that important, sure, but Flippy Broderick was, and Broderick would penalize them if they disobeyed him. They were watching vids while guarding Michaelis's roommate, Hector. Sonny motioned for Franz and the other two caretakers to search Michaelis's room while he watched Hector.

Sonny pulled a chair up in front of the vids screen, directly across from Hector. For now, he just stared him down.

After a good minute, Sonny looked at the time on his comlink. The game would be beginning in fifteen minutes, and he'd been hoping to watch, but this was too important. It was annoying.

Hector was fidgeting nervously. "You're Sonny Joseph, right? Your team won NSF last year."

Sonny ended the fawning before it went any further. "Shut up until we ask you to speak," he said.

Sonny stared at him again. Hector looked down uncomfortably.

Eventually, the three musketeers came back down the hallway from Michaelis's room. They had a number of files and a sizeable backpack, all of which they placed on the table in front of Sonny. Franz looked proud of himself.

"What's in the bag?" Sonny asked nobody in particular. He began scrolling through the files. The other caretakers carefully pulled out the backpack contents.

Most of the files were old school papers and technical articles. One of the files, however, was interesting. It had what looked like contacts, transactions, and news clippings relating to a number of illegal black market activities. Many of the transactions were linked to someone named Chooly Fantonesta. Jackpot.

The backpacks contained a number of gel packs of different colors and what looked like some form of wicking mechanism. Explosives? There was also a mini-assault rifle tucked away, in addition to some ammunition and computer flash drives.

At first Sonny was ecstatic, as it validated his intuition that Michaelis was up to something, but then he quickly grew concerned. This was well beyond anything he'd envisioned. The stuff was all contraband, and who knew what was on the flash drives. He knew there had to be organized illegal activity going on in the Outworld, but he hardly expected to find it this easily, and especially not in some chubby teenager's room.

Explosives and guns? He made a mental note to be more careful. Even caretakers didn't even have access to these kinds of weapons. They mostly used shockers to incapacitate any Outworlders and were only given guns only during emergencies.

Sonny held his head in his hands and rubbed his temples. When he glanced up again at Hector, the poor Outworlder looked as if he was about to weep. He was sweating profusely and his eyes were darting between the backpack contents and the faces of the caretakers.

"You can start talking," Sonny said.

It came out in a torrent. "I had no idea those were in his room. I don't even know Michaelis well, you've got to believe me. I'll tell you everything. I haven't done anything wrong!"

Sonny wasn't really listening. Hector clearly didn't know about the stuff in Michaelis's room. If he did, he wouldn't have stuck around when they chased after Michaelis.

"Who is Michaelis working with?" Sonny asked.

"I—I really don't know. This is all so crazy." Hector was shaking his head.

Sonny stood and grabbed the mini-assault rifle. He made a sideways nodding motion toward Hector. His musketeers thankfully got the hint to come over and restrain him.

"What are you doing? I don't know—"

Sonny turned the gun around, and with the butt, smashed Hector in the face. A bloody tooth jettisoned from his mouth, and a fresh gash oozed blood from his right cheek.

Hector grimaced in pain and held his jaw. At least he wasn't crying, yet.

"Are you ready to answer my question?" Sonny asked.

Hector spat a wad of bloody saliva into his hand. "He...he's been busy and secretive lately, going out on his bike, working on his computer, or going to the computer lab. He hangs out with his friend Luisa a lot. Otherwise, he sticks to himself."

"Luisa who?"

"Luisa Vincent. I think that's her last name. They're old school friends or something. I met her once—"

"You can shut up again."

Sonny needed to think. Of course he knew Luisa. She had a real shot at making the Inworld, so why would she mess with this Michaelis guy? She was even in the first Outworlder game to be held in the dome today, an opportunity of a lifetime...

Sonny's skin crawled. He glanced at the assault rifle and explosives again. Something was rotten here; something was very wrong.

Sonny stood up and made for the door. "See what else you can find," he said to the other caretakers. "I'm going to the Parkdome."

He looked at the news feed on his comlink. The game was about to begin.

CHAPTER 43

Tristan watched the dozens of hovering vid cams panning the arena. They swiveled and spun on numerous planes, enabling the complex cross-camera coordination required for 3D hollowvision viewing.

Ardrey and the Phaser Frenzy team captain were being escorted out, presumably for pre-game comments with the media. As Ardrey walked away he looked back at the team. His gaze persisted to the extent he was craning his neck awkwardly until he was out of sight.

Did he suspect something? He was truly an enigma.

Tristan tried to focus on the game plan; not the Shock Hawk game plan, the other one. But he found it difficult. A feeling of nervous anticipation built reflexively with the roar of the spectators. Luisa seemed to be caught up in the moment as well.

He looked up at the clock. The game was supposed to begin in ten minutes.

He closed his eyes to shut out the noise, forcing himself to go back through it one more time.

The first phase would begin immediately after the game. Tristan and Luisa would break off from their caretaker escorts and make it to the south dome wall. There was supposed to be a gathering in the arena atrium, and they hoped that during the celebration they could sneak away, or at least get a head start. Judging by how complacent security had been so far, Tristan was hopeful it would work.

Once they reached the south wall, they were to find the locations where Michaelis had said they should plant the biogel explosives. Former attacks directed at the dome wall exterior had failed because there was a force field created by structural columns along the walls of the inner dome. This force field would magnify the strength of the polystyrix material. Unless they took out at least two of these columns, it would be impossible to penetrate the shell from the outside.

Once Luisa and Tristan's bombs disabled the force field, the OPM's rocket launchers would help expand the hole in the wall between the columns and they would enter the dome.

If they accomplished this first phase, Tristan would be satisfied. Depending on their level of success, they would have to make a decision on whether or not to go to the next phase, which was more of a long shot.

With the help of the OPM forces, they would find their way to the caretaker control hub to disable the citywide electronic firewall on communications, so Michaelis's message could be sent out to all of San Francisco.

With the symbolism of blowing a hole in the dome wall, combined with this message, they might be able to convince the people of San Francisco that they didn't have to live under Inworld authority. Anyone who read the message would be forever seeded with doubt about the Inworld and its place in society, and that seed would grow to something bigger over time.

It was so far out of the realm of contemplation for the caretakers that it just might work.

But his heart thumped in his chest, unrestrained by his platitudes. Whatever their success, he would probably die or be caught by the caretakers in a matter of hours.

Ardrey returned to the bench. He reiterated the Shock Hawk strategy. They all nodded absentmindedly.

There was less than a minute left on the clock. Tristan took a deep breath, stood up from the bench, and made his way to his position.

☢ ☢ ☢

Neither team made any ambitious maneuvers at first. Tristan took the odd shot at the Phaser Frenzy from his cover position.

The acoustics were different than he was used to. Each Ket pulse was louder. The plexmold, if that's what it was, would glow ominously when hit by stray shots.

The Frenzy began moving up. First, they tried to assault the Shock Hawk's right flank. They were trying to assert a numbers advantage on the four Hawks located in that vicinity.

Tristan saw an opportunity to pick off one of the advancing Frenzy players. He could make his way to another cover block and put his target in a precarious position. This might help equalize the numbers disadvantage the Frenzy were trying to create.

He fired several times above his cover block and made his move.

"Tristan, hold." It was Ardrey with a tightbeam comlink message to him.

Tristan retreated to his initial cover position. What was Ardrey thinking? The right flank was surely going to get slaughtered.

Tristan fired a few shots to try to slow the Frenzy advance, but held his position.

Ardrey messaged him via tightbeam again. "Coming in on your left."

Did Ardrey want to double-team the Frenzy surge? It seemed a risky maneuver just to make it to Tristan's position. But Ardrey was the captain, and a damn good one at that, so Tristan didn't question his orders.

Tristan poked his head up and gave a blast of covering fire as Ardrey ran to his position.

Ardrey sat down, looking away from the action, as if disengaged from the battle. Tristan was still taking the occasional shot to try to slow the Frenzy.

"Aren't we going to try to contain the surge on our right flank?" Tristan asked.

"No," Ardrey answered. He patted his hand on the ground beside him.

Tristan made his way over while staying low. Ardrey was taking off his headset, which would disconnect him from the rest of the team. He was signaling for Tristan to take off his own headset. *This was not normal.*

Tristan's heart skipped a beat.

"Tristan, listen to me," Ardrey yelled over the noise of the arena. "I know about you, Luisa, and Michaelis."

Tristan was crouching in front of Ardrey, but he staggered backward after hearing Ardrey's words. He lost his balance and fell on his behind. Ardrey continued to yell, even more loudly. "I know you're planning something. Don't do it."

Tristan slid further away by forcefully digging his heels into the floor.

Ardrey was becoming harder to hear over the roar of the arena crowd. He leaned forward, but not enough to expose himself to Ket pulse fire the way Tristan was doing. "Tristan, listen to me—"

Phaser Frenzy had found Tristan's blatantly open position and a flurry of Ket pulses danced around him. He continued to backpedal. Thinking fast, he got to his feet and bounded forward.

Below he could see Ardrey shaking his head, yelling to him unintelligibly as Tristan's arc rose above him.

His trajectory was chosen completely at random, so Tristan was lucky he didn't jump into certain elimination. He ended up landing in the upper left side—an area where there was little action. The Frenzy had already advanced well out of the vicinity, so Tristan posed no real threat. A few stray shots went past, but most of the Frenzy ignored him as they correctly deduced his action was of no real consequence.

The spectators must have been scratching their heads.

He ran for cover and took stock of the situation. How did Ardrey know? Had he told the caretakers? Any way he saw it, there was no way Ardrey would let them pull it off. He was on the cusp of his certain entry into the Inworld, so better to have them found out than be perceived as an accomplice.

Fuck. Fuck, fuck, fuck.

Tristan would have to find Luisa, explain the situation, then bolt for the arena doors.

He was about to direct a tightbeam communication to Luisa when he realized he hadn't reattached his headgear. He tethered his ear bud and cheek mic around his ear and refastened his mask over top.

A stream of communications inundated him.

"I've got four on me; Ella and Quince are down." It was Jared on the right flank.

"Hold your position. Right flank is lost. Sorry, Jared. Marty, Danil, rotate one block left to get a better angle on the right flank assault." It was Vernon, second in command. Was Ardrey down?

There was a pause.

"Damn it, Tristan, what are you doing over there? Answer me!" It was Vernon again.

Tristan ignored him and sent a tightbeam communication to Luisa. "Luisa, what's your location?"

"Tristan, what the hell are you doing? Are you going to help us or what?"

"I need you to meet me at the middle-left, near the exit, for a strategic maneuver," Tristan responded. Hopefully, she got the hint. Gamers never referred to the arena exits in these communications because every arena had different exit points, making it disorienting.

"Dammit, we're down to five, and I need to help Vernon hold the line," she responded.

Tristan tried again. He sent her another tightbeam, talking slowly, trying to take her out of the frenetic mindset of the game. "This is more important, Luisa. There's been a change in plan." The vids would be recording all this, but Tristan was sure it was inconspicuous enough.

"Oh. Okay. Middle-left?" There was a pause. "I'll try. I may not make it."

"See you there."

Tristan bounded up again from his position toward the middle-left exit. He could see the full scope of the battle below him. It didn't look good for the Shock Hawks. He counted eight Frenzy against five Hawks, and excluding Tristan and Luisa, it was more like eight against three.

There wasn't much time.

Some Phaser Frenzy players surely saw Tristan's bound, but no one fired at him. He was still outside reasonable range. And they must have thought he had completely lost it. He could imagine the spectators debating his actions. "I told you he was crazy. Sure, he had a good game in the NSF playoffs, but his erratic play was bound to be a liability eventually." This would certainly fuel the naysayers about him. He would be blacklisted forever.

He gritted his teeth. None of that mattered anymore.

As he descended from his bound, he saw Luisa rise from her location at the bottom left among concentrated bursts of Ket pulse fire. Whereas Tristan was removed from the action, Luisa was in the heart of it. A flurry of Frenzy fire followed her up and tracked the progress of her arc. She was an easy target, taken out almost immediately on the beginning of her upward movement. The angle of the Ket fire returned to more planar targets.

He heard Vernon on the comlink, "Luisa, what are you—" At that point, Tristan decided to remove his headset. Luisa could no longer communicate via her comlink, so there was no point in staying online to hear Vernon's complaints.

Luisa landed short of Tristan by about thirty feet. The last component of her Ketrix pack shut down after the bounding safety interrupt had finished. Her teal collar and waist lights extinguished.

He ran over to her as she removed her powerless headset.

She looked at him sheepishly. "This better be good," she said.

"Ardrey knows about us. He told me. We need to get out of the arena as soon as possible."

Her eyes widened and darted back and forth. "We'll have to make a run for it when they collect us after the match."

"No, we need to leave now," he said. "Ardrey could rat us out at any moment."

"Now? How do we—"

"I have an idea. Pretend you're injured and follow me."

Typically when players were eliminated they stayed in the arena, lying where they were last shot until the end of the match. On rare occasions, when someone was injured badly, they would be let out of the match early.

Luisa was considering his idea. It looked like she agreed because her leg suddenly buckled under her. She arched her back to hold the leg melodramatically.

He supported her and they hobbled to the side exit together. It was a plexmold sliding door with about twenty feet of clearance. Two caretakers stood behind it, next to the door controls. These caretakers watched them with no small amount of disgust. There was no respect for compassion in the Ket games, so leaving before the end of the match was seen as weak, whether you were injured or not.

Tristan made a revolving motion with his hand so they would open the door, as if they didn't get it.

After a pause, the caretakers grudgingly pressed a button on a side panel and stood waiting as the door slid open. Tristan pretended to have trouble moving Luisa's weight.

Luisa was getting nervous. She whispered through her mock wincing, "Maybe you should have told me what the plan was, or do you really have one?"

The two caretakers were impatient and wanted to get the door closed as soon as possible. It drove them to move through the threshold into the arena to grab Tristan and Luisa.

Which was the moment Tristan had been waiting for. He locked his arms around Luisa and bounded. His objective was to jump over the caretakers, through the gap above their heads into the exit corridor. If he timed it well and used just the right amount of effort, he would clear the caretakers while not hitting the top plexmold. Tristan and Luisa would then be projected into the corridor by the force of the bounding jump.

It was risky because he knew the Ketrix mobility field would be cut as soon as he passed the plexmold threshold, but he hoped the momentum would be enough for them to at least get past the caretakers.

It didn't work out as planned.

Tristan had never jumped while holding onto another player, and he overcompensated badly. He went up at too high of an angle, and both their torsos slammed into the plexmold above the door, which made him release his grasp on Luisa. She fell fast, while he was lowered more mercifully, still supported by the bounding safety interrupt. Luisa ended up landing right on top of one of the caretakers, breaking her fall and getting tangled up with him.

As Tristan descended he carefully timed a roundhouse kick to the face of the other caretaker, who was surprised by the turn of events. The kick knocked the caretaker down. Upon landing, Tristan grabbed Luisa's arm, forcefully extracted her from the messy heap she was in, and ran beyond the two discombobulated caretakers.

They entered a large gantry way used by bottom-level spectators. Tristan continued to hold Luisa by the arm and cut to the right, accelerating into a sprint. There was a lift at the end of the hall that would bring them up to the level that led to the Theater chamber.

Inworlders gawked at them and shrank away as they rushed past.

When they were still a good hundred feet from the elevators, a torrent of blue and gold uniforms flowed out of the adjoining corridor ahead of them, blocking their progress to the lifts. Tristan and Luisa skidded to a stop. Behind them, some two hundred feet away, more blue and gold uniforms were emerging from entry points on the gantry way. Tristan looked at Luisa for help. She also froze, indecisive.

Suddenly a pulse of energy wracked Tristan's body. He doubled over and fell down. His body shook in agony.

The next few moments were hazy. He captured only brief glimpses of the scene as he writhed on the ground. Luisa had joined him on the hard floor, succumbing to similar convulsions. Flashes of gold and blue surrounded him. Eventually the shock waves left him, and his captors scooped up his inert body.

His heart sank at the realization of his capture, and his head pounded with the aftereffects of the shocker pulses.

He was coherent enough to know two burly caretakers were pulling him forward, with his feet dragging behind him. He managed to lift his head up enough to peer at the collection of blue and gold uniforms attending to the scene. Even through his shrouded senses, he could see among them the contrast of a black and teal Shock Hawk uniform. It was an all-too familiar figure. He was nodding to another caretaker as they discussed his fate as casually as they might be discussing the weather.

In a burst of rage, Tristan struggled against his captors. He briefly escaped their grip and launched himself at Ardrey, but the shocker had sapped his strength. He only made it a few feet before they stunned him one more time, and then subdued him.

He was wracked by pain and confusion as they lifted him away from the scene. His head bobbed until he could no longer keep it up. All his energy, all his remaining stamina, fled from his body, and he lost consciousness.

CHAPTER 44

Michaelis crawled out of the back alley trash pile, trying to shake off a smelly piece of synth-crab patty packaging stuck to his back. He'd only spent several minutes in his hiding place before thinking better of it. There was too much to do, and it would be better if he distanced himself from the robot lanes.

His next stop was a clothing store a block away. It was a quaint little shop for trendy customers, or at least anyone with some sort of fashion sense. Luisa might have frequented this store from time to time, but certainly not Michaelis.

He splurged on a new outfit: tight red khaki pants with a yellow hoodie made out of thin windbreaker-type material. It was hardly appropriate for inciting a rebellion, but it would have to do as a disguise. Plus, it was better than smelling like garbage.

He cautiously left the store and made his way over the robot lanes via a bridge sufficiently distant from where he'd come through the fence. There was no sign of caretakers. He was hopeful they didn't know where he'd exited the lanes.

There were more people about in the streets on the west side of the lanes. People were tending to their errands or other business on a Saturday. He felt like he must be blending in.

It didn't offer him much consolation.

The caretakers might know everything. If they didn't, it was simply a race against time. They would find his records, the assault rifle, and the explosives, and they would launch a thorough investigation. If they tied him to Luisa and Tristan, it could be disastrous. His flash drives were heavily encrypted, but they might be able to crack it with Inworld hackers and supercomputers. Then there would be no chance of ever sending any message to the people of San Francisco. They would be able to immediately block the malware worm he'd developed.

He quickly proceeded toward the computer lab, hoping to collect the backup flash drives he'd stashed in his locker. Since he'd used an alias for his logins, he doubted the caretakers would be looking for him there.

This particular lab was in the newly minted trade school building in Parnassus. Composed of ugly, blocky buildings, the school looked sterile and institutional. There were only two people inside the lab, and the caretaker monitor was heavily engrossed in his own terminal, ignoring Michaelis altogether. Michaelis grabbed the flash drive from his locker and made a swift exit.

The time he'd spent making a duplicate copy had actually paid off.

He walked downhill toward the rendezvous point, which was a decaying house with a large basement garage. One street farther down was the Parkdome wall, just outside where Tristan and Luisa were supposed to plant the biogel bombs.

He looked at the time on his handheld comlink. The explosions were due to occur in thirty minutes. It also meant he was now a good twenty minutes late. He hoped the OPM hadn't gotten cold feet.

The street was eerily quiet as he walked up the house steps and rang the bell.

After a minute, John opened the door. "You're late," he said.

Michaelis expected him to be angry, but instead he sounded nervous. "Yes, something unexpected came up." Michaelis decided not to elaborate. No sense inciting any more trepidation than necessary.

John's eyebrows arched.

"We don't have much time," Michaelis said. "Can you take me through the plan again?"

John didn't push his curiosity. "Yes, of course. Come with me."

Michaelis was introduced to nine nervous-looking OPM "militia" men sitting around the living room and brandishing a variety of equipment and weaponry. They were a ragtag group with little experience, who were limping, swearing, and scratching themselves in inappropriate places.

John escorted him to the garage, where Michaelis was pleased to see an impressive array of weaponry. They had jury-rigged two jeeps with what looked like machine guns. They also had a number of rocket launchers lined up on the floor with stacks of rockets. It all looked antiquated, but John assured Michaelis that everything worked.

"We have two other OPM cells ready," John explained. "One down the street and another on the north side of the dome. Once we hear the dome wall explosions, we'll be able to start moving in the heavy artillery."

John glared at Michaelis, looking for some kind of affirmation. It felt strange that their plan was so dependent on Michaelis and his friends, and a far cry from their original encounter in the woods when they were treated as second-class citizens.

Michaelis nodded. "Good. That's good," he confirmed.

As John went through more aspects of the plan, Michaelis partially tuned out. He'd heard it before, and his thoughts had moved to his friends. A growing sense of guilt and concern took hold, knowing they might be in jeopardy.

John led Michaelis up an old wooden staircase to the second floor. There they found Sergeant Noah, who was in charge of the squad getting ready downstairs. According to John, Noah was the only one who had real combat experience. He'd been involved in supporting the Inworld to put down Outworld riots in Arizona before he realized he was fighting for the wrong side. Michaelis had never heard anything about these riots, but it sounded like the kind of thing the Inworld would have kept under wraps.

Noah was glancing back and forth between a map laid out in front of him and the vids. John and Michaelis sat across from him.

There wasn't much to do but wait, so they sat quietly for a while. They were to formally prepare for action in ten minutes.

The empty time weighed on Michaelis, and he realized he owed it to the OPM to inform them of his near-capture. They had put their lives at risk, just like he did.

Michaelis tried to keep his voice firm. "There's something you should know. There were caretakers at my apartment this morning. They chased me and I escaped, but they must have found my backpack, which had explosives and flash drives. There was nothing that could tie me to you, but I'm not sure why they were there."

Noah just shrugged it off, but John looked flustered. He began pacing around the room until he stopped and asked the obvious question. "Should we abort?"

Michaelis said, "There's no sign that Tristan and Luisa have been compromised, and I never told anyone about our rendezvous point. Let's just wait it out."

John continued to pace. "It doesn't sound good. How do we know for sure your friends aren't compromised?"

Noah was shaking his head.

John noticed. "What is it Noah?"

"You guys are too smart for me. I'm glad I am not in charge of these big decisions. I'd rather just watch the Ket games."

Michaelis and John both ignored the sarcasm and stepped in front of the vids screen. "How are they doing?" Michaelis asked.

"I hope your friends are better at planting bombs than playing Ket."

The game was wrapping up. On the screen, Tristan was holding onto Luisa, who appeared injured, and he tried to launch the two of them out of the arena with an ill-conceived bounding maneuver. After a struggle, they made it out of the arena.

One of the commentators was focusing in on the event. "This is unheard of," he said. "They will be apprehended, I assure you."

It wasn't part of the plan. Something was wrong. Michaelis wiped away the beads of perspiration forming on his forehead.

The vids began playing the event at the arena entrance over and over again, and Michaelis could feel Noah and John's eyes boring into him.

He held still, not meeting their gaze.

Noah seemed to tire of staring him down. He said, "Either way, let's get ready. If something doesn't happen soon, it won't ever happen."

They descended the stairs down to the garage and joined the other militia. The nine OPMers were nervous, fidgeting with their weapons.

Their edginess did nothing to calm Michaelis's already-frayed nerves.

CHAPTER 45

Luisa never quite lost her senses. She'd been stunned only once, whereas Tristan had been stunned multiple times. She might have preferred that. It would have been better than experiencing the pounding headache that followed the shocker hit, and the bruising manhandling of her captors.

She was stripped of her uniform, including the biogel explosives, dressed in what looked like hospital garb, and thrust into a room with four chairs and a small table. Tristan, now awake, was pulled into the room shortly afterward. The caretakers just threw him onto the table and closed the door behind them. He was unable to remain in rigid form, so he slid off the table and landed on the floor, barely putting his hands out to catch his fall before his face hit.

He forced himself to crawl to the wall while breathing heavily, and tucked his legs under him into a sitting position.

"Are you okay?" Luisa asked.

"I think so." His voice sounded raspy.

"Any idea how to get out of this?" she asked.

He just shrugged. He was still recuperating.

A blanket of despair began to envelop her. It looked like they were done for, to be executed after who knows what kind of torture. She had expected this day would come, but she'd hoped it wouldn't be for nothing.

She wondered if Michaelis could still try to make something happen with the OPM rebels—maybe figure out another way to send their message to the people. But it seemed just as hopeless. Michaelis's hacking wouldn't be any match for the Inworlder firewall. He'd said numerous times it would likely fall flat, the communication halted at the first server it reached, unless they could shut down the network security firewall from the inside. Besides, now that they'd captured Tristan and Luisa, the defense systems would be on higher alert, eliminating any advantage of surprise.

No message would get through, and anything that did would have little impact because they hadn't set off the explosives. There was no chink in the Inworld armor for them to expose.

Such was her mindset as she was sitting there, forlornly reviewing their situation, when Sonny Joseph entered the room.

"Oh my," he said. "What a sad little pair you make."

Luisa crossed her arms, glaring. Tristan could barely glance up at Sonny, but his jaw was clenched.

Sonny said, "You've made a lot of hard choices—bad choices—in your lives. You have to know your limits. Just because you can't make it to the Inworld doesn't mean you should lash out against it."

He came closer to her. "What's really sad, Luisa, is you could have made it. People kill for that opportunity, but you blew it with some misdirected sense of morality. What a waste."

Luisa continued to glare defiantly. Sonny turned to the hinged shape of Tristan against the wall.

"You're an even sadder case, Tristan. We beat you last year, fair and square. Your arm was broken, but just because *you* are broken doesn't mean the system is broken. You should have just accepted you might not be good enough, like all Outworlders do, eventually."

Tristan didn't react.

Sonny backed away from Tristan. "So why don't you give me your side of the story? I'm not going to tell you you'll get any kind of pardon...but maybe we'll be more *lenient*. And be careful. We already know about Michaelis, so if you feed us some BS, I will make sure you, *and* your families—" He smiled at Tristan. "—will be fully prosecuted."

He knew about Michaelis! Her heart sank even further.

Tristan's eyes widened, and his face became flushed. After what happened with his brother, it would be horrifying for him if his parents were caught up in this.

Sonny could see his words were having an effect. "Oh, yes, your parents will most certainly be impacted. What did you think? We have to make an example of you. But maybe, just maybe, we'll spare one of them."

Tristan forced himself up from the floor and stood on shaky legs. He lifted his head to face Sonny as if a twenty-pound weight was tied to it. Then to Luisa's amazement, he jumped at Sonny, landing a hard right hook.

Sonny fell to the back of the room, a flash of fear crossing his face. Tristan was about to advance again, but two caretakers quickly entered the room and restrained Tristan before he could move.

Sonny regrouped. He swiped at his cheek to check for blood, but found none. His menacing look returned. "Well, so much for leniency."

He was advancing on Tristan.

Luisa knew what was going to happen next. She stood up. "Sonny, wait. I can tell you what you want to know."

Sonny surprised Luisa with a knuckled backhand to her face. She fell over the table awkwardly.

Tristan had exposed weakness so Sonny needed to humiliate Tristan in return. "Restrain them," Sonny said without taking his eyes from Tristan. One of the caretakers already had a good hold on Tristan. The other went to hold Luisa down.

The minutes that followed were painful to watch. Sonny punched Tristan several times in the face and stomach. Tristan took it well, absorbing the blows without flinching, but his resolve was being eroded. Sonny didn't ask him any questions, nor did he give him any more ultimatums. He just wanted to see him in pain. Tristan might have mere minutes to live, rather than hours or days.

Sonny wrenched Tristan's index finger, twisting it so it extended grotesquely upward from his hand. Tristan cried out, no longer able to withstand the pain.

Sonny smiled with glee. "Now that's better. And we're just getting started..."

Sonny went in to grab another finger. The other caretakers turned their heads away, grimacing in disgust. Luisa also had to close her eyes.

The door opened.

There was another voice. "Mr. Joseph, sir. I have an urgent message from an Outworlder named Ardrey Percival."

Luisa opened her eyes. Sonny turned around, looking annoyed.

"Who is Ardrey Percival? Do you mean Ardrey Wren?"

The caretaker looked down at his notes. "N-no sir I believe he specifically said his name was Ardrey Percival, and he said I should tell you the message was from him. He was in the match today."

"That's Ardrey Wren, you idiot."

The caretaker looked unsure of himself. He shrugged deferentially to Sonny.

"Never mind. Why don't you tell him to give you the message?" Sonny turned back to Tristan.

But the caretaker didn't leave. "S...sir, he says it's urgent, and for your ears only. He wouldn't give it to me."

Sonny sighed and shook his head. "Okay. Tristan—" and he turned to her, "—and Luisa, we are far from finished. I look forward to returning soon."

Sonny wrung his hands and backed away to the door. "By the way, if this message from Ardrey is what I think it is, it looks like we may have rounded up the rest of your little gang of losers. Maybe we'll have a reunion? Doesn't that sound like fun?"

Their response was a hollow silence.

Sonny smiled and pointed to the caretakers restraining Luisa and Tristan. "You both come with me. I think Tristan may have shit himself, so you probably don't want to stick around." He grinned again and exited the room.

The other caretakers followed.

Luisa crawled over to Tristan and kneeled in front of him. She tried not to look at his distended finger. Blood matted the front of his hair, and the beginnings of a black crescent was forming under one of his eyes.

"Are you okay?"

"Yeah...yes, I think so." He was wincing in pain, while at the same time looking disoriented, frowning, and holding his head, as if in concentration.

"You might have a concussion. Do you think you have any ribs broken?"

"No, I'm fine Luisa. Let me think for a second."

He somehow managed to get on his feet again. He hobbled about the room, hunched over, oblivious to his gnarled finger.

"Think about what?"

"Just please...let me think," he answered. "Why?" Tristan asked the air in front of him.

"Okay," Luisa said, throwing up her hands. Tristan kept pacing. Occasionally he would vigorously rub his head, as if trying to scare off a pack of fleas.

"What's wrong with you?" Luisa asked. "I really think you may have a concussion or—"

"Just give me a minute." He held up a finger on his good hand.

Tristan was murmuring and nodding to the air in front of him.

"Son of a bitch. Son of a bitch."

Tristan was clearly delusional. Maybe she could convince Sonny to relent if it was clear that Tristan had a concussion. It might save Tristan for a few days, before the hanging, flogging, or whatever else was planned.

Tristan stopped pacing, backed to the wall, and slid down to sit beside her. He was still concentrating deeply, or at least trying to.

She realized, in those few minutes, that she feared losing Tristan. Her family was gone, and all she had left were Michaelis and Tristan. Michaelis had probably been caught, unless Sonny was lying. Tristan could be her last friend in the world.

Even Tristan might already be gone. He seemed broken, lost to self-delusion.

She didn't cry though. She had nothing left, not even tears. She had cried too many in her life, and she wouldn't give Sonny the satisfaction. Nothing mattered now except that.

Gradually Tristan became more subdued, murmuring every few minutes. Luisa focused on the clock. Every minute was another step toward their inevitable fate.

Oddly enough, the next time she looked at Tristan, a grin was spreading from one side of his battered face to the other.

"Don't worry, I didn't shit myself," he said.

He's completely lost it.

That's when the walls shook.

A second shockwave hit the room, jarring Luisa from her seat.

A deep rumble followed.

Tristan stood up, seemingly unperturbed by the incident. With almost surgical precision, he wrenched his distended finger back into place with his good hand.

He stared at the door with his fists clenched.

CHAPTER 46

Michaelis waited nervously. It had been thirty minutes since Luisa and Tristan had wrestled past the two caretakers and exited the arena. The faces of the OPM members were glancing his way with greater frequency.

John turned his back on the recruits and pulled Michaelis to the corner.

He spoke quietly. "On the vids they're talking about a security incident where some of the team members have been apprehended. Maybe we should abort?"

"A *security incident* doesn't mean Luisa and Tristan have been caught. We knew they might have to modify the plan as they go."

John looked doubtful, but nodded. He wasn't willing to push the issue, yet.

They stood there, waiting uncomfortably. The air was thick with tension.

"I'm going to see if the vids will give us more information," Michaelis said. He climbed the stairs without waiting for an acknowledgement.

Michaelis was hoping to get away from the probing eyes of the

OPM soldiers, but when he entered the room Noah was still there, watching the postgame show.

Michaelis asked, "Anything new?"

"No. Any idea what I should be looking for?"

Noah was sitting cross-legged and aloof, like it was any other day. Michaelis touched the rough welding of his glasses. It was the only thing that gave him comfort. "No," he said, "the plan has changed, I'm sure. I was wondering if they described the security incident in more detail."

"Nope," Noah said.

Michaelis turned his attention to the vids. The commentators were asking team members pointed questions about the Shock Hawks falling apart.

Nobody seemed to have a good answer, so they showed the pregame interviews of Ardrey and the Phaser Frenzy captain again. It wasn't entertaining, or enlightening. The program was coming to an end. Michaelis changed the channels, searching in vain for more information.

"I doubt you'll find anything else," Noah said. Michaelis continued to search. He returned to the original channel, and a series of ads began.

The ads only amplified the uncomfortable atmosphere in the room. It was worse than silence, as Noah would glance over at Michaelis, as if expecting to glean information based on Michaelis's reaction to the meaningless commercials. Michaelis kept his face devoid of emotion. It was like when he had been in trouble in Hex Strategem. You can't let them see you sweat, or they all turn on you like sharks sensing blood in the water.

Michaelis was grateful to hear someone running up the stairs. One of the scouts entered the room.

"Sir, there's been some kind of—what sounds like—an explosion. But it was from the dome interior, not the wall. John said we should move."

Michaelis was surprised, but maintained his composure. "Yes, right. They're probably on their way to the wall now. I'll be right down."

He paused and addressed Noah before he walked to the stairs. "Are you coming?"

CHAPTER 47

Tristan had been in a haze since waking up. His head pounded, and aches emanated from every precinct of his body.

The beating by Sonny had been surreal. He tried to maintain his dignity, but he knew he'd lost control as the barrage overwhelmed him.

There was a break in the clouds when Sonny stopped his onslaught. What Sonny said before he left the room stayed with him, perhaps because it was so strange.

Why did the caretaker give Ardrey the name Ardrey Percival instead of Ardrey Wren?

The fog descended on him again after Sonny left, and his tortured body tried to regroup, but he kept this thought with him. It nagged him. It chased after his flagging attention. He searched for associations. Why would the caretaker give Sonny another name? Or did the caretaker have it right, and Ardrey did, in fact, give him that name? It seemed such a random occurrence, yet too specific to be dismissed as a simple clerical error.

He realized it was the name Percival itself that was bothering him, more than the odd discourse between Sonny and the other caretaker. It sounded familiar. He searched the interstices of his mind, leaving no stone unturned, cutting through the fog by sheer force of will.

The image that came to him was an electronic stencil of the name Julia Percival, hovering in the air. It was followed by stencils of the names Henry Percival, Ryan Percival, Javier Yammin, and a blurred image of another name. The scene resolved itself. It was Union Square, nine years ago. The names of those individuals were listed on the hollowvision screen for all to see. Sound came through to him as the caretaker announcer listed crimes against the Inworld.

Could Ardrey actually be the Percival boy Peter Hastings had told him about—the one named Zachary Percival who lost his parents that day in Union Square?

As soon as the thought hit him, skepticism also surfaced. This was the same Ardrey who had broken Tristan's arm and stolen his strategic plans. No way. And Peter had said the boy died—a freak accident on the robot lanes.

So it couldn't be him. No way.

But perhaps out of delirium, or perhaps out of desperation, Tristan allowed himself to consider the possibility.

Another shockwave hit him. If Ardrey was Zachary Percival, could he have the Inworld data finger they were looking for?

He murmured aloud, forcing himself to think. More archives were opening in his mind as the fog abated. His reviving synapses delivered new information.

The Zachary boy was dead. Peter said so. But then, if Ardrey had the data finger, was it possible he'd used it to fake the death report? Peter did say he didn't know where the report came from, and it *was* missing some caretaker protocol information.

"Son of a bitch," he whispered. It seemed so implausible.

Could the security camera in the cabin up in Treble have been Ardrey's custom security camera, watching for intruders? Could he have seen Michaelis that day? If he did, and he was against the Inworld, why wouldn't he join them?

He paced around the room as Luisa looked on with an air of incredulity.

Maybe Ardrey thought it would be too risky? Why not watch them, follow them, and see how they fared without risking himself and the all-important data finger?

Okay, fine, but why would he associate with Sonny Joseph? Was it possible Ardrey's contact with Sonny could have been a way of tracking what the caretakers were thinking? Know thy enemy?

It was possible. Tristan's pulse quickened.

But then, why risk letting Luisa and Tristan join his team? Tristan and Luisa would help him get in by being on a winning team...and maybe he needed to have allies on the inside?

Tristan's heart was pounding erratically. "Son of a bitch," he said again.

He sat down against the wall again.

It was a complicated hypothesis, but he couldn't deny the possibility. It was Ardrey—his nemesis, the bane of his existence—but any chance, however remote, was enough to keep him thinking. That's what Tristan needed, then and there, as he sat battered on the floor. He needed hope.

His abused gray matter eked out one more thought, or rather it was a familiar sensation. He'd the same feeling when Ardrey looked at him in pain when he broke his arm, as well as the time when Ardrey had taken the Ket pack off the Wired Warrior player in the NSF finals.

Tristan pushed himself to recall the boy from his dream—breaking from the crowd in Union Square, running toward the podium, screaming. Like the image of his brother hanging, the child wailing in Union Square was something he had tried to suppress. But now it came rushing back, and he could see the similarity with Ardrey. This was what finally convinced him. And if Ardrey was in fact that tortured boy, then what burned inside of Tristan burned inside of Ardrey, perhaps even brighter.

Tristan smiled with hope as the argument continued to gain traction. The blight that was Ardrey in his psyche was gradually, systematically taken down, piece by piece.

And maybe, just maybe, Tristan and Luisa were part of Ardrey's plan. Maybe that's what he was going to tell Tristan before he bounded away in the game. Maybe that was why Ardrey gave the caretaker the name Percival...

The audacity of these revelations made him giddy. It awakened him from his intense concentration, and he became aware of Luisa's presence next to him again.

"Don't worry, I didn't shit myself," he said, smiling. She stared back at him, looking concerned. He would have to convince her when they weren't being watched, but hopefully, if he was right, Ardrey would help.

Moments later, an explosion rocked the room. The well of hope inside Tristan grew. He stood up and wrenched his swollen finger back into place without flinching, his vigor restored by a flush of adrenaline. He didn't know what was in store next, but he was going to be ready for it.

CHAPTER 48

It took Sonny time to reach Ardrey. He was being held outside the command center several levels up and Sonny first had to navigate through a number of caretaker security people questioning him about the incident with Tristan and Luisa. An expletive-laden comlink message from Flippy Broderick was also requesting answers. He would need to send out a report soon.

A mass of Inworlders was leaving the arena and monopolizing the lifts. He had to wait his turn because most were the admin caretakers. Gold and blue had to defer to the black shirts—always.

Soon he'd be a black shirt as well.

Ardrey was waiting for Sonny on a balcony that overlooked the expanse of the Theater chamber. Two caretakers were standing guard next to him.

Sonny was curt. "This better be good. What is it?"

Ardrey glanced back and forth at the two caretaker guards. "I believe there's a bigger scheme at work here. Can I talk to you privately?"

Sonny took Ardrey's arm to walk to a more secluded area. "There isn't much time," Ardrey continued, "but I think I can get the names of the perpetrators if you let me interrogate Tristan and Luisa."

"Why do we need to talk privately? Do you think there might be caretakers involved?"

"I overheard Luisa and Tristan talking about 'help from caretakers after the game' in the locker room. I didn't think anything of it until after they were apprehended."

Sonny made sure Ardrey witnessed his skeptical frown. "And why do you need to interrogate them?" Sonny asked.

Ardrey looked down at his watch. "There isn't much time, and there are things I've heard or seen that I could reference in the interrogation —to get them to talk." Ardrey looked nervous. He was fidgeting, with his hands in his pockets. He was almost always closed to emotion. Something was certainly bothering him.

Sonny disengaged from the conversation and peered out over the expanse of the Theater chamber. It sounded a little weak, but he had no reason to disbelieve Ardrey. He was a lock for the Inworld, so he wouldn't do anything to screw up his chances.

Sonny had tried to obtain information from Ardrey in the past, but Ardrey hadn't given him any good leads. Now that they knew Luisa and Tristan were conspirators, he might have some valuable info. So yes, his story was plausible.

What worried Sonny wasn't that Ardrey would be a traitor, but that he would compete against him in his rise in the Inworld. Ardrey was cunning. When he did make it, Sonny wanted him on his side, or even better, under him, so he could use him. He would be a considerable asset.

Sonny turned back from the vista of the chamber to face Ardrey again. He spoke loudly enough for the other caretakers to hear. "You've got a lot of nerve making these requests, Outworlder. The only reason I'm not reprimanding you is because you may have useful information, and we're in a crisis situation."

Sonny pointed at the other caretakers. "You two, keep watch on him. I'll be back." He couldn't acquiesce to his request for an interrogation, especially in front of these other caretakers. Better to not give him any sense of equal footing. Besides, he liked doing the interrogation alone, and he was relishing getting back there as soon as possible.

Ardrey's face went blank, but he still fidgeted with his hands in his pockets. The other caretakers went to his side.

That's right, Sonny thought. *I'm the boss.* Sonny walked away from the trio back toward the lift.

That's when the explosion hit.

Sonny stumbled to the ground and looked back toward the balcony. From his vantage point, he could see a piece of debris fly up in a spiraling arc into the Theater chamber.

The two caretakers had grabbed hold of the balcony railing, first to steady themselves, then to help them lean over and look down toward the source of the explosion. Sonny joined them at the railing. A significant hole had been blown into the Theater chamber wall to the right of them. Flame-lit debris defiled the pristine chamber near the hole.

It had to be related to that sniveling loser Tristan and his crew.

He also realized what this meant for him—how it would change people's perceptions. A minute ago, Sonny was the hero who'd caught two conspirators, but now he might be blamed for this explosion. He needed to get to the bottom of this, and fast.

The first thing was to secure the area near the blast. He pointed to one of the caretaker guards and barked out an order. "You, come with me and arm your shocker."

Sonny paused in mid-stride. He would still need to continue the interrogation. His original attempt to put Ardrey in his place was over-ruled by this incident. Better to have him close by.

He pointed to the other caretaker. "You, take Ardrey down to the command center and wait for me there."

Sonny grabbed Ardrey by the collar. "But don't think you're getting in the interrogation room. You'll be lucky if you aren't detained for weeks just because you're here."

Ardrey stared back, wide-eyed. Sonny let him go.

The two duos took separate lifts, Ardrey and one caretaker to the command center, and Sonny with the other to the main terrace of the Theater chamber.

He looked over at the help. The caretaker with him was named

Marcus. He was the only one he'd seen who didn't look frazzled. He looked ready, and focused.

They can't all be useless.

CHAPTER 49

After the explosion Luisa had become tense, ready for a flurry of action, but since then she'd returned to a more relaxed sitting position on the floor. Tristan was still standing by the exit.

Eventually Tristan turned his ear toward the door as if listening for more sounds. She couldn't hear anything.

"Are we expecting someone?" Luisa asked, at her wits end.

Tristan turned to her, his finger to his lips.

She shrugged in defeat.

A few minutes later, the door opened. It was Ardrey, and he was alone.

Luisa braced herself for the inevitable conflict, but Tristan was just standing there, unsurprised by the presence of his long-time nemesis.

Ardrey had his hands up, and he looked nervous. "I hope you got the hint. We need to get out of here."

He had left the door open. This would be a perfect opportunity to try to escape. Maybe Tristan had the same thought.

Tristan didn't pounce, though. Instead he replied calmly, "I got the hint."

Ardrey looked relieved. "Okay. I need you outside. I've secured the control center, but there isn't much time. Things aren't going according to plan."

"Just one question," Tristan said. "Did you have to break my arm?"

Ardrey wrinkled his nose. "That was an accident," he said. "I needed to win so I was in a good position to get into the Inworld this year."

Tristan didn't look convinced.

"Listen," Ardrey continued, "if you hadn't triggered the alarm, I would have been able to take control of the whole city from the inside, instead of being in the precarious position we're in now. So what do you say we call it even?"

Tristan was unmoved.

Ardrey glanced at his comlink. "The explosion will only divert them for so long." He abruptly left the room, leaving the door ajar.

Tristan took a step forward to follow, but then looked back to Luisa and paused. "Listen Luisa, I know it's hard to believe, but Ardrey is with us."

"What? How can you, of all people, believe that? Didn't you see him with Sonny Joseph earlier? What's this hint you're talking about?"

"The name Percival—it's complicated. And yes, I know how it looks with Sonny Joseph, but I'm pretty sure it was all part of Ardrey's plan."

"What plan?" Luisa asked.

Tristan went back to holding his ahead again. "Look, Ardrey has the data finger, and he's on our side. We need to help him. You're going to have to trust me."

After a moment's hesitation, his sense of urgency got the best of him, and he darted out the door.

Her head was spinning. Now she knew why Tristan was acting so strangely. He had been trying to make sense of all this. She didn't have time to sift through it in her mind the way he did. She had to decide her allegiance right away.

Ultimately she had nothing to lose by leaving the room, though she was determined to stay cautious. It could still be some sort of ploy for her to give up Michaelis and the OPM.

She followed them out.

She'd known from her unpleasant journey here that they'd been kept in a locked office in the vicinity of the caretaker command center. The main hub of activity was just down a short corridor from where she'd just exited. She walked down the corridor in that direction.

Before the end of the hallway there was a closed door on the right from which she could hear muffled yelling, but she couldn't be sure. Perhaps this was where Ardrey had put any caretakers he'd overcome.

She continued into the command center.

The four caretakers whom she'd seen buzzing around were gone, replaced by just Tristan and Ardrey. On one side a monitor was smashed, looking like the result of some altercation. Tristan and Ardrey were in the midst of conversation while Tristan was putting his Shock Hawk uniform back on.

"Luisa, good," Ardrey said. "Here's a caretaker uniform for you. Put your Shock Hawk uniform back on first, though." He pointed to a small stack of Shock Hawk uniforms on the floor.

The caretaker uniform she understood, but why the Ket uniform? Before she could ask, Ardrey continued his explanation to Tristan. "Since we set the alarms off early it's going to cause problems. Many of the security functions—the city-wide ones—have been relayed to the other Inworld command center, which is out of caretaker control." He pointed to the west.

"What security functions?" Tristan asked.

"We can control maintenance robots and climate systems from here, but we can no longer access city-wide communications. There's a master control system we need to find in the Old Inworld, but the only way to get there is with help."

"Okay, so...that's why you need us," Tristan said.

"Yes, but more than just you. The way to the Old Inworld command center is long and we may face more resistance. Which means—" Ardrey paused, looking sheepish. "I've followed you on occasion. I know you have some contacts on the outside..."

Tristan said, "I was beginning to think you had all the answers."

"If you hadn't tripped the alarms early it would have worked out fine," Ardrey said defensively.

Tristan glanced at the clock on the wall. "Okay, we hadn't contemplated anything this grandiose, but I think we can get you some help, if they haven't given up on us."

Luisa jumped in. "No! This has to be a trap. How do you know he has this data finger? If you tell him it could compromise everything."

Tristan frowned for a moment, considering the possibility.

Ardrey put his hands up. "I know it's hard to believe. Why don't you check for yourself?" He pointed to an active terminal next to him, and motioned for Luisa to sit down.

She approached the terminal cautiously. In the corner of the screen she could see a schematic of the caretaker dome area in detail. It was a command console.

"Just don't run any new programs," Ardrey said.

Presumably the SCA program was running in this console, and through it Ardrey had some control of the caretaker portion of the Inworld security systems. She sat down and tried to verify this wasn't some illusion—some fake program put together by the Inworlders.

Using the keyboard controls, she zoomed into areas where it appeared she had control of live cameras, seeing inhabitants milling about, or looking out windows in the Theater chamber. The console showed a list of robot units in the caretaker dome that were on override, under the control of the console, their usual programs on hold.

She needed a test, something to show Ardrey did indeed have control. She zoomed into a far corner of the dome near a Theater chamber balcony and ordered a bot to traverse about fifty feet in one direction, which would ostensibly lead it off the balcony. The cameras showed the robot doing just that. It wheeled the fifty-foot span and fell over the edge as nearby caretaker onlookers watched, perplexed at the bot's behavior.

Ardrey spoke up. "Okay, okay, do you believe me? I do plan to use those bots for something productive."

It was remarkable. What she did couldn't be easily faked.

"Okay, I believe you," she said. "Sorry."

She looked up at Tristan who had been watching her control of the console from over her shoulder. "I'm sold," he said.

Ardrey looked exasperated. "Good," he said.

Tristan and Luisa hastily explained their original plan.

"The way will be crawling with caretakers and who knows what other obstacles," Tristan said. "I'm not sure how much you can help with that." Tristan pointed at the console. "And, of course, there is always the chance the OPM have given up on us. They were expecting this to happen earlier, and they may be nervous we were compromised. I mean, we *were* caught."

Ardrey nodded. "Yes, well, I have programs that will help us get to the Theater chamber wall. As for the OPM, let's just hope they stuck around."

"Right." Luisa and Tristan nodded.

They finished donning their gear. Ardrey had found their biogel explosives, which they strapped on carefully under their clothing. They also grabbed short and long-range shocker devices that Ardrey had found in the weapons store.

They were ready. With a quick set of keystrokes, Ardrey activated a program on the console. Afterward he detached a portable unit that still contained the SCA data finger.

They all nodded in readiness and faced the door. "The maintenance robots have been reprogrammed and will buy us some time," Ardrey said, "but the confusion will only last so long."

On the monitors Luisa could see a host of eight caretakers outside the main door, trying in vain to figure out a way to get it open using pry bars and the security keypad. Behind them, an onslaught of mainte-nance robots was congregating in the vestibule. The caretakers would occasionally glance over at the bots. They just stood there, for now.

Ardrey pressed a key on the portable unit.

The robots advanced. There were about thirty highly varied bots, from small wheeled cleaning units Luisa had seen before, to larger transporter units with grasping arms, to much more intricate, humanoid bipedal units with more advanced motor functions. These machines were designed to do everything from cleaning the facility, to providing transportation, to serving food, to carrying out factory opera-tions. Here, however, they all moved with a common purpose.

A few caretakers backed away from the door immediately when they saw the bots advance, but others stood there, stupefied, unable to conceive the robots could be moving against them. In some cases, the bots actually ran into the caretakers and knocked them to the floor.

When those same bots thrust their grasping mechanisms out as well, the remaining caretakers scattered.

The way was clear.

With another keystroke, Ardrey opened the door, and the trio advanced through rapidly.

CHAPTER 50

The epicenter of the blast was a bathroom facility next to the Theater chamber. The caretakers first on the scene told Sonny they'd found no source of natural incendiary or accelerant nearby. Someone must have fixed a bomb to the wall that the bathroom shared with the Theater chamber.

It was no accident.

But why? It seemed like an insignificant chunk of the building. Two people were injured who'd been walking by the site. Nobody was killed. While the wall fragments had projected far out into the chamber, the actual quantity of debris was relatively small. Inside the building the wreckage hadn't gone beyond the interior wall of the bathroom.

It must have been one of the Outworlders, or at least was made to look like one of the Outworlders. According to some of the caretaker security personnel, a number of Shock Hawks and Phaser Frenzy players had used this bathroom when walking out after the game, but none of the useless caretaker sentries remembered specifically which ones. Their protocols had been way too lax.

After several comlink calls, Sonny determined that even though the Outworlder gamers were all accounted for, they were at various stages of exiting the Inworld. Some were still in the arena atrium talking to fans or reporters, some in the Theater chamber, and some already in the panhandle exit.

Caretaker security heads were going to roll for this.

He sent a comlink message to have all the Outworlders from the match rounded up for questioning. It would take time.

His biggest problem was containing the caretakers. There had never been a need for crowd control in the Inworld, and all the pretentious dark shirts were asking him questions he was forced to answer. Much of his time was spent giving a canned rendition of events. "We don't know the cause of the explosion. There are two people injured, but not seriously. We'll get to the bottom of this."

He was like a broken protocol bot caught in an infinite loop, answering the same thing over and over.

He finally worked his way to the end of the crowd and made a break for the main building, walking at a brisk pace up the steps to the entrance.

At that exact moment, Flippy Broderick walked out of the building. Sonny tried to evade him but Broderick's eyes caught him.

Broderick marched over and surprised him with a backhand slap to his face. Sonny fell on his side and slid down the steps. His right cheek was smarting. "What in Myra's name is going on here?" Broderick said, looming over him. "I thought you had this under control."

Broderick's considerable height seemed doubled because of his vantage point on the stairs. After Sonny stood up and composed himself, he gave Broderick the same answer he'd given all the others. "We don't know the cause of the explosion yet. There are two people injured but not seriously. We'll get to the bottom of this."

"Does this have anything to do with the two Outworlders you captured?"

"Unknown, sir. I'm on my way to interrogate them."

Broderick's nostrils flared. He seemed to be searching for some way to further rebuke Sonny. "You're on the hook for this," he said. "You better figure it out."

"Yes sir," he answered.

After some time staring down at him, Broderick finally let him off. "Well. Get to it."

"Yes, sir."

Broderick walked past him and headed down to the Theater chamber to survey the damage. Soon he would be the one caught up in the morass of questions. *Better him than me*, Sonny thought.

Sonny marveled at the turn of events. Broderick wasn't even subtle about it. He would make sure Sonny was going to take the fall. And it was no idle threat. He'd heard Broderick wasn't bashful about scapegoating his people if it suited his interests.

When he reached the command center vestibule there was a group of caretakers standing several yards from the door. A number of robots stood in their path. They stopped their animated conversation in mid-sentence when they saw Sonny.

"Why aren't you in the command center?" Sonny asked.

"The bots attacked us, out of nowhere."

Another caretaker chimed in. "It's like the bots had a mind of their own—"

Sonny decided to take a page from Broderick's book and slap the caretaker hard across the face. He said, "Get a hold of yourselves. This is someone's idea of a practical joke. They're just bots. Stun them and see if that disables them, or grab a hold of them and take out their command chips."

But Sonny knew this was no practical joke. This had to be linked to the explosion, and to Luisa and Tristan. The situation was deteriorating quickly. Somebody might even have control of the command center, and if they could get control of the command center...

He walked away from the befuddled caretakers. As he paced, he looked at his comlink messages. There was nothing from the caretaker who had escorted Ardrey. It was mostly useless crap: questions from black shirts, a preliminary report on the explosion.

He sent a message to the caretaker who had escorted Ardrey. *Where are you and what is happening in the command center?*

There was no response.

Could Ardrey be linked to this? It seemed so unlikely, given his imminent entry into the Inworld, but it was impossible to know for sure.

He glanced through the rest of his messages quickly. There was a new text message he'd been awaiting from Franz, to whom he'd given a special assignment. It read: *We have the target and we are on our way to the dome. Where should we take him?*

Fenton Kittredge. The caretakers interrogating Michaelis's friends and roommates had linked him to Tristan, Michaelis, and Luisa. This might be his chance to get some answers.

He texted back. *Bring him to sector fourteen, via the emergency exit above the Nineteenth Street entrance. Find a room, and bring something heavy like a mallet or a hammer.*

No more quibbling with these Outworlder lowlifes. It was time to get to the bottom of this.

CHAPTER 51

There was an eerie quiet as they weaved through the hallways, the only sounds being their soft footfalls and the occasional keystroke on the control console. Ardrey was taking them through a little-used section of the Parkdome, and he'd run programs to lock doors or barricade them with robots to keep their passage free of caretakers.

Tristan had lost his sense of direction some time ago. For all he knew, they could be in the Sidiodome or Marindome.

They arrived at a lift door. Ardrey opened it with a keystroke, and ushered them in. He finally broke the silence, telling them in a low voice, "Okay, so listen closely. This lift takes us up to the Theater chamber."

The lift began rising while Ardrey turned his console screen to them. "We'll be here." He pointed at a spot on the map of the Parkdome. They would enter the chamber about a quarter-mile from their target.

"I can't cordon off this area, and it's near where I set the bomb, so there will be people around. I've disabled the main security systems, so we're free and clear from automated threats, but caretakers can still pursue us. We should pretend like we belong, plant the bombs, and make a break for it back to this lift. We'll hole up somewhere and hope your friends break through after that. Tristan, you take the right column. Luisa, you take the left." He pointed to two dots on the map along the Parkdome wall.

"How do we pretend like we belong there?" Luisa asked.

Ardrey showed a confused frown. "I don't know. Act like an Inworlder."

Luisa threw her hands up in the air.

"And, oh yeah," Ardrey added, ignoring Luisa's reaction. "In case we need it, I might turn on the Ketrix mobility field in the Theater chamber. Be careful, though. You each should have enough juice in your Ket packs, but the field generator hasn't been turned on in years, so I'm not sure how well it will work."

Tristan looked at Luisa with eyebrows raised. "Wait. You mean the Theater chamber is like a Ket arena? I can bound in there?"

Ardrey nodded. "When they first invented Ketrix fields, the whole Theater chamber was used as a sort of Ket playground. They stopped using it because it created too much chaos."

At least now they knew why Ardrey had asked them to wear the Shock Hawk uniforms underneath.

The lift stopped. "Are you ready?" Ardrey asked.

"Yes, ready," Tristan volunteered after reading Luisa's resigned expression.

They entered the Theater chamber, marching purposefully toward the south wall. Ardrey had the portable console unit stowed under his arm.

Again the bright blue expanse of the synthetic sky temporarily blinded them. When Tristan's eyes adjusted, he saw a crowd of gold, blue, and black-uniformed people milling about, no more than a hundred feet away. Billows of smoke still puffed out from the wall. People were mostly gawking at the hole, but a few were also picking up debris.

As they approached one of the tall, ornate towers, Tristan became aware of a significant number of onlookers. They were mostly focused on the damage caused by the explosion, but their eyes would occasionally stray toward the three of them as they made their passage on the walkway.

Hopefully, they were far enough away to not recognize them, or otherwise too preoccupied by the aftermath of the explosion. He kept his head down, as Luisa and Ardrey were doing. Any of them could be recognized as Outworlders easily. They were famous, and now infamous. They moved hastily but not so fast as to draw attention.

They reached a small pond preceding a thicket of trees. Some distance ahead was a bridge over the pond—their way across into the woods on the other side.

At the bridge, they paused momentarily. This was where they would part ways. "Are we good?" Ardrey asked.

"Yup," Luisa answered. Tristan also nodded.

Tristan looked to see if the way was clear. A young Inworlder couple was meandering in the park beyond the bridge, but otherwise there was nobody ahead of them or on the adjoining pathway. People must not be using the Theater chamber much, given all that was happening.

But when Tristan looked behind him, the way wasn't clear. A group of four caretakers in gold and blue were jogging toward them from the scene of the explosion. "Shit, look." Tristan pointed to the incoming caretakers.

"Go!" Ardrey said.

Tristan ran forward across the bridge, pulling out his shocker as he went. Luisa trailed him. Ardrey followed them from further behind, typing into the console while following them across the bridge. "Change in plan," he yelled after them. "Set it for two minutes instead of five, got it?"

"Yup," Tristan called back. Luisa also nodded.

Tristan branched off to the right, following the pathway on the other side of the bridge. Behind him, he heard Ardrey shout a warning to the couple, who had become frozen in their tracks on the pathway. "You're in danger!" he said. "There's another explosive hidden in this area. Please leave the area immediately."

The couple quickly started heading over the bridge.

After staying on the path for a hundred feet, Tristan leapt into the thrush of trees, putting his arms in front of him to ward off branches and keep them from poking them in the eye. The trees had thick, staunch limbs, and he had to sometimes break them off to make progress.

After another hundred feet, he nearly ran face-first into the dome wall. There was some sort of hollow-vision image on the wall projecting the continued thicket of trees. The distortion was only discernable once he was within a few feet, otherwise it was almost impossible to tell the wall from the rest of the forest.

The force-field power column should be nearby. He ran up the length of the wall to his right, dragging his hand along it to guarantee he was still against it, and ensuring no protrusions were lost in the illusion. He ran about fifty feet, but couldn't find anything. According to Michaelis, there should be a discernable physical outcropping of the wall. He thought he must have overshot it, so he went back to where he originally intercepted the wall and tried the other direction. Just a few feet farther on he stumbled upon what looked like the trunk of a larger tree, but when he touched it he realized it was a distinct column extending out from the flush surface of the wall.

This had to be it.

He frantically took out the biogel packs, plugged in the timer pack and linked the mixing tubes together. When the explosive components of the pack were exposed to a temperature of sixty degrees centigrade it would cause a chemical chain reaction, resulting in an explosion. The timer was a simple device that calibrated the speed of mixing of the two reagents that brought the exothermal reaction to sixty degrees.

He adjusted the mixing speed on a dial to reach sixty degrees in two minutes and stuck the pack to the base of the column, then ran back the way he'd come.

CHAPTER 52

Sonny left the small office he'd been using and threw the bloody pipe segment down beside him. His two caretaker associates had objected to his methods. Youssef, who was deputy of internal security, even threatened to take it up with Broderick, and he could have since he was of equivalent rank, but Sonny went ahead with it anyway. They watched him like he was a rabid animal.

Good. Fear can be a strong motivator.

He'd broken Fenton on the third strike. If he'd given up more information earlier, he might have saved his hand. Now, Sonny wasn't sure he'd be able to use it again. Many of the bones had been crushed and would heal dysfunctionally.

Sonny had learned much of Tristan and Luisa's plans, or at least whatever Fenton knew. They were ambitious, and for the first time, Sonny realized the Inworld faced a real threat, especially if these OPM misfits were helping them.

He doubted it would have any real impact in the long run. Sure, there might be some casualties, but the cards were stacked against the rebels, and cooler heads would prevail.

In fact, he could see the positive side of this whole affair. Yes, they would have to quash this little rebellion, but this was his chance to shine by revealing the plot and be instrumental in dismantling it. The more the severity escalated, the greater his opportunity to increase his authority.

But first he needed to ensure he wasn't being used as a scapegoat. He began preparing a comlink text message to Broderick to ensure there was a record of events that protected him.

Before he could finish, his comlink chimed on an emergency voice channel. It was Marcus, who had been rounding up the Ket game players. "Sir," Marcus said, "a caretaker patrol is chasing what looks like the Outworlders Tristan Mardukas and Luisa Vincent through the Theater chamber."

"Where are they?" Sonny asked.

"Near the southwest corner, heading east, sir."

"Understood. Keep me posted." Sonny disconnected.

His mind raced. If they were heading for the south wall, it was likely they were planning on setting off their explosives there. Fenton Kittredge had told him this was one of the scenarios they had considered.

There wasn't much he could do about it without access to the internal security systems, but it did give him an idea of how he could cover his own hide.

So he finished the note to Broderick, with some modifications.

Sir,

I am aware of the perpetrators. Two of them are Tristan Mardukas and Luisa Vincent. They are collaborating with an outside rebel group called the OPM, or Outworlder Peoples' Movement, targeting the southern Parkdome wall for the next attack. I had tried to stop the earlier bomb placement but was not given sufficient influence over security protocols, nor sufficient manpower.

I am unable to stop the southern dome wall attack for the same reason. Your assistance would be appreciated.

Sonny Joseph

He sent it to Flippy Broderick, but made sure to copy the Inworld security marshal. This would make it clear Sonny had figured out the plot. And given the severity of the situation, it was justified copying the marshal.

Then he sat and waited.

After a minute, the caretakers with him shifted nervously. Franz asked, "What should we do now, sir?"

Sonny ignored him.

"You need to tell us what's going on, Sonny," Youssef said. "This is not how we do things."

Sonny ignored Youssef as well. He occasionally glanced at his comlink inbox.

A distant explosion shook the room.

The caretakers braced themselves, and then began pacing. "Was that an explosion?" Franz asked. "Sir, shouldn't we do something?"

Again, Sonny didn't respond, unfazed by the explosion or the questions from his caretaker associates. He kept waiting, scanning his comlink.

There was another explosion.

That's when the call came from Broderick.

He was yelling. "Who the hell do you think you are you little punk! Never send a message to the security marshal unless I ask you to! You'll be lucky if you aren't working at the robot docks after this crap. You're responsible for all this, I hope you know."

Sonny held the handheld comlink device away from his ear, letting him finish. He responded calmly but defiantly, "On the contrary, sir, I can't be accountable if I'm not given what I need to address the problem. This is what I need. First, to be promoted to captain of internal security, and secondly, all caretaker security details should be reporting to me immediately."

There was silence on the line, then Broderick went on another tirade. "Are you insane? Just be glad you're not here. I'd turn your face into a bloody pulp, you little shit. I don't—"

Sonny cut him off. "*Sir*, time is running out, and don't think I've captured everything I know in that note to you and the marshal. This is the biggest crisis caretaker security has ever faced, and I'm the best man for the job. Give me what I need, or face the consequences!"

With relish, Sonny hung up the comlink. Youssef and Franz looked at him with jaws open, incredulous.

The comlink beeped at him again. He let it ring. Sonny checked his fingernails melodramatically. He had Broderick by the balls. He was the only one to do the job, and the security marshal would know it. It was Broderick who would be working by the Outworlder docks if he didn't give authority to Sonny.

Sure enough, a few minutes later, there was a broad comlink communication from Flippy Broderick promoting Sonny Joseph to captain of internal caretaker security.

Youssef and Franz were still staring at him. He said, "Look at your comlink inbox, then do exactly as I say."

CHAPTER 53

A flurry of sparks and energy pulses lit up the pathway. The air felt thick with charge as the echoes of stun-gun shots reverberated in Tristan's ears.

Ardrey had taken cover behind a tree and was trading shocker fire with the four caretakers on the other side of the pond. Tristan was a few trees behind, and Luisa was just across the path.

Tristan looked back nervously in the direction of the bomb he'd planted. Michaelis had said the blast radius could be as wide as five hundred feet. He yelled up at Ardrey, "We could take heat from the bombs. We need to get across the pond."

Ardrey fired once around his tree without aiming. He turned back and yelled, "Cross-arcing pattern, when I give the word."

After a brief moment of confusion, Tristan understood. They were going to bound over the caretakers.

With his back to the tree, Ardrey pulled out his portable console and began stroking keys. Tristan could see two caretakers carefully advancing toward the posts on the far side of the bridge. They appeared to be preparing to make a blitz across.

According to Tristan's watch, they had about thirty seconds before the first explosive blew, maybe less if Luisa set hers earlier.

Ardrey looked up from his console at Tristan. His eyes reflected the electrical blaze of a missed shocker pulse. "I'm turning on the grid. Are you ready?"

Tristan wasn't really sure, but he nodded anyway. Luisa was on the other side of the pathway, coiled like a spring.

Ardrey pressed another key.

In the minute that followed, the barrage of sensory stimuli that assailed Tristan were almost too much for his mind to process.

First the lights went out, and not just one or two—all of them. The near-blinding sunshine reverted instantly to pitch-black. It was as though someone had punched him out, but he remained standing, and he felt no pain. He heard cries of astonishment and fear from the distant tower dwellers.

The darkness was soon followed by neon-like nodes illuminating all around him, forming a lined grid in every direction on the Theater chamber sky. When his eyes began to adjust, the grid lights revealed forms of people and trees nearby, mostly as dark contours cut out of the grid.

He heard, "Go now!" from Ardrey a few feet ahead and saw his pale shape rise from where he stood, like a celestial body trailing faint wisps of Ketrix energy in the dark—a celestial body that began firing bright lightning strikes from his shocker device down toward the bewildered caretakers.

Tristan followed with his own bound, crossing Ardrey's trajectory with the intention of landing about fifty feet to the left of him. In the games, a cross-arcing pattern was typically used to incite enemy confusion. Doing this would maximize enemy losses while not letting them easily target one bounder at a time.

His heart beat erratically as he accelerated into the gloom. He felt like he was moving much faster than in the games, and the shroud of darkness made the experience much more harrowing.

There was nothing but a vast chasm of black below him, but soon shocker fire shot up at him, grossly missing him. It revealed his enemy's position. He fired back, but only once, to keep them suppressed.

His upward arc crested, and he began descending. Having passed over the caretakers, Tristan redirected his attention ahead. He noticed much of the neon grid was obstructed from view.

He squinted and moved his head to different angles, trying to make sense of the obstruction. When he realized what it was he unintentionally let out a cry of alarm. He was right in front of one of the Theater chamber towers, meaning he must have bounded half a mile. He could only guess the Ketrix mobility field was stronger in the Theater chamber.

And then the explosion went off behind him. As he continued descending from his bound, the shockwave hurled him forward, and he careened off the surface of the tower wall. It was painful, but with the exception of some bruises, he seemed to be uninjured.

Fortunately, the bounding safety interrupt on his Shock Hawk uniform was still functioning. He continued downward, this time vertically, not knowing when he'd finally land.

Behind him, dancing flames lit up the southern dome wall, and the thicket of trees had been set ablaze near the explosion site. Burning debris was strewn about the area or was gradually terminating in landfall, like flaming meteors in the neon sky. There was no clear hole in the wall, nor any real visible damage to be discerned from the heart of the explosion, although details were obscured by the fire and shifting clouds of smoke.

Faint outlines of people could be seen exiting the tower, whether to gawk or flee he couldn't be sure.

Luisa was just finishing her bound behind him when the second explosion went off.

Tristan still hadn't quite touched down, so his body again pummeled the tower, this time hitting a window and cracking it.

By the time he finally landed, the second explosion had brightened the scene considerably. He heard more cries of fear. Mass confusion was probably a good thing for them, although the additional light could expose their positions.

Tristan ran to the middle of the pathway in the general direction he'd seen Ardrey heading on his bound. Luisa trailed behind, jogging cautiously on a path that would soon intersect his. He waited for her to catch up.

"Are you okay?" he asked.

"No worse for wear," she answered. A thin grin could be discerned in the flickering light. "You look a little beat-up."

It was true. After the shocker pulses, the beating by Sonny, his swollen finger, and now being thrust into the tower by the explosions, he was feeling countless aches and pains, but the adrenaline kept him going.

They heard Ardrey before they saw him. "On your right," he said.

They followed his voice and found him near one of the towers. Dark shapes were moving in the shadows nearby, so Luisa and Tristan approached cautiously. At first Tristan worried it was a caretaker ambush, but it turned out Ardrey was surrounded by a number of his robot servants, with their lights off.

"We need to find cover nearby," Ardrey said. "Follow me." He led them into the nearby tower.

Several bots joined them. Tristan was trailing a humanoid-shaped one, which had a lurching gait and metallic skin, without any semblance of a real face. It was nothing like any robot Tristan had ever seen in the Outworld. As they entered the tower, an orifice opened in the robot's chest and a small flashlight appeared. It lit their way in the dark corridors of the tower.

They made their way into a lift, which promptly jerked them upward ten floors. Service robots lined the hallways outside the elevator. Ardrey must have programmed them to keep the way open.

They ended up in a small room that opened to an expansive balcony. Outside Tristan could see the southern wall of the dome.

Ardrey said, "This should be a good vantage point to see if your friends join us. I hope they come through soon, because I can't keep this up forever."

The three of them walked out onto the balcony while the robots remained in the room, motionless.

The fire had spread. Along the dome wall, smoke and flame encompassed their entire field of vision. Clusters of caretakers had gathered around the area, but they were doing little aside from watching in helpless amazement.

"We'll need to assign bots to help contain the fire," Ardrey said. He went back to the portable unit and reassigned some of his robot minions to address the problem.

Ardrey finished his commands and looked down over the railing of the balcony toward the ground below. "It looks like the caretakers lost track of us. They must be busy dealing with the aftermath of the explosions. How will we know whether the bombs worked well enough?"

Luisa answered, "We won't know for sure until the OPM tries to break through. Michaelis said the plan had a high probability of success, if we could lay the bombs in the right place."

"So now we wait?" Ardrey asked.

"Yes, we wait," Tristan confirmed. He leaned over the balcony rail and gazed at the location where the hole had been made. Little could be discerned beyond the fires.

It felt strange to be idle with the burning maelstrom below, but they had no choice. It was Michaelis and the OPM's turn, unless they had fled already, and in that case there was nothing else they could do.

CHAPTER 54

Michaelis lifted the binoculars to his eyes and directed them toward the curving Parkdome wall where it radiated out next to Lincoln Avenue. He found the rusted-out mechanic's garage John had pointed to as a reference point. The explosion was supposed to occur near the Parkdome wall area directly across from that.

The fact that an explosion had already gone off was confounding. There were no marks on the wall as far as he could see. Did Luisa and Tristan fail to make it to the target? Was it some form of improvised diversion?

Michaelis was positioned with two jeeps parked down Fourteenth Street, away from Lincoln. Another two jeeps were parked on Sixteenth Street. With each set of vehicles were ten OPM soldiers, and six others were at strategic lookout points within a block or two, watching for any caretaker activity. There were other jeeps on the other side of the dome, similarly armed, primarily for scouting purposes.

They kept all the weapons concealed. While the jeeps and men would certainly look suspicious, they could pass for a construction team or even a film crew. Pedestrians wouldn't think there was any immediate cause for alarm.

Michaelis upheld his air of confidence, even though it made him uncomfortable, and even though he was probably transparent to the uncertainties that plagued him. He made a mental note to add this to his list of things he wasn't meant to do. No skulking around in abandoned cottages or leading men into battle.

The first dome wall explosion finally hit, and there could be no denying that was what it was. The ground shook and there was a roar that reverberated down Lincoln Street. He couldn't see the source from his vantage point.

Noah, who was with the other group, reported in. "An explosion at our force field column, but no visible damage on the outside."

John followed with a broadbeam comlink message. "We're in business. Everyone be ready for action." The OPMers all donned their flak jackets, and Michaelis followed suit with his own gear. The OPM troops brandished their weapons and unveiled their rocket launchers: one jeep-mounted and another two shoulder-mounted.

Two men from Michaelis's group started heading toward Lincoln to take a closer look.

John spoke tersely into his comlink. "Where are you going? Get back and find some cover!"

Most of the OPM weren't disciplined soldiers, but rather passionate volunteers, and this was a perfect example. Recognizing their error, they turned back, but not soon enough.

The second explosion was much more dramatic. The sound was deafening, and now that the force field had been compromised, part of the polystyrix dome wall blew out and shrapnel glanced off the street. It shattered office windows on the other side of Lincoln Avenue, and a large fragment took out a wall of the rusted-out garage across the street, causing the roof to slump.

Unfortunately, the two soldiers who had advanced onto the street were knocked down, and one took some shrapnel in his back. He cursed and writhed on the pavement.

Michaelis had ducked instinctively, but after the shockwave passed, he stood tall to survey the situation.

A small opening had been formed in the wall at what would have been the center of the second explosion, and black smoke billowed out of it. Radiating from this center were visible cracks in the surface of the dome that spanned out across their field of vision westward toward the first explosion at Sixteenth Street.

The remaining wall material had also been altered. In a vertical swath in front of them, the glossy sheen was gone. It looked more like concrete than the ominous black texture that characterized polystyrix material. The sheen must have been a byproduct of the force-field energy permeating the material.

Several cars had been driving along Lincoln nearby when the explosion hit. One had flipped over, and the other drivers had stopped in surprise. No one appeared injured, other than the overeager OPM volunteer.

Two of the OPM soldiers ran out to lend assistance to the injured man. He was moaning, but didn't appear mortally wounded. The rest of the group was standing around, digesting the transformation of the dome wall.

John began barking orders. "Get these people out of here for two blocks in each direction. Use the cars to form a barricade of Lincoln on each side." Then, into his comlink, "Noah, are you there? Noah, come in. Situation report. Good. Fire the first volley just to the right of the original interior explosion. I want a nice clean entryway blasted out. We'll launch the second volley on our side. Let me know when you're in position and fire on my mark."

It took several minutes to extract the driver from the flipped car. The others they ushered away at gunpoint, and commandeered the stranded vehicles to where John had instructed. A few minutes later the way was clear and they were in position.

One of the OPM checkpoint sentries approached them. "Sir, we have two caretakers approaching from the southwest."

This was inevitable, of course. They had anticipated caretakers would investigate the situation on the outside, though Michaelis had hoped they would have more time.

John frowned. "Take them out by any means necessary."

They heard gunfire from several streets over. John was pacing.

"Sir." It was a broadbeam voice comlink from another sentry. "One got past us and is coming your way."

The caretaker was on his enercycle, speeding down Lincoln while looking back at his erstwhile assailants. OPM soldiers near Michaelis advanced into the street and took aim. Surprised by yet another group of rebels, the caretaker tried to speed up to get past quickly. In the distance, Noah had stepped out from Sixteenth Street onto Fulton and took the first shot, knocking the caretaker off his bike from behind. The cycle skidded on its side and wiped out in a heap.

They didn't want anyone to get hurt, but it was necessary. They all knew there were going to be casualties.

"Remove him from the blast area," John said, "and get into position right away." The troops sprang into action, pulling the limp caretaker to the side, and then moving quickly to their spots.

John gave the order. "Noah, fire when ready."

The blast was as loud as the second wall explosion, and when Michaelis looked up over his cover, a sizeable triangular-shaped chasm had formed in the dome wall; the tip had to be five stories high, and the base stretched about forty feet along Lincoln. It wasn't clean, however. Sizeable amounts of rubble still blocked the way.

"Focus on the rubble with the next volley," John said via broadbeam.

Michaelis took cover again. Another series of blasts turned the triangle into more of an archway, and much of the rubble appeared to have been blown away from the dome wall. The way in now looked sizeable enough.

As the smoke subsided, Michaelis tried to peer into the dome, but he saw only darkness. It was supposed to be brightly lit with the synthetic sunlight of the Theater chamber. Was the smoke too thick inside?

"Let's move," John ordered.

Michaelis watched John with some awe. His training was taking over, and any unease he may have shown about the mission was gone. Michaelis jumped into one of the jeeps, following the commands in earnest.

A team of four would stay behind to hold defensive positions in nearby buildings. They left them a jeep.

The three remaining jeeps, with Noah's leading at the front, drove ahead. They navigated the bumpy rubble with deliberate caution, and were soon swallowed up into the smoking chasm in the dome wall.

CHAPTER 55

On the tower balcony, Tristan watched with some relief as Michaelis and the OPM troops drove through the dome wall.

As it turned out, the OPM encountered little resistance from the Caretakers. The few who remained in the area were dumbstruck by the explosions and the conversion of the Theater chamber into a Ketrix mobility field. After that, facing a platoon of heavily armed assailants was just too much. Most fled immediately.

A couple of the more courageous caretakers did try to find defensive positions. They fired long-range shocker pulses at the oncoming vehicles. These shots missed badly, and they stopped firing altogether when the OPM returned fire with guns. The last two caretakers withdrew in the direction of the command center.

The rebels had secured the area, for now.

Tristan, Luisa, and Ardrey hailed the jeeps from the tower balcony and exited the building. To be sure they weren't taken for caretakers they approached the jeeps with hands in the air.

It took a while for Tristan to figure out who was who in the flickering light. The OPM troops were all wearing inconspicuous dark flak jackets and safety masks. Michaelis made his way to the front and his short stature and archaic spectacles couldn't be mistaken, despite the fact he was wearing an uncharacteristically stylish pair of red khaki pants and a yellow hoody.

"Nice threads." Luisa quipped.

"It's a long story," Michaelis responded.

A weight had been lifted upon seeing each other, but it was a curt reunion between the three friends. Michaelis and the OPM were maintaining a high state of alert, and casting curious glances toward Ardrey.

The troops spanned out in an array surrounding the group, while the three huddled with John. Ardrey hung back a few feet with his hands up, wary of the suspicious looks being cast his way.

Tristan and Luisa hurriedly laid out the situation. It was difficult to determine whether John and Michaelis grasped it in totality. As Tristan and Luisa continued to explain, John received a call on the comlink and stepped a few feet away.

Michaelis appeared to be gaining comfort with Tristan and Luisa's rendition of events, but their attention shifted as they overheard John's conversation, which was becoming heated.

"How many are there?"

"Are they armed?"

"Okay, okay. Get out of there. Go to the south side in the dome and take a defensive position to protect the entryway."

John hung up his comlink and turned to the others. "The north side units are under attack. They lost one of the jeeps. It sounds like the caretakers are being supported by a group of repurposed utility robots."

One by one they all turned to look at Ardrey.

"Yes," Ardrey said. "I was afraid of this. As I said before, with the alarm tripped, centralized control of anything outside of the caretaker part of the Parkdome was moved to the west, to the Old Inworlder section. Plus the Sidiodome may have its own defense systems. Bottom line is, I can control robot units in the caretaker part of the Inworld, but I have no control outside of that. Someone must have figured this out and is improvising control of the bots on the outside."

Tristan asked, "Can they come into the dome from the outside and attack us?"

"Yes, I think so," Ardrey responded.

They stewed over this for a moment.

"So it's only a matter of time," Luisa chimed in.

John said, "I think we need to hole up in one of the towers and wait for the OPM reinforcements. We can do some real damage, retreat, and get the word out about the OPM to the people."

Tristan had been watching Michaelis during this discourse. He had been holding his head in his thoughtful way, fingering his glasses, and taking his time to synthesize everything. "I'm...I'm not quite sure it's the best idea to stay here," Michaelis began hesitantly. "We'll eventually be overrun. There are more than ten times the number of bots on the outside, and we have to deal with the caretakers as well, who'll be back in greater numbers. Unless significant reinforcements arrive soon, I'm not sure we could hold a defensive position."

John looked annoyed. "We would only hold out long enough for our reinforcements. The first wave will be here in about thirty minutes. After that we should be able to hold our own."

"If they make it here in time," Michaelis countered. "The outside defensive forces may have noticed them. They could be intercepted."

John frowned. "Fine. I'll check on them." John took out his comlink handheld again, stepped aside, and tapped on the screen to begin a call.

Ardrey had been standing one step removed from the conversation. He raised his hand like a student patiently waiting for the teacher to call on him.

"Yeees?" said Tristan. Nobody else looked like they wanted to offer him the floor.

Ardrey said, "As I've explained to Luisa and Tristan, I think the best option is to take the city-wide command center for the San Francisco area. That would allow us to control all internal and external robots, and external communications. It's the only way we can defend the city and try to convince the Outworlders to support us." There was dead air for a moment. "Which means we have to infiltrate the Old Inworld area to the west."

John hung up his comlink call to refocus on the discussion. "Wait just a minute. The agreement was we would do some damage here to show our symbolic resistance, and then pull back. Now you want to go to the Old Inworld? Even the caretakers don't go there because it's so cramped and hard to navigate. How do we know what security systems we would face? Also, who the hell is this guy?" He wagged his finger at Ardrey. "Why should we trust him?"

Luisa cringed, and Michaelis frowned. Tristan was going to have to stick up for him. "Look, John," Tristan said, "I know it seems strange, but Ardrey is controlling the robots, and he helped us blow that hole in the wall. I don't think they would allow that to happen if he was a plant. He also has been preparing for this day his whole life, so I'm sure he has good ideas of what might be needed to be done to be truly successful."

Ardrey stood quietly, letting Tristan speak for him.

John was still on edge. Never mind Ardrey, he'd met Tristan only recently. "Fine, so he's not a traitor, but it still seems like a crazy plan to me. I mean, no one has been in the Old Inworld for decades. We have a beachhead, and reinforcements are coming, so why give that up for some high-risk commando mission?"

Michaelis spoke up. "John, I hear what you're saying. This won't be easy. But I think I have a good grasp of the situation, and I think Ardrey is right. We can't hold out here forever, but perhaps more importantly, our impact will be fleeting if we don't get the word out. The people need to know why this happened, and the only way to do that is gain control of city-wide communications."

John raised his eyebrows. He was at least listening to what Michaelis had to say. He looked around at the group and walked away, frustrated. After a moment of glancing at the glowing fissure in the dome wall, he went and spoke with some of his troops.

Tristan wondered if he was going to ignore them altogether, but eventually he did come back, followed by Noah. "Okay, I'll give you some help, but the majority of our forces stay here to defend this position. I'm not going to throw this opportunity away on some suicide mission, but I can't stop you, either. Noah and his squad will go with you."

He turned away and walked toward his men. Apparently this wasn't a debatable point. Before he was more than a few feet away he paused and craned his neck back toward them. "Good luck."

It was only slightly more audible than a whisper, but it was an indication that even though they disagreed, they were still on the same side.

It wasn't the amount of help they were hoping for, but they would have to make do. And maybe John was right; maybe it was a long shot.

Noah, for his part, seemed unperturbed by their chances. "So, the Old Inworld now?" he said. "Ballsy. What's the plan?"

Searching glances again eventually found their way to Ardrey again. On cue, he obliged by turning the console display around for everyone to see.

CHAPTER 56

Sonny put his comlink down on his office desk and sighed. When he wasn't barking orders, he was answering his subordinates' stupid questions.

Finally, they were getting it. Youssef had helped to set up a command relay post in the Sidiodome. Central Inworld authorities had granted him the ability to control the external robots through the relay, and he was assembling a small army of robots around the city. Most of these could only serve as roadblocks or a means of scaring people, but there were still a good many humanoid ones with more advanced functions that could be programmed to attack people. They had no shockers or other weapons, but they were fearless.

His team had finally blown through the caretaker control center door, and he was surprised to find it empty. He assigned a group to figure out how to regain control of the caretaker area from the Outworlders.

Now he was staring at the back wall of his office. He had set up a projected map of the Parkdome, including all the main levels. It was frustrating he couldn't even pull up the Theater chamber cameras. All he had was a twenty-year-old rendering of the area, and his only reports of the scope of the devastation in the Theater chamber came from the cowardly caretakers who'd returned. If he didn't need every man, he would have reprimanded and reassigned them.

When he spun his chair back around, he was met by a line of subordinates extending out of his office.

He pointed at the first one. "You. Speak."

"Sir, we've managed to capture and reprogram two of the internal robots. It takes some time but we have the team together that can do this. The two—"

"Fine. Reprogram as many as you can, move them to this sector, then wait for further orders."

He nodded and left.

"Go away," Sonny said to the others.

"But sir," the first in line said, "you had—"

"Go away!" Sonny said angrily. "All of you." This time they backed away. One of them had the presence of mind to close the door behind them.

He massaged his forehead. He needed time to think.

There was a stray round on his desk that he'd taken from Michaelis's rifle. He rolled it along the table. That was the other thing he'd done: outfit his troops with a cache of guns they'd found. This was war, not play-fighting with shockers.

He paced the room and finally returned to face the projection of the dome architecture on the back wall. "Okay, Tristan, Michaelis, Luisa. If I were you, what would I do next?"

CHAPTER 57

The ten of them marched on. Michaelis discussed the plan with Ardrey while the others watched for trouble. Ardrey spoke succinctly, with little emotion.

Michaelis liked him from the start.

Ardrey explained that they faced a problem with the internal wall that bifurcated the Old Inworld and caretaker sections of the dome. It was made out of the same material as the exterior dome wall and was locked down by a force field. To break the wall, they would have to blow out the force field from the other side. But there was one weak point. The Inworlders had made a tradeoff when they created the arena for viewing the games, and that tradeoff was security. With some light explosives, it should be possible to blow out the plexmold in the arena viewing area to access the western part of the Parkdome.

A growing assembly of robots was collecting in front of and behind them. One of the humanoid protocol droids was scouting ahead, at times even picking up litter and debris to create a clear path.

"I could get used to the escort service," Tristan quipped.

"These aren't all the ones I requested. Some of the robots are no longer responding," Ardrey said, focused on his console.

They had proceeded north through the center of the Theater chamber, then turned west. As they left the glow of the wall fissure behind them, it grew darker and the neon lines of the chamber ceiling were becoming more apparent. Eventually Ardrey led them through a door at the western end, where a brightly lit hallway greeted them. After a few corridors, stairs, and lifts, they found themselves at the entrance to the Ketrix arena where the interleague final had been played earlier in the day.

"We need to move quickly," Ardrey said. "I don't have enough bots to cover all the entrances."

Noah instructed two of the OPM militia to plant explosives at the locations Ardrey indicated. Michaelis watched thoughtfully while at the same time peering up at the plexmold walls. There were no silhouettes visible through the glassy material. Perhaps the Inworlder side was empty.

A series of shots rang out. *Bullets.*

Michaelis dropped behind a row of seats and slowly lifted his head above them to look out. He couldn't find the source of the gunshots, but one of the OPM soldiers had fallen on the arena floor. He was unmoving and bloodied.

"Upper left. Two caretakers," Luisa called out.

Tristan was suddenly up in the air, bounding to the southwest side of the dome. Michaelis also saw Luisa moving to the southeast. More shots rang out.

It was exciting to watch Ket on the vids, but even more so close-up, in person. In this particular arena, the walls amplified the spectacle. The reflections made it look more like six figures were bounding from as many angles, rather than just Tristan and Luisa.

Soon they were out of Michaelis' field of vision, and the reflections on the plexmold also descended past his viewing horizon.

More bullets rang out.

"Got them." It was Luisa on the comlink.

Michaelis stood up taller and surveyed the situation. There was an opening high up on the glass where two caretakers were limp, curled over a railing, the victims of Luisa's marksmanship.

"Let's blow the wall out and move on," Ardrey broadbeamed. "They surely reported our position."

CHAPTER 58

Tristan peeked over at the chair he'd been using for cover after the latest explosions. Sweat spotted his brow. He wiped it away before it could drip into his eyes.

The arena plexmold had shattered easily at the heart of the explosion, and two large cracks propagated out from the blast center. The hole was about thirty feet wide, plenty of room to get through.

Before they entered the fissure, Ardrey issued a few words of caution. "I have a map of the Old Inworld part of the Parkdome from quite a while ago, but I don't have any up-to-date views. I'm not exactly sure what we might come across."

The group of nine stepped carefully through the jagged hole in the glass, and climbed down over the mound of rubble on the other side. Ardrey, Tristan, Luisa, and Michaelis were in the middle of the line. Leading them were thirteen of the more humanoid robots that Ardrey still had control over. Two dozen others trailed the party.

They entered a hallway leading due west. There was no sign of life.

The walls here were different. There were no visible light fixtures, but all the surfaces gave off a faint white glow. It made it hard to discern any contrast or movement, as there were few shadows. If you were to squint, the vertices of the hallway were lost completely, as if you were floating in a white, empty space. Tristan reached out and touched the walls. They *felt* real, at least.

They wound through various corridors, all nondescript, empty, colorless, and shadowless. On quite a few occasions, the layout didn't match the map Ardrey was using. At first they thought this was because the map was from the SCA program—from nine years ago—and the Inworlders may have changed the layout since then. Ardrey was somewhat baffled by this, however, because he'd downloaded the latest map from the caretaker command center, and even that was wrong.

"According to the map, we'll be approaching one of the main thoroughfares soon," Ardrey said. "There should be many cramped accommodations. It could be complex and difficult to navigate."

Once they were at the end of the hallway, they opened the door with their weapons at the ready.

The interior was nothing like Ardrey described.

It was a cavernous room—also white surfaced—that was several hundred feet long. In the center was a large white hollowvision screen hanging in the air. In the distance, two figures rose from chairs near the hollowvision and scrambled away hastily.

Not quickly enough, though. Their robot escort sprinted forward to catch up with them and block their path. The two Inworlders shrieked in terror, and the robots closed in on them, clamping them by their arms with vice-like metal grips.

The rest of the bots fanned out, creating a perimeter around the two captives and the approaching squad of Outworlders.

Tristan marveled at the massive hollowvision cube floating in the air. It had no clear source for projecting the cubic hologram. The crystals appeared to be completely suspended, with no visible wires or supports. It was much like the one used that fateful day when his brother was hanged, but even larger and more impressive. Surrounding this hollowvision were tables and white, curvilinear chairs designed to tightly fit a person's body. There was nothing else in the room—just thousands of square feet of empty space from end to end.

And now that he was a few feet away, he was able to get a better look at their captives.

Tristan's first reaction was to ask: are they even human? Dressed in bleach-white garments, they were pale, stringy looking and very tall—maybe seven feet in height. They had no hair on their faces, heads, or bodies. One looked vaguely female, judging by the subtle curves in the shape of her body.

Their faces were human enough, and demonstrating emphatic emotions of fear and concern. "Please, do not harm us Outworlders," the man said. "We can give you...a place here, inside. We can give you anything you need."

"Quiet," Noah said with authority. His troops searched the captives. The Inworlders shrank away and grimaced at every touch, as if the Outworlder hands were burning their skin.

Tristan had always pictured Inworlders with rosy cheeks and powerful musculature, but these people looked more like the undead. Had cocooning people in the domes for so many generations, living a life of leisure, created these...things? This wasn't the shiny he'd expected.

And where was everyone else?

Noah, Ardrey, Tristan, and Luisa walked away from their captives and discussed the situation.

"We need to take them with us," Noah said.

"Why?" Luisa asked. "They might get hurt if we use them as hostages. They're so...fragile-looking."

"So what?" Ardrey said. There was a glint in his eye.

"I didn't come here to kill Inworlders," Luisa said.

"I didn't either," Ardrey said, "but ask yourself, how many Outworlders could be protected from the elements—from contamination—in this room alone? Yes, their bodies may appear to be fragile, but they're rotten with greed. I won't shed a tear if they die."

Luisa frowned. Tristan had to admit it sounded harsh.

Noah looked annoyed by the moral dilemma. "Either way, they could report us, and they may have valuable information. We'll find out on the way."

The rest of them nodded slowly. It really was the only option.

So they took their fearful captives along. Tristan was given the task of trying to extract information from them as they continued westward toward the command center.

"Listen, if you cooperate, you'll be fine," Tristan said. "I'm Tristan. What are your names?"

"Tristan Mardukas!" The female one with the green eyes said, just now recognizing him. Her eyes blazed with fear and awe. "My name is Malika York, and this is Neldon Palestine." The Inworlder man offered a diminutive wave while still maintaining his distance.

"Where is the Inworld command center?" Tristan asked.

Neldon answered readily. "At the Nexus, of course."

Tristan looked to Ardrey. Ardrey said, "I see the spot labeled on the map, but it's just a big circle."

"What else is there?" Tristan asked.

"It is the main hub for entertainment and transport," Neldon continued. "If you are looking for the Parkdome triumvirate, they have long since left to Myrantia. We are some of the few who remain—a tour of duty, as it were."

"What do you mean by *tour of duty*?"

"Oh, it's exceedingly boring. We must stay here in San Francisco to man our production posts, but at least the new releases came out yesterday—*Starla the Space Witch*, and *Federal Detectives*, and *The Blue Standard*. Those are the only tolerable ones. We do enjoy the Ket games, although we would rather not—no offence—*participate*."

"Uh-huh." So a tour of duty was...watching the hollowvision? Tristan decided not to probe any further on that topic. There were more important questions. "And what is this triumvirate?"

"Expansion, Entertainment, Production. They control the primary mandates."

When it was clear Tristan wasn't getting it, Malika said, "They rule the Inworld—for San Francisco, at least."

Ardrey interjected. "Should we expect any kind of resistance in this...Nexus?"

"I don't know." Malika looked at Neldon who had an equally vacuous look. "We are not responsible. We leave security matters to the caretakers."

"Where is everyone?" Tristan asked.

"What do you mean?"

"Where are all the people? There is supposed to be more than a million people in the Parkdome."

Malika's eyebrows raised and she broke into a laugh. "I'm sorry, but...no, Outworlder. Most have emigrated to Myrantia. And of those few hundred who remain, most fled when it became clear the Old Inworld would be breached. Alas, we had to stay because of our tour... and if we weren't so caught up in *Starla the Space Witch*." Malika cast an annoyed look at Neldon.

There was the reference to Myrantia again, but Myrantia was supposed to be a fairy tale—where Mother Myra would take the dead Outworlders and relieve them of their pain. Tristan couldn't tell if these Outworlders were deluded, and everyone had already died, or if this Myrantia was actually a real place.

Tristan stared at the Inworlder's awkward, angular gait as they walked along beside them. His impression of the Inworld had been first shaken by seeing the cold emptiness of the corridors. Now, seeing the inhabitants shattered any remaining vestiges of his childhood imagination. He finally had his answer to what lay behind the glossy black exterior of the Parkdome: nothing. The Inworld was, in fact, an empty shell, with a few remaining hosts holding on to a lost legacy.

Unless there was something to this Myrantia place, but where could it be? There was only so much space left in the Parkdome, and there were no other dome cities named Myrantia, as far as he was aware.

They reached the end of the corridor, where there was a large door replete with ornate metal arcs and crystalline patterns.

Ardrey said, "The Nexus—or whatever it is—is just beyond this door. Like I said, on the map it's just a big circle—maybe slightly smaller than the Theater chamber in dimensions, so I don't know what's inside. But if they've mustered any sort of defense, it will be in here, so be ready for a fight."

They all nodded solemnly. Ardrey pressed a button on the side wall, the door opened, and they entered.

It was indeed similar to the Theater chamber in size, but that was where the likeness ended. The ceiling wasn't sunny blue but rather had a yellowish aura. There were rows of outcroppings that looked like rooms with viewing areas that hung from the ceiling.

Below the ceiling, across the broad span of the room, was a plethora of huge hollowvision cubes. Interspersed among these cubes were what looked like sculptures, paintings, and odd-looking artifacts, as though it was one part huge museum, one part media center.

The immense walls of the chamber formed a mosaic of different styles of architecture. Barely visible in the darkest corners and abutments was some old Edwardian styling, likely a remnant of the early dome architecture they saw in the Theater chamber. In other areas, overlaid on top of this, or renovated into it, were more angular minimalist decorations, with glimmering silver paneling and more crystalline ornamentation. Balconies were built into the Edwardian foundation in this style. In still other places, another style overtook the minimalist one consisting of a darker sheen with a mossy green paneling.

Just offset from the center, rising above the sculptures and hollowvision cubes, was a red track-lit tower that tapered up all the way to the ceiling a good twenty stories high. "Is that the command center?" Tristan asked, pointing at the tower.

"No, that's the tube station," Neldon said. "It's there." He was pointing to the center of the chamber where a three story tall building was circled by robust pillars. It wasn't the biggest building, but it was the most institutional-looking.

"Are you sure?" Ardrey asked.

"Yes," Neldon answered, shrugging. He could have been lying, but he didn't even seem fearful, or nervous. Maybe he thought there was no chance they would succeed, or maybe he didn't care about much of anything except *Starla the Space Witch*.

Tristan glanced around at the sculptures, paintings, and audiovisual displays. Judging by the size of the chamber, there must have been several hundred of these placed throughout. On the hollowvision cube closest to him was a large screen playing a vid featuring images of another dome city, but it was no city he'd seen before. The cityscape was a series of domes layered onto each other, and a number of spires shot up from the domes, unlike San Francisco or Seattle.

Tristan had become so hypnotized by the novelty of the room that he hadn't been actively looking for any threats. There appeared to be no one immediately ahead of them, but then his attention returned to the center building in the distance. Pulsating red lights had begun cycling on the outside. An alarm had been set off.

Noah wasn't as easily distracted. He'd been scanning the chamber with his binoculars. "There's a group of caretakers entering the chamber on the far left. I count at least thirty of them. They're still far away, but closer to the command center than us."

He pulled down the binoculars and paced forward stealthily to a sculpture area that looked like it might provide some protection. "I think we'd better find some cover," Noah said.

They all followed his lead.

CHAPTER 59

As soon as Sonny received the reports of shots fired in the Inworld Ketrix arena, he knew where the Outworlders were heading. Sneaky bastards. If they could gain access to the Old Inworld command center, they could get control of the whole city.

He met with his top deputies and strategized.

They mapped out the fastest way to intersect them and immediately headed in that direction. It required leaving the Parkdome and heading along Lincoln to re-enter in the Old Inworlder section, via an emergency exit farther to the west. Along the way he also took on additional forces, including more caretaker troops, better weapons, robots from the external city, and internal robots they had reprogrammed.

The hardest part was convincing the Inworlders to let his squad into the dome in the Old Inworlder section, since Inworlders had never let caretakers into that part of the Parkdome before.

The security marshal, who was somewhere in the Sidiodome, conveniently tucked away from the action, refused vehemently at first. Sonny had to explain all the possible scenarios, including how if the situation got worse they might even have to meet with Outworlder people face-to-face. After some heated conversations, the argument finally worked; they were granted access to the Inworld from outside the dome, just south of the Nexus where the command center was located.

In fact it turned out Sonny's arguments were more than convincing. With overarching city command at risk, initial dismissal turned to pleading for their safety, and as they made their way west, the messages kept coming in on his comlink granting more power, including transferring satellite control of the remaining elements of citywide security to him. The Inworlders could take this authority away at any time, but it felt good to have more responsibility than any caretaker ever had.

They also granted him access to two robots that had been an experimental law-enforcement project from years ago. He was skeptical of the usefulness of just two additional bots, but when he entered the Old Inworld section of the Parkdome and they stood waiting in front of him, his opinion changed. They were eight-foot tall drones with thick, heavily armored limbs. Each had large energy cannons strapped to its arms on each side. They were old, and made grinding noises when they moved, but he had no doubt they would be formidable weapons.

His squad entered the Nexus to find a panoply of strange artifacts and audiovisual equipment. When they fanned out to take positions, he spotted the Outworlders, far away to the east. There was still time to stop them before they could reach the command center.

He ordered several groups of caretakers to spread out and begin moving on the Outworlders' position. As for his two new best friends—the well-armored security bots—he put them in the heat of things, directly in front of the command center. They could probably take anything the Outworlders threw at them.

He gleefully plugged away on his console, working commands for the security bots while watching his forces advance. It reminded him of his days on Amber Lightning, and the exhilaration he once felt before a big game.

"Okay, Shock Hawks," he mused. "Let's play."

CHAPTER 60

Tristan reloaded his rifle and fired at the security bots. Despite his terrible aim he scored a hit, but the bullet just glanced off the bot's tough metal shell.

The two huge security bots were a force to be reckoned with. They stood in front of the command center blowing their massive energy pulses at the oncoming Outworlder-controlled service robots. Many of the higher-end humanoid bots had already been pulverized. Some had just stopped in their tracks, others had started to catch fire, and still others had been knocked down and were unable to get back up, spinning out of control as a result of some kind of short circuit.

Ardrey wasn't far away, sitting in front of his mini-console behind their precarious cover, occasionally glancing up to check on the battle.

Noah was just beside Ardrey, barking out orders or firing at the oncoming caretakers.

Luisa and Michaelis found themselves on the left flank, bogged down by fire from advancing caretaker squads. The occasional caretaker would try to move forward and they would try to pick them off. It was slowing the caretaker advance, but with limited success in reducing their numbers. Their hapless Inworld captives were tied up next to them, their eyes firmly closed as if they could relegate the experience to a bad dream.

Tristan scanned the chamber with his binoculars again. Far away in the distance, he could see Sonny Joseph glance in their direction from behind his cover. He was on a console as well, typing intently or giving commands. He must be running the show for the caretaker side.

Figures it would be him.

As for Tristan, he remained on the right flank with one of the OPM soldiers. He was farthest removed from the caretaker advance or robot pulse blasts.

It was all happening so fast. Unless they did something different, this would only lead to only one possible conclusion. Michaelis, Luisa, and Noah were firing furiously, and Ardrey was struggling to maneuver the robots to their advantage, so only Tristan could take stock of things. He was the only one who had time to think, never mind act.

He rubbed his head. The OPM volunteer next to him was firing the occasional shot, but the enemy was too far away or too well protected for the shots to be effective. Still, he looked over at Tristan reprovingly, as if to say: *Why don't you chip in?*

Because he had an idea, that's why.

"Stay here," Tristan said as he scurried away from their position, moving further up into the chamber. The OPM volunteer stared back at him between shots, shaking his head.

Tristan moved cautiously from cover to cover. He was on the far right side of the Nexus, several hundred feet from the main action. Ahead were a number of hollowvision cubes, artifacts, and display platforms that would hopefully obscure his approach. He was closing in on being in a horizontal line with the command center.

Up ahead there was an opening between the myriad artifacts and hollowvision cubes. This was where the red tower rose up several stories tall to touch the ceiling of the Nexus, tapering in circumference with each segment. The base of the tower was a series of open archways that created an atrium, with four silver cylindrical pillars forming a quadrant in the center. The atrium was massive—each archway the size of a small house.

Navigating around the tower area would take too long, so Tristan sprinted directly across, pausing just inside the first archway. Once closer he could see the interior pillars had doors with buttons on them. They were elevators, and one opened when he approached, possibly triggered by a proximity sensor. Inside there was a panel labeled *subfloors* and scores of buttons.

He moved across to the other side of the tower and scanned the area. There was a good chance Sonny would try to outflank them by going around the command center on this side, so he was watchful for any movement.

As his head swiveled left and right, he caught sight of the ground underneath him, and his heart jumped. Within the confines of the tower atrium, the floor was transparent and spotless, revealing a huge open expanse filled with interweaving, translucent tubes, like the arteries of a giant subterranean behemoth, connected by the needle-like pillars of the cylindrical lifts. Huge multilevel constructs were cantilevered to the walls on the sides. These supported racks of hundreds of large shipping containers. The tubes and containers were stacked into the depths below him as far as he could see.

A feeling of vertigo came over him. He felt as though he might fall into the abyss at any moment.

When he purposely pulled his gaze away from the ground, his eye caught a huge map on the ceiling of the archway. It depicted what must be this elaborate system of underground conduits—thousands of them, ninety floors deep. And that wasn't all. There was a larger scale map featuring numerous dome nodes he recognized, including the Park-dome, Sidiodome, Marindome, and even the Seattle dome system, but beyond that were even bigger nodes to the west, in the middle of what should be the Pacific Ocean. The largest of these, a dot on the map a good ten times the size of the Parkdome, was one called Myrantia.

He had always known the Inworld had an underground transport system but this was something else. It was gigantic, and it suggested there were much larger cities to the west, deep under the ocean. The work they had uncovered at Ocean Beach was just the tip of the iceberg. The Inworld authorities had in fact been honest that they weren't extending the Parkdome. Instead they were maintaining the roof of this transport system. They didn't need to extend the Parkdome if they already had huge cities under the ocean.

They had all the space they needed, and more.

A series of explosions rattled the tower around him. He doubted it was an encouraging development for the Outworlders.

He needed to focus.

When he was sure the way was clear, he moved ahead to his next cover location near a series of flickering hollowvision cubes. As he arrived, he caught sight of movement that didn't look like another hollowvision image. He halted and peered with his binoculars from behind his cover. A number of caretakers were methodically moving forward, toward the Outworlder positions. They were progressing faster than he was; speed was their priority, rather than stealth.

When he thought they might be out of his line of sight, he moved to a nearby hollowvision cube and found cover on the side that didn't coincide with the path of the caretakers.

Then he waited.

It seemed like ages, though he knew only a minute had passed. The hollowvision was showing an old film that was unfamiliar to him. Up close, the figures in the hollowvision looked so vivid and real. It was like being transported to that earlier era—as if he could reach out and grab the woman with the tight-fitting embroidered dress and kiss her on the mouth from where he was sitting.

There was no way to hear the oncoming caretakers with all the background noise, and he needed to know when he was clear to move. If he advanced too soon, he would certainly give up his position. So instead of looking around the corners, he tried to stare through the hollowvision. He knew if they were to pass close enough on the other side, they would appear as apparitions in the hologram.

Eventually silhouettes could be seen bobbing behind the cube, as if the hollowvision movie director had screwed up the lighting, and there were shadows from the supporting crew showing up on the set.

Yes, he could have gotten the jump on them there. He could have taken out some of them—perhaps all of them. It would have prevented them from doing a deadly flanking maneuver, or otherwise getting into better defensive position in front of the command center. But what he needed to do was more important. So he waited.

When the caretakers were sufficiently distant, he continued on his original course, moving slowly at first, then rapidly. He'd lost precious time, and the others might not be able to hold out much longer.

CHAPTER 61

From his vantage point in the command center, Sivian Constantinople shifted in his chair, rearranging his sprawling limbs into a more relaxed position. It was the first time he'd moved since the battle began. As the tide went in favor of the Inworld, he allowed himself this additional comfort.

Sivian had felt a piercing dread when the Outworlders first entered the Nexus. Just knowing that a multitude of weather-beaten, Tyband-contaminated Outworlders were in close proximity was profoundly unnerving. Yes, he'd always wanted to see one up close, but his mind changed quickly when they entered. And although the doors to the command center were said to be nearly impenetrable, he'd never been anywhere near a gunshot or explosion of any kind, so his fear betrayed his confidence in the robust security systems. He had agreed to be on security reserve, but he was worried it had been the wrong choice—that he should have fled in the tubes to Sidiodome or even Myrantia like his friends.

It was supposed to be an easy job—one that made him feel important. A few hours of boredom every week. Not...this.

Gradually, however, a feeling of exhilaration overcame his fears; the caretakers were routing the Outworlders.

Sivian had always been a devout watcher of the Ket games, never missing any of the playoffs. And now, he realized, this was like being in the center of a match, in an indestructible shelter with the battle in full tilt around him. A visceral energy he'd never felt before filled him as the shots fired just outside the door.

The monitors showed the huge security robots blasting steady, rhythmic pulses of energy toward the Outworlder positions. They'd been doing this consistently for many minutes, suppressing any movement or return fire from the rebels.

While the Outworlders were pinned down, ten caretakers were methodically advancing on their position, adding to the suppressing fire as they went. Five were to the left of the security robots, and five were to the right. They navigated around the scraps of destroyed Outworlder-controlled service robots that lay in shambles on the Nexus chamber floor.

Sivian looked to another monitor that showed where Sonny Joseph was positioned. Sonny was sitting back from the front lines with a few of his caretaker deputies, relaying orders via comlink or typing commands into his console. Sivian experienced a strange cocktail of disgust, fear, and awe as he took in Sonny's appearance. Sonny still had the weathered look of an Outworlder—and he harbored the kind of malice and drive that no Inworlder would ever know.

Maybe that's what the Inworld needed—to fight fire with fire. Sonny was a necessary evil—and proof the caretaker system worked.

The one oddity on his screens was an Outworlder straggler who had split off from the main group. Sivian wouldn't have noticed him except that the command center had twenty monitors, covering all vantage points within the Nexus, and he caught the movement out of the corner of his eye.

This straggler had managed to run through the transport tube station, evading a small troop of caretakers coming through the area, and was now directly behind the command center, moving rapidly toward the rear of the caretaker position.

Sivian considered sending a tightbeam message to Sonny Joseph, but then thought better of it. He didn't want to communicate with any caretaker if he didn't have to. Just thinking about it made him queasy, and Sonny probably already knew about the straggler. Even if he didn't, what could the Outworlder do against twenty caretakers? Sivian assured himself that Sonny Joseph, NSF league winner, could handle it, and it would be best to not interfere.

So his attention shifted. He lost track of the straggler and focused on the main group. There was an advance forming on the right of the chamber. With two of the remaining Inworld service robots on point, a band of five caretakers charged on the right flank of the Outworlders.

The caretakers ran toward the Outworlder positions, firing furiously. Three overwhelmed Outworlders were forced out and ran back toward the other remaining cover positions.

All caretaker firepower instantly focused on the exposed Outworlders. An energy burst from a security robot hit one of them square in the chest and blew him back to the chamber wall. The victim's trajectory sent him right through one of the hanging vid screens, amplifying the effect of the original energy burst with a flurry of shooting sparks and shattered electronics. The other two Outworlders were taken down less dramatically, capitulating in a barrage of fire from a number of angles.

Sivian felt a rush. To be a part of this! What a story for his friends to hear. He licked his lips as the caretakers recalibrated their cover and mobilized for a final advance. The caretakers were preparing to go in for the kill.

Sivian pulled his chair up closer to the bank of monitor screens, as if doing so would allow him to get an even better purview of the battle.

CHAPTER 62

Sonny was happy to see his flanking maneuver work to perfection. There was no way out for the pitiful Outworlders and only a handful were left.

On his console screen he shifted and zoomed out his vantage point of the battle. He commanded only small advances for his squads. Most people would expect Sonny to announce to the Outworlders that it was hopeless—that they should give up. Sonny didn't want to give them that out. So he waited, hoping they would make a move. And he couldn't make a last push to overtake them. There were two Inworlder prisoners tied up with them. If the Inworlders were injured in his attack, his new authority might not last long.

"Come on," he said, "do something."

Almost on cue, something did happen, but not what Sonny expected. Rifle shots rang out around him as one of his nearby deputies was taken down.

The shots were coming from *behind* them.

Sonny and the two other deputies in the area immediately took cover.

It was clearly some kind of sneak attack, but how did they get through unnoticed?

He glanced at his display unit and zoomed in on the area behind them after finding the appropriate camera. There was Tristan, firing away. Sonny panned out and saw no one was with him.

It was a desperation move—some vain attempt at trying to take revenge. In fact this whole insurrection might be some grandiose act of jealousy by Tristan.

Sonny scanned the main skirmish area on his console one more time. The other Outworlders were pinned down, so there was no rush. Sonny found himself actually reveling in this chance to get into the action himself—and even better, to be rid of Tristan once and for all.

More fire was coming from the same location. Maybe it was some sort of suppressing fire, or maybe he was trying to finish off his first victim.

Sonny put down the console and picked up his rifle. "Okay, you want to play, let's play." He pointed at Youssef and yelled over the noise. "Come with me."

They moved up in a staggered fashion, giving each other covering fire as they went. The return fire continued intermittently.

Tristan always did like to use the element of surprise, even before he decided to specialize in suicidal clown-show bounding maneuvers. This was just another example, but he was giving away his position too early. He might have even had a chance at hitting Sonny if he'd done it right.

Eventually, Sonny and Youssef closed in on where Tristan had appeared on the console. *Now,* he mouthed to Youssef and they jumped out.

Tristan wasn't there. His weapon had been strapped to a tangle of curved, looping metal—one of the Inworlder artifacts—and set on a repeating fire pattern.

Sonny immediately crouched down, found some cover, and signaled for Youssef to do the same.

He sent a comlink message to Franz, whom had been left behind at the command area. *Franz, take cover. We found a weapon firing on auto. He could be nearby.*

Sonny's mind raced. What was the purpose of this little distraction?

Whatever the reason, they should ignore it and get back to the main battle. He could send some robots to investigate or check the monitors from the other parts of the Nexus.

So they started making their way back to their command area, from cover position to cover position.

Franz hadn't responded. "Franz, confirm status immediately," Sonny tightbeamed.

There was no response.

He sent out a broadband message. "Deputy Marcus bring a squad of five to converge on the command area. Kill anything that moves. Franz may be out. Youssef and I will be coming in from the west."

"Yes, sir." The response was immediate this time.

Sonny's pace quickened.

They arrived back at the clearing he'd been using to coordinate the attack and peered out from his cover to scan the environs. Franz was lying in the middle, blood oozing from his temple. The other caretaker who'd been left in the command area—a beefy private with only a few brain cells—wasn't anywhere to be seen.

But Sonny could make out the unmistakable outline of boots extending from behind one of the artifacts, boots that shifted slightly. Whoever it was sat at the base of a significant sculpture that rose to the ceiling. It depicted a defiant snake, hissing a forked tongue in Sonny's direction.

In case it was a trap, Sonny circled around to the other side, where he'd be sure to maintain his cover, but also to see if the boots were attached to the person he suspected.

They were. Tristan was sitting there, a patch of blood on one shoulder, typing away at Sonny's console. He was oblivious to his surroundings and exposed to fire from several angles. A rifle lay beside him on one side, possibly Franz's. On the other side was the unmoving crumpled form of the beefy private who had been with Franz, pushed up against the base of the sculpture.

Sonny's mind rewound to the first thing he'd noticed.

He was typing away at the console.

Sonny's heart raced. With deliberate calculation, he lifted his rifle and aimed at Tristan.

Sonny's synapses converged on one thought: *Stop him from typing.*

Sonny fired.

Tristan spasmed convulsively with the force of the projectile. The bullet hit him in the upper chest, forcing his body to slide away along the base of the sculpture. He was on his side, the console lying in front of him.

Sonny approached Tristan cautiously, his rifle aimed forward, while glancing side to side in case any other Outworlders were around.

Before Sonny could react, Tristan somehow slinked away behind the far corner of the statue, pulling the console from behind him as he went.

Sonny closed the distance and cautiously rounded the sculpture artifact, gun leading. A smear of blood had painted the corner and continued along the other side. Sonny followed the trail. The red streak ended, but drops continued on the ground, and he spotted Tristan's form staggering away, clutching the console to his chest as if he was using it to contain whatever might be spilling from his wound. He had broken free from the denser cluster of artifacts and was running awkwardly across an open area toward the transport tube tower.

"Enough," Sonny said. He took aim and fired.

The bullet went through Tristan's shoulder and out the other side, past the tower, to crash through a hollowvision screen in the distance. A sheen of blood sprayed over the glassy floor as Tristan toppled under an archway.

Sonny ran to Tristan, who had retracted into a fetal position. Amazingly, his eyes still flickered with life. He was clutching the console with white knuckles.

Sonny wrenched the console from Tristan's hands and examined it. It appeared dented, scratched, and covered in blood, but the control program was still running. Tristan was mouthing something into his comlink mic. It came out as an unintelligible whisper.

Sonny kicked him in the head, knocking off the mic and earpiece. It slid several feet away.

His eyes scrolled over Tristan's battered body. It reminded him of when Tristan shattered his arm in his last league game. Here he was again—a loser, a pathetic picture of humanity, crumpled up and broken. "Lots of points for effort, but again you lose, Tristan. Haven't you learned anything?"

Tristan's body wasn't moving, except for his labored breaths. He would probably die soon.

Sonny opened up the console and scanned it. Sonny's control program had been modified, and Tristan had changed the access credentials. "What did you do?" Sonny said. "Tell me, or I will finish you off here and now."

CHAPTER 63

The caretakers closed in, and then did nothing. Sivian watched for interminable minutes, eyes glued to the screen, anxious for the inevitable charge against the Outworlders. What were they waiting for?

The caretakers wallowed there, lingering behind various strategic cover points. Their positions couldn't be any better.

Nothing.

Sivian was still riveted. He didn't want to miss the final blow to the Outworlders.

Were they arranging some kind of surrender? Did they need to capture them alive?

Then something happened—something Sivian would never have expected.

The juggernaut security robots had been laying steady bursts toward the Outworlder positions. They stopped. This in itself wasn't surprising. The Outworlders were pinned down, with or without the security bots, and maybe the caretakers were hoping to flush them out.

The security bots moved. The suppressing fire went quiet as all eyes fixed on them. The hydraulic machinery of the massive legs of the bots could be heard cycling even from Sivian's position behind the doors of the command center. One advanced to the northeast corner of the building, and the other crossed over and stood on the other side of the doorway, exactly where the other security bot used to be. They stopped at their new positions and froze.

A few caretakers looked back with eyebrows raised. The Outworlders alike could be seen stealing furtive glances above their cover, trying to see what was amiss. The moment of silence was only interrupted by the sporadic intonations of the few remaining active vid screens in the area.

The security bots came to violent life again. They fired, but not at the Outworlders.

The security bot nearest the door began releasing powerful blasts of energy, swiveling a few degrees after each volley, targeting the exposed backs of the caretaker positions directly in front of it.

The first wave of caretakers was caught totally unaware. They were hit squarely, leaving huge burn marks on their tunics. Their bodies twisted like rag dolls against whatever hard surface they had been using for protection. Others faced a more gruesome finale. They were thrown significant distances, with a force that propelled them through the protrusions and curves of the eccentric artifacts nearby.

The second security bot was doing much of the same, but with less precision. Its blasts fanned out to cover the entire right side of the chamber—a wide angle—and its targets were more spread out and less exposed. Only a few caretakers were hit by this bot, and most on that side managed to use the extra seconds to find new cover and regroup.

The security bots stopped firing.

Sivian took a deep breath. His feeling of exhilaration was gone, replaced by the paranoia he'd felt at the beginning of the battle. He scanned the carnage on the screens. What had been the site of a minor skirmish was now a full-blown war zone with debris and bodies every-where. Somewhere a lone cry of agony rang out, likely the only struck combatant who wasn't dead or unconscious.

The security bots began firing again.

In the second wave, other caretakers were caught in the barrage, although many had found protection. The security bots seemed to adopt a more rhythmic suppressing fire routine, similar to what had been used on the Outworlders only a minute ago.

The caretakers who weren't dead or injured were under deep cover, and difficult to spot. Sivian overlaid their identity beacons on the map and he could see there were still quite a few on the right flank. They seemed to be regrouping.

Sivian scanned the monitors from right to left again, and something caught his eye in the middle. A channel of carnage had been left by the security bots directly in front of the command center. None of the caretakers dared venture into the crossfire of the two security bots—but here was a man, running at full speed, hurdling islands of smoking debris in a beeline toward the command center. He was running erect, without cover, ignoring the security bots.

And the security bots were oblivious to him. Instead they continued to fire on each side of the command center, keeping everyone else firmly entrenched in their cover positions.

Sivian got a better look at the running man as he came closer. It was one of the Outworlders—the one called Ardrey. Of course, Sivian knew who he was—he was quite an impressive gamer. But was he crazy?

Why don't they shoot him?

The caretakers were bogged down by the security bots and weren't able to fire at the renegade Outworlder. In fact, in their defensive positions they might not have even seen him running. And there was no reason for them to look—no reason to believe someone could be so audacious as to run through the middle of the melee, through the crossfire of the two juggernauts.

At first Sivian thought the security bots' programs had failed—indeed they were known to be unreliable—but now he rethought this supposition. *Do the Outworlders have control of the security bots?*

It was all happening so fast. A well of nervous energy was building inside Sivian. Ardrey had run through the main carnage of the battle and was out of the forward monitor range.

He tried to calm himself. He was safe. The doors were impenetrable. *But Sonny Joseph controlled the security bots?* Sivian came to the realization that it had been the lone Outworlder at the back. He must have taken control from Sonny.

But before he could react to this epiphany, the command center doors slid open. The running figure, not hesitating for a second in his stride, shifted his angle only slightly, and was *running directly for him.*

Sivian couldn't move. It was too fast, too unexpected. He sat frozen in his chair, overwhelmed by fear. In an instant, Sivian felt the cold metal of a rifle barrel fixed to his forehead, and the grotesque panting Outworlder was looming over him. "Patch control back through the caretaker command center," Ardrey commanded, "and give me the access codes."

Sivian could only wither in his chair.

"Right now!"

CHAPTER 64

Ardrey guided Luisa and the rest of the rebels through the battlefield to the relative protection of the command center. They had the advantage of knowing with pinpoint accuracy where the caretakers were, thanks to the chip locators implanted in their shoulders, so it was easy to move unimpeded.

Relentless fire from the security bots also helped.

Once in the command center, Luisa paced as Ardrey, Michaelis, and the one remaining OPM private worked feverishly at the control consoles. Noah had also survived. He scanned the monitors from a few steps away.

They had far-reaching authority over the city's security systems. Virtually all the bots in San Francisco could be controlled from the command center. Ardrey had been mobilizing some of these to interfere with the attack on the Outworlder rebels on the outside, but it was a lot of guesswork which robots to use and how to control them.

He had also been trying to bring in reinforcements, and had marshaled as many robots as possible to head for the Nexus, but it would take them time to arrive. He had to figure out how to open numerous doors along the way using the command console.

They weren't out of danger yet. Through the view screens and the chip implant locator, Luisa could see at least two dozen caretakers left in the Nexus, and they appeared to have organized themselves into a defensive position in and around the big red tower. They had grenades and grenade launchers. If they were to find a way to blow a hole in the wall of the command center the Outworlders would be in trouble.

And they had Tristan. All she knew was what Ardrey had told her—he was alive but hurt. Tristan wasn't answering his comlink anymore.

"Ahem," Luisa cleared her throat loudly.

Ardrey and Michaelis stopped what they were doing and looked back at her curiously.

"We need to get Tristan out of there," she said. "What's the plan?"

Ardrey winced. "I'm not sure how we can do that. If we lose the command center, we lose everything, so we can't open the doors, and we need the security bots to stay in front to defend it. We have to focus on recruiting as many bots as possible, and not only for us. John and the remaining OPM need reinforcements in the Theater chamber."

"How badly is he hurt?" Luisa asked.

Ardrey's eyes wavered. "The truth is, I don't know. He didn't sound good, but I have no idea. Like I said, he's not responding to his comlink."

Luisa continued pacing. Noah and the others were showing signs of discomfort with her line of questioning, as it was taking attention away from controlling the bots. *Screw them*, she thought. They wouldn't be there if Tristan hadn't risked his life.

Michaelis added, "Luisa, do you think Tristan would want us to risk losing everything going after him?"

He was right, of course, but it felt as if they were leaving him to die.

But she had to admit, he may already be dead.

CHAPTER 65

Tristan was floating in and out of consciousness, his instinct for survival battling the alarm bells in his brain. It was hard to move his limbs. Pain came over him in rippling shockwaves.

For whatever reason, Sonny had left him by the thick, curving pillar of one of the red tower arches. Maybe he enjoyed seeing him in pain. Or maybe it was because there was no sense wasting a bullet on someone who was going to die soon.

Sonny and his men had set up a small perimeter out of rolling carts filled with metal boxes, one archway over from where Tristan lay.

He heard the cries from other parts of the Nexus chamber, and it *sounded* like there was a shift in focus by the security bots, but he couldn't see much beyond the artifacts circling the tube station area.

It took all the effort he could muster to push himself into a sitting position against the pillar. His comlink wasn't far out of reach, but it had been crushed by Sonny's boot. Retrieving it would be pointless.

Sonny was splitting the caretakers into two groups. He sent them out into the surrounding artifacts in the direction of the command center.

Sitting there with little to do but absorb the pain and try to remain conscious, Tristan's mind wandered.

He thought of his many bike rides through San Francisco. He passed by the ever-present Parkdome and rode through the vacant downtown streets. He arrived in Lincoln Heights, and a sunset blossomed into view. He'd spent many days and nights there. To him, the view represented a hope for a better future, a better place. This was the place he'd fought for, why his mom took her demerits, and why his dad worked so hard every day.

Tristan's eardrums reverberated with the crack of gunshots and—unmistakably—the sound of the security bot energy blasters coming to life again. This was followed by an explosion, and then two more—grenades. The energy blasts from the security bot ceased, and there were cheers. The caretakers must have taken one down.

Indeed, the two caretaker groups returned, and they began plotting another assault, presumably on the remaining security bot, or the command center itself.

The pool of red was growing around him, and he was incredibly thirsty. He slowly managed to drink the rest of his canteen, panting between gulps. His head bobbed and he gritted his teeth. He couldn't let the demons overtake him. This wasn't over.

But what could he do? His rifle was gone—he'd left it by the snake statue.

There was one other option.

Slowly, methodically, he used his one good arm to push first against the pillar, and then the floor, moving back inches at a time, until he reached one of the cylindrical lifts in the center of the tower. The door opened for him, and he gripped the side of the opening to slide inside. He left a swerving trail of blood on the transparent floor behind him. It looked like a ghastly distorted reflection of the red pillar where he had been sitting.

He was so thirsty.

He pressed a button at random from the myriad buttons on the wall. Only then did Sonny look back, searching for Tristan. His eyes found him in the lift. Sonny didn't flinch or even call out in alarm that Tristan was getting away. Instead, his expression morphed into one of disgust. He mouthed one word: *coward.*

Sonny had always been confident. People were attracted to confidence in the Ket games, and it helped him build strong teams. Ultimately it helped him win games and gain entry to the Inworld. But Tristan had always thought it was only a matter of time until his confidence became overconfidence—until a mistake or oversight cost him a match.

It never had, until now.

It wasn't only the console and the rifle that Tristan had taken from the caretaker named Franz; there was one other item. Tristan fumbled in his pocket, took out the grenade, pulled the pin, and rolled it forward. It tumbled out the door toward the caretakers huddled with their own guns and grenades, just before the lift door closed in front of him.

CHAPTER 66

They stared dumbfounded at the monitor focused on the red tower. The explosion in the tower area was followed by two more —some kind of chain reaction from the caretakers' remaining grenades. Those few caretakers that survived staggered out from the billowing smoke in all directions, coughing and disoriented.

And that was just the beginning. One of the arched pillars crumbled and the tower listed, until another pillar crumbled, shifting the tower like a pendulum, until yet another pillar disintegrated. Luisa thought the huge structure might crash on its side like a falling tree, but instead it was swallowed into the ground, casting up an even larger cloud of soot and dust and debris as it disappeared beneath the surface.

Tristan, or what was left of him, would be somewhere at the center of it all.

"We should take advantage of the confusion," Michaelis said, returning to his senses, "before they regroup and take out the last security bot."

Ardrey peeled his eyes away from the monitor, nodding slowly, and focused on his console. "We've assembled a good number of bots in reserve," he said. "I'll put them to work."

The bots began converging on the billowing cloud from distant entrance points into the Nexus, and advanced toward the confused and disparate caretakers. Most of these bots were the humanoid kind that threatened to grip them with pincers. Others would simply scurry around in such a way as to annoy and confuse them.

Meanwhile, the remaining security bot took off obliquely away from the command center, and eventually angled back toward the caretakers. The command center was no longer defended, but it was the only way to flush them out.

Sonny Joseph was nowhere to be seen—probably killed in the explosion—so the remaining caretakers had no leadership. A couple did fire back at the frenzy of bots with their rifles, but most fell once the security bot made it into the area. Cover was hard to find with the now-gaping hole in the ground where the red tower used to be, and with the pervasive smoke and dust obscuring everything. While the caretakers could barely see a few feet in front of them, the robots had the advantage of knowing the layout, and also where the caretakers were with pinpoint accuracy because of the beacons implanted in their shoulders.

Their numbers dwindled quickly, until only two caretakers remained. Battered and dusted gray with ash, these two had the presence of mind to raise their hands in surrender.

Luisa wasted no time celebrating. She immediately exited the command center and headed toward the smoldering hole in the Nexus floor.

Feelings of guilt rose within her as she navigated through smashed hollowvision cubes and ashen artifacts. Why didn't someone go with him? Could they have done something more to save him?

When she reached the giant hole she lay down to peer over its jagged edge.

The huge maze of interweaving tubes was mostly intact, except a swath directly below; it had been obliterated by the collapsed station tower, and it had taken two of the cylindrical lifts along with it. The smoke was dissipating, but the debris still fed several wisps that lingered through spaces between tube lengths. When one of these wisps finally cleared, she spotted Tristan.

He was lying face up on a platform next to one of the cylindrical lifts that remained standing. Two tubes met the platform on either side, keeping it upright. He must have escaped on the lift before the explosion, and then made it onto the platform, if one could tell by the trail of blood.

He was alive, but he looked ghastly. His eyes were slits and his lips were moving, but nothing could be heard.

Luisa couldn't help herself. She burst into tears. "Dammit, Tristan, stay awake." She was yelling into the abyss. "We'll get you out soon."

But it was a lie. There was no way to reach him.

"Don't leave me!" she yelled again. "Don't leave me like all the others!"

CHAPTER 67

Tristan's life hung by a thread—like a feather he could drop at any time. But the feather was heavy, so heavy; more like a stone tied to his neck, pulling him underwater. He could feel his essence slipping away, but his mind raced defiantly against the forces that sought to expunge him.

He could hear Luisa yelling, encouraging him to hold on, but he didn't know where she was. There was smoke, and a whirlwind of tubes nearby that spun like a merry-go-round.

The voice triggered memories of Luisa. He could see her laughing on the cliff near the docks, then crying in her apartment next to Rex. He could feel them embracing on their only night together.

He felt a sense of loss at the brevity of their relationship, but also some solace that he'd shared some time with her. It was a vestige of happiness to hold onto in his otherwise tumultuous existence. In his haze, he managed to smile.

The smile was also driven by another feeling, one unfamiliar to him: satisfaction. He knew if they gained entry to the command center, things could change, or at least they could make a visible tear in the fabric of the Inworld system. Even if their control was short-lived, they'd be able to get the word out that the Inworld wasn't invincible, that they'd been lied to. The balance of power could shift.

He wanted so much to let go, but he couldn't. Luisa's voice, everything they had fought for, reminded him there was something he wanted more: life.

He managed to push himself along the platform with his one good arm, toward the tube. An arced segment of the tube opened, just as the lift door had opened, when he came near. He slid over the threshold, into a barely visible transparent vessel nestled inside the transparent tube. The door closed behind him and beeped.

A pleasant woman's voice spoke. "Welcome. This vessel's destination is Myrantia. Do you wish to proceed?"

"Yes," he croaked. Blood dribbled from his mouth and spilled on his shirt.

The door shut and a green light winked at him. He felt gentle movement, and heard a hum all around him, like a distant bee buzzing. It might have been the vessel moving, or maybe he was hallucinating. He couldn't tell.

Soon these sounds became imperceptible. His eyes couldn't stay open. He could see only a slate of darkness. Even the sharp pains of his wounds began to diminish.

Finally, an image appeared to him from the pitch. It was an animal —a deer—lying on its side by a path in the woods. It jumped up from its slumber, as if disturbed by Tristan's presence, and vibrantly pranced away down the mountain path toward the lake.

The image faded, and darkness engulfed him.

EPILOGUE

Luisa stared across the expanse of the bay from their familiar spot in Lincoln Park. It was at this very clearing where they had discussed their ambitious plans only weeks ago.

It was a relatively clear day for San Francisco. The fog was tempered enough that they could see across to Marin. There were no shapes she could make out on the Golden Gate Bridge. Beside her, Ardrey and Michaelis looked across the same vista, armed with binoculars. They didn't seem to notice anything either.

Ardrey looked down at his watch and glanced back over his shoulder. "When will they be here?"

One of his subordinates sat behind him on a makeshift bench, typing away on a console. "Sir, it looks like they're less than two minutes away from the bridge. We have two security bots in position at the first bridge column."

Michaelis glanced back. "And the charges?"

"Armed and ready."

A few days ago the Outworld rebel leaders had ordered that explosives be laid throughout the city, in case of external attack by another dome city. Many had questioned the necessity, but this new development put an end to that.

Two of the new OPM recruits hovered close by with rifles ready, crowding Luisa out to sneak peeks at the console screen between squinted glances at the bridge.

Luisa had come to Lincoln Park at Michaelis's request, after she'd stopped by the command center. She had expected the usual monotony, but instead encountered a frenzy of activity. They had spotted twenty armed robot vehicles coming toward San Francisco from the north, and they were moving fast. They knew they were unfriendly because they had already blasted through a checkpoint set up in the North Bay. Reports came in about them being heavily armed, destroying any vehicle that dared to stand in their way.

With less than an hour's notice, they had taken whatever steps they could to defend against them. The Outworld rebel leaders had decided to announce the attack on the city over the loudspeakers. This was risky because it might incite panic—the first true test of the city's allegiance to the ragtag group of insurgents. But in the end it might allow cohesion and the possibility of a more coordinated defense.

The results were mostly positive. Some people fled, but others armed themselves, preparing for conflict. At first blush, it appeared the city had taken to their new leaders.

Ardrey and Michaelis continued to glance through their binoculars nervously every few seconds.

Michaelis—a leader, a general. He was on par with Ardrey and the three other OPM generals in terms of responsibility. This was her friend whom she had known for so long and once perceived as a meek, socially-awkward individual. It would bewilder her when his newfound authority would result in looks of awe from his subordinates.

Many people looked at her in the same way, as they did anyone who was a part of the original rebel group. They were heroes, or so it was said, but she didn't feel like a hero. She felt as though she'd lost everything. The focus on their rebellion had subsided, and it left her with the ghosts of her past.

And the last person she'd let in, the last person she'd opened up to, was gone. His tube vessel had disappeared on its way to Myrantia, and there was no coming back. Ardrey and Michaelis had insisted they had to block off the underground tube conduits to other dome cities, for security reasons.

Even if Tristan was alive, he was probably gone for good.

How can you be a hero if you've won nothing?

She avoided anyone who wore that look of awe. She didn't want to hear their compliments or see the sparkle in their eyes.

And then there was Ardrey.

She knew Ardrey had experienced a particularly difficult life. He'd been traumatized as a child, and had needed to be cunning and devious just to survive, but she worried he could be—at times—ruthless.

Her first hint was that she learned he'd had some injured caretakers killed after the Nexus chamber battle. She'd seen the corpses later in the cleanup and some had fresh security bot shots across their chests she hadn't seen when the battle formally ended. It had to have been Ardrey's doing, and while she felt little remorse for the caretakers, she found his behavior disconcerting.

Or maybe that was what they needed. Through his study of the SCA program over all these years, he had the broadest education on the dome systems. He was the closest thing to their president, prime minister, or chief executive. They needed his cunning and, if necessary, ruthlessness—just to survive.

So it was all working. The problem, she knew, was with her and her alone. She could see it in Michaelis's eyes and the looks from the OPM people. Her only solace was that she hadn't fallen back into drinking. Rex, who was now a happy resident of her new Inworld residence, had always managed to keep her spirits from cratering.

But she would still cry when she was alone, and the weight of the void remained as heavy as ever.

"Here they come," one of the armed men spoke up.

"I see them," Ardrey said. "Damn, they're coming fast." He put away his binoculars and circled to the control console. Luisa saw only tiny specks at the far end of the bridge. She followed Ardrey and Michaelis to their seats to watch.

The security bots started firing at the oncoming vehicles. The shots glanced off the front shielding of the sleek-looking drones. Turrets rose from the top of the vehicles and began firing back at the bots. The screen went dead. Both of their bots were down, almost instantly.

"Ardrey?" Michaelis asked. He sounded nervous. His finger was ready to make a key press. Ardrey looked back grimly. "Yes. Do it."

Michaelis pressed a key and glanced up from the keyboard toward the bridge.

A series of explosions ignited the middle of the bridge and a split second later the group was shaken by the soundwaves from the blast. Luisa saw various points around the epicenter continue to light up under the clouds of smoke and sparks that surrounded the structure. The sound of wrenching metal could be heard, and debris rained down into the waters of the bay.

All eyes turned back toward Michaelis as he refocused on his console.

After a few moments of intense concentration, he said, "It looks...it looks like we got them. Or at least the bridge is severed in the middle, and none of them made it over."

A series of sighs and nods pervaded the group, and there was some handshaking and congratulations. They all went to work again, coordinating fire crews or trying to determine if any of the attackers were still operational on the other side of the bay.

Luisa stood transfixed, watching the bridge consumed by an inferno, the metal twisting and buckling. It was hypnotizing to watch. It moved her, to see this landmark be in such peril. The bridge had been rendered useless. They had altered the shape of the city to save themselves.

It was at that point, staring at the destruction of the Golden Gate Bridge, that it sank in. It wasn't over. What she and her friends had started wasn't finished. The fight would continue.

Her guilt and depression turned to shame. Her moping was self-centered and trivial. She should be contributing. They needed fighters and builders, and she was as able as anyone.

Michaelis and Ardrey were talking feverishly. She clenched her fists, walked up to them, and bowed her head.

They stopped in mid-conversation and looked at her curiously.

"I've been a dark uniform. I'm ready and willing to help. Tell me what needs to be done."

Later that day, Luisa came back to Lincoln Park and again stared over at the bridge. The fires were out and the smoke had dissipated, revealing a mess of twisted steel and concrete dangling toward the waters of the bay from both sides. The suspension cables still kept the bridge together precariously, but the road itself had been reduced to a gaping hole, under which a section of the Inworld tube that had connected the Sidiodome to the Marindome had also been severed.

The sun was setting the world alight in a deep orange, diminishing the contrast of the crippled structure against the horizon. It was as if the sky and the bridge were wrought out of the same crimson iron.

She stared out at the twilight for a brief time, enough to take it in and commit it to memory; to see the sky, the setting sun, the gentle Marin headlands, and the hole in the bridge and remember it. It was a blight on the beauty of the bay, but it seemed fitting, a necessary scar to be worn by the city of San Francisco, to keep it wary and at the ready. And maybe, also, a warning that Inworlders weren't welcome here anymore.

She walked forward and approached the cliff face. Pausing for a moment, she said, "I miss you." It was for all she had lost: her family, and for Tristan. She needed to say it. She needed to let it go.

The wind was picking up, and a gust blew some of the sand off the cliff nearby. She watched the particles twist and turn in a spiral, away from her toward some other home on the cliff. Now out of sight, there they would rest until uprooted once again.

It wasn't like her to be sentimental, but it felt right. She needed to pay her respects and move on. It's what Tristan would have wanted her to do.

She looked down at her watch and it read 7:25 p.m. There was a meeting at the command center at eight. She'd be late if she lingered, and she'd planned on getting there at least fifteen minutes early.

She backed away from the cliff toward her bicycle, which was lying in the grass nearby.

On her way out of the park, she rode past a boy in the street. He was no more than eleven or twelve, with stiff spiky hair and prominent cheekbones. He caught her attention because his mask was off. It worried her that a boy might be that irresponsible—that he might even be a walkoff. But when she came closer she realized his mask was off for a reason. It was on his lap, and he was painting it. Curious, Luisa directed her bike toward him to see his allegiance.

The colors on the mask were unmistakable. They were the teal and black of the Shock Hawks. He saw her similar mask and smiled shyly as she rode by.

She rode purposefully back toward the Parkdome, her mask concealing a burgeoning smile of her own.

AFTERWORD

Thank you for your interest in my work. I hope you enjoyed it.

I would greatly appreciate any posted reviews, even if brief. As a self-published author, gaining exposure is challenging, and readers are much less inclined to discover books with fewer posted reviews. I hope I can be inspired again, for this world or the next.

If you enjoyed A Toxic Ambition, you may also enjoy my other books and series, which are featured in the subsequent pages.

With gratitude,

Erik A. Otto

ALSO BY ERIK A. OTTO

Detonation

An epic dystopian tale that is a cautionary reflection on our own innovation-obsessed culture. It follows two societies that are connected, but centuries apart, and their struggle against a superintelligent machine.

Named to *Kirkus Reviews* Best Books of 2018

"A highly entertaining and absorbing combination of philosophy and action featuring robustly individualized characters."

"…a future world that vibrates with conflict and ideas."

— *Kirkus Reviews* (starred review)

ALSO BY ERIK A. OTTO

A Tale of Infidels

The first book in an epic fantasy series that deals with prejudice and political
intrigue in a medieval setting, with prophesied gravity-defying events and
stories of mythical beasts as regular undercurrents to daily life. It follows cast-
out characters who face a desperate fight for survival and recognition.

"Rich, layered and thoughtful world building..."

"...characters are well developed and intriguing."

— *Kirkus Reviews*

A TALE OF INFIDELS is a finalist for the Foreword Indies Book of the Year
Award.

ABOUT THE AUTHOR

Erik A. Otto is a former healthcare industry executive and technologist, now turned science fiction author. His works of fiction include A Toxic Ambition, Detonation, Proliferation, and the Tale of Infidels series. Detonation has been named to *Kirkus Reviews* Best Books of 2018. The first two books of his Tale of Infidels series have been finalists for the Foreword Indies Book of the Year Award.

In addition to writing, Erik is currently serving as the Managing Director of Ethagi Inc., an organization dedicated to promoting the safe and ethical use of artificial general intelligence technologies.

Please visit Erik's website at erik-a-otto.com for more information or to sign up for updates on new releases.

9 781732 136144